JURY DUTY

Peter Cawdron

thinkingscifi.wordpress.com

Paperback ISBN-13 : 979-8506891468
Hardback ISBN-10 : 979-8506900030

*"In all our searching,
the only thing we've found
that makes the emptiness bearable
is each other."*

Carl Sagan

FIRST DOWN

"What the hell are you doing?" Nick says, leaning to one side on the old, worn couch, trying to see the TV. "Get out of the way, woman!"

With a beer in one hand and the remote in the other, he turns up the volume. It doesn't negate Sandra's defiance. She stands there between him and the screen with clenched fists held by her side. A slight tremble betrays her nerves. Her knuckles turn white, but not from anger. There's desperation in her eyes. She's fighting her fear of confrontation. It would be easy to walk away. Nick would love that, but she's not moving, which annoys him even more.

At best, she can only block part of the widescreen TV, but it means Nick is missing the defense rush the quarterback.

A ball sails into view on the screen.

From somewhere up high in the stadium, a camera zooms in, tracking the ball's motion down field. A wide receiver sprints toward the end zone, leading the throw without looking for the ball. He pulls up just short of the line and pivots, cutting across the field with barely five yards to go. Years of practice tells him precisely where and when the ball will arrive. The safety anticipates the wide receiver's route, chasing him, watching the subtle motion of his helmet, knowing that will signal him turning for a catch. Rain blows in squalls, sweeping across the field. The

1

wide receiver twists sideways, looking over his shoulder precisely as Sandra steps in front of that part of the screen.

The commentator yells, "*Intercept!*"

"For fuck's sake," Nick says, slamming the TV remote onto the couch beside him.

Sandra has tears welling up in her eyes. "You need to read this. You can't ignore it."

"Later," Nick grumbles, unable to formulate an entire sentence. Anger seethes within him. On the screen, a tangle of bodies pile up at the twenty-yard line. The ball pops out, rolling on the grass.

"*First down!*"

"I'm leaving."

It's only with those two words that Nick realizes Sandra has set a suitcase by the door. Her son is already in the car, just visible through the curtains. He's sitting in the front seat with his smartphone out. He's distracted, looking at something entirely meaningless that nevertheless demands his absolute attention. Fucking teenagers.

"Come on, baby," Nick says, struggling to suppress the anger he feels welling up inside. Although he'd like to think he's desperately trying to hold on to their relationship, the reality is he's at the limits of his interest. There's a football game on. Sandra needs to calm the fuck down. She always does. Eventually.

"You hit me," Sandra says. Her long, blonde hair, normally so straight, is ruffled and in motion. She jabs at the air, pointing at him. "I told you, if you ever hit me it was over!"

"It was just a push."

In the haze of his alcohol-soaked mind, Nick's not sure if he's lying. He's belittling what happened, but what else can he do? He doesn't have a time machine. He can't undo the past. Goddamn it! She's always going on at him about something he did last week or last month. He doesn't care.

Nick finds it impossible to take his eyes off the screen. The snap is called. Bodies collide. Arms push and shove. "I was rough—too rough. I said I was sorry."

"Not good enough."

"It was a mistake. Okay? I made a mistake. There. Are you happy now?"

Happy?

Nick's deflecting her concerns as effectively as any offensive tackle cutting off a linebacker. This was never about happiness. Sandra's not exacting revenge. She's cutting her losses. Nick can't help himself. He can't leave his comments at that. Ego compels him to say more.

"It takes two to tango, babe. You. You made me so angry. But you know I didn't mean to hurt you. I would never hurt you."

Sandra stops by the door.

"Goodbye, Nick."

"And what's this?" he finally asks, holding up the envelope. Based on the return address, it's a formal notice from the county clerk.

"Read it, Nick. Read it carefully."

Nick tears open the letter, but his eyes are on her.

"You're nothing without me. You know that, right? Look at you. You're fat and old. Do you really think you can make it out there alone?"

"I'm thirty-eight," she replies, but her words ring hollow. His strike deep. There's no denying her age or weight. Neither should count against her, that much is clear from the look of exasperation on her face, but society says they do. She wants to say something clever. The hurt shows in the furrows of her brow. She desperately wants a retort. She wants to say something that will negate his cruel jab, but her lips falter.

3

Sandra walks to the door and picks up her suitcase. She's careful not to turn her back on him. Tears run down her cheeks. Her hands are shaking.

For a moment, she stands there staring at him. Why? What the hell does she want? Is she hoping for something more? In the blurred tunnel vision of his myopic mind, he's already done everything he can and now he's through with her. He just apologized. Again. But then he verbally lashed out at her, which is contradictory and yet surprisingly consistent for him. Is there any hope for them as a couple? Any hope for him? What could there be? Her bottom lip trembles. She goes to speak, but no words come out.

With a half-empty beer bottle in one hand, Nick pulls the letter out of the envelope. He unfolds it and glances at the subject line. Nick doesn't need to read the whole thing. The title tells him everything he needs to know.

"You fucking bitch!"

He throws the bottle at her, but his aim is lousy. Whether it's the adrenaline coursing through his veins or the alcohol impairing his judgment, he misses. Back in high school, Nick was an outfielder on the baseball team. He could hit the catcher's glove on home plate time and again, but that was twenty years ago. As much as he'd like to think he's still in the groove, he'd throw his shoulder out these days. The bottle flies wide, hitting the door frame. Sandra barely has time to cringe. Glass shatters beside her, showering her with fragments. Fine splinters catch in her hair. Beer sprays along the wall.

"Get out! Get the fuck out of my house, you goddamn whore!"

Sandra runs for the car. She pops the trunk and tosses her suitcase in, slamming the lid shut. The young teen looks up in alarm.

Inside the house, Nick kicks over the coffee table in anger, sending magazines flying. Empty beer bottles roll across the

4

carpet. Screwed up in his left hand is an official court filing.

18 USC 997 (v) Domestic Violence Firearms Surrender Notice

"You want my goddamn guns?" he mumbles under his breath. "Well, you can have the fucking bullets!"

A car door slams outside. In the kitchen, Nick yanks open a drawer. He lifts a tray containing tableware, exposing a hidden cavity. His fingers wrap around the pistol grip of an old nine-millimeter Glock.

Nick marches to the front door with the gun in his hand. He pulls back on the slide, loading a round from the magazine. His bare feet pound on the wooden floor. Echoes resound through the empty house like thunder.

The car engine roars to life after a few false starts. Sandra throws the gear shift in reverse, but before she can peer over her shoulder and race down the drive, she sees Nick standing in the doorway. He raises his gun and stares along the barrel.

"No, no, no," she yells, pushing her son's head down below the dash of her old convertible and reversing along the driveway.

Nick has never shot anyone before, but he's thought about it. A lot. He's trained for this moment with paper targets at the gun range. They say killing someone is hard, but that's a lie. It's as easy as squeezing a trigger.

His finger tightens on the thin, curved, precision-machined metal. In the movies, sweat breaks out on the shooter's brow. Nick feels no such compulsion. His hands should tremble, knowing the pain he's about to unleash, but they don't. For him, this is revenge. She deserves this. This bitch has fucked up his life.

As soon as he saw the domestic violence notice, Nick knew he was now on a register in some goddamn federal database somewhere. The US Government never forgets and neither will he. Nick waits, but not out of pity. He's leading the shot, anticipating the motion of the car, making sure he's not going to miss. That's the problem with hatred. One shot on target is worth more than an entire magazine emptied in anger. This is no beer bottle slipping from his fingers in a fit of rage. No, this is calculated.

His eyes shift focus, moving from the tritium sight running along the top of the Glock to her head. He lowers his aim, settling on her torso. A shot to the head is gruesome and a sure kill, but it has a high risk of missing. The kick of the gun, the precision of his aim, the speed of the car—these all contribute to his accuracy. A shot to the upper torso is better. Heart and lungs. Larger target.

Is this who he really is?

A murderer?

Even he's not sure in those few seconds. He's slept with this woman for over five years. Are love and hate two sides of the same coin? They're both the offspring of passion, but are they interchangeable? Does the fury of the moment outweigh everything that's gone before? And what's next? Killing is easy. Living with the consequences ain't.

Nick wavers. He hates himself for it, but life should be measured by something other than a mere eight grams of lead being accelerated to over a thousand feet per second.

Fuck this shit! Pulling a trigger is simple. Killing someone shouldn't be so goddamn easy.

Sirens sound.

The police are close. They're already turning onto the street. The cops had to be waiting for him. Damn it! She set him up royally. Sandra glances back at him as the rear tires of her car hit the road. Her eyes—the intensity in them screams at him. They're piercing, telling, knowing. She understands something crucial about what's unfolding, something he missed.

That bitch!

Nick's being played. She's fucked him over. Five years of living together has taught him her tells. Sandra never was any good at Poker. He ejects the magazine from the gun. No bullets. She emptied the Glock before handing him that *fucking* envelope.

Smart.

All those times he whined about his old Glock—she was listening, thinking, plotting, planning. She knew the slide didn't catch anymore. The worn springs. The bent mag follower. She'd seen him get frustrated with the damn thing at the range. She knew he wouldn't realize the gun was empty.

Police lights flash in the gloomy half-light of the coming evening. Red and blue lights flicker over the surrounding homes. An engine roars. A patrol car rides up over the curb, bouncing on spongy suspension. It races over the lawn, crushing a low wooden fence. Another police car races in from the other direction as a helicopter flies low overhead. Its rotor blades thrash at the air like a swarm of angry hornets, sending out a wall of noise. An armored SWAT vehicle clips the front of Sandra's car, sending her skidding sideways as it pushes through toward him. It rides up onto the lawn, cutting him off from her.

"What the—"

Nick could run inside. He could dart out of sight in that fraction of a second before the officers pile out of their vehicles, but he stands there bathed in the headlights. He raises his arms, still holding the Glock and the empty magazine.

"Drop the gun!"

It's empty, but he does as he's told, giving both the gun and the magazine a flick. They land on the grass beside the concrete path. Nick is expecting the classic, "On the ground," but with the Glock lying a few feet away, the officers have other ideas. One of them runs in with his gun drawn, pointing it at Nick's chest. The other officer yells, "Turn around. Keep your hands in the air."

Nick complies, but not to be compliant as such. It's a reflex response to authority.

The sheer speed with which the officers move is overwhelming. He hasn't had more than a few seconds to consider his options—of which there are none. Suddenly, his hands are twisted down and around into the small of his back. Handcuffs are locked in place.

Nick is shoved inside. He stumbles and falls into the couch. The officer drags him onto the floor, pushing a knee into his back and pinning him to the carpet. The commentator on the TV yells, *"Touchdown! The Bulldogs have done it! With 18 seconds on the clock, they're through to the Sugar Bowl!"*

All Nick can see are boots and trouser legs rushing into his home. The knee in the center of his back pushes hard, applying pressure to his spine and ribs, squishing him against the carpet. There are dozens of police running through his house. They check the kitchen. Boots pound up the stairs as police check the bedrooms.

"Nicholas James Ferrin? Born 14th August, Charleston, South Carolina to Jonathan Mark Ferrin and Elizabeth Jasmine Ferrin of Mt. Pleasant, South Carolina?"

Amidst the haze of alcohol and the blur of pain in his shoulders, Nick becomes acutely aware he's never thought of his parents this way before. Johnny and Bee, that's how they were known to family and friends, and only ever as Mom and Paps to him.

"Ah, yeah," he says as the fog in his mind slowly clears.

The year was missing from their question.

Why didn't the police officer include the year of his birth? That seems like a surprising omission given the other details they're focusing on. His date of birth is on the application form of every ID he's ever had. It's as though they're acting on partial information. What the hell is going on?

Nick is expecting them to read him his rights, not question him about his parents. Something's seriously wrong. Something other than threatening to shoot his girlfriend.

Would he have done it?

Would he have gone through with shooting Sandra if there was a round in the chamber?

Nick's not sure, but it wasn't murderous intent rattling around in his head, it was the desire for payback. It would have been easy. He can still feel the machined metal trigger beneath his finger, noting how the grooves felt against the soft flesh on the inside of his knuckle. He was overwhelmed with anger, with adrenaline surging through his veins. He would have hated himself afterwards, but even with his doubts, in the blur of the moment, it would have been all too easy to pull that goddamn trigger. She was right to remove the bullets.

Nick's waiting for the police to question him about Sandra and the gun, but all the talk within the room focuses on his identity, not on what he was doing when they arrived.

Two police officers drag Nick to his feet, holding him by his shoulders. Another officer looks at a computer tablet, examining an electronic mugshot of him. Nick has been arrested before and charged with several misdemeanors, but he's never been convicted of a felony. Not until now.

"Let me see his face," is spoken from somewhere behind him. The accent is European, the kind that reveals English as a second language. Nick barely has time to take in the stranger's appearance as the man steps past the overturned coffee table. Whoever this is, he's not a cop. He's wearing an immaculate three-piece suit with a brilliant red tie, but he has a thick, full beard and straggly hair sitting just off his shoulders. It's as though someone forced a muscle-bound surfer into a suit for a day.

"Yeah, that's him," the foreigner says.

"Get him out of here," the senior officer says with disgust.

To Nick's surprise, the handcuffs are removed.

The police officer pushing Nick out the door says, "I don't know what the hell you thought you were doing out there, but pulling a gun was all kinds of stupid. You almost got yourself killed."

A helicopter circles the house, bathing the lawn in a brilliant white light.

Rather than being bundled into the back of a police car, Nick's escorted to a military Hummer parked in the middle of the street. Two soldiers dressed in fatigues stand by the open rear door. They're carrying side-arms. Nick never served in the military, so he's unsure what the various designations mean on their caps. One of them has a dark badge with several chevrons pointing up. The other has a solitary bar reminiscent of the capital letter I. Neither of the soldiers is that old. They're kids, to his mind at least. Teens. Maybe early twenties. Shaved heads. Barely shaved cheeks. Pale skin. Sunburnt necks. Their name tags are attached with Velcro:

WILLIAMS   US ARMY

COOPER   US ARMY

Cooper's a woman, although it took a second glance for Nick to realize that. Her eyebrows aren't quite as bushy and her chest protrudes just a fraction more than Williams, while her shoulders are slight and her waist pulls in. Other than that, she looks like she could kick his ass down the street and back again, barely breaking a sweat.

Williams gestures to the rear door.

"Get in."

With all that's transpired, Nick is sullen, shuffling rather than walking toward the olive drab Hummer. Five minutes ago, he was watching football, drinking beer and enjoying a lazy Saturday. Then Sandra left him. He flew into a murderous rage and would have shot her if she hadn't outwitted him. Then the cops bundled him to the carpet, handcuffing his arms behind his back and kneeing him in the spine. Given what could have happened, his injuries are nothing, but the carpet burn on his cheek and the ache in his right shoulder are real. Now, the military is taking charge. Life is a blur.

"What's going on?" Nick asks feebly, but Cooper is already shoving him in the back of the vehicle. Another, older soldier is talking with the senior police officer and the foreigner. His cap has two stars on it. Nick doesn't know what rank that signifies, but he's clearly above Cooper and Williams. The officer climbs in the front passenger's seat as Williams starts the engine. The foreigner pushes in the rear of the Hummer beside Nick, sandwiching him in the middle, with Cooper on the other side.

"Who are you?" Nick asks, looking around and seeing several more police cars with their lights flashing. The vehicles are spread out on either side of the road.

"Major General John Sanders," is the response from the front of the Hummer. "This is Corporal James Williams and First Lieutenant Jasmine Cooper."

"Jazz," Cooper says, but without the smile he expects to accompany an informal introduction. "And that's our Russian friend, Dmitri."

"UN Observer," Dmitri says, pulling off his red tie and undoing the top button on his shirt. Indignation hangs from his words. "I'm here to ensure the US complies with its treaty obligations."

"Sure," Jazz says, rolling her eyes and shaking her head.

The word, "Treaty," stumbles from Nick's lips, but it's an echo, not a question.

The Hummer weaves its way down the street, working around the police cars partially blocking the road. Several police cruisers provide an escort, with one in front and two following close behind.

"Am I under arrest?" Nick asks, rubbing his wrists and looking at the red marks left by the cold, hard steel. Deep down, he already knows the answer. The US Army doesn't have jurisdiction over American citizens on US soil.

"No," the general replies, watching the road ahead.

"Then I'm free to go?"

The Russian laughs.

Nick isn't impressed. "Can I ask what's going on?"

"You can ask," the major general replies, turning in his seat to face Nick. "But I'm not going to answer you."

Jazz says, "Let's just say your options are limited."

"I have rights," Nick says, but he's bluffing. He's seen too many goddamn awful, stupid TV shows. He has no idea what rights he has in any given context—especially as he just threatened to kill his girlfriend.

"Your rights have been suspended," the major general replies. "Article One of the Constitution, Section Nine, Clause Two states, '*The privilege of the writ of habeas corpus shall not be suspended unless... public safety may require it.*' Right now, your options are to sit there and shut up or spend the next couple of years in solitary confinement until this crisis is over."

No one likes being talked down to, least of all Nick, and yet, beyond the resentment festering in response to the way he's been treated, there's a gnawing sense of uncertainty. Years in solitary? Crisis?

The general doesn't give a damn about him and his feelings. With callous disregard, he says, "My orders are to escort you to Charleston Air Force Base where you'll be flown to Ramey Air Force Base in Puerto Rico before flying on to South Georgia."

Nick shakes his head, somewhat in anger, somewhat in dismay. "We're going to Georgia via Puerto Rico?" He quickly becomes wrapped up in that obscure point, missing the real question—*why?* Nick turns to the Russian crammed in beside

12

him and says, "We could drive there in under an hour. What the hell is going on?"

The burly Russian just smiles.

"No, not Georgia," the general says, turning back toward him with a smirk on his face. "*South* Georgia."

Nick still doesn't get it.

"In the South Atlantic. It's an island in the middle of the ocean. Twelve hundred miles off the southern tip of Argentina. Just above Antarctica."

"But—But why would you do that?" Nick asks.

"Don't you know?" Jazz replies with sarcasm dripping from her words. "You're the chosen one."

CHOSEN ONE

"You don't like me, do you?" Nick asks as they sit inside the pressurized cargo hold of a C-5 Galaxy waiting for takeoff. Jet engines whine, idling outside.

Jazz replies, "I'm not here to be your friend. I'm here to do a job."

"And what is your job?"

"To keep you alive. I'm an Arctic warfare specialist. Although, in this case, it's the Antarctic we'll be dealing with, and that's worse, far worse."

Questions bounce around in Nick's head. He isn't sure where to start. Dmitri walks over to them, sitting down on the other side of him with a couple of water bottles. He offers one to Nick, who waves it away with a polite, "No, thanks." Defiance is all he has, even when offered something helpful. Passive-aggressive much? Almost immediately, Nick regrets those two words, but his pride says, *too late*, even though his parched lips scream otherwise.

Without saying anything, Dmitri insists, waving the bottle one last time. "Are you sure?"

Reluctantly, Nick concedes.

The interior of the C-5 Galaxy is massive, living up to its name. By Nick's reckoning, the cargo hold is well over a hundred feet long, easily twelve feet high, if not higher, and is probably about twenty feet wide. As there are no windows, instead of sitting in the fuselage of an airplane, he feels as though he's inside a warship.

The hold is full of equipment. Instead of being packed in tight, the equipment has been placed throughout the aircraft, being spread out to balance the load. Thick strapping secures dozens of crates. There are a pair of snowmobiles on a wooden pallet. Tall radio antennas have been attached to the rear of each vehicle. They've been bent over, forming an arc that ends by the front skids, but even so they reach up to within inches of the ceiling. The snowmobiles have been painted bright orange, no doubt to aid with visibility.

Behind them, there's a large, clunky, orange industrial tractor with four independent tank-like treads instead of wheels. The box-shaped cabin lacks any aerodynamics and could house ten people at a pinch. The clunky engine bay at the rear makes the tractor look like something from the 1950s, while the paint job reveals the machine is brand new. Old-fashioned bulky windshield wipers hang down from above the cab. Thick metal arms extend from clunky electric motors on the roof. These are for scraping ice rather than clearing snow or shifting water.

The loadmaster checks the strapping on the cargo. He calls through to the cockpit via his headset, letting the pilots know they're ready for take-off.

"So Puerto Rico and then South Georgia, huh?"

"We need to stop for fuel," Jazz says by way of explanation.

"On our way to Antarctica?" Nick replies in disbelief.

Jazz nods.

One of the aircrew checks his seatbelt, making sure it's uncomfortably tight.

The three of them are seated on the side of the plane facing inward. Not exactly survivable in a crash. There's no safety demonstration. No blurb about putting on oxygen masks or grabbing lifejackets if they ditch in the sea. The unspoken assumption is, if it comes to that, they'll probably be dead already.

Jazz says, "Normally, we'd take you along the supply route out across the US to Hawaii, then south to Christchurch in New Zealand. The final leg is over the Southern Ocean to McMurdo in Antarctica. The problem is, the Pentagon wants you there yesterday, while the White House is stalling, wanting clarification."

"I don't understand," Nick says, shaking his head. "Why?"

Jazz replies, "If we get the green light, we need to get you in before winter closes the continent. The Brits have a base on South Georgia. So we'll touch down there to drop off supplies and refuel."

"No," Nick says. "Not why are we going this way. Why are we going there at all? What the hell am I supposed to do in Antarctica?"

"That's classified," Jazz replies. "I'll tell you as soon as I can."

Nick says, "Did it ever occur to you that you might have the wrong man?"

Jazz laughs. "Oh, you're kidding, right? Did it ever occur to *me?* Hell, yes."

Nick is silent. He's insulted by the enthusiasm in her response.

She adds, "Do I think you're the wrong man for the job? Absolutely. But it's not my call. It's his."

Dmitri says, "I have confidence in you."

"That's not what I meant," Nick replies. "Surely, there's been some kind of mix-up—a misunderstanding."

"Nope," Dmitri says. "No misunderstanding."

"But you've got the wrong guy. I'm an electro-mechanic. I

never went to college or into the army. Sure, I've made a few mistakes along the way, but whatever this is, I'm not your man."

"You like football, yes?" Dmitri asks.

"Yes."

"You drink beer?"

"Yes."

"You love America? The Fourth of July? The Constitution? All of the Amendments?"

To be honest, Nick's only aware of the first few, particularly the second, but, "Yeah, sure."

"So you're an average American."

"I guess."

Dmitri slaps his hands together in a muffled clap, "Then you're the right man. That's why you're here."

Here, though, is in the back of a military cargo plane accelerating down the runway. The whine of the engines grows ever louder.

"Are you going to tell me what this is about?" Nick yells over the noise rattling around within the hold.

"As soon as we're airborne and out over international waters," Jazz replies. The C-5 Galaxy lumbers into the air. Her comment does not inspire confidence.

Once the plane climbs to cruising altitude, soldiers begin milling around the cargo hold. Several mechanics pop the hood on the snowcat. They start tinkering with the engine, working on it as though they were in a garage somewhere on the ground. As he's a mechanic and technically not a prisoner being held under arrest, Nick unbuckles and joins them.

"Can I take a look?" he asks, standing by one of the tank-like treads immediately below the engine bay.

"Sure," one of the military mechanics says.

Nick climbs up under the watchful eye of Jazz and Dmitri.

"Oh, man. This is old school," he says, getting his first good look at the engine.

"Yeah, she's a beauty," the mechanic says. "Naturally aspirated V12 diesel with even torque all through the range. She purrs from just a few hundred RPM right up to four thousand."

"No fuel injection?" Nick asks, surprised by the simplicity before him. "No electronics?"

"Nope," the mechanic says. "Nothing to go wrong. Reliability beats efficiency. I've seen one of these babies keep running for over six hundred miles across the ice in the dead of winter with a cracked head. We had temperatures plunging to a hundred below but she just kept humming. I had to clean out the rocker cover every couple of hours because the condensate and oil kept mixing. There was this soapy sludge that would form under there. It would ice up, but she kept on trucking. This baby is bulletproof."

Nick's eyes follow the thick wiring for the glow plugs, the steel pipes forming the exhaust manifold, the fan belt and the antifreeze plumbing, recognizing all the parts. The entire engine has been painted what he could only describe as shit-yellow, which clashes with the orange of the vehicle, but he understands why. Any leaks will be immediately visible. If a gasket goes and oil starts to ooze from the sump, it'll be obvious.

"Beautiful, huh?" the mechanic says, realizing Nick's admiring the engine.

"It's quite something."

"Jacob Smith, Private, First Class," the mechanic says, offering a friendly hand. They shake, although Nick is a little cautious and not quite as enthusiastic. He's still trying to assess the dynamics within the crew. "They call me Bear. I'll be your driver on the ice."

"Oh," he replies. "Nicholas Ferrin, nobody, no class. They call me Saint Nick. I'll be your extra baggage on the ice."

Nick's trying to imitate Bear's military swagger, but his joke falls flat. Bear, though, doesn't seem to notice. He smiles, saying, "Welcome to the team, Nick."

"Thanks, I guess."

The C-5 Galaxy is buffeted by turbulence, reminding Nick he's in the air. He's not at a trade show admiring the latest engineering innovation, or in this case, a classic engine design. He's being dragged to the underside of the world.

"So you're a mechanic?" Bear asks.

"Electro-mechanic. Nothing old school like this," he replies. "While I was in high school, I spent my summers volunteering with the New York Fire Department, but their old diesel engines are still a world away from this beauty."

"She's a legend," Bear says.

"Yep."

Dmitri beckons Nick over. He drops to the deck and staggers a little as the Galaxy sways with a crosswind.

"We have clearance to fill you in on a few things."

That gets his attention. Nick sits in a canvas seat. Aluminum rods on either side of the thick canvas pretend to give the seat some form, but they fail at any measure of comfort. Jazz hands him a thin paper cup with a plastic lid on it. The heat of the coffee radiates through the walls of the cup, forcing him to switch hands. He removes the lid and blows on the surface, trying to cool the drink without spilling it. Black. Probably no sugar. Probably instant. This is a caffeine hit and nothing else. There are no macchiatos or cappuccinos in the unfriendly skies of the US Air Force. Barista is probably a term ridiculed by the flight crew. Nick sips at his coffee. It's as bitter and angry as he expects.

"This is going to sound crazy," Jazz says.

"No more crazy than being hauled onto a military transport bound for the South Atlantic," Nick replies.

Dmitri says, "Four hundred and thirty thousand years ago."

He pauses, looking for a response from Nick, but from Nick's perspective, this day simply could not get any weirder. "Something crashed on the Antarctic continent."

"Something big," Jazz says. "Something not from this world."

"Aliens?" Nick asks, genuinely surprised.

"Aliens is a bit cliché," Jazz says. "These aren't your little green men in flying saucers or monsters with acid for blood."

"So what are they?"

"That's what we're trying to determine," Dmitri says. "Best we understand it, they were explorers. Imagine Columbus or Magellan, but traveling between planets instead of continents."

"And this is for real?"

"You're sitting here, aren't you?" Jazz says, gesturing to the cargo hold.

Nick is stunned. Is this a joke? The presence of the snowcat, the aircrew, and the soldiers all reinforce her point. The drone of the engines is all too real. There must be some other rational explanation, but the hard lines on her face tell him she's serious.

"So you're telling me there are aliens in Antarctica?"

"*Were*," Dmitri says.

"The craft is buried under a mile of ice," Jazz says.

Dmitri adds, "You have to remember, this happened long before there were humans. Around this time, our ancestors were covered in hair. They probably looked more like apes, but stood upright. Their brains were about two-thirds the size of ours. Natural selection still had time on its hands before we arrived on the scene."

"You've seen photos of Antarctica, right?" Jazz asks. "It looks like a frozen wasteland, huh? Just a barren, flat stretch of snow and ice, and the odd mountain range."

Nick nods.

"Well beyond that, miles below all the snow and ice, there are canyons and crevasses etched into the rock. They form a network easily fifty to sixty miles longer than the Grand Canyon. There are subsurface lakes teeming with microbial life—all interconnected—all in defiance of the mile or more of ice they're buried beneath."

"And that's where the UFO is?" Nick asks.

"Yes."

For a moment, Nick sits there stunned, wondering how the hell he got caught up in all this and why it has any relevance to him. He was happy watching football with a beer in hand.

"And what does this have to do with me?"

"You've been selected for jury duty," Dmitri says.

"Jury duty?" Nick asks.

Just when he thought things couldn't become more surreal, the idea of serving on a jury shocks his mind.

"You're familiar with the concept, right?" Dmitri asks.

Somewhat offended, Nick replies, "Oh, yeah. I get what a jury is. What I don't understand is why you need one."

Dmitri explains. "Juries have existed for at least two and a half thousand years for one purpose and one purpose alone."

"To ensure justice?" Nick says.

"No," Dmitri replies. "To ensure justice was never the sole domain of the elite. To prevent kings, queens, and princes from perverting justice. Juries keep life and death decisions in the hands of common people."

"I don't get it," Nick says. "No one died, right? No one got murdered down there, did they?"

Jazz says, "We don't know what we're going to find beneath the ice, but we do know it will irrevocably change our world. Whether that's for the better remains to be seen, but who should decide how this power is used? The military? No. What about the government? Ours or his?" She laughs. "Would you trust either of them?"

"What about scientists?" Nick asks.

"They would be a good choice," Dmitri says. "But there too we're faced with an elite. No, the UN decided that the only way to ensure impartial decisions were reached was by means of a jury of peers. If decisions are to be made, they need to be something the average man and woman can understand and agree upon. We need a jury of equals, not elites."

"So I'm a juror?" Nick asks in disbelief, pointing at himself.

"You're a contingency," Dmitri replies. "Ten jurors were chosen. Two civilians from each of the five permanent members on the United Nations Security Council."

"Wait," Nick says. "I'm confused. You said I was a contingency. So I'm not on the jury?"

"You're a reservist," Jazz says. "One of the American jurors fell ill. If we have to evac them, you're the replacement."

"So I'm on standby?"

"Kinda."

PUERTO RICO

Much to Nick's surprise, after landing in Puerto Rico and taxiing to a halt, the front of the C-5 Galaxy opens. The nose cone rises above the plane as a ramp lowers, allowing them to exit beneath the cockpit. Nick boarded the plane through a side door and assumed the rear of the craft would open. He's taken back by the sheer size of the open nose cone.

Several ground crew usher him and the others to one side of the tarmac as the hold is rearranged and a helicopter is loaded within the belly of the craft. Its rotor blades have been turned so they're in line with the hold. Somehow, this monster of an airplane swallows the chopper whole, with its gaping jaws stretched wide—something Nick wouldn't have believed possible had he not seen it for himself.

Even though it's night, the heat and humidity are overwhelming.

"Where's the sun?" Dmitri asks as they sit on the back of a military flatbed truck parked just off the tarmac on the lush, thick grass between runways. "I feel as if I should be wearing sunscreen."

"Not quite Moscow, huh?" Nick says.

"No."

Dmitri takes off his jacket. He removes his tie and rolls up his sleeves. Sweat soaks through his white shirt.

Spotlights illuminate the plane. Thousands of bugs swarm through the air, attracted by the lights.

Nick reaches for his pocket, instinctively searching for his smartphone, wondering what the time is, but his phone is charging on the kitchen counter back in South Carolina. He feels naked without it, unable to connect with anyone. He's not even sure which timezone Puerto Rico operates on. It's a US territory and gets hit with hurricanes, but his knowledge of geography is limited to North America. Beyond the Atlantic Ocean, the various countries in Africa, the Middle East and Europe all become a blur. As for the Caribbean and South America, they're the land of poverty and dictators—or so he thinks. He sits there quietly, trying to grasp what's happening to him.

"It's a lot to take in, huh?" Dmitri says.

"Yeah."

Nick doesn't mean to be rude, but he's distracted. Although there's a lot of activity on the tarmac, Nick's not dumb. He notices how four soldiers have been assigned to them, casually keeping watch as the rest of the crew work with supplies and refueling efforts. Lieutenant Cooper has disappeared somewhere, leaving him with the Russian.

Dmitri says, "I remember exactly where I was when I first heard about the craft."

Nick's tired. It's been at least five or six hours since Sandra walked out on him, which must make it ten or eleven at night. Dmitri might be chatty, but Nick just wants to go to sleep. He wants the nightmare to end. It won't, but it would be nice to think he'll wake up tomorrow in bed with Sandra by his side. That'll never happen. Perhaps she's why he's so compliant, willing to be dragged along by the current. There's nothing for him back there in South Carolina. Nothing but popping hoods on electric cars and hooking up diagnostic computers that can do the job far better than he ever could. That and football. And bowling. And beer. Some life. The rat race is a never-ending treadmill, but Nick's not even making an effort. Metaphorically speaking, he's fallen face-first on the rapidly turning tread and has crumpled at the end like some chump in a GIF.

"It will be like that for everyone," Dmitri says, still talking about the alien spacecraft. "Everyone remembers where they were on 9/11. For those that weren't born back then, it's as haunting as Pearl Harbor. Even for us Russians, the imagery of civilian planes plunging into skyscrapers and exploding in a ball of flames is somber. It's sobering. This is like that, you know. It's one of those world-changing events that defines us all in some way."

Nick nods, but only to be polite. He's annoyed with himself. Damn it, Sandra. He loves her. He hates her. It's better this way, he thinks. Being dragged halfway around the world is merciful. What would he have done if the cops hadn't arrived? Oh, he wouldn't have gone after her. No, he would have marched around the house for a few hours, drinking heavily, breaking shit and cussing. He would have drunk himself stupid, collapsed on the couch, or more likely the floor, having pissed his pants. He'd wake the next morning in a smear of sticky vomit, blinded by the sun, with a jackhammer pounding inside his head. Then what? Beg for forgiveness. Rinse and repeat the monotony of life. Fuck it all up again.

"Why so glum?" Dmitri asks. "You are now a part of history. Out of the *billions* of people on this planet, you have the chance to make a difference."

"A difference?" Nick says, trying not to laugh. "Me?"

Oh, it's flattering. Perhaps that's why Nick doesn't mind going along with the madness. Everyone wants to be a hero. Nick dreams of being John McClane. What red-blooded American male doesn't dream of *Die Hard*? Shoot all the bad guys. *Yippee Ki-Yay, motherfucker!* But that's not the kind of difference Dmitri's talking about. Being sequestered on a jury? Really? Nah.

27

Nick's dreams have justice dispensed down the barrel of a gun.

Attention is a drug. Ego is intoxicating. Nick would like to believe Dmitri. He'd like to think he can make a difference, that he might somehow be the hero of his own story, but Nick breaks everything he touches. In a rare moment of honesty, he shakes his head in disagreement. Sandra was right to leave him.

"You have a chance to do something for all of humanity," Dmitri says softly, but he doesn't understand. Nick's afraid he'll fuck this up just like everything else.

"How did you get involved in all this?" Nick asks, feeling uncomfortable with Dmitri's attention and wanting to move the conversation along.

"Me?"

"Yes. You. Where were you?"

"I was in a break room at the United Nations building in New York. Shitty little room. It was a closet, really. No windows. Barely big enough for a small table, a single chair and a microwave oven. We had a coffee maker—filtered, not one of those fancy pod machines—and a small sink. There was a bar fridge under the table, but the milk kept freezing. I hated that goddamn fridge. Frozen salads are—they're horrible. Ah, the glamorous life of a Russian diplomat."

"And that's where you first heard about it, huh?" Nick asks.

"Yep. If there were more than two people in that room, you came back later. So I open the door and hit someone in the back.

"*Sorry,* I say.

"*No, come in, Dmitri.*

"My boss is in there along with five other people. Come in? It's all I can do to squeeze my head around the door. And then he tells us...

"*They found an alien spacecraft.*"

Dmitri shakes his head. It's as though he's struggling to believe it even now. Nick is content to listen.

"*They*—who's they? I think my boss is confused. *Found*—how do you find a UFO? I thought UFOs found you. If they even exist, I'm pretty sure they abduct you, right?"

Nick laughs. "Right."

"I mean, are we talking about crop circles and anal probes or what?"

Nick shakes his head, grinning at Dmitri's absurd but utterly honest recollection.

"So Markoff has us all in this tiny room because he's paranoid about you Americans listening in—only you guys found it, not us. He tells us your ambassador presented the US findings to a closed session of the Security Council.

"So why are we talking about this in a broom closet? Because Russia doesn't know if it should believe America. We don't want you to think we're gullible, or worse, stupid. It was madness. Was this a test? A trap? Moscow thought it was something to make Russia look silly. I thought we looked silly talking about it in a closet."

Dmitri laughs.

"So you really do work at the United Nations?" Nick asks, already knowing the answer but happy to keep the conversation going, finding Dmitri's recollection fascinating.

"I was one of many UN attachés for the Russian Federation, specializing in the industrialization of scientific research, so Markov says to me, *Dmitri, I want a write-up on the implications of the alien craft by morning.* Me? He's the only one that heard the Security Council briefing. How am I supposed to write a report? It was crazy. Insane. So, yeah, I remember exactly where I was when I first heard about all this."

"How long have you known?" Nick asks, gesturing around him. "I mean, how long has all this been going on?"

"Awhile," Dmitri says. "We don't know quite when the American's first knew. Officially, it's been about 18 months, but I think they knew something was up for several years before that.

"They set up an ice-core drill that passed within a couple of hundred feet of the craft, so they knew before then—or at least they suspected. We think that's the point they realized they had found something that didn't originate on this planet.

"Antarctica is pretty damn hostile. It's difficult to do anything on any scale without attracting attention. I think they knew they couldn't mount a serious expedition without arousing suspicions of mining or oil exploration—all of which are banned. So it became a question of what they said and when. My guess—and it's only a guess—is that they learned all they could before telling anyone else about this thing.

"We Russians have a drill site exploring the nearby Lake Vostok, about four hundred kilometers away, so they knew they couldn't keep this a secret forever. It was only a matter of time before someone else figured it out.

"The craft is on Wilkes Land, well within the Australian Antarctic territory. I suspect the Aussies turned a blind eye for a while, but even they would eventually wonder what the Americans were doing without a clear subsurface scientific target."

Nick asks, "What does it look like?"

"Beyond blurry radar imaging, I don't know. Like you, this is my first trip to the ice. I know they're still digging down there. It's one thing to drill an ice core. It's entirely another to excavate a shaft a mile deep and build a base. The material strength of ice isn't like that of rock. We have to reinforce the walls with steel rods or they'll collapse. Ice compresses nicely, but any tension, any twisting or stretching and it shatters. We're building a research center beneath the ice, but we have to move slowly and carefully.

"The pressure beneath the ice is as extreme as the weather above. Being under a mile of ice, the spacecraft is probably crushed beyond recognition, but there's much we can learn from any species that can traverse the stars. Even something as small as a computer chip could hold secrets in its design that could propel us hundreds of years ahead."

Nick nods. Sweat drips from his forehead.

"What about Jazz?"

"Jasmine?" Dmitri asks, apparently surprised Nick would seek his opinion. "This is her second tour down there. She's a genuine war hero. Heroine, I guess. She saved a lot of lives in the Himalayas. We are lucky to have her on our side."

"Huh?" Nick replies. He goes to say something when he spots the distinct form of a woman marching across the tarmac. Her arms swing in rhythm with her stride. She's determined, coming straight for them. Her tight lips and narrow eyes speak of barely contained anger.

"Come with me," Jazz says. It's an order, not an invitation.

Sheepishly, Nick drops down off the flatbed, landing in the long grass. Dmitri is silent, but he watches them intently. Nick walks up to Jazz, who grabs him by his upper arm, marching him away from the truck.

"Do not let him isolate you."

"What? Why?"

"Nick, he's Russian. He's the enemy."

"He was just trying to be nice, explaining what he knew."

"You need to be smarter than this," Jazz says. "The Russians always have an angle. Always. They're always playing you for something. Nothing comes free. Absolutely nothing."

"But isn't this like an international partnership?" Nick asks, confused. "I thought we were all in this together. For the good of humanity, and all that stuff."

Jazz brings him to a halt by a portable generator rattling away in the night, powering the spotlights that flood the tarmac, turning the night into day.

"Let me make this perfectly clear to you," she says, talking down to him as though he were a child. "We are at war."

Nick is silent.

"Make no mistake," she says, taking advantage of the diesel generator to hide her words from anyone other than him. "There's a reason all sides in this endeavor are using military assets to get to that thing—and it ain't for the lols. You think we've found an alien spaceship?"

Her eyebrows raise, looking for a response from him before she continues.

"We haven't. We've found a treasure chest. X marks the spot. Think Aladdin's cave—gold and diamonds glistening in the half-light, dumped in piles cascading on themselves, riches beyond anything you could imagine. That's the way these guys see this thing. Make no mistake, whoever controls the secrets of that machine will rule the world."

SOUTH GEORGIA

No sooner has the C-5 Galaxy roared back into the night than Nick falls asleep. The drone of the engines, the voices around him, even the lights become irrelevant. Like the white noise of waves crashing on the rocks, washing up over the sand, the ambiance helps rather than hinders the march of sleep.

When he wakes, the deck of the cargo hold is bathed in a soft red light. With pressure building in his bladder, he wanders to the toilet, still half-asleep. Guards watch him. They're indifferent, being neither warm and friendly, nor angry or suspicious. Like Jazz, they're simply doing their job—and that leaves Nick cold. He wonders about their orders. He's curious how much they know. Would they trade places with him or shrink from the role if given the chance? If he were in their position, the heavy-set civilian from South Carolina wouldn't scream *Hero!* His stained t-shirt, faded shorts, and worn tennis shoes are embarrassing next to their rugged, functional military fatigues.

Nick's a wannabe, a has-been. As much as he doesn't want to admit that to himself, it's true. Perhaps that's why he was so mean to Sandra. She was the right person with the wrong guy. Like a rip tide at the beach, when the waves appear calm, the undertow is deceptive. Even when Nick seemed relaxed and rational, he wasn't—just brooding. His mood swings were out of frustration. Blaming others is an easy-out for his own failings.

How the hell did he get here? And not *here* as inside the cargo hold of a military aircraft being buffeted by turbulence, but *here* as in middle-aged, overweight and as grumpy as a sewer rat? Perhaps that's it. He's frustrated at the realization his dreams have all died. Whatever happened to the twenty-year-old jock full of piss and vinegar? Nick was ready to take on the world, only the world passed him by without so much as a word. Poor Sandra, she bore the brunt of the storm.

Nick takes a drink of water, not feeling comfortable with where these thoughts are leading. Perhaps it's the radical change of setting that's made his failures so painfully obvious, or maybe it's the hangover. Maybe it's the lack of any decent sleep. He feels like shit—physically and emotionally.

What lies ahead? Nick screws the cap back on his water bottle, winding it slowly and methodically, taking his time. No rush. He's not going anywhere. Well, he is, but not through any volition of his own. For him, there's nothing to hold onto but now. Nick has no illusions or nostalgia about the past. No hopes or dreams for the future. All he has is now. That arrogant jock with the powerful right-arm throw and visions of making it in the major league was only ever kidding himself. And now he's heading to Antarctica to examine an alien spaceship. Nick shakes his head. Life couldn't be any more surreal.

Dmitri has draped a blanket over several seats on the far side of the hold and has curled up asleep. Jazz has disappeared somewhere. She's probably asleep as well.

"How far out are we?" Nick asks a young airman.

"Just over an hour, sir," the clean-cut, lily-white, stick-thin teen says. Where are all the muscle-bound stereotypes? Where are the real heroes? Where's *The Rock* with his thick chest and rippling muscles?

As for being called *sir,* that's incongruous with reality. The idea that Nick's worthy of respect is insulting to anyone with any real integrity. For him, such an acknowledgment heightens the dissonance he feels. It's as though he's stepped into a parallel universe. Nick knows it's not flattery, that the military thrives on respect and affords that to everyone, but it feels misguided—misdirected. Save it for *The Rock* when he gets here.

Nick nods as the airman adds, "We'll be waking everyone soon."

Another crew member comes over, handing him a pile of clothing along with a pair of boots. With one hand on top and the other underneath, she says, "You need to get changed before we land."

Nick takes the clothing from her, looking carefully at what he's been given. Black, lace-up boots with thick soles, a white singlet and underwear, and a bright orange jumpsuit—clothing that's unlike anything anyone else is wearing.

"Prison issue, huh?"

"High-Vis," the crew member replies. "We wouldn't want to lose you in a snowstorm."

Nick returns to the bathroom and changes. The underwear is multi-layered and immediately warm. Rather than pulling the jumpsuit up over his shoulders, he wears them as trousers with the arms wrapped around his waist. The standard-issue singlet is as white as the driven snow. The clothing's an improvement over his dirty shorts and torn t-shirt, but he still comes out looking like a mechanic.

The cabin lights are on, flooding the cargo hold with a brilliant, white, sterile light. Jazz greets him with coffee in a recyclable cup, handing it to him as she asks, "Sleep well?"

Nick rubs the back of his neck, still feeling a little stiff. "Well enough, thanks." He sips at the coffee. Either the brew has improved or he's desperate for a caffeine hit and his tastebuds are sleepwalking.

"Do you want to see it?"

A rush of adrenaline beats him to saying, "Yes," although it seems Jazz has something other than an alien spacecraft in mind. Nick was expecting photographs or video footage, but she leads him to one side and pulls on a cover, exposing a window. Outside, the light is blinding. The sky is a brilliant blue, almost iridescent, without any clouds. Whitecaps dot the waves. Given their altitude, those are some big ass waves. A mountain range dominates the horizon. Tall, bleak, dead stone peaks rise from the ocean. Their slopes are covered in snow and ice. There's no green anywhere, not even down close to the coast.

"See that, the thick column of ice in the valley? That glacier has endured for twenty million years. It's got individual ice crystals as large as baseballs."

Up until now, Jazz has been all business. Nick is surprised by her excitement. Looking out at the mountains, she seems genuinely warm. For a moment, the bitter cold is gone. Sunlight reflects off the dark waters.

"Beautiful, isn't it?" Jazz asks.

"But that's not Antarctica, right?" Nick replies, unsure where they are.

"Oh, no," Jazz says. "South Georgia is just a baby. Wait until you see Antarctica. It's a sight you'll never forget. Imagine the entire continental US, reaching from New York City to LA, from Florida to Washington State—all of it buried under *miles* of ice."

"We're coming in for landing," one of the aircrew says. They return to their seats as the plane banks.

"So there's like an airport down there somewhere?" Nick asks, sneaking one last look out of the window.

Jazz says, "I wouldn't call it that. The Brits built a runway just north of the Norwegian village of *Husvik* to assist in defense of the Falklands. It's set between the mountains in a broad, flat riverbed that was once buried under a glacier. This time of year, the runway is mostly clear of ice. Strap in tight. The landing

36

might get a little bumpy."

"And from here," Nick asks, "the next stop is Antarctica, huh?"

"Oh, yeah. You're getting the express pizza delivery service."

"But not via Hawaii?"

"Hawaii might sound nice," Jazz says, trying to make light of the insanity of his situation. "But it would have been torture. It would have been just like Puerto Rico. They would have kept you sitting on the side of the runway in the sweltering heat and humidity while we refueled. Normally, we'd wait here, but I suspect they want to get you down there before winter sets in. We'll know for sure as soon as our orders are cut."

They.

This is the first time there's been any mention of the decision-makers behind all this madness. Mobilizing military assets on this scale is not trivial. At a guess, it's some politician somewhere. Soldiers follow rather than give orders. Jazz and Dmitri are blunt instruments. Their role is to obey. Someone else is doing the thinking, running through scenarios and coming up with ideas.

Nick wants to ask Jazz, *Why me?* But he understands the game. There are answers and then there are reasons. The two concepts are entirely separate and distinct. Dmitri has already answered his questions, but he hasn't provided any reasons. He's told him the party line. He's told him what *they* want him to believe while avoiding any actual reasoning. Fuck. Nick is screwed. He's so totally screwed. He may be a dumbass, second-rate mechanic from South Carolina, but he's seen enough movies to know when a patsy is being set up for a fall. It's the distance between vague answers and actual reasons that's the giveaway. This journey isn't going to have a fairytale ending.

The C-5 Galaxy banks, beginning its approach.

From where he's seated, Nick can stare out the far window on the other side of the aircraft. He watches as the frozen landscape comes into view. Jagged cliffs drift past. Snow-covered hills stretch along the distant shore. Fresh rock falls lie scattered across the ice.

For the longest time, it seems as though the aircraft isn't going to touch down. Nick expects to feel the bump of wheels against the runway, but the plane continues to descend. The engines whine as though they're in pain. Outside, the crags and cliffs appear stupidly close, rushing past the window. Turbulence buffets the gigantic military cargo plane, pushing it around like a toy. To his horror, Nick feels the fuselage skew sideways. The Galaxy is flying in one direction while pointing on a slightly different heading, off to the side. A few of the veterans hold onto straps hanging from the bulkhead as though they're expecting to be thrown around. Nick reaches up, copying them. White knuckles grip at the webbing, swaying as gale-force winds rattle the aircraft.

Jazz has a pair of military headphones clamped over her ears. She's listening to whatever conversations are taking place in the cockpit. With deft calmness, she says, "One hundred meters." Her voice is barely audible over the roar of the engines. "Fifty... Twenty..."

Nick is expecting her to say, *Ten*, when the plane hits with a thud, sending a shudder through his body. This isn't Puerto Rico. The engines are frantically thrown into reverse, shaking the superstructure of the aircraft. Four turbofan engines scream in agony. To Nick, it feels as though the Galaxy has landed on some rough field covered in rocks. He grits his teeth, expecting the plane to crash into the hillside. Sharp vibrations rock the fuselage. Outside, boulders the size of houses rush past the wings. Snow and ice cling to the lifeless rock. The pitch of the engines as akin to a banshee howling in a storm.

Slowly, the plane comes to a halt before turning and facing

back the way it came. The Galaxy taxis for a few feet before coming to a halt.

"There. That wasn't so bad," Jazz says, and it takes him a moment to realize she's entirely serious.

"An equal number of take-offs and landings," Dmitri says, looking distinctly pale. "That's all I ever ask for."

The front of the aircraft cracks open, rising slowly under massive hydraulic pistons. Light floods the cargo hold. Within seconds, the temperature inside the aircraft plummets fifty degrees. Goosebumps break out on Nick's arms. Instantly, his breath leaves a trail of vapor in front of him, drifting in the air like a fog.

"Oh, damn."

"Feels good, doesn't it," Jazz says, zipping up her jacket.

Nick is regretting not having his jumpsuit on properly. He struggles with the sleeves, working the thick material up over his shoulders, already shivering as a stiff breeze curls within the cargo hold.

"How cold is it out there?" he asks, feeling the frozen air chilling his cheeks.

"In Celsius or Fahrenheit?"

"In real temperatures," Nick says with his teeth already chattering.

"Oh, this is nothing. At a guess, it's hovering around freezing, perhaps a little below," Jazz says. "Wait till you get hit by the wind."

"Why does it feel so damn cold?" Nick asks.

The snow in Charleston is rarely more than an icy sludge in the gutter. Nick's been skiing up at Beech Mountain. He loves being out in the woods in winter. The term *skiing,* though, overstates his experience. Nick spent most of his time wobbling on shaky legs and falling on his ass.

Jazz hands him a lined winter hat, a scarf and some gloves,

39

saying, "Put these on. The South Atlantic cold always hits newcomers hard. I think it's the moisture. We're at sea level, so it's a wet cold. It gets into the bones."

"Damn," Nick says, slapping his hands together and trying to get some warmth into his fingers as he flexes them within his gloves.

"Oh, you are going to love Antarctica. It's like being on another world."

He follows her down the ramp as soldiers begin unloading supplies from the hold. A diesel tractor pulls the helicopter out of the plane.

As they walk into the sunlight on the edge of the runway, Nick turns to Dmitri, echoing his comment in Puerto Rico. "Where's the sun?"

Dmitri just laughs.

Clouds drift in front of the sun, casting a shadow over the team. The temperature drops again. The blue skies Nick saw while on approach are gone. Dark clouds curl over the mountains.

Jazz says, "Let's get you to the quartermaster and get you properly kitted out."

They climb up on the icy treads of a snowcat and clamber into the high-set cabin. Dmitri wraps a fluffy arctic jacket around himself. Nick's expecting the interior to be heated, but the seats are icy cold while the air is frigid. The view, though, is breathtaking.

The runway has been built from ground-down, compressed rock. Ice has formed in patches. Wind blows snow flurries across the ground. To either side, the narrow valley opens out into towering mountains covered in brilliant white snow.

Ice glistens like turquoise as the sun breaks through the clouds for a moment. Dark patches of granite line the hillside, being too steep for snow to settle. In the distance, calm waters open out into a sheltered bay. The sea is as smooth as glass. A handful of icebergs dot the ocean, rising just above the water, serene and sure. The sun sits low in the sky. Light glistens off the bay.

After a fifteen-minute drive, they approach a collection of huts half-buried in snow and ice. Radio masts rise above the roofs, each one being supported by half a dozen guide wires securing them against Atlantic storms. Steel barrels sit up against the side of the motor pool. A variety of decrepit snowmobiles, plows and tractors have been arranged in various states of repair, or disrepair, depending on perspective. The shell of a burnt-out snowcat sits raised on a steel frame acting as a jack, having been stripped of its treads and most of its parts. Several of the windows have been removed. Mounds of snow have piled up on what's left of the seats. Icicles hang from beneath the engine bay along with unplugged wires.

The quartermaster's hut is next to the frozen motor pool. Although the temperature is below zero, there's little to no wind in the sheltered bay. With the sun streaming into the courtyard, it feels pleasant outside. It's crisp but not unbearable. The quartermaster has propped open the long side-panel on his hut, letting the sunlight in. He chats with Jazz as he puts together Nick's survival kit.

Nick is issued a breathable waterproof jacket that has plenty of padding. The jacket has a thick fleece lining built into the hood. Nick's also given several sets of quick-dry thermal underwear and woolen socks, snow goggles, over-trousers to help with thermal insulation and reduce the amount of wind that can reach his legs, a pair of over-gloves, a backpack, a set of ski poles to assist with hiking, but much to his disappointment, no skis, not that he'd do anything other than hurt himself with them.

Jazz leads him inside the base and through the maze of interconnecting walkways to the dormitory to show him his bunk.

Privacy isn't a big concern on South Georgia. Ten bunks

have been built out of wood, covering three and a half of the four walls within the room. The corners are being used as shelves for storage.

"You'll sleep here, right below me. Lunch is in ten minutes so freshen up."

"Lunch?" Nick asks, expecting breakfast.

Jazz checks her watch. "It's a little before two. Sunset is at four. We're going to have to hustle to get your first lesson in before dark."

"Lesson?" Nick says as Dmitri throws a pack on an empty bunk at the end of the row.

"On how to survive in Antarctica," she says. "I don't know how long they're going to keep you here before moving on, so I've got to get you prepped. Could be hours. Days. Months. A year. Who knows? It depends on what happens to Smith and how nervous they are at the Pentagon."

"Smith's the other juror?" Nick asks, not sure which point he should challenge. A year. An entire fucking year stuck on South Georgia? Awaiting something that may never happen? From the tone of her voice, even that sounds optimistic. Then there's the whole survival thing. Just how bad is it going to be down there? Nick thought he'd be stuck in a nice warm hut. He has no desire to go out on the ice. And who the hell is Smith? Nick stumbles through the phrase, "The guy I'm replacing?"

"Chad Smith. The juror you *might* replace."

"If no decision has been made, why am I here?" Nick asks, looking in his newly acquired personal grooming kit at a very basic single-blade razor and a Bakelite toothbrush that appears to have been magically transported from the 1950s. Nick has scrubbed toilets with brushes that had softer bristles than this monstrosity. He tosses it back into the case, unsure what to think.

Jazz is blunt.

"Down there, nothing stops. If we lose a juror, they keep

making decisions without him—leaving only one American representative. We can't let that happen. Everything hinges on whether Smith makes a recovery."

"What happened to him?" Nick asks, noting Jazz didn't use the term *full* recovery. The omission of that one word seems deliberate. Her attitude leaves him unsettled. Nick's aware he's on the verge of the unknown in more ways than one.

Dmitri and Jazz exchange a quick glance before she says, "You need to focus on here and now."

Nick goes to say something, but she cuts him off. "Ten minutes. Mess hall. Don't be late."

Dmitri rolls out a sleeping bag and climbs on his bunk with his boots still on. He flicks through a book, but he's not focused. He's not reading anything.

As there's no one else around, Nick says, "It's no bed of roses down there in Antarctica, is it?"

"It's important," is all Dmitri offers in reply.

"And dangerous."

"Crossing a street is dangerous," Dmitri says. "People forget that."

Nick nods, half-heartedly agreeing, mostly disagreeing but unable to muster a counterpoint. He tosses his kit bag on the bunk and wanders off to the communal bathroom before lunch.

As he's late getting to the mess hall, half of the tables are already occupied. Most of the men on the station have full beards, although that's probably for practical reasons rather than aesthetics, allowing them to stay warm without a scarf. Nick can't help wonder, though, if none of them want to risk cutting their own throats with the "safety" razors issued by the quartermaster. If they were that safe, they'd still be popular, but Nick's only ever seen these chrome T-shaped relics on display in a barber shop window. They're better than the old switchblades, but he prefers his electric razor.

Lunch is cold baked potatoes topped with cold bacon, sour cream and grated cheese, a stupidly thick slice of black bread, and a stick of butter that's easily three to four inches long. Nick sits down next to Dmitri, opposite Jazz on a solid wooden bench, and places his tray on the table in front of him.

"Looks delicious," he says. Dmitri turns to him with a quizzical look on his face, apparently unsure whether that's a lie or a lame-ass joke. Jazz doesn't bite. Right about now, prison food is looking decidedly inviting to Nick.

"Eat up. We've only got a few hours of daylight."

Nick spreads a little butter on his bread, but the butter's cold and the bread's stale.

"You need to eat all of that," Jazz says, and for a moment, he thinks she's kidding. The dull look in her eyes suggests otherwise. As he takes a second bite, watching the motion of her fork pointing at his plate, he realizes she's not talking about the bread. She's gesturing at the butter. "Every last bit."

"You're kidding, right?" he asks, looking to Dmitri for support, but Dmitri's grinning. He's on the verge of laughing. It seems he knows what's coming next.

"Out here, your number one concern is warmth," Jazz says. "And the most basic way to stay warm on the ice is by burning calories. You need a lot of them. At least six thousand calories a day."

Nick stares at the barely touched stick of butter as Jazz continues.

"The only way your body can absorb that many calories is by consuming high-energy foods. We set meals based on calorie-density. You might have shied away from donuts and greasy food back home, but not here. Out on the ice, you'll use every last calorie, I promise. If anything, you'll lose weight, not gain it."

Nick works the butter into his cold potato, determined not to eat raw butter on its own. Jazz provides a breakdown of their afternoon.

"We'll cover the basics today. There's a nice four-mile hike along the shore that curls up to the ridge that'll give me the opportunity to demonstrate some basic survival techniques."

"Four miles?" Nick says in alarm. Back home, walking the length of the mall to the parking lot is a chore, but that's probably less than a quarter-mile.

"Each way," Jazz replies, and for the first time since they met, she smiles. Nick's not impressed. Sadist. "It'll be dark long before we get back, but that's good."

"How is that good?" Nick says with a mouthful of overly dry, stale bread and cold butter.

"You don't get it, do you?" she says. "You're not on Earth. Not anymore."

"Well, technically, you are," Dmitri says, trying to allay the sense of alarm on Nick's face.

Jazz ignores Dmitri.

"Antarctica is like no place on Earth. Living on Mars is easy by comparison. You think I'm joking, don't you?"

"I—I don't know what to think," Nick confesses.

Jazz says, "On Mars, all you have to contend with is the need for breathable air and staying warm. Down in Antarctica, you might as well be on another planet. Somewhere like Hoth.

"It's winter. Base camp is locked in perpetual darkness. If you're lucky, you might see a slight glow low on the horizon for maybe an hour, but you won't see the sun. Not for months. And when you do, it'll be a pretender, a tiny ball of light that refuses to provide any warmth at all."

"Oh, tell him about the sun," Dmitri says with a sense of glee Nick finds unsettling.

"Yeah, the sun. Okay. What does the sun do during the day?" Jazz asks Nick.

"Trick question, right?" he replies. Nick chews on his stale bread. "At a guess," he says, "It shines?"

"It rises in the east and sets in the west," Jazz says. "But not down there."

"I don't get it. What does the sun do over Antarctica?" he asks.

"When it rises, which is like *never* in winter, it moves in an arc low along the horizon. The sun never reaches high noon. It never gets above you. At first, for barely an hour, it'll peek over the mountains and then retreat back into the darkness. By the time you get to October, the sun is up and doing circles in the sky. It's never directly overhead, but it never sets either. Not for four months." She gestures with her finger, twirling it around her head as she adds, "It just loops and loops and loops and the day never ends."

"Loops?" Nick asks, confused.

"Around and around the edge of the horizon," Dmitri says.

"It really is like being on another planet," Jazz says. "You probably don't realize it, but we instinctively rely on the sun for a sense of time. But in Antarctica, the sun lazes around the sky, distracting you. You lose all sense of direction. And this is important—if you get lost, you *cannot* rely on the sun. If you get separated from your surface team and can't see any landmarks, it's crucial you stay where you are. Wandering around under the maddening sun won't help. You'll think it will. You'll be convinced you're going in the right direction, but you'll only make things worse for the rescue team."

"Four months," Dmitri says, raising four fingers. "Four months of darkness in winter and four months of unrelenting daylight in summer. It's crazy down there. In summer, there's no way to tell if it's noon or midnight."

"And in between?" Nick asks, genuinely curious about how radically different the seasons are in Antarctica.

Jazz says, "The days grow shorter in autumn and longer in spring, changing at an astonishing rate until either the darkness or the light is banished for months on end."

There's something about the way she speaks. For her, this is personal. She's talking about Antarctica the way a boxer might speak about an opponent in an upcoming fight. There's a sense of defiance tinged with respect.

"Then there are the katabatic storms. That's something you sure as hell don't get on Mars. The wind howls across the frozen plateau at upwards of two hundred miles an hour for weeks on end. It's like a hurricane without an eyewall, driving snow and ice at you like hail, making it almost impossible to walk outside."

Nick keeps chewing. He's fascinated. He gets that the point of her diatribe is to scare the bejeezus out of him—and it's working—but it's also mesmerizing to hear about another world on Earth.

"When the wind picks up, your body becomes a sail. It sounds crazy, but we'll practice hurricane-walking on the ridge. You need to bend at the waist to almost ninety degrees. Keep your chest facing down at the ice or you won't make any headway. Look up and you'll be blown backwards like a bunch of ten-pins being struck by a bowling ball."

"The chill," Dmitri says with a little too much delight. "Tell him about the chill."

It's almost as though he's recounting a checklist of points to drum into the new guy.

Jazz obliges. "Then there's the wind chill. It can turn negative forty into negative eighty in a heartbeat. With the wind chill, temperatures have been known to sink well below a hundred. You think breathable air is a problem on Mars? Hah. You ain't been to Antarctica. Exposed skin will succumb to frostbite within minutes, at some points, in mere seconds, and as for your lungs? Anything below eighty is going to hurt like *fuck*. We even had one guy drown out there on the ice."

"Drown?" Nick asks with a mouth full. "On the ice? How is that possible?"

"It was a hundred and twenty below with the wind chill. We were on the edge of the plateau, surrounded by granite-like ice cliffs and packed snow. He didn't have enough fur covering his face."

"He wanted to see," Dmitri says, clarifying her point. He's trying to be helpful, but his demeanor is unsettling. He wasn't there. Losses like this must have become almost lore among the team. They must talk about them at length, trying to figure out what could have been done to save a life.

"See what?" Nick asks, reluctantly mopping up more butter with his stale bread.

"There was nothing to see other than the whiteout," Jazz says.

"He should have said something to someone," Dmitri says.

Jazz shakes her head, recalling the incident. "Within minutes, he was coughing up blood. He never even realized he was drowning as fluid filled his damaged lungs."

"Damn fool," Dmitri says.

"He only lasted fifty-eight days," Jazz says as though that's notable.

Nick wants to ask whether that's fifty-eight days down there or fifty-eight days after that incident damaged his lungs, but either way, the point's clear—he's dead now. Dmitri shakes his head. It seems he knew the man.

Jazz chews on a piece of jerky. "Hell, Mars is easy by comparison. All those flash fancy spacesuits and shit. We get none of that."

"I get it," Nick says, trying to eat the last of his butter with a bit of bread crust. "You're trying to scare me."

"I'm trying to build respect," Jazz says. "Antarctica is vicious. Unforgiving. Worse than Everest. Antarctica's a bitch.

She'll kill you in under a minute given the chance."

"Have you?" Nick asks, curious about the comparison she's drawing. "Have you climbed Everest?" He knocks back a lukewarm mug of coffee. Jazz doesn't bother saying yes. She seems offended he would even ask.

"Everest is a walk in the park. Do you want to know what I remember most about Everest? Do you *really* want to know what sticks in my mind about conquering the world's highest mountain?"

"Sure," he replies. "The cold? The view? The thrill of standing on top of the world?"

"The bodies."

Jazz shakes her head. Up until this point, Nick assumed Jazz was giving him the usual hazing, wanting to scare the new guy. Now, he's not so sure. Her eyes are ten thousand miles away, somewhere on the upper slopes of the North Face, gazing at a corpse buried in the ice. "Every one of them. Every *goddamn* one was a highly motivated, well-trained, fully-equipped, experienced climber. And every one of them was dead."

Her eyes focus on him.

"Do you want to know what motivates me out there on the ice? It's simple. I'm sick of leaving bodies on the trail."

Nick swallows the lump in his throat.

HIKE

After lunch, Dmitri and Jazz lead Nick through the rabbit warren of corridors within the base.

"This is the mud room," Jazz says, leading him into the external staging area within the network of huts. There's no mud, but there's plenty of ice scattered around the rubber mats lining the floor, particularly over by the external door. If anything, it looks like they're about to walk into a commercial freezer.

As much as he doesn't want to admit it, Jazz is right. This is nothing like the snow-capped mountains of the Carolinas. Life on South Georgia is akin to being on another planet. Antarctica will be worse. There might not be any pressure doors or spacesuits hanging on the walls, but the staging area operates like an airlock, separating two entirely different worlds. Boot prints have become embedded in the crushed ice.

A double-glazed window provides a glimpse outside. With the sun sitting low above the mountains, the temperature is plunging across the island. The mud room acts as a buffer against the bitter cold. As they walk along the narrow room, the temperature plummets, dropping below zero before they reach the far door. The outer door opens. Nick is momentarily blinded by the light reflecting off the brilliant white snow.

Once outside, they don ski goggles. Jazz shows Nick how to adjust the hood on his jacket so it narrows around his head, warming the incoming air. His hood, though, also narrows his field of view. Nick can only see the world through the small furry opening. His peripheral vision is gone. He's either looking down at his boots or along the path. To either side, there's nothing but a blur of fur.

The temperature falls along with the sun. Out over the bay, a warship sits anchored among icebergs. Its straight lines and gunmetal grey hull are distinctly out of place among the sea ice and the distant, rocky peninsula. That frigate is an alien intruder in a primitive, hostile land. Nick wonders if the view before him isn't that dissimilar to the one that occurred hundreds of thousands of years ago in Antarctica when the alien spacecraft crashed.

Rocks crunch beneath their boots as they trudge along the shoreline. Granite boulders the size of houses dot the landscape, each capped with snow, frozen in the ice.

Occasionally, penguins waddle down over the loose pebbles toward the waves lapping at the beach. They disappear beneath the dark water with barely a splash.

"You have to respect the cold," Jazz says as they trek inland, following a rocky trail leading up to an antenna mounted on the ridge. "Most places on Earth, you can survive for roughly three days without water and a month or so without food. As soon as you factor heat into the equation, everything changes, regardless of whether that's Siberia or the Sahara.

"Without a constant 98 degrees, your internal organs are in deep trouble. Out here, all it takes is a drop of a few degrees—just four degrees—no more. If your core body temperature hits 95 you're succumbing to hypothermia and on the verge of death. Down there in Antarctica, the cold can kill you in under four minutes, so the survival equation goes—breathable air, then warmth, then water, then food.

"That's the critical path. Never reverse any of the components. It doesn't matter how thirsty you think you are, don't drink ice water. If you're holed-up in a snow cave waiting for rescue, don't drink anything cold."

As the slope of the hill increases, Nick breathes in deeper. Cold air rushes into his lungs. Jazz seems to anticipate a question he's thinking about but hasn't asked.

"If the cold hurts your lungs, it's okay. Close your hood a little more to heat the incoming air, and keep going. If it stops hurting, you're in trouble. At that point, your body is passing through a physiological milestone leading to frostbite, hypothermia, organ failure, and death. And all in under four or five minutes if you don't have shelter. If you *can't* feel the cold, you're in a bad way. If you're cold and you suddenly feel unusually warm, you're seconds away from dying. Remember that."

Oh, how could he forget?

Jazz picks up the pace, taking long strides, stepping up over large rocks and propelling herself on. She pushes up with her thighs, hitting a fast pace. Dmitri is behind Nick. The big Russian is in his element, following so close he's almost stepping on the back of Nick's boots.

Nick is already struggling, sucking in the frigid air. Jazz seems to bounce along the track. Dmitri is relaxed, moving with ease.

Jazz looks back over her shoulder, saying, "Your body will shut down in stages." Her comments are unsettling. It's almost as though she's predicting his death. "Your core will want to maintain its temperature, so it will sacrifice the extremities. Toes, then feet, then legs. Fingers, then hands, then arms. Anything to keep the vital organs in your torso alive.

"If you can breathe, nothing else matters beyond staying warm. Nothing. Don't drink ice cold water. Don't eat frozen food. It's just not worth it, no matter how hungry or thirsty you are."

"But we're going to be inside a base, right?" Nick manages between breaths.

"Right," Dmitri says from behind him, only his tone of voice is not convincing. Jazz doesn't respond. She steps onto the next rock, springing up the side of the slope, using her ski poles to guide her on.

After a few yards, she says, "Sometimes, the warmest place is in a snow cave."

"How do I find a snow cave?" Nick asks.

"Find a snowdrift and dig. Stick a walking pole outside. Tie something colorful to it as a flag. That'll let people know where you are."

Nick nods.

"It sounds strange," Jazz says. "As you'll end up lying on the snow and ice, but you'll be warm in a snow cave. Everything's relative in Antarctica. If it's eighty below with the wind chill, burrowing into a snowdrift can raise the temperature in the air around you to a balmy thirty above. Even though it's still below freezing, that's a difference of over a hundred degrees. Anything around freezing is like the inside of a fridge. It's cold but bearable. You can survive that for a few days."

"But there is going to be a base, isn't there?" Nick asks. "I'll be inside it, won't I?"

"Right," Dmitri says again. His dry repetition isn't reassuring.

"Then there's the white-out," Jazz says, reaching up and grabbing the side of a large boulder half-buried in the ice and working her way around the edge. Nick watches where she places her hands and boots, determined to replicate her motion.

She says, "Whenever you go outside down there, hook up to a support line. Never go anywhere without clipping on, even if it looks fine out. If you're moving between huts in the dark, *always* connect to a safety line. The wind can come out of nowhere, and when it does, it'll bring snow. As Antarctica is locked in perpetual darkness during winter, it's difficult to anticipate snow flurries or an oncoming blizzard.

"As soon as a storm hits, you'll find yourself in a white-out. Snow and ice will come at you so hard and fast you'll barely be able to see your own legs. You'll have a light on your helmet, but it'll only make it worse. If you're not hooked up, you'll go tumbling. Once you lose that line, you have no bearings, no way of knowing which direction you should be moving in.

"Remember, there are far more wrong directions than right ones, so if you get blown to one side, don't rush. Look around for lights, buildings, vehicles, fences, anything that will give you shelter or a sense of direction. If you have to move, go no more than twenty feet. If you haven't found the safety line, retreat back the way you came. Backtrack. Follow your own footsteps to where you fell, then venture out on another angle. Try to move in a star-like pattern, always returning to the point you first got lost rather than wandering off.

"What you think of as a straight line will be akin to a drunken walk in those conditions. If you walk off confidently in one direction, you'll almost certainly get lost in the dark."

South Georgia is rugged. Were it not for the gravel trail they're following, Nick's sure this hillock would be untouched by humanity. The slope is steep, but it's consistent. Loose gravel shifts beneath his boots. He digs in with his ski poles, pulling himself up onto a thin strip of frozen dirt as the track narrows.

"Be careful," Dmitri says from behind him. "Don't put weight on your ski poles. They're a guide, not a support. You don't want to get in the habit of leaning on them. Use them to probe the ground around you. They're an assist. Something to help you keep your balance. Don't treat them like climbing gear."

"Got it," Nick says between breaths. He's trying. He wants to lean on the poles, but Dmitri is right. Put too much weight on them, and if they slip, he'll go tumbling down the slope.

"Come on," Jazz says, calling out into the wind, seeing him falling behind.

Nick pushes himself on, wanting to keep up with her. He tries to match her pace. To his surprise, she's able to continue talking without losing focus.

"I was down at *Vincennes* last winter when we lost our first researcher."

"Dr. Maxim Vasnetsov, from the Russian Academy of Sciences," Dmitri says.

Jazz says, "He'd been gone for no more than fifteen minutes when the station chief dispatched six of us to go out after him in a blizzard. We moved in pairs, linked together by rope.

"We searched out to a quarter-mile with spotlights. When the storm finally lifted, we found him huddled on the ice. Poor bastard was barely twenty feet from one of the huts when he died. I must have walked right past him as he was in my zone, but the storm was so bad I never saw him. We were convinced he'd gone further. If only I'd tripped over him, he'd still be alive. Shit happens, I guess."

Up until now, Nick assumed Jazz was simply a hard-ass, but there's sorrow in her voice. She blames herself for the loss. She's never forgiven herself. That strikes him as profound. She took it personally. But that guy wasn't some other Nick Ferrin. He wasn't a chump they dragged out of his living room during some stupid football game. He was a researcher. If anything, that's worse as he would have been properly trained and prepared for life on the ice.

Jazz falls silent, trudging on up the hill. Nick's sure she has far more to say but that's enough for now.

It's almost an hour before they approach the ridge. Jazz continues talking him through survival techniques, coming up with some new anecdote every ten minutes or so, but it's all Nick can do to focus on placing one thick, heavy boot in front of the other. For what seems like an eternity, the rocky rim of the hill is little more than a distant illusion, and then suddenly, they're there, with their goal barely twenty feet above them.

A massive radio antenna rises above the barren ground. Taut guide wires keep the structure in place. The wind howls like a lion roaring into the gloom of twilight. A small wooden maintenance hut sits nestled into the side of the hill below the antenna. As the hut is beneath the ridge, rocks have collapsed around it, half-burying the metal roof and piling up against the walls. Ice binds the rocks together like mortar.

Jazz turns to Nick. "Have you ever summited?"

"Ah, no," he replies. To the best of his knowledge, summit is not a verb.

She gestures, waving politely with her hand and beckoning him on up the track. "Please. Be my guest."

Jazz and Dmitri remain on the narrow stone path beside the hut. Nick picks his way along the rocks, avoiding the ice. He clambers up toward the ridge. Snowflakes drift around him, being lifted by the swirling breeze. Working hand over hand, grabbing at large rocks, he scrambles up the mountainside.

Nick clears the rim, stepping up onto the ridge, and is hit with a blast of wind unlike anything he's ever felt.

The hood on his jacket balloons. It's ripped off his head by the sheer force of the wind. The loose material catches like a sail in a squall, causing him to stagger backward. The ferocity of the wind is overwhelming, striking him in the chest. It wraps around his arms and legs, chilling his face. The noise is overwhelming. It's like a freight train roaring past inches from his ears. Whereas moments before, he was warm, now the cold seeps through his clothing, slithering beneath his jacket and wrapping around his legs like the clammy tentacles of some invisible monster. The chill creeps into his bones.

Nick fights to step forward, struggling not to lose his footing. It's difficult to move. He's on the verge of toppling backward. The wind seems to lighten him. It's as though it's trying to lift him off the ground. The storm toys with him like a child.

A gloved hand rests in the center of his back. Jazz pushes his upper torso forward. Her motion is calculated, pressing between his shoulder blades, causing him to lean into the wind.

"Over. Right over," Jazz yells above the howling gale. She's beside him, but she's bent at the waist. She keeps her head down, staring at the rocky ground. "This is hurricane-walking. Wide, slow steps... lean into the wind... trust the wind to take your weight... big sweeping steps... use your poles as a guide."

It feels entirely unnatural to stumble on with the grace of Frankenstein's monster, albeit staring solely at the ice and rocks a few feet in front of him. Once he's facing down, Nick dares not raise his head for fear of being bowled backward by the wind. He has visions of being knocked over the edge of the ridge and rolling down the rocky slope.

"That's it," Jazz yells. "Work your way into the storm. Use the wind. Imagine you're leaning on a shopping cart. Keep your legs pumping."

"H—How?" he yells. "How do I go back?"

"Slowly," she replies. "As you turn, you're going to take a broadside from the wind. It'll shift your center of gravity. Take your time. Use your poles. Stay down. Don't straighten up until you're off the ridge."

He offers her a thumbs up, but any change in posture is met with the vicious strength of the gale. It's almost as though the storm has a mind of its own. It's vengeful, wanting to beat him into submission.

Turning away, Nick steps off the ridge, watching the placement of each boot. He picks rocky spots with care as he slowly sinks below the wind.

"Damn," he says as he reaches the hut half-buried on the side of the hill.

"Yeah, quite something, huh?" Jazz says. "You really can't explain it. You have to experience it."

"That was crazy," Nick manages. He's aware his body temperature has plummeted. He pulls his hood up, shivering, shaking heat back into his muscles. His cheeks feel as though they're frozen solid.

Jazz and Dmitri sit on a couple of large rocks beside the tiny hut. Nick joins them. His hands are trembling. He slaps his gloves together, working warmth back into his fingers. Jazz tosses him an energy bar.

"Is this what it was like?" he asks. "When you lost him?"

Although that conversation took place over an hour ago, Jazz instantly picks up on his concern.

"Worse." She gestures with her head, nodding toward the antenna. "Up there, you're facing winds under a hundred miles an hour and a wind-chill factor of about ten to fifteen degrees. That night, we were hit with one-sixty and forty below before factoring in the wind chill. And it was dark. The snow and ice cut through me like a knife."

Dmitri's body language is telling. He raises his snow goggles, resting them on his forehead. His eyes dart between the ice clinging to his boot laces and the surrounding rocks. He's not comfortable talking about this. He knew Maxim, and not just as an acquaintance. Nick doesn't want to open old wounds, but he has to know. This could happen to him. He feels compelled to learn more.

"And when you found him?"

Jazz replies, "He wasn't in any pain. He'd curled up against a snowdrift to get out of the wind. He should have dug in. He froze to death. When we found him, it looked like he was waiting for someone to offer him a hand to get up."

"I've never seen a dead body," Nick confesses. His choice of wording is telling. Not a dead *person*. A body—devoid of life. For him, it's difficult to conceive of anything more than a mannequin. "I mean, I've seen skeletons, but not an actual body." In Nick's mind, they're different, even though they're not.

"It is not a sight you would wish on anyone," Dmitri says.

Jazz chews on a granola bar, talking with her mouth full.

"First time I saw one was on Everest. I thought this guy was resting under an outcrop. He looked so calm. Peaceful even. A light dusting of snow sat on his jacket. I think it was his gloves that threw me. His jacket was dull green, but his gloves were bright red. They looked vibrant and new, with barely any ice on them. I thought he'd fallen behind one of the lead expeditions and was resting out of the wind, but then I realized his lower torso was buried in ice. His legs were completely covered. That's when I knew he'd been there a long time."

Jazz still has her goggles on. The curved, mirrored surface reflects the lifeless landscape, hiding her eyes, but like Dmitri, her gaze is distant. Her head barely moves as she speaks. She's staring off at the horizon, looking out over the bay, but not at the warship or the icebergs.

"I'll never forget that moment."

"It's the eyes," Dmitri says, finally looking over at her. She nods but doesn't reply. He says, "They stare right through you."

"They do," she finally says, busying herself. Jazz buries the plastic wrapper deep in her backpack, making far more effort than is necessary.

Nick is intrigued by the dynamic before him. Jazz doesn't trust Dmitri, and yet there's a bond between them. Also, this isn't some distant memory. Jazz might be describing a stranger on Mt. Everest, but her mind is on the researcher she lost in Antarctica.

Nick's unsure how he knows, but he feels as though he's picking up on the subtleties in their body language. Dmitri wasn't there, but he knew the guy. They were friends. Jazz feels as though she let them both down. It seems neither of them have closure. They're still processing what happened. With that, Nick feels the cold on another level. He lifts his goggles, resting them on his head. The cool air bites at his eyebrows. There's something primal about the bitter wind, something that needs to be experienced, not ignored. Vapor forms on his breath.

Out over the bay, the sun sinks below the jagged hills on the distant peninsula, plunging the land into darkness. Clouds roll over the mountains, swamping the land in a mist.

"Time to go," Jazz says, slapping her thighs and getting to her feet. It seems enough has been said about their loss. She changes the subject. "At night, in the dark, your footing is important. Don't let fatigue make you lazy. You may not be able to see very well, but plant each step as though it were your last. If you don't, it may well be.

"Sprain an ankle on the ice and, depending on how far you are from base and how bad the weather is, you'll leave your team in a difficult position. Do they carry you? Or do they set up camp and call for help? Do they split the team and leave someone with you while they go for help? It's hard to know what the right decision is when you're freezing to death. Do yourself a favor. Don't sprain your ankle."

Jazz swings her backpack up over her shoulders and hunches forward, trudging off along the track.

The cool of the evening descends. Their boots crunch on the ice and rocks as they follow the path winding down the slope.

"During the day, you look where you're going," she says, leading the way. "Not at night. In the darkness, you need to look around on either side of the track. Keep scanning the ground. Keep your eyes moving. Your night vision relies on the fringes. That's where you'll pick up the real detail, out of the corner of your eye."

As they march along, Nick watches the subtle motion of the hood on her jacket, picking up on the frequency with which she's running her eyes over the rocks. He copies her. It's hard work. Who would have thought looking around would take so much effort, but she's right. If he relaxes, looking only at the fall of her boots in front of him, the rocks become a blur in the darkness. It would be easy to trip and stumble. Looking around, though, even just a few feet on either side of the track, brings the darkness into focus.

Going downhill is harder than climbing up. After an hour, Nick's thighs are burning from how they've steadily resisted the fall of the land. His calf muscles begin to tremble. The faint lights of the base station, nestled in against the hill, are a long way off along the coast. It takes Nick a while before he realizes they're following a different track.

Red flashing lights mark a helicopter flying low over the water, returning from the warship. The sound of rotor blades drifts on the wind.

Another hour passes in silence before the crackle of a radio takes Nick by surprise. He's expecting to hear someone talking to them, but Jazz has an earpiece in so all he catches is her reply.

"Copy that... We are just over a mile out... Understood. Archangel, out."

"Any news?" Dmitri asks.

"We're wheels up at twenty-three hundred."

"Really? So soon?"

"The weather's closing in down there. Mikhail doesn't want to wait any longer. As it is, we'll be landing to flares in the darkness."

"At McMurdo?" Dmitri asks.

"Yep, then overland to *Vincennes*."

"No choppers, huh?"

"They're grounded. It's going to be tough enough getting a Galaxy in this late in the season. Damn, it's going to be a long haul across the ice."

Nick is quiet.

Neither of them talk to him even though they're talking about dragging his ass across the frozen southern continent in the dead of winter. Right about now, a warm, safe prison cell sounds appealing. Like a leaf caught in a river, swirling with the current and flowing downstream, Nick's being swept along by the events around him. With each passing second, he's being dragged further away from his home in South Carolina. He wants to say something, to challenge Jazz and Dmitri, but to what end? He shouldn't be here. Nick shouldn't be anywhere near Antarctica, let alone an alien spacecraft buried beneath the ice. This is crazy. Insane. Unthinkable—to him, at least. And yet, he can already see lights flickering along the track leading from the base to the airfield. Someone's driving a snowcat back out there, no doubt prepping the aircraft for departure.

Whatever's happening in Antarctica, it's got Uncle Sam rattled. Marshaling aircrews and equipment to survive in such a harsh environment is a colossal undertaking. And for what? For him? To get him in the jury box? It doesn't make sense. Joining the debate halfway through is going to leave him starved of context. He's going to be lost on even the most basic concepts. Besides, there's been no crime.

Although Nick understands the UN's reasoning in appointing an impartial jury, it strikes him as profoundly shortsighted, but what other choice is there? Placing that level of responsibility in the hands of average, everyday, common men and women seems crazy. There's too much power in too few hands, but decisions have to be made. He figures they couldn't hold a public vote on outcomes. Hell, getting the public to pick between just two parties is hard enough without the complexity that must arise from this discovery. Then there's the way voters can be swayed. The pundits and prognosticators would have a field day. Nick understands why they've gone with a small, select jury to avoid conflicts of interest among soldiers, politicians, and even scientists. What he doesn't understand is why him? There are almost four hundred million people in America, and they chose a washed-out mechanic?

At a stretch, Nick figures he broadly fits the demographic they're after. Middle-aged. Not too young or old. Healthy. Kind of fit, if only modestly so, but he's not overweight—at least, not in his estimation. He figures he's got just enough padding for a North American winter. He's average enough. White. Male. Middle class. High school educated. No kids, so there are no dependents. No partner—not anymore, so there's no one to miss him beyond Mom and Dad and a few work buddies. There has got to be millions of other people like him. Certainly, the Twitteratti would challenge a white southerner being chosen for jury duty. Not woke enough.

It's supposed to be a jury of peers, right? Whoever's selecting the jury should be responsible for diversity, not him. He's there to represent his strata in society, not everyone on the planet. To properly represent the people of Earth, a jury would have to contain hundreds, if not tens of thousands of people from various cultures and ethnic backgrounds. Ten people from the permanent members of the UN Security Council sounds horribly limited.

Regardless of the structural issues with the jury, Nick struggles with his personal involvement. He does not want to be here. Perhaps that's why they think he's ideal for the role. Anyone that wants to be part of this madhouse is the kind of person they need to avoid.

In the confines of his own home—his personal Fort Knox— Nick loves to brag about his prowess. A bit of ego never hurt. Well, Sandra would disagree, but she was like that. She was always on about privilege as though it were the toss of a coin. To his mind, privilege is a fuel tank. Some people are running on empty. Others have a quarter of a tank to play with. Still others have the needle on full. In his mind, he isn't a billionaire or one of the Hollywood elite, so he has no problem with what little privilege he has. So someone has less. Someone is always going to have less. Sandra didn't like it when Nick talked like that. He wonders what she'd think of the jury. She'd probably hate it.

A knot forms in his stomach. Nick feels sick, but he knows

it's not physical. He's heard of imposter syndrome, but this ain't it. It's not a syndrome if you really are an imposter.

Trudging down the frozen ridge in the darkness, all pretense is stripped bare. This is wrong. Unequivocal. No doubt whatsoever. Nick can't rationalize what's happening to him as somehow noble or deserving. Funny that. In his imagination, he's always been the hero. Now the opportunity has arisen, he'd rather lounge on the couch watching football.

Courage is easiest from the sideline of a football field. When a two-hundred-pound linebacker capable of bench pressing an easy four hundred came crashing through the scrimmage, Nick found his legs going to jelly. Nick was sacked once. That's all it took to snap his left arm like a twig and knock him out of his senior team. In the cold, his arm still aches, reminding him of the folly found in unbridled bravado. Monday morning quarterback—that's the role that suits him best.

He could refuse, but he wouldn't want to be seen shirking his duty. Nick's not sure he could face being labeled a coward and dragged back to the US in chains. What if he got sick? He could sprain his ankle while he's here on South Georgia. Nah, they'd still drag him on that godforsaken aircraft. Getting a bout of gastro might delay things. As it is, he feels nauseous, although whether that's because of all that damn butter or just his mind unraveling is debatable.

They can't force him onto the plane, can they? Back in South Carolina, Nick was taken by surprise. He was in shock at how crazy things got with Sandra and the cops. He was drunk. He wasn't thinking straight. Now, though, with the snow drifting across the frozen rocks in front of his boots, he has clarity.

"Don't think too much about it," Dmitri says from behind him, apparently reading his mind. "Everything's going to be fine."

And just like that, the machinations of his mind evaporate.

Like a prisoner on death row being marched to the execution chamber, all hope is gone. Everything's going to be fine. Hah! The chances of that are slim to none. Even Nick knows that. He has no idea what he's walking into down there in Antarctica, but this sure as hell doesn't feel like jury duty.

A gloved hand grabs firmly at his shoulder as he works around a rocky ledge. He turns. Ice clings to Dmitri's thick beard. The Russian smiles, revealing crooked teeth.

"You're okay, Nick. Don't worry. I believe in you. You're going to do fine down there."

Maybe Dmitri's right. Maybe everything will run smoothly in Antarctica and he's getting all worked up over nothing.

Lies are a poor substitute for truth, but they're all he's got.

THE CALL

"You get one call," Jazz says, holding out a satellite phone within the relative warmth of the commons room inside the base at *Husvik* on South Georgia.

"But not to a lawyer, right?"

Dmitri bursts out laughing. "You don't have a lawyer."

That bland cliché even evokes a smile from Jazz. She shakes her head. Nick was half-serious, but he knew the answer before that quip left his lips.

Jazz unfolds the thick stalk of an aerial and powers up the device. The digital display flickers as it springs to life. "Dial two zeroes and three ones before entering any US landline or cell phone number."

Nick takes the phone and stares at it for a moment. Who the hell should he call? Has anyone even noticed he's gone? Other than his parents, does anyone care? Hell, most of his calls these days are over the internet, using an email address instead of a phone number. He only knows a few numbers other than his own.

Nick's at an age where most of his friends are acquaintances. Sure, they'll miss him, but not for long. Within a week, they won't even notice he's gone. His bowling team will call in a replacement. Oh, he's got a few high school buddies, but those days are gone. They've settled down. Wife, kids and a mortgage. No more hell-raising. On those rare occasions they do catch up, there's nostalgia for the old days, but they all know those days were pretty shitty back then. Nah, all he has is his folks—only they love to talk about everyone and anything but him.

What could he tell them?

No, there's only one person he can call. Jazz stands at a distance, leaning against a wooden door jamb, no doubt wanting to listen in and make sure nothing untoward is said. Ooooooh, aliens under the ice. Who would believe that shit anyway? Are you drunk, Nick? That would be the reply. No, Jazz has nothing to fear from his loose lips as no one would believe him anyway. They'd just laugh him off.

He punches the buttons, raises the headset to his ear and waits. There's a slight hum on the line and the odd crackle.

"Hello?" a warm voice says with utter innocence.

Nick pauses, waiting a little too long before saying, "Sandy."

There's silence on the line, but that's better than being cut off. He breathes deeply, looking briefly at Jazz, knowing she has no idea who he's talking to or how this conversation is burning in the depths of his heart.

"Listen, I just wanted to say—"

"Don't," Sandra says, cutting him off.

A knot rises in his throat, surprising him with how much can be communicated by a single word. She's right. What would yet another hollow apology accomplish? Not a goddamn thing. He wants to explain that this call is different, but for all she knows, he's half-drunk, calling her from the alley behind some seedy bar. Nick picks his words carefully.

"You deserve better, you really do."

"I'm not doing this, Nick. Not again"

A knife plunged into his chest wouldn't hurt as much as

those few words, but she's right. Too many times. Too many mistakes. Too many re-dos that always led back to the same damn place.

"I'm not calling to get you back. I'm not."

Sandra doesn't reply, but in his mind's eye, he can see her. He can see the tears welling up in the corner of her eyes, the tension in her lips and jaw, the determination and anguish.

"I'm not calling to say I'm sorry. Well, I am, but to blurt out those words would only hurt you, and I get that. I understand. I'm not trying to gaslight you. Honest. I'm—"

"What are you trying to say, Nick?"

"I—I had no one else to call." He laughs, but it's reluctant, bitter and twisted. His own voice condemns him as the punchline of a sick joke. "Crazy, huh? When it comes down to it, you're all I ever had, and I was stupid and mean and selfish and dumb."

Sandra doesn't reply, but he knows she's biting at her bottom lip. She does that when she's upset.

"I just wanted to say goodbye—and I mean it. This isn't some stupid trick to gain sympathy. I wish—I hadn't been such a fool. I wish you nothing but the best."

"Are you in some kind of trouble?"

He laughs, looking up at the paint peeling off the ceiling. Now it's his turn for tears. Oh, she knows him so well.

"I should be, but no. It's—complicated." He looks at Jazz, but she's staring at her feet, ignoring him while listening intently nonetheless. "You'll do great. I know you will, Sandy." Nick doesn't know that, but he's happy to lie to himself. "You're smart. You're kind. You're caring."

Again, her silence speaks volumes. This isn't her Nick.

"You take care of yourself," he says.

"You too," she replies with genuine warmth, and that's it. That's all he can deal with. The uncertainty is too much.

"Bye."

He lowers the phone. His finger hovers over the end-call button, wondering if there's anything else she wants to say. If she said anything at this point, he'd be able to hear her, only just, perhaps not the exact words but at least the tone. There's silence on the line. Nick feels empty. If he could make out just one word, he'd know she said something more, but she doesn't. This really is the end.

To be fair, she doesn't owe him anything, but that doesn't lessen the hurt. Perhaps that's the thing that stings most within his madly beating heart—the realization that she's able to move on without him. The pain he feels is self-inflicted through his own pigheaded arrogance and anger during that goddamn stupid football game. Ah, the arrogance of past mistakes. If he hadn't yelled at her and shoved her into the table last week, she'd never have taken out that court order, and he'd have never pulled a gun on her. Nick feels as dumb as dog shit at how his ego escalated into utter stupidity.

He presses the button, ending the call, wondering what else he could have said, curious about what she's thinking thousands of miles away. He wonders if she'll ever find out what happened to him. Hah. What happened to him? Damn. In his mind, the future is already in the past. Deep down, he suspects his life is over. There's nothing he can put his finger on, no reason to think he's going to die in Antarctica, and yet a sense of dread hangs heavy over him.

Dark clouds descend on the bay. He can see them out the window. He can feel them in his heart.

Jazz walks over, holding out her hand for the phone. Reluctantly, he surrenders it.

"Good call," she says. Dmitri nods as well, but neither of them look him in the eye. They know he's fucked up his life. Given the chance, he would have fucked up Sandra's life as well out of pure spite. Perhaps that's what upsets him most—seeing the demons laid bare within his own soul.

For her, that call will be an oddity. Oh, at some point, she'll drop by the house to collect a few things. She'll see his car in the garage and perhaps come back later when she knows he's at work. On seeing his old Dodge still there, she'll knock, figuring even he couldn't be drunk a couple of days later. When there's no answer, she'll use her key. She'll tread carefully through the house, surprised the mess hasn't been cleaned up. It'll take some time before she realizes he's not there. Maybe she'll have someone with her—just in case. Before long, she'll know something's wrong. His phone and wallet will still be there, along with his motorbike and car, but he'll be long gone. If he's lucky, she might file a missing person's report. What will the cops tell her?

Nick knows Sandra well enough to know she'll come by the house a few more times, strategically looking to catch him in a quiet moment. Normally, he'd leave for work at eight in the morning. She might swing by half an hour earlier, but he won't be there. Again, nothing will have been moved. Will she worry about him?

At a guess, there's got to be some government cover story. If she digs deep enough, someone will spin a yarn about him being arrested or moving interstate. By that time, she'll have retrieved her furniture and be done with him. She'll check his firearms and be able to account for all of them except the Glock, which she'll assume was taken by the police as evidence.

Sandra won't be able to rule out suicide in some remote part of the nearby woods. Perhaps she'll contact his parents. Nah, by that point, Sandra will have settled elsewhere. Far from being the center of her world, he'll be some creep she used to know.

Nick wishes he'd slowed down and controlled his hot head. It seems it took dragging him halfway around the world to realize how much of an asshole he's been to her, but the past cannot be changed.

Will she ever forgive him?

Should she?

Nah. This mess is on him, and he knows it. Mistakes ain't a parking ticket. They're not something that can be paid out by swiping a credit card and zeroing the balance. Forgiveness isn't his to demand. It's hers to give. The passage of time will soften the rough edges, but forgiveness is something he can never earn. Even if she does forgive him, nothing changes the past. All forgiveness does is make those bitter memories a little more bearable. Nick knows that's not what he needs. He's had too many easy outs. If he's ever to make something of himself, he's got to change, regardless of how painful that might be.

"Are you okay?" Jazz asks. For once, it's not duty driving her interest. She's genuinely concerned. Perhaps she can see the pain lining Nick's face and the way he tries to hide behind a fake smile.

"Fine."

One word isn't an answer.

It's a lie.

CHANGE OF PLAN

The base at *Husvik* is a menagerie of humanity. Scientists, base staff, engineers, flight crew, naval officers and cooks all keep busy in the cold. Accents are a tell. The quartermaster is from Chile, while the operations manager is Australian. The Norwegians are polite, speaking English with a distinct European tinge that sometimes spirals into their native tongue. One of the cooks is from Qatar. The other is from Vietnam. The cuisine, though, is supersized European mush. The British sound regal. Even when talking about some of the more mundane aspects of life, like fixing a toilet cistern, their conversations sound like a matter of life and death. The Americans are more relaxed, or so Nick thinks.

"Change of plans," one of the senior US aircrew says, pulling Jazz aside within the dining room. Given the commotion at the tables, there's no way of overhearing what's being said, but Dmitri looks worried. Nick's sitting across from him. The Russian smiles, stuffing some bacon in his mouth.

"I'm sure it's nothing," Dmitri says, chewing on a fatty strip of meat.

Liar.

Nick wonders how much he should care. Perhaps something that worries them will be a pleasant surprise for him. Maybe they've changed their minds. Maybe the White House has vetoed the Pentagon's plans and he'll be hauled back to the US.

Over the cacophony of voices, he hears Jazz object to something that's been said to her. "Goddamn it! This is bullshit."

Her lips tighten as she straightens, clenching her fists by her side. She doesn't like what she's hearing but she's unable to argue. Finally, she nods and returns to the table.

"What's up?" Dmitri asks.

"There's been an accident. McMurdo is closed for the season."

"What? What kind of accident?"

"A C130 Hercules was refueling on the ice. Something went wrong. They're not sure what, but it sounds like whiteout conditions. It seems they had the props turning over to keep the engines warm. McMasters thinks one of the fuel trucks clipped a prop and—*boom*—no more airfield."

Nick stops eating. This is great news. Well, not for the poor bastards that got fried on the ice, but if there's nowhere to land, they'll have to take him back stateside.

"So, what's the plan?" Dmitri asks.

"You saw the frigate in the bay, right?" she says.

"No way."

"Oh yeah."

"What?" Nick asks.

"There's been a change in plans," Jazz says. "We're steaming south on the *Te Kaha* to *Halley*, a British base just off the Ronne Ice Shelf."

"And from there?" Dmitri asks.

"Overland to *Vincennes*."

"That's got to be a thousand miles!"

"Closer to fifteen hundred," Jazz says. "The Brits have fuel dumps at staging points, but it's going to be a long crossing."

"On the polar plateau? In winter?" Dmitri asks with his fork hanging from his fingers.

"Yep."

"Fuck," he says, followed quickly by, "How big an expedition?"

"Three cats."

"That's all?"

"Yes."

Dmitri says, "I—I."

Nick asks, "I take it that's bad?"

Jazz just laughs, looking at him in disbelief. "You really don't get it, do you?"

Nick shakes his head.

Dmitri says, "You're about to understand what misery really means, my friend."

Nick is smart enough to know now's the time to be quiet.

"It'll take weeks to cross the ice," Dmitri says, pleading with Jazz as though she has the power to change this decision. "We won't get there until late winter or early spring."

"Not if we ride right up on the plateau," Jazz says.

"Out in the open?"

"We'll cross the East Antarctic Ice Sheet, passing in front of the Argus Dome. If we avoid the mountains, we can make good time."

"And drive into the heart of a winter polar storm?" Dmitri asks. "We could get lost. Stranded. Nothing could be this urgent. They should wait until spring when we can land at McMurdo. At the very least, we could fly by chopper to *Vostok* and on to *Vincennes*."

Jazz bites her lip. Nick can see the machinations of her mind. She's trying to figure out what she should say.

"They found something."

Jazz is pensive, but it doesn't seem that big a deal to Nick. Of course, they found something. That's the whole point of being down there, to dig up an ancient UFO, but Jazz adds one final word that changes everything.

"Alive."

"What?" Dmitri says. "No. No. No. You're kidding, right? That's not possible."

Jazz simply shrugs.

"That's what they're saying. The Pentagon is rattled. The Kremlin is going nuts. Downing Street wants to go public. Even the Chinese are struggling to keep a lid on this. Whatever's happening down there, it's scaring the bejesus out of all sides. I need Nick down there on standby. If Smith dies, Nick needs to be ready to step in. The US will not be sidelined on this."

Dmitri nods. "When do we leave?"

"Now," she replies. "The weather is closing in. *Vincennes* is already past the last sunset for the season."

"Last?" Nick asks.

Dmitri explains. "The last sunset before three long months of darkness."

"Winter is falling," Jazz says, getting up from the table. "The weather up on the plateau is going to get bad. Real bad. The sooner we move, the better our odds."

"Okay. Let's do this," Dmitri says. He scoffs an extra scone, shoving it in his mouth as they head for the door. Crumbs adorn his beard. He licks his fingers with glee. Nick might be terrified, but Dmitri is excited.

They head for the dorm to gather their gear. Nick isn't looking forward to going back out in the cold. His legs are sore from the march up to the antenna. Although his bunk bed is narrow, with a stiff mattress, he was looking forward to crashing in the insanely soft, padded sleeping bag that's been issued to him.

"The adventure begins, huh?" Nick says as they don their external gear and shove items into their packs.

Jazz doesn't reply.

"This is history in the making," Dmitri says. "You should be proud. You're a part of something marvelous, something that will change our world."

Nick nods and finishes packing. They meet in the ready room. It takes a few minutes to don his external heavy weather gear. His boots are stiff.

Base staff push through the narrow passage, coming in from the cold. With their jackets hanging open and frost on their beards, they mumble in anger. Nick doesn't pick up much of what's said as most of the comments are in Norwegian, but he recognizes a few phrases.

"...bloody stupid..."

"...someone's going to get killed..."

"...wait for fucking dawn, for Christ's sake..."

"Time to go," Jazz says, pushing him ahead of her toward the main door.

Nick stumbles out onto the snow, being careful with his footing. With the coming of night, the slush around the doorway has frozen solid, forming a slick layer of ice. His boots slip, but he keeps his balance.

A helicopter hovers low over the equipment yard, kicking up flurries of snow. A belt descends from its undercarriage. Bear stands on the pristine snowcat from the cargo hold of the C-5 Galaxy. He hooks up chains to various anchor points. The constant thumping of the rotors overhead makes it impossible to talk. Jazz yells something, holding the hood of her jacket in place so it doesn't blow off. She points toward the shoreline.

Out across the bay, the warship is lit up like a Christmas tree. Navigation lights flash on the communications mast. Spotlights illuminate the rear deck. Brilliant white lights turn the darkness into daytime, reflecting off the still water. Sailors move with purpose. A spotlight ripples across the ocean, being directed toward the shore.

An inflatable zodiac boat races in toward the beach. The water is churned white behind it, forming a V-shaped wave that ripples across the bay. Rather than stopping as it gets close, the boat rides up onto the pebbles, pushing waves over the loose rocks. Several sailors get out. They're wearing black wetsuits along with what looks more like a thick Day-Glo collar than a lifejacket. They fit Jazz, Dmitri and Nick with similar lifejackets, explaining that these devices will inflate automatically if submerged in water. A small white strobe light on Nick's shoulder flashes every few seconds. No one's taking any chances on his exact location.

Pebbles crunch beneath his boots as he walks down to the boat. Waves lap at the shore. Nick climbs over the sidewall, followed by Jazz and Dmitri. The boat is much larger than it seemed on approach. Although the sides are inflated, the boat has an aluminum hull. Seawater sloshes around his boots. They sit three abreast in the middle of the boat. A couple of sailors push the boat back out into the dark water, jumping into the front as the depth reaches waist height.

The driver is seated behind a spray shield mounted at the back of the inflatable. As the boat drifts back, he lowers the propellers. Two massive outboard motors roar into life. The zodiac turns away from the shore and races out across the bay. The wind whips over the craft. The water is as smooth as glass. The inflatable skips across the sea. The front of the boat rises with a steady rhythm, splashing back down every few seconds as the hull skims along. One of the sailors is mounted at the front as a lookout. He pulls on a rope, peering into the darkness as they cut across the bay. The wind whips around them. Nick finds it difficult to look straight ahead. He hunkers down, pulling his hood tight and looking to one side.

The helicopter flies low over the water with the snowcat hanging beneath it, racing toward the frigate. Bear is still standing on the roof of the cat. He's holding onto one of the chains. Not exactly standard operating procedure, but he seems to be enjoying the ride.

The inflatable decelerates and turns, riding in on its own wave as it pulls alongside the warship. A rope net has been lowered over the side of the hull. It's easily twenty feet wide and reaches down to the waterline. The sailor kills the engine and they drift to a halt.

"Three points of contact at all times," Jazz says, standing in the inflatable and holding onto the thick rope for support.

Nick nods and sets his mind on the climb, reaching out and grabbing the rope. He positions his boots, rocking with the sway of the zodiac, and steps up. A couple of sailors wait at the top. As he comes level with the deck, they grab his arms and haul him up.

"Gidday, mate," one of the officers says with a sense of warmth that surprises him. "Sorry about the climb. Normally, we'd bring you in beneath the helicopter deck, but we're a bit busy down there."

Nick looks along the length of the frigate. The helicopter hovers over the rear deck, lowering the snowcat. Sailors work with guide ropes to keep the cat from twisting through the air. Bear looks like he's just conquered Mt. Everest. He's loving this.

Once Jazz and Dmitri are onboard, the officer says, "If you'll follow me." He leads them along the side of the vessel.

Nick hangs back, saying to Jazz, "Um, they're...?"

"They're from New Zealand," she says. "No one knows the Southern Ocean like the Kiwis."

"They're a long way from New Zealand."

"They're on assignment to support the Brits."

The three of them are led through a steel bulkhead door and up a flight of steep stairs to the bridge. Nick is careful to step over the various bulkhead doorways so he doesn't catch his shins on the plate steel. The bridge is a hive of activity. Red lights allow the crew to retain their night vision, painting both the controls and the sailors with an eerie dim glow.

"Commander Simonds," Jazz says, saluting a woman in fatigues.

"Welcome onboard the *HMNZS Te Kaha*," the commander says, returning the salute. "Well, you yanks are nothing if not surprising."

Jazz laughs. "This is Nick Ferrin, bound for *Vincennes*."

"Lucky you."

"What are we dealing with?" Jazz asks as Dmitri waves hello to the commander. It seems they know each other quite well.

Commander Simonds leans against a broad console with a paper map unfolded before her. She brushes her hand across the worn paper, talking as she describes the journey.

"We're just over fifteen hundred kilometers from *Halley*. This old girl is good for 25 knots in these waters. We'll make good time while we're sheltered by the South Sandwich Islands. Once we hit the open ocean in the South Atlantic, though, a lot is going to depend on the weather. The forecast is for gale-force winds coming off the ice. It's going to be damn cold down there. Also, we're going to lose daylight as we head south. That makes everything more difficult."

Dmitri nods.

"ETA?" Jazz asks.

"I'd like to have you down there in five or six days. It'll be tight, but if we don't gun it now and the weather sets in, things are going to get nasty. We've got a short window we can squeeze through, but we can make it. Any questions?"

"Ah," Nick says, raising his hand as though he were in school. He grimaces slightly, knowing this is a dumb question but wanting to ask it anyway. "What if we run into icebergs—I mean, I can see icebergs out there in the bay. Doesn't that make it dangerous?"

Commander Simonds chuckles lightly, addressing Jazz as she says, "He's a cute one, huh?"

She looks up from the map, saying, "Oh, we want to see icebergs. Lots of big white-tipped bergs dotting the horizon. Nothing would make me happier."

Nick's confused, so the commander clarifies her point.

"Because that means we've made it across the Southern Ocean. There's going to be pack ice in close to Antarctica. The ice sheets are growing at this time of year, forming as the surface of the ocean freezes. Icebergs help calm the waters. They're big enough to slow the swell. They deflect the wind. Besides, you're on a warship. This ain't the Titanic. There's nothing I love more than sailing among icebergs."

She taps the open ocean on the map, pointing roughly halfway between South Georgia and Antarctica, saying, "This is the danger zone. Right here. In this region, we're going to get hit by circumpolar storms. As we pass through here, you'll be praying for icebergs."

"Gonna be rough, huh?" Jazz says.

"Oh, yeah, but we're up for it."

She folds up the map, saying, "Johnson will show you to your quarters. Anchor's up at twenty-three hundred, once we've got your equipment stowed."

"Thank you, commander," Dmitri says.

TE KAHA

Nick wakes a few times during the night, relieving himself occasionally, but dawn never seems to come. He goes back to sleep, but not because he's tired. Depressed would be a better term. His life has spiraled out of control. For once, the madness is not of his own making or his own obstinate stupidity. A dim light glows over a metal sink in his shared quarters. It must be four or five in the morning by his reckoning. He's tired of sleeping—something he would have never thought possible.

The ship sways. Somewhere deep within the superstructure of the vessel, two massive diesel engines drive the frigate on. A slight hum reverberates through the steel walls.

Dmitri and Jazz are already up. Early birds.

Nick runs some water up through his hair and stares at the ghostly image in the mirror. There's a note taped beneath the glass.

Come up to the bridge when you're ready.

Ready?

For what?

The end of the world?

An alien invasion?

Nick brushes his teeth. Hah, what a distinctly human thing to do when faced with the unknown, but routines calm his weary soul.

As much as Nick would like to, he can't grow a beard. After the last few days, his cheeks and chin have grown a little bit of bumfluff. A rather pathetic mustache has appeared over his lips, but no beard. If anything, it's as though someone's pranked him and stuck pubic hair on his face. Nick lathers his face and shaves. Mentally, that act gives him a lift.

Warships are built for battle. Every wall is a bulkhead. Nick pushes down on the stiff metal handle and pulls the watertight steel door open. The lights in the corridor are blinding. He steps over the rim, closing the door behind him. A sailor standing beside the cabin stiffens, coming to attention.

Nick's unsure of the protocol. Is he a guard? As if in response to the confusion on his face, the sailor says, "Ensign Temuera. I've been assigned as your aide."

Okay, so a polite guard. Got it.

"Ah."

"The bridge is this way, sir."

Ensign Temuera leads him down a series of nondescript corridors, seemingly turning at random and darting through bulkheads before leading him up a ladder pretending to be a set of stairs. Pipes run along the walls. Bundles of wires hang from racks lining the ceiling. The walls have been painted so many times the scratches reveal older coats of grey paint rather than naked steel.

"Ah, there you are," Jazz says as Nick is led on to the bridge.

"Just in time," Dmitri says.

"For what?" Nick replies, seeing them seated in raised chairs at the back of the bridge. In any other context, these would be industrial-grade bar stools but with seatbelts hanging to either side. They're conveniently out of the way, allowing the crew to move around without interference.

Dmitri points at the windows. "Sunset."

"What time is it?" Nick asks, seeing the sun off to the side of the frigate, sitting low on the horizon, lighting up clouds as it dips toward the sea.

"Just after two in the afternoon."

Commander Simonds asks, "Coffee?"

"Ah, yeah. That would be great. Thanks."

The ocean is like glass. A broad swell undulates across the surface, rolling into the distance.

"We're making great time," the commander says, handing him a Styrofoam cup. Vapor rises from the pitch-black coffee. "Hitting thirty knots. We might just edge out the coming storm."

"I sure hope so," Nick says, sitting at the rear of the bridge and warming his hands against the cup.

"Sleep well?" Dmitri asks.

"Like a log."

"Good."

"Ah," Nick says, speaking under his breath. "How much does everyone know?"

"Don't worry. We'll let you know if we're in an insecure environment," Jazz says. "Everyone here is in the loop."

"Really? Everyone?"

"You're surprised?" Commander Simonds says, taking the central chair by the navigation desk.

"I figured this was like beyond top secret. You know, to prevent rumors."

The commander says, "The best way to stop rumors is to keep people informed."

Nick is stunned. She continues, saying, "We're military. We've sworn an oath to do our duty. You don't think we can keep a secret?"

"But aliens?" Nick says. "That's kinda big news. What if it

gets out?"

"Oh, it gets out," she says. "But no one believes it. And anyone that actually knows is quick to dismiss it. You see, if it was a rumor, they'd have doubts. My crew have no doubt. They know. And because they know, they're quick to scoff at the idea in front of outsiders."

Nick is speechless. The commander's confidence is baffling.

"By knowing, they're in a position to protect that information."

Nick feels as though his head is about to explode. "And everyone's okay with that?"

Commander Simonds smiles, saying, "Don't underestimate the value of camaraderie, especially in the navy. When it comes to it, no one gives their life for something as abstract as a country or a flag. Whether it's a foxhole, a helicopter, or a warship, they give their all—right up until their last—for the guy or gal next to them. After all, what is a country other than its people?"

"And then there's pride," Jazz says. "The crew know they're making history. They know they'll look back on this and tell their grandkids they were there when First Contact became a reality."

"And no one's broken ranks?" Nick asks, feeling incredulous at what he's hearing.

"A few have tried," Jazz says. "And, from all accounts, they're enjoying their extended time in solitary."

Nick sips his coffee. Apart from being black, it's quite good. It's an improvement over the sludge he was given by the US Air Force.

Jazz says, "I've got a bunch of stuff to run through with you about your role as a juror and the precedence of past decisions."

Dmitri's deadpan expression must suggest now is not the time as she adds, "But there's no rush."

Nick gets to his feet. He's hungry. Ensign Temuera starts moving as well.

Nick gestures to him, asking, "Is this really necessary?"

Commander Simonds points out at the vast, open ocean, saying, "The water temperature out there is five degrees. The average survival time in these conditions is under four minutes. Our mean time to respond to someone overboard is three minutes. In that time, we need to sound the general alarm, secure for an emergency turn, cut the throttle and throw the *Te Kaha* into a two-to-three kilometer wide U-turn while simultaneously launching multiple search and rescue teams on high-speed inflatables. By the time they hit the water, we have less than sixty seconds to get to you. And all that assumes we know the exact moment you hit the water, so yes, I want someone watching you twenty-four hours a day."

Reluctantly, Nick nods.

"Besides," the commander says. "How else are you going to find the galley?"

"Good point."

"This way," the ensign says, leading him back downstairs to the mid-decks.

The galley is a slightly wider portion of the main internal corridor, with fold-out tables off to the side. No thought has been given to aesthetics, although there are colored prints of the New Zealand forest stuck to the aluminum cupboards. Ensign Temuera explains how the crew eat in shifts. The kitchen runs sixteen hours a day with self-service available twenty-four hours. He introduces Nick to Eddie, the head chef.

Eddie's a Māori with the build of an NFL linebacker. Given how narrow the kitchen is, Eddie's surprisingly agile, moving about with ease. His face has been intricately tattooed. Back in the US, Nick's seen the odd facial tattoo, but they tend to be scrappy. If anything, they speak of a criminal underclass, but Eddie's native tattoo is different. Its appearance is fearsome, majestic. Dark green lines form intricate patterns swirling around his cheeks and curling over his nostrils. There's a hypnotic symmetry to the design. Lines bend over his brow and down toward the bridge of his nose.

Eddie smiles warmly in defiance of his tattoos, rattling off a quick greeting with, "*Kia ora, kia ora,* bro!"

"Ah, hi."

"So you're the new kid, huh?"

"Yeah. I guess so," Nick replies. It's been a long time since he's been called a kid.

"Watch chew won?"

It takes Nick a moment to decipher a coherent statement from Eddie's thick accent.

"What do I want?" he replies, stunned at how his mind struggles to interpret a question spoken in his own language. "Ah, I dunno. Do you do burgers? Or an omelet?"

"For you, I can whip up an omelet," Eddie says, pointing at an open carton of eggs on the stainless steel benchtop. "You hungry? You want sex?"

"I what?" Nick says, struggling to process what's being said. He recoils, shaking his head in disbelief, but Eddie seems oblivious to how uncomfortable he feels.

"Four, five, or sex?"

"Oh, the number of eggs?" Nick says, laughing. "Ah, three. Thanks."

He holds up three fingers to make sure there's no misunderstanding.

"You're a bantamweight," Eddie says, chuckling. He cracks two eggs at once, striking them on either side of a skillet and dropping them on the sizzling cast iron. He tosses the shells in the waste and cracks another two eggs all within a fraction of a second. Nick's about to point out that's *four* eggs when Eddie splashes a little milk on top of them along with a handful of cheese and then proceeds to mix them in the pan.

"The secret," Eddie says, tilting the pan and whipping a steel whisk around at a frantic pace, "is to aerate. Keeps the mixture nice and fluffy."

Handfuls of bell pepper, diced tomatoes and ham are tossed into the skillet. Eddie flips the omelet like a pancake, sending it sailing into the air and catching it with aplomb before returning it to the burner.

"Smells good, huh?"

"Smells great," Nick replies.

Eddie slides the omelet onto a plate. There's so much grease he doesn't need a spatula. Eddie almost loses the omelet as the ship rocks with the ocean swell, but he recovers, tipping the plate with care.

"Thanks."

Nick sits at a bench facing Eddie as he works. He's fascinated by the big man.

"So, where you from?" Eddie asks, chopping carrots as though he were a ninja. Somehow, he never hits his fingers. When he moves on to tomatoes, Nick does a double-take to ensure there's no blood in the red pulp.

"Ah, South Carolina."

"That's in America, right?"

Nick laughs. "Yes." It's never occurred to him that his home state is anything other than renowned, but he can see how it must seem like some foreign, obscure place to someone from the other side of the planet.

Bear walks up, greeting Nick with a pat on the shoulder and taking a seat beside him as he says, "Hey, I see you've met the most important person on this rust bucket."

"Damn straight," Eddie says, chuckling. He points at Bear with his oversized chopping knife, adding, "Coffee?"

"Sure."

"What are you up to?" Nick asks Bear as Eddie serves him a drink.

"Stripping Lucille."

"The snowcat?"

"She's a beauty, but she's got to lose some weight. You wanna help?"

"Sure," Nick replies, inhaling the last of his omelet and glancing over at Ensign Temuera, who's doing his best to remain invisible.

"Thank you. That was awesome," Nick says, acknowledging Eddie. "Man, you are one helluva cook."

Eddie's face lights up with a smile. "*Haere rā*, my friend."

Nick has no idea what that means, but he waves goodbye. He's fascinated by the big man.

Bear leads Nick through the rabbit warren of corridors within the *Te Kaha*, through a hatch and down a ladder leading to the hangar bay. With each rung, the temperature seems to fall by ten degrees.

Bear hands him a heavy coat and a pair of gloves, saying, "Cold, huh?"

"Like a freezer."

"This is the maintenance bay for the chopper." Bear points at the windows on the sliding garage doors at the rear, saying, "The flight deck is out there."

Floodlights illuminate a helicopter sitting on the pad. Ordinarily, it would be rolled inside the bay to protect it from the weather. Instead, dozens of straps hold it on the deck. They extend from the skids, the tail boom and even the rotors, fixing them in place. Icicles hang from the fuselage. There's no railing around the flight deck, but there is netting to catch anyone that falls off the edge.

"Once I've stripped this baby down, we'll push her to one side and wheel the chopper back in here."

"Ah," Nick says as though he understands.

"Can you hand me that torque wrench?" Bear asks, pointing at a tool kit.

Nick hands it to him, saying, "You're trying to conserve fuel, right?"

"Yep."

Bear removes the short ladder leading up to the cab of the snowcat.

"On a long haul like this, shedding weight will improve speed and mileage."

Nick nods.

"Help me with this guard rail," Bear says, standing on the flatbed back of the snowcat. "We'll use straps to hold fuel barrels in place."

Ensign Temuera stands back, out of earshot.

Nick tries to put on a brave face, but his heart sinks lower.

"What's the matter?" Bear asks as they start working on the flaring over the rear treads.

Nick lets out a solitary laugh. He's not sure why but he feels he can trust Bear. Perhaps it's because they're both mechanics. Maybe it's because Bear's the only person that hasn't asked anything of him. Bear seems genuine.

"I am so far out of my depth."

"We all are."

"You don't understand," he says. "I mean like—I shouldn't be here. I really shouldn't. You could literally pick anyone in America and they'd make better decisions than me. I've—let's just say, I've made my fair share of fuck ups."

Bear nods but doesn't say anything.

The snowcat runs on four independent sets of tank treads. Nick's used to seeing bulldozers with oblong treads on either side, but the treads on the snowcat are triangular. Bear begins removing the sheet metal covering the cogs that drive the treads. He tosses them aside.

Nick says, "I know nothing about outer space. How the hell am I supposed to make decisions about extraterrestrials?"

"You're afraid you'll make the wrong decision," Bear says, moving around behind the snowcat to work on the far treads.

"Yes," Nick says rather emphatically, as though such a conclusion should be obvious.

"It's not a coin toss," Bear says. "There are no right or wrong decisions—just decisions. I mean, think about it like where you're going on holiday next year. It doesn't matter if it's Florida or Canada, right? Hawaii or Italy? You make your decision based on the moment. On whether you want pineapple or goat's cheese on your pizza."

Nick nods.

"And you won't be alone. You'll be part of a team—a jury."

"I still don't get why they need a jury to make decisions."

Bear stops for a moment, crouching beside one of the treads and looking up at him.

"It's to stop arguments. Say China wants to remove a component for analysis, but the US says it should be left intact until we understand its function. Both sides will present their arguments, and you guys decide. You look at the pros and cons. Or say the scientists want to drill through a bulwark, but the military says no—you guys make the call."

"And if they agree?" Nick asks.

Bear laughs.

"It's a green light."

"Seems like a flaw," Nick replies, taking one of the panels from Bear and laying it aside as they move on to the front tread.

"How so?"

"What if everyone agrees on a really bad idea?"

Bear laughs.

"You can't get these guys to agree on the weather. Hey, can you hand me that screwdriver?"

Nick grabs a long flathead screwdriver and gives it to him. Bear digs around behind one of the panels, clearing out some gunk.

"Honestly," Nick says, "When I think about going down there and making decisions on stuff I barely understand, it makes me feel sick."

"I think you're going to make good decisions."

"Why's that?" Nick asks.

"Because you doubt yourself."

"And doubt is good?"

"I'd rather someone that doubts himself than some asshole that's convinced he's always right."

Nick nods. Bear's got a point. The only thing is, up until a few days ago, the asshole Bear's describing was Nick. Sandra wouldn't trust Nick to pick out a dress from her own closet, let alone decide on alien tech. And as for that goddamn football game Nick was so intent on watching when she left—hell, he's worried he'll be provoked by something equally dumb down in Antarctica. Everyone's reasonable until they ain't.

Wasn't it Pavlov's dogs that heard the dinner bell and came running? Pavlov described saliva dripping into empty bowls. Yeah, ring that damn bell and Nick will be there, panting with excitement. Will someone down there figure out how to punch his buttons?

Not much scares Nick. He's never been afraid of the dark. Horror movies are a bit of a laugh. Oh, sure, the jump-scares get him, but mostly because he's been surprised. This, though, this scares him. On Friday nights, whenever Sandra would ask what he'd like from the local Chinese takeout, he'd be fraught with indecision. More often than not, he'd go with an old favorite. He's predictable. Lame would be a better term, and he chides himself for being so damn soft.

Nick takes solace in one point—the multinational team of scientists, engineers, and military support have been doing this for almost eighteen months. For over a year, they've been able to make this work. He only hopes he doesn't embarrass himself.

STORM

An alarm sounds in the dark of night.

Nick opens his eyes, feeling disoriented. Something's wrong, but it's not a fire. There's no smoke. A rucksack slides across the floor, slamming into the far wall. Dmitri tumbles after it, still in his sleeping bag. Rather than rolling, he falls toward the wall. Jazz is awake. She has her arms wrapped around the bunk support. Her pillow tumbles past, while her legs fly out in the same direction.

In the fog of Nick's groggy mind, it's as though the cabin has been upended, but that makes no sense. It's only then he realizes he's suspended in midair. Rather than resting on the mattress, Nick is in motion as well. His head buckles as he hits the end of the bunk. Nick's back arches as he crumples, colliding with the empty bunkbed above him. Jazz is shouting something, but he can't hear her. Warnings sound over the speakers in the ceiling, but Nick can't make out individual words, just a haze of noise.

Dmitri is on his feet with his legs spread wide. He kicks with one foot, trying to free himself from his crumpled sleeping bag. He's holding onto the wall by the sink, swaying like a drunken man, barely able to stand.

Nick swings his legs over the edge of his bunk, holding on to the upper bunk. As he was hot, his sleeping bag was unzipped, acting as a blanket so he doesn't get tangled like Dmitri.

Jazz has her hand out, signaling for him to stay where he is. The door to their cabin swings open, slamming into the bulkhead.

Out in the corridor, an ensign yells, "Everything is fine. Everything is going to be okay. Stay where you are." Only he's standing almost sideways in the hatch, clinging to the upper rim of the door as the *Te Kaha* rocks. He sways as the rucksack slides back beneath Jazz.

Dmitri's bleeding from a split on his forehead. He staggers over toward Nick, pushing a hand towel against his temple. Nick finds himself sliding along his bunk, naturally making room for him.

"Oh, that smarts," Dmitri says, sitting on the edge of Nick's bed.

Nick's bunk runs along the side of the hull while the others are set on the back wall. Together, they form an L-shape. The cabin door has swung open into a catch, preventing it from swinging back. Light spills in from the corridor. Sailors run past in the hallway.

"Stay here," Jazz says, running for the door. She pushes past the ensign who's pleading for her to remain in the cabin. To hell with this, if the *Te Kaha* is going down, there's no way Nick is waiting around for the icy cold water to rush in. He slips on some trousers and chases after Jazz. The deck beneath him surges, pushing against his feet as the warship rides up a wave. For a moment, it's like being in an elevator rushing skyward. The waves they're riding must dwarf the vessel for size.

The ship rocks, swaying in a storm. Rather than running along the corridor, Nick finds himself pushing on the wall as he chases Jazz. Water drips from hatches as sailors work to close the upper deck. The internal ladders are all set well away from the external hatches. Seawater must be flooding in from somewhere.

A couple of sailors push along the corridor wearing cold water immersion suits. Although these look like wetsuits, they're bright orange and baggy. Thick black zippers. Reflective patches. Black rubber boots. But with all that, it's the flag that's incongruous. Mentally, Nick knows he's on a New Zealand frigate, but seeing a pure white flag with red stars and the Union Jack in one corner makes him uneasy. He'd rather see the Stars and Stripes. Regardless of how competent the Kiwis may be in antarctic waters, Nick would feel at home with the US Navy.

Jazz rushes up the ladder to the bridge. Nick follows close behind her.

Rain lashes the windows. Lightning ripples through the darkened cloud banks.

"Now is not the time," Commander Simonds fires off at Jazz. She's holding on to a rail, leaning beside one of her officers. He points at a wave towering over the *Te Kaha*. The pilot works with the helm, facing into the monster.

Nick assumed it was night, but the clouds are backlit by a cold winter sun. Visibility is less than a mile, but he doesn't need to see far to know what's coming.

Whitecaps stretch along an aquatic ridge line. Far from being waves, the *Te Kaha* is riding mountains in the ocean swell. A wall of water sweeps down toward them. The gun-metal grey bow of the warship plunges into the massive wave. Spray explodes from the hull. The forward gun disappears beneath the ocean as the deck is swamped. The *Te Kaha* is driven on by its massive engines. It rides up and out of the wave. Windshield wipers sweep across the windows, desperately trying to clear the spray.

"You shouldn't be up here," the commander yells as the ensign following them scrambles onto the bridge.

"I—I have to see this," Nick says from behind Jazz. She turns, only now realizing he's followed her.

Jazz is about to say something, probably wanting him to return to the cabin when Commander Simonds says, "For fuck sake, if you're going to be up here, strap in at the back!"

The two of them rush to the seats behind the navigation desk and buckle in.

The *Te Kaha* clears the top of the next wave, giving them a broad view across the ocean swell. The depression before them opens out like a valley. The crest is capped with smaller breaking waves, while the hollow in between is smooth by comparison. The ocean is streaked with white spray. It's only when the warship drops into the trough that Nick's heart rises in his throat. This is a rollercoaster running out of control, plunging into the depths. Not only is the *Te Kaha* rushing down toward the base of the next wave, it's swaying with the wind.

Waves crash over the sharp bow of the warship. Salt spray explodes from the hull, racing out across the water.

The next wave isn't as large, allowing the warship to ride back up and over it without any trouble. From the crest, though, several other waves come into view. Nick clenches, seeing what's coming.

A wave the size of a high-rise looms before them. Within seconds, it's towering over them, blotting out the sun. When the bow of the *Te Kaha* hits, a wall of white spray shoots out across the sea. The forecourt of the vessel disappears beneath the ocean along with the cannon. This time, though, it's not just the spray hitting the windows. For a moment, the bridge itself is submerged by the wave. The superstructure of the frigate shudders under the impact.

Looking out the windows, all Nick can see is the emerald green of the deep sea. Then, as suddenly as it came, the water recedes. The *Te Kaha* drives up, cutting through the surface. The windows are lashed with spray. Finally, the horizon appears through the torrent of water rushing off the roof of the bridge.

Commander Simonds holds onto the bulkhead above her.

"Yeehaw!"

She could be riding a bull at a rodeo.

"Damn, that was big!"

The *Te Kaha* comes thundering back down on the other side of the wave. Yet again, the bow of the warship stabs at the ocean, cutting through the dark water. Simonds is busy, talking with her crew about weather patterns, wind speeds, wave heights, and the angle of attack.

The storm is relentless.

The *Te Kaha* faces up toward the sky before plunging back into the depths. It's all Nick can do not to vomit. He has to keep his mind busy or he's going to paint the floor yellow.

Radar images sweep across consoles stretching along the bridge. The crew are wearing fire suits not unlike those used by Formula One racing drivers. Their hair is hidden beneath white fire-retardant material. Thick headphones cover their ears. Throughout it all, they're unwavering. The *Te Kaha* might be taking a pounding, but if the crew have any misgivings, it doesn't show. They speak calmly into microphones positioned just inches from their lips. That's when it strikes Nick. Far from being driven by just one or two people, the entire crew is working together to ride the storm. He overhears discussions about ballast loading, equalizing fuel tanks, displacement pumps, and the communications array. In that moment, it strikes him that the *Te Kaha* is alive. Despite the ferocity of the storm, everyone's working together as one.

Even the commander is calm. At first, Nick mistook her passion for anger, but she's directing rather than controlling her crew. She talks with them rather than yelling at them, discussing options rather than demanding a response.

Commander Simonds moves between stations, bracing a split second before each thundering impact as waves crash over on the warship. At one point, she steals a quick glance at the two of them and cracks a slight smile. Damn, she's enjoying this way too much.

The wind whips spray across the deck as another wave

submerges the frigate's main gun, but Nick's relaxed. He's found his rhythm. The calm, methodical actions of the crew have put him at ease.

"Are we having fun yet?" the commander asks, moving back beside the two of them. That they're the last of her concerns doesn't go unnoticed by Nick.

"I'm good," Jazz says, but the way Jazz grips the armrests suggests otherwise.

"We're doing fine," the commander assures her. "We took a freak wave from the starboard side, but other than that, we're okay. We can ride this out."

"H—How?"

"How long?" Commander Simonds says, completing a question Jazz could barely manage. "It's going to be a long day, I'm afraid. But don't let this worry you. The *Te Kaha* is an ANZAC class frigate. She's built for days like this. She can take one helluva beating and still keep rocking."

Waves crash over the forward gun, spraying the windows yet again.

"This is all perfectly normal," the commander says as the warship rides up and over the ocean swell before that familiar sinking feeling hits yet again. Four thousand tonnes of steel plunges back down into the sea.

Jazz is pale.

"We have sedatives," the commander says, gesturing to the ensign to come over. "I can have the ship's doctor give you an antiemetic to help with nausea."

"Yeah," Jazz says, timing when she gets out of her seat. The ensign helps her down the stairs, bracing as another wave strikes.

"And you?" the commander asks.

"I'm fine," Nick says, surprising himself with how he's perked up. "Being able to see what's happening helps."

Commander Simonds laughs, shifting her weight as the *Te*

Kaha rocks with the impact of another wave breaking over her bow.

"Okay. Well, if you need anything."

"Oh, you'll be the last person I'll bug," Nick says. "You've got your hands full."

The commander smiles and makes her way back to the helm.

For Nick, there's something strangely satisfying about the way the *Te Kaha* refuses to surrender to the relentless onslaught of the squall. It's the mastery of nature. As small as their vessel is within the vast open ocean, as immense and powerful as the storm is along with the thundering impact of each wave, somehow humanity has prevailed.

Nick is riding upon the triumph of several thousand years of engineering prowess. A single wave could kill him—kill all of them—and yet the waves can't get to them. They're protected by more than reinforced glass and thick plate steel. Their salvation lies in the design workshops and architectural drawings of yesteryear.

Someone thought about this exact moment decades before it occurred. Someone calculated the force they'd be hit with and decided, hell yeah, we can tame this beast. Did they ever actually ride a frigate in a storm like this? Hah. They didn't need to. They'd seen it in their mind's eye. With over forty thousand horsepower being produced by the diesel engines, they knew they could conquer even these immense waves.

"There you are," a voice whispers from behind Nick.

Bear slides around and into the seat Jazz was in, tightening the buckle as another wave pounds the *Te Kaha*. Salt spray rushes at the windows with a rhythm Nick finds strangely reassuring.

"Thought you might need this," Bear says, slipping a small steel water bottle from his jacket and handing it to him.

"What's this?"

"Antifreeze."

MANA

After three days, the storm becomes the new norm. Actions that would have seemed insane when they first left South Georgia are now somewhat habitual. Walking down the corridor toward the galley requires an utterly alien level of coordination. Sailors pass each other with their arms out, ducking and weaving through the passageways as they keep their hands up, ready to tap against the walls, countering the sway of the frigate. They're pinballs bouncing around a rickety old machine.

Nick loves the rough weather. As the warship rises, riding over a wave the size of a luxury hotel in Vegas, the floor drives up beneath his feet. Then there's a lull—a brief moment when the vessel begins to fall as it crosses the crest of the wave. At that point, his sense of weight fades. His feet skip across the grating. The deck drops away. His outstretched hand prevents him from hitting his head on the steel ceiling. And he rides down with the warship. Then the dance unfolds again.

The *Te Kaha* rolls with a steady rhythm, making this bizarre form of walking somewhat predictable. To his surprise, it's enjoyable. His reactions have become somewhat autonomous. Life onboard the *Te Kaha* is abnormally normal in the midst of an antarctic storm tearing through the Southern Ocean.

Drinking coffee is all about timing. Nick has learned to sip on the up-stroke, just after the warship dips into the trough of a wave. Coffee tends to slosh when going down in the ocean swell, but not when rising up. If anything, it's strangely calm at that point. Going over the top of a wave with a full cup, though, is an invitation to be scalded by hot fluid. Nick finds it funny seeing everyone drinking at once, and then not drinking at all in a surreal sense of unspoken coordination.

Ensign Temuera has lightened up and occasionally swings by to check on Nick, but he's no longer shadowing him.

Eddie still flips omelets—storm be damned. Nick tries not to stare at his facial tattoos. They're sacred. They speak of a culture beyond anything Nick could ever imagine. The soft green stripes mirror each other, being interlaced on either side of Eddie's face. The design is organic, almost natural in its styling. It's as though dozens of silk ribbons have been caught in the wind and rain. They've curled over Eddie's cheeks and forehead, leaving their mark on his skin. Nick is fascinated by Eddie. There's something regal in the way the cook carries himself.

Bear continues playing around with Lucille in the equipment bay at the rear of the *Te Kaha*. The helicopter has been moved inside, so there's not a lot of room to get around, but Bear doesn't mind. If anything, life back there is less extreme. The weight of the engines and the design of the frigate is such that the stern is more stable than the bow.

Nick wakes on the fourth day feeling unsettled. He sits up and hangs his feet over the edge of the bed. Jazz and Dmitri are both still asleep. No motion. He gets up, instinctively reaching for the walls and ceiling, trying to find a rhythm that no longer exists. The *Te Kaha* sways slightly. The diesel engines hum as the warship plows through the ocean.

There's a knock on the door. Nick opens it. Jazz stirs.

"Commander Simonds requests your presence on the bridge."

"Oh. Ah. Sure," Nick replies, grabbing some trousers and slipping them on. He shoves his feet in a pair of boots and tightens the laces as he steps out into the corridor. The ensign leads him along the now-familiar passageways with their pipes and conduits and takes him up the ladder to the bridge.

Nick arrives to see a relaxed commander lounging in one of the chairs with a huge grin on her face. At first, he assumes it's because they've ridden out of the storm, but she points behind him, saying, "I thought you might like to see a berg."

"Oh, wow," Nick says, walking over and reaching for the windowsill.

Jazz arrives on the bridge behind him.

Stars dot the sky, breaking through the night. Lightning flickers through distant cloud banks low on the horizon. The ocean is choppy, being whipped up by the wind. Whitecaps dance across the waves, but it's the backdrop that catches his eye. An iceberg rises from the depths. Rugged white cliffs lead up to a plateau easily a hundred feet above the waterline. Chunks of ice fall away from the leading edge, crashing into the sea, sending huge waves across the water.

The iceberg is easily four times the length of the Te Kaha and twice as tall. Even though they're hundreds of yards away, it towers over the warship. The water immediately around the base of the iceberg is an iridescent blue, highlighting the iceberg's sunken base. It's an ice mountain hidden in the ocean.

To his delight, a bay opens out on the side of the iceberg. There's a ledge nestled into the icy crag, curling around to what looks like a pearly white beach. Water laps at the smooth edge, slowly melting the ice.

Cracks run through the iceberg, threatening to tear it apart, opening huge crevasses in the cliff face.

The warship glides past.

"Amazing!"

"Yeah, quite something, huh?" Commander Simonds says.

"Where are we?" Jazz asks.

"We're in the Weddell Sea, a couple of hundred kilometers off the coast of the Brunt Ice Shelf. We've sailed into the lee of Maud Land, so for now, we're sheltered from the storm. It's quite late in the season for icebergs. Normally, during winter, they're much closer to land. They tend to get caught in the growing ice sheet."

A helicopter flies in low across the ocean. Its red navigation lights flicker in the darkness. The Sikorsky circles out wide around the warship before approaching the landing pad at the rear of the *Te Kaha*.

Commander Simonds says, "We've run a couple of recon flights to scout our approach to the coast. There's a lot of ice out there. Temperature's dropping fast."

"What's the plan?" Jazz asks as the commander rolls out a map on the navigation desk.

"The Brits are already in motion," she says, tapping the map. "They departed *Halley* a couple of days ago, heading in toward the Shackleton Range. The idea is we'll fly you as far as we can inland. To maximize our range, the chopper crew will return to *Halley* rather than the *Te Kaha*. That'll give us an additional hundred and fifty kilometers to play with. The crew will winter at *Halley*. We'll pick them up in the spring."

"And the fuel depots?" Jazz asks.

"There are three dumps," she says, tapping the map in three spots. "At the base of Fuji Dome, Argus Dome, and Amundsen-Scott, but Amundsen is off your route. It's there if you need it, but it would be one helluva detour."

"Understood," Jazz says.

It's only then Nick realizes Bear is peering over his shoulder.

Bear says, "Lucille's got the coordinates locked in. The challenge is, we're only going to have the Brits with us as far as Fuji Dome."

"They'll get you through the glacier field and up onto the plateau," the commander says. "But they're running smaller cruisers. They don't have the range of your cat."

Jazz nods. "Thank you, commander."

"We've got about four hours before we reach our closest approach to the coast. My advice—get Eddie to cook you up some grub. That's going to be the last decent meal you'll get for a while."

"Sounds good to me," Bear says, slapping Nick on the shoulder. They head back below deck as Jazz continues talking with the commander.

The *Te Kaha* is a hive of activity. Sailors rush through the passageways, moving with purpose, pushing through doorways and down ladders.

Eddie grins as they approach the galley.

"Brother. You are going to Antarctica. Hot damn!"

Nick barely knows Eddie, but he loves his unbridled enthusiasm.

Bear smiles. "We came down here for some more of your world-famous Ōtāhuhu omelets."

"Awe, nah," Eddie says. "You fellas are getting the prime cuts. Commander's orders."

"Nice," Nick says, squeezing into the bench seat running along the front of the galley, giving him a view of Eddie working his skillets. Eddie has four of them on the burners, cooking up sautéed mushrooms, fried potato scallops, onions, and a rich gravy.

"How do you like your steak?"

Nick and Bear reply in unison with, "Medium rare."

"Too easy."

Eddie uses a pair of tongs to turn roast pumpkin and zucchini over on a hot grill. He bounces between the various dishes, moving like an octopus with eight arms.

"I am so going to miss this," Nick says.

"Oh, you sure are," Bear replies, laughing. "Just wait till you're scooping corn beef out of a cold can in the middle of a blizzard. Remember this moment. Remember the smell."

Eddie smiles. He lets the steaks rest on a wooden chopping board and cleans up with a cloth.

"You fellas are going to love this," he says, dishing up the vegetables onto a couple of plates. He slices the steak into strips, fanning them out on the plates.

"That," Nick says as the plate is slid toward him, "is a work of art, my friend."

Eddie has a deep, chesty laugh. "He, he, he!"

Nick and Bear begin eating as Eddie excuses himself. He comes back several minutes later with a small blue box. To Nick's surprise, a number of the crew have gathered around, blocking access to the galley from both sides.

As they finish their meal, Eddie speaks with a level of pride and passion Nick has never known.

"Nicholas James Ferrin. It has been our honor to serve you on board this warship."

Nick puts down his cutlery, giving Eddie his undivided attention as the big man continues.

"*Te Kaha* means be strong. Down there in Antarctica, you must *kia kaha*, you must *remain strong*, for you represent not only America, but all of us. *Nga Iwi Taketake o te Ao*—all the people of this Earth.

Eddie opens the box, presenting Nick with a Māori war club carved from jade. Unlike a European ax, there's no head of iron or wooden handle. Instead, the ax unfolds like a wave on the ocean. There's a knot at the base of the handle. From there, the ax fans out, with most of the weight forming a rolling curve. Nick's never seen anything like this. To him, it screams of a lost world.

The intricate carving suggests the ax is designed for precision blows. The rounded head has a thin edge, but it's not sharp. It's not difficult to imagine it cleaving a skull in two. Although this war ax is a miniature replica, it's still six inches in length. This is something to be worn with pride.

The inscription inside the box reads:

Te kaha wahaika mana

Kia kaha, kia whakahaere

To be powerful, be in control

"This is the *wahaika*," Eddie says, pointing at the words inside the box. "It is made from *pounamu* or greenstone. It's on the coat of arms for the *Te Kaha* as it represents our *mana*—our pride, our integrity, and our humility."

There's something regal about the way he speaks. Being American, Nick would pronounce *mana* like nana, but Eddie says *mun-nah* with the emphasis on a low, guttural *m*.

"Do not be mistaken. The *wahaika* is a symbol of both war and peace. My great grandfather was from the *Ureweras*. He would tell me that *mana* was: *Te mūrau a to tini, Te wenerau a to mono, Te manu tīoriori*."

The crew close ranks, swelling around them, filling all the various areas within the galley, listening intently to Eddie. Nick has made a lot of dumb mistakes in life, but dismissing Eddie as being just a cook is not one of them. Eddie clearly has the respect of the crew. For them, he's a spiritual leader. There's no doubt Commander Simonds understood this when she sent Nick down here for breakfast.

Eddie strikes his chest with his fist as he translates his great grandfather. He hits with such aggression and passion his chest reverberates like a kettle drum.

"The dread of all, the scorn and envy of thousands is the

songbird that dances in the trees!"

Nick has no idea what that means.

Eddie removes the ornate club from its plush velvet padding and hangs it around Nick's neck. The jade is stunning. A thin black cord runs through the handle, forming a necklace.

"This is *mana*," Eddie says. "When my people would go to war, there was no mercy. No surrender. We took no prisoners. All would die. And so we developed the *haka*—a war dance. It was an alternative to war. A deterrent.

"The *haka* was a song. A chant. A threat. The beating of the chest. The flex of muscles. The rush of passion. We would dance with our weapons—the *patu*, the *taiaha*, and the *wahaika*. Such is the dance of the songbird. These displays were a chance to avoid war. Sometimes, the bravest thing is not to fight."

Nick nods, swallowing the lump in his throat.

"When you're down there," Eddie says, "don't forget us. Do not forget why you are there. Do not forget the *Te Kaha*. Do not forget your *mana*."

"I won't."

ΛNTARCTICA

Icebergs dot the sea.

Spotlights illuminate the flight deck.

Icicles hang from the railings running along the *Te Kaha*.

Bear hangs out of the open side of the Sikorsky helicopter as it hovers above the deck of the frigate, allowing the wind to whip inside the cabin. Nick hunches against the chill. His zipped-up jacket and fur-lined hood struggle to keep his cheeks warm. Jazz is beside him. Being thinner, she feels the cold more. She's adopted a posture with her legs up on the seat and her arms pulled in close to her body. She barely moves, not wanting to lose heat. Damn, it is cold with the helicopter door open.

Bear is wearing a harness with a climbing rope anchoring him to the fuselage. He's stepped down, half out of the chopper, with one boot on the skids. He holds his arm out, signaling for the pilots to drift slightly further forward.

A steel cable hangs from the underside of the helicopter. Down on the deck of the warship, sailors attach chains to Lucille, leading them from the four corners of the snowcat to a central hook. Over the radio, a sailor talks through the approach.

"Ten meters out... Slight crosswind... Steady... Down five."

Although the frigate is at anchor, vapor billows from its twin chimneys as hot air collides with cold. For Nick, it's unnerving to be so close to the *Te Kaha*. The gunmetal grey warship is imposing from the air. Radio masts reach up from the mid-deck. The Sikorsky is below the height of the antenna array and radar domes on the bridge.

"Albatross, you have four points of contact. You are clear to take the weight."

"Copy that, *Te Kaha*."

The pilot eases the Sikorsky higher, gently taking up Lucille's weight. Sailors use guide ropes to control the motion of the snowcat as it clears the deck.

"Albatross, the package has fifteen meters separation. You are clear of the *Te Kaha*."

"Copy that. Albatross withdrawing."

The helicopter drifts backward, giving the crew time to release the guide ropes as the stern of the warship comes into view. Bear closes the side door.

"God speed, Albatross."

With that, the helicopter rises, pulling out to one side of the frigate as it gains altitude. Crew members line the bow of the warship, watching as the helicopter passes at a distance of several hundred meters.

Moonlight reflects off the water. Icebergs drift in packs. Looking down on them from above, they go from pure white to iridescent blue beneath the sea. In the distance, sheer walls of ice stretch along the horizon. Clouds hide the distant mountains, revealing only their rocky slopes.

"We got lucky," Jazz says, talking over the radio.

"How so?" Nick asks, pushing his hood back and adjusting his headset so it sits directly over his ears.

"The weather is being kind. We've got cloud cover down to four thousand meters, but that'll let us get at least a couple of hundred kilometers inland."

Even though Antarctica is shrouded in perpetual darkness

for the next three months, the ice is crisp, clean, and bright. Nick sits by one of the windows, staring out into the night, watching as they cross the coastline.

Glaciers pass beneath the helicopter. Occasionally, rocky outcrops are visible, breaking through the snow, but for the most part, there's nothing beyond the white ice. There's no sign of life anywhere. Jazz wasn't kidding when she said it was like being on another planet.

There's talking over the radio, but Nick blocks it out. The sheer size of Antarctica is daunting. Nick's aware he's only seeing a small portion near the coast.

After almost two hours, Jazz taps him on the shoulder, pointing in the distance. A faint blue strobe light blinks on the horizon.

"That's the Brits."

The helicopter descends, talking to the ground team as it circles a makeshift camp on the ice. Tents lie half-buried in the snow beside two orange snowcats. Their spotlights are on, illuminating the darkness, providing the pilot visibility as he approaches. Out on the fringes, dark shadows move, reaching for guide ropes flicking in the wind. The helicopter sways as it brings Lucille in. Once the US snowcat is safely on the ground and the chains are released, a winch activates, withdrawing the cable.

The Sikorsky swings around, turning on its own spotlights, and lands on the other side of the makeshift British base. The side door opens. Jazz jumps out into the blizzard being kicked up by the rotor blades. Dmitri hands their packs and supplies to Bear, who passes them on to Jazz. She casts them to one side on the frozen plateau. It's time to disembark.

Dmitri gestures for Nick to go first. Bear helps him down onto the skids of the helicopter. This is it. With a single step, he's passing from one world into the next, leaving civilization behind. Jazz takes his gloved hand and guides him away as the others jump down.

Within seconds, the navigation lights on the underbelly of the helicopter disappear into the gloom. The thump of the rotors is replaced by the howl of the wind whipping across the desolate plain. Nick feels abandoned.

Soldiers run in, grabbing their packs and carrying them over to Lucille. Bear is already standing on the tracks of the vehicle, checking something in the engine bay. Another snowcat pulls alongside, dragging a sleigh with barrels of diesel stacked on the rear deck. Bear yells above the growing storm and attaches a pump, filling the empty tanks on Lucille. Dmitri climbs in the cab. He stacks the backpacks at the rear as Jazz gets on the radio. Nick is numb, but not from the cold.

"You okay?" Jazz asks as he climbs in the back of the snowcat.

"Yeah, good."

Liar.

Jazz knows but doesn't care. Dmitri overhears what's said, but he continues busying himself, packing away goods on the shelves at the rear of the cabin. Caring is a luxury item not found in Antarctica.

Lucille has two rows of bench seats rather than individual seats. Behind the seats, there's a mattress and the storage area. For now, backpacks clog the gap.

Bear climbs in the driver's side, stepping up from the front treads. He slams the door and starts the engine. Lucille springs to life. Snowflakes are caught in her headlights. The British team pack up their tents, leaving chaotic boot prints in the snow. The lead British snowcat pulls out in front of them, with the other following behind them.

"Okay," Bear says. "Let's get this show on the road."

"What about crevasses?" Dmitri asks. "Are we going to have to make any crossings?"

"Are you worried about falling through the ice?" Bear asks.

114

"We cheated and flew over most of the crevasses. They tend to be close to the coast, where the glaciers start to break up. The one saving grace of a winter crossing is anything that opened up on the plateau last summer will be buried by now."

"Good to know."

Nick leans over from the back seat, poking his head between Bear and Jazz. "Looks pretty bleak out there."

"It is," Bear replies, "but we've got ground radar and GPS. We'll be fine."

Jazz has a map out. She draws lines with a grease pencil, marking their position and heading using an old-fashioned compass. She writes in the margin, noting the time, direction, and estimated speed of the snowcat.

"Don't mind me," she says, looking across at Bear, "I'm old school. I trust dead-reckoning over satellites."

Bear seems to find that quaint, grinning at her as he speeds up, messing with her equations. He ensures the lights on the British snowcat are visible through the driving snow.

"You laugh," she says. "But just you wait till a solar storm hits and we lose our bearings."

Bear doesn't bite. He sets the throttle and sits back, watching the old-style metrics in front of him.

The snowcat is more like a tractor than a car. There are only two pedals, both of which are mounted on huge steel bars protruding from the deck of the vehicle. The clutch and brake are clumsy, being designed to operate with thick boots. There's no accelerator as such, just a throttle set below the steering wheel. It's a thick bar moving along grooves in a steel plate, allowing the engine to be set at a precise, steady rate. Not only does it ensure consistent fuel consumption, it makes the calculations Jazz is doing realistic. There's little to no variation in their speed as they trundle over the ice.

"How fast are we going?" Nick asks, seeing the tachometer

along with dials showing oil pressure and engine temperature.

"At the moment, about fifteen miles an hour. Out on the plateau, we can hit twenty plus."

"And that's fast?" Nick asks.

Bear laughs. "Oh, for Antarctica, that's like racing around in a Lamborghini. Twenty miles an hour might not sound like much, but you have to remember, we run day and night without stopping. If we could travel as the crow flies, we'd eat that up in three days. As it is, we'll probably cover fifteen hundred miles in about four or five days."

"Oh," Nick replies.

Jazz says, "The only time we'll stop is at the fuel dumps. You're going to have to shit and piss in the bucket behind the backseat, but it's not all bad. Bear smuggled some chocolate off the *Te Kaha*. Compliments of Eddie."

"Wonderful."

Lucille rides up a gentle slope. For the longest time, there's no change in the view out the windshield. Snow flurries rush across from the side, blurring their vision. Their headlights are good for about twenty to thirty feet. Beyond that, the dim glow of navigation lights on the British vehicle are barely visible in the darkness.

"Do we have guns?" Nick asks out of curiosity.

"Yes," Jazz replies. "Why do you ask?"

"I was just wondering if we might run into polar bears."

"There are no polar bears in Antarctica."

Dmitri says, "It's too damn cold."

"Oh. So why do you have a gun?" Nick asks. "Are there like killer penguins or something?"

Jazz laughs.

"Procedure," she says. "Standard military deployment. Just in case."

Nick can't let that go.

"In case of what?"

"Nothing," Jazz says, turning back toward him with her arm resting along the top of the bench seat. "Honest. There's nothing out there in the darkness."

Neither of the other men say anything which Nick finds strange. He's expecting them to reinforce her position, but they don't. There might not be anything in the darkness, but there is something beneath the ice.

"We're going to be running shifts on driving and navigation," she says, changing the subject. "Bear and Dmitri for eight hours. Then the two of us while they rest. Through the night, we'll switch and run two four-hour shifts to keep everyone frosty."

"Oh, I'm frosty all right," Nick says. "Are you going to turn on the heater?"

"It's on," Bear says, looking over his shoulder and grinning at Nick.

Time becomes immaterial.

Nothing beyond the double-glazed glass seems to change.

Were it not for the rocking of the cabin, they could be sitting still on the ice with the engine idling, watching as the driving snow slides sideways through their spotlights. Minutes pass like hours as boredom sets in.

Without the sun, it feels like it's always midnight, but the digital clock on the dash reads 16:07. It's just after four in the afternoon. Fuck.

Jazz and Dmitri swap spots, clambering over the bench seat, but Nick finds the cold creeping in anytime he shifts his arms or legs. To keep warm, he stays still.

"Who knows a good ghost story?" Bear asks without taking his eyes off the driving snow.

"Ghost stories, really?" Jazz says, rolling her eyes.

"Sure," Dmitri says. "I know one. It's called the Former Soviet Republic."

"What about you?" Bear asks, glancing over at Nick. "Have you ever seen a ghost?"

"There's no such thing as ghosts," Jazz says rather emphatically.

"No," Nick says, ignoring Jazz. "No ghosts. The closest I've come is a skeleton."

"A real one?" Bear asks, surprised.

"Unfortunately."

"Come on then," Bear says. "We're all skeletons on the inside, right? We're a bunch of bones brought to life by blood and sinew. Tell us about your skeleton."

"Well," Nick begins. "This is going to sound kind of crazy—like something from a Stephen King novel—but I swear, it's true. Every word."

No one speaks. For a moment, Nick loses himself in his memories. Instead of traversing a glacier in Antarctica, he's back in South Carolina, where he ought to be.

"In high school, we had this skeleton hanging at the back of the biology lab. To me, skeletons are creepy. They're us laid bare, stripped of everything that makes us human. Every day I went to class, there it was, giving me a greeting from beyond the grave."

"And it was real?" Bear asks. "You know, not like a Halloween skeleton or something."

"Oh, yeah. It was real," Nick says. "Over time, I found it fascinating. Skeletons are different. They're not a dead body. Well, they are and they aren't. They don't look like anyone. They don't look like they were ever alive, but they were.

"After about three months, I cracked. I had to know who it was, where they were from, what they were like. It turns out, that collection of yellowing bones was a teenaged girl that died in a flood in Bangladesh about two decades earlier.

"I doubt she willingly donated her bones to science, but there she was, with a metal screw drilled into the top of her skull. She was doomed to hang from a steel frame. A metal bar bent back over her head and down beneath her dangling feet. The base of the frame was rickety as hell. It's amazing she never fell over. It seems she was cursed to haunt our classes forever, destined never to graduate. I thought it was sad. Once she died, she could never grow old.

"Anyway, she disappeared for a few weeks. No one thought anything of it, but I missed her macabre reminder of our fleeting time on Earth. It turns out, she was on loan to another school. Lucy was cheating on us, or so we joked.

"So one day, I was called to the admin block with a friend and asked to take Lucy back to the lab, only that seemed cruel. We were teens. All three of us. It seemed wrong to have one of our own condemned to a lifeless existence, never experiencing friendship or joy, so we decided to take Lucy on a tour of our school.

"First stop was a classroom with a solid wooden door. We knocked between bursts of laughter. The teacher was in the middle of class, so she called out, *Come in*, but poor Lucy couldn't open door handles with her feeble stick-like fingers and boney knuckles. We knocked again. Somewhat irate, the teacher yelled, *I said, Come in!* To which, we knocked even louder. Finally, the teacher threw open the door, yelling, *Who is it?* On seeing Lucy, she screamed. Within seconds, she was chuckling in delight and calling us rascals. I think Lucy would have approved. Certainly, the teens in the class roared with laughter.

"From there, Lucy wandered throughout the school, sticking her head around the corner of a door, peering through the glass, and tapping on windows with her zombie-like hands. Each time, both teachers and kids alike responded with shock and then delight at this macabre interruption to their otherwise mundane day.

"Sure beats being locked in a cupboard, huh, Lucy?

"Eventually, with the hour almost up and the corridors about to be flooded with kids rushing to their next class, we returned to the biology department. For once, we knocked with genuine resolve. We were here. Our task was complete. The lab assistant opened the door and screamed, which confused me. She was the only one actually expecting Lucy on her metal stand.

"I don't know what happened to Lucy after that. They started keeping her in a locked cupboard. I think someone must have complained about our whirlwind tour. Like me, they were probably freaked out by her empty, hollow eye sockets staring at them.

"We only ever saw Lucy on the odd occasion when they let her out for discussions about anatomy. As horrific as her death must have been, I'd like to think she would have enjoyed that one sunny afternoon traipsing around our high school thousands of miles from where she was born and raised.

"Whenever I saw her, I'd wonder about the life that once animated those bones. I would have liked to meet Lucy. The real Lucy. She always left me feeling numb at the realization we were both the same—that our only difference lay in time and chance. So yeah, that's it. Not really a ghost story, but it's all I've got."

"Huh," Bear says, lost in thought, staring out into the darkness.

DECISIONS

An eerie green glow breaks through the clouds like some alien monster lurking in the darkness. For now, the storm has abated. Antarctica is locked in a perpetual night. It's a little after 11 AM, not that Nick cares. For him, not seeing the sun ever is utterly dispiriting. Jazz wasn't kidding when she said Antarctica was worse than Mars.

"Don't wander off," Jazz says as Nick gets down from Lucille, dropping from the ice-covered steel tracks into the snow. It's been three days, and he has to stretch, if only to remind his legs they still work. The wind curls around the snowcat, chilling his cheeks. Hell has frozen over. He tightens the hood wrapped around his face.

Bear drags a thick black hose over to Lucille. Like a snake, it winds its way from the barrels forming the fuel dump to the Day-Glo orange snowcat. Most of the barrels are buried in snow, forcing Bear to chip away at the ice to open their access ports. An aluminum frame rises from the middle of the plateau. Although it looks like a radio mast with steel wires holding it in place, it's a flag pole, marking the location of the fuel reservoir. A tattered flag rattles in the gale descending upon them. The red, white and blue of the Union Jack are barely visible in the darkness.

Their escorts have already turned around, having pulled into the other side of the fuel dump as they prepare for their run back to *Halley*. Dmitri and Jazz talk with the British team. Headlights fight the darkness.

"What is that?" Nick asks, pointing at the sky.

Bear stands on Lucille's tracks, watching as diesel is pumped into the tank.

"Aurora Australis. The southern lights. Beautiful, huh?"

"I guess."

For Nick, the green glow is foreboding.

Although they haven't had much to do with the British teams, seeing their headlights disappear into the oncoming storm is disconcerting. They're heading in the opposite direction. From now on, the American team is on its own—just four of them pushing on into the antarctic winter. Bear fills up the empty diesel barrels on the back of Lucille, extending their range.

"Does it ever freeze?" Nick asks.

"The diesel?" Bear replies. "We're using a class-four mix. There are so many additives in this stuff, it's barely fuel."

"Huh."

Jazz is anxious to get going. She said the weather forecast provided by meteorologists at *Halley* wasn't encouraging.

Within a few miles, the wind increases, buffeting the snowcat. The cabin rocks in the gale-force winds as the storm returns. Hail strikes the metal roof, making it difficult to think, let alone talk. On they drive, seeing nothing beyond the reach of their headlights. Snow flies sideways, whipping along the ground. There's no horizon, just a blur where the darkness defeats the light.

"So, how does it work?" Nick asks, trying to take his mind off the feeling of being lost. "The jury."

"Okay," Jazz says, reaching into her rucksack and pulling out a bunch of papers. "Let's go through a decision."

She thumbs through the papers with her gloved fingers,

struggling to separate them.

"All right, this was a decision made last month. It's a ruling between the US and China on meta-materials."

"What are those?"

"Ah," she says, scanning the page. "They're materials that have unusual properties. Things that aren't found in nature."

It sounds boring, but Nick doesn't say that.

Jazz says, "The US wanted to release the structure and composition to the broader scientific community under the guise of a peer-reviewed research paper on emerging materials for use in space exploration."

Now it sounds like psychobabble.

Jazz holds up a photo to show him what it looks like at an atomic level.

Nick says, "So, basically, it's a waffle minus maple syrup."

"Don't joke about waffles," Bear says.

"This is a microscopic image of the actual material recovered from the outer layer of the alien craft," Jazz says, walking herself through the notes in front of her. "Ah, it's a lightweight ceramic nano-truss capable of withstanding loads almost a million times its own weight without losing its shape. It absorbs energy rather than reflecting it, making it appear jet black."

"Oh, okay," Nick says. Finally, something about this deliberation sounds important. It's still obscure, but clearly this material is impressive. "Why did the Chinese want to block its release?"

"Hang on," Jazz says, scanning the content in front of her. "They argued it could be used to build supersonic kinetic weapons with the impact energy of a tactical nuke. So no explosives, just insane speeds. They suggested this kind of missile would be virtually invisible to radar."

"Oh," Nick says. "That doesn't sound good."

"Which way would you vote?" Jazz asks.

Fuck.

Nick doesn't have enough information. The jury had to be presented with more than that. He has no idea what to say. Even here, within the confines of the snowcat, he's aware of the expectation to side with his country. Is it treason to question intent? To want some assurance how this will be used? Jazz looks at him as though the answer is simple. He should just blurt it out, but Nick takes this seriously, after all, such a weapon could be used against a warship like the *Te Kaha*, destroying it in the blink of an eye. What would happen if such a device slammed into a building in downtown New York?

"There must be more arguments," Nick says, trying to buy himself some time. He's acutely aware Dmitri is watching him with curiosity. It seems Jazz wants unquestioning loyalty while Dmitri is looking for something else—a spine. As for Nick, his motivation is simple. It's not that he's struggling with indecision. He doesn't want to be a fuck-up. He wants to reclaim all that was lost to his arrogance. Sandra was right to walk out on him. He hit her. Oh, he claimed it was just a push, but that wasn't true. The crazy thing was, even in the heat of the moment as she stood there by the door ready to leave, she never called him out on that lie.

Jazz stares at him, narrowing her eyes.

"They must have debated this," Nick says, pleading for more information. "I mean, we're down here to learn from this thing, right? So we've learned about a new kind of wonder material. There must be lots of applications. I mean, it's swords and plowshares, right? It's all a question of how we use this material. It could be used to make planes more lightweight, saving fuel."

Jazz nods. She likes his logic, but Nick's not fooled. She likes it because it supports the US position.

"And there must be more to the Chinese argument," he

says. "Why wouldn't they want this material?"

Jazz skims through a few pages, saying, "Hmmm. This material only forms under extreme temperatures and pressures. There are only three experimental labs capable of recreating it."

"All of them in the US?" Nick asks.

"Yes."

"Okay, so they're afraid of the US gaining a strategic advantage over them."

"I guess."

"Well," he says. "They're right. We would use it to make bombs. I mean, we've got the biggest military in the world. We *love* our bombs—especially the expensive ones that make people rich."

"You're not helping the argument," she says.

"I'd vote, no," Nick says.

There's silence.

Jazz glares at him, gritting her teeth.

"What was the final decision?" he asks.

Begrudgingly, Jazz says, "It passed with an injunction limiting the use to civilian projects for a period of 18 months."

Nick nods. That makes sense as a compromise. It's only now he realizes he's being called on to make decisions that will shape the future of life on Earth. Nick had assumed this was about First Contact, but it's not. *Vincennes* was built to exploit alien technology. To him, the real question is, who were these aliens? Where did they come from? Where have they gone? Are they still out there? How can we contact them? But it seems human progress is more important than contact.

Bear says, "Hey, ah. Boss lady."

"What?" Jazz snaps, still irritated by Nick's decision. She does not look impressed at being interrupted. No doubt she wants to dissect Nick's response and school him on the appropriate US-centric perspective. Ordinarily, Nick would be the first to yell, *USA. USA!* But he feels conflicted by the insistence on loyalty. Nick's not good at much, but the one thing he excels at is in being stubborn.

Perhaps if Jazz hadn't demanded loyalty of him, he'd have been more obliging. He would have probably walked into that trap without a thought, but being pushed provoked pushback. This particular demon has always been part of his personality. Oh, he tries to be as rational and logical as the next guy, but deep down, Nick knows he's an emotional pinball. What logic was there in taking out his frustrations on Sandra? Hell, it was easy to justify the argument as her fault, but she was sick of his self-centered bullshit. If only she'd sucked it up and let him have his way. Yeah, *#AITA.* If he'd posted on Reddit, asking, '*Am I the Asshole?*' thousands of people would have taken delight in setting him straight with a definite '*Yes.*'

Bear asks Jazz, "You're still keeping your dead-reckoning up to date, right?"

Jazz offers a pensive, "Yes. Why?"

Nick is in a daze. He can hear what the others are saying, but his mind is still unraveling at the implications of being part of the jury.

Nick is a red-blooded American. Nothing stirs his soul more than 80,000 fans standing to sing the Star-Spangled Banner before a game of football, and yet to be loyal to America feels like a betrayal of humanity. Should he put the US ahead of everyone else? For all the hype, being drawn into discussions that potentially impact every single person on the face of the planet is unnerving. Politics is bluff and bluster. It's all a bit of fun and games until someone gets bombed. Cheerleading is fine when it's your side claiming divine providence, but when everyone's equally invested and passionate, the limits become obvious. Patriotism is shortsighted and in need of a new pair of prescription glasses.

What difference is there between Americans and the Chinese? Or the Russians? They're all equally blind to the folly of their own unquestioning loyalty to country over species. But when billions of lives are at stake, it's fair to say there's a need for a little sobriety. As a drunk, Nick understands this implicitly. Is that it? Are all nations drunk on their own ego? Are they blind to their own humanity?

Nick is glad Bear interrupted Jazz.

"GPS is playing up. I'm seeing our position shifting sideways, then back again. Dropping in and out. The damn thing is coming back with different altitudes. Crazy shit."

Jazz asks, "Solar storm?"

Dmitri asks, "Can we be hit with a solar storm when we can't even see the Sun?"

"Those auroras," Jazz says. "There's plenty of activity out there that can fuck things up down here."

"The radio's gone quiet," Bear says as the snow howls past the headlights. "I can't even raise the Brits. We're on our own."

Jazz pulls out her map and flips it over, grabbing her compass and pencil.

"Okay, we're still on the same heading as we were at 14:00, right? Any change in speed?"

"Hard to say," Bear replies. "I've set the throttle at 1,500 RPMs, but our speed over the ground will change depending on the incline. On average, we're hitting 18 to 20 miles an hour."

Jazz says, "I was within a hundred yards of the fuel depot, so I'm happy with my calculations, but any change in bearing or speed has to be noted and time-stamped."

"Understood," Bear says, looking at the map with her.

Jazz is distracted.

She double-checks her calculations, checks her compass, and talks with Bear about the effect of wind shear on their heading. Given visibility is down to fifteen feet, Nick hopes Jazz is correct. There's an awful lot of darkness out there. If there are any features beyond the windswept icy plain, Nick hasn't seen them. He tries not to think about the possibility of missing *Vincennes* in the dark, or a mechanical failure causing them to fall short.

Jazz works the radio, checking different channels and frequencies. Nothing. For the next few hours, she tries at regular intervals. Static is all they hear in reply.

The wind picks up, buffeting the cabin, raging against their intrusion into the eternal night of an antarctic winter. Lucille is flawless. Despite the cold, she continues trundling on over the dark horizon.

VOSTOK

Two days trundle by without any radio contact. The world beyond Antarctica could have been vaporized and they wouldn't know it. The storm has become worse, something Nick didn't think was possible. The snow and ice howling past the headlights creates a white blur. It's cold in the cab of the snowcat. Damn cold. No one talks much. The focus is on double and triple-checking their course.

Bear has the makings of a beard.

Nick scratches at the fuzz on his cheeks and neck, longing for the opportunity to shave again.

Jazz has always kept her hair immaculate, but living in a snowcat makes that impossible. Like the others, she gets itchy, ruffling her hair and scratching at her scalp. No one says anything, but on those few occasions she pulls down the hood on her jacket her hair is an utter mess, sticking out on odd angles.

Jazz has drilled Nick on the decision-making process within the base. While she sleeps, Nick asks Dmitri, "Why is she so strict?"

"Father won't tolerate interference with jurors."

"Father?"

Bear leans over the seat, talking a little too loud for Nick's liking and almost waking Jazz.

"Artificial Intelligence," he says. "Dumb as dog shit, but it runs everything."

"I don't understand."

"No one trusts anyone down there," Dmitri says, "So everyone trusts Father. His code base and machine-learning algorithm are shared by all nations at *Vincennes*."

Bear says, "And he gets cranky if anyone corners a juror. Jazz is coaching you now so she won't need to later."

"Not that she won't try," Dmitri says.

"Not that *you* won't try," Bear says, looking over his shoulder at the burly Russian.

"Anyone thirsty?" Dmitri asks, shifting the subject. No one answers.

Water has to be heated before they can drink it, but not to the point of boiling as that wastes electricity. Their instant coffee is tepid. Plain water tastes strangely metallic.

"Hungry?" Dmitri asks, fetching a can from the storage area. Nick never wants to see another goddamn can of sardines as long as he lives. Dmitri eats the stuff like it was candy.

Jazz stirs. Nick's not entirely sure she wasn't listening in.

"What did I miss?"

"A whole lot of nothing," Bear says as snow and ice whip past the windows. Out beyond the headlights, there's nothing but darkness.

"Have you told Nick about your plans for next season?" Dmitri asks.

"What? No?"

Jazz looks awkward. She shifts in her seat. She's not happy with Dmitri bringing this up.

"Come on," Bear says. "Spill the beans. Hell, I'd talk about anything right now just to pass the time."

"It's not a big deal," Jazz replies, shutting down the

conversation.

"What is?" Nick asks.

"My personal life."

"Oh."

"I'd rather keep it out of this," Jazz says as though Nick was the one that brought it up.

"She's getting married," Bear says.

Jazz hits him across his chest, swatting him with her outstretched arm.

Bear laughs, letting out a fake, "Ouch!"

"It is cause for celebration," Dmitri says.

"You really are bored," Jazz says. "Wedding plans are nothing if not painful."

"She's getting married in London," Dmitri says.

"Ontario?" Nick asks.

"United Kingdom," Bear says.

Jazz asks, "Why don't you just get on the radio and let everyone know?"

Bear plays along, grabbing the radio microphone and broadcasting, "Hey, *Vincennes*. Jazz is getting married. Please put some champagne on ice for us. Over."

There's no reply. Boredom has turned this into a game for Bear and Dmitri. The two men laugh. Even Jazz plays along.

"No invite for you."

"Couldn't afford the flights," Bear replies.

Nick says, "Getting married in the middle of a multi-year expedition to explore an alien spaceship is..."

"Is what?" Jazz asks, challenging him.

"I dunno?" Nick replies, trying not to offend her. "It's unusual, right? I mean, this whole damn thing is unusual."

Bear grins. "Love doesn't take a holiday."

"I will shoot you," Jazz says, leaning over the seat and punching him playfully on the arm.

Dmitri laughs.

"All right. All right," she says. "I give up. Yes, I'm marrying Captain Jon Danes of the British Expedition. There. Are you happy now?"

"At *Halley*?" Nick asks.

"He was stationed at *Vincennes*," Jazz replies. "He's spending the winter back in Europe, although it's already summer up there."

Bear has a smirk on his face. He sings, "Summer loving—"

Jazz pushes his shoulder, rocking him to one side. They both laugh.

Dmitri says, "Our little girl is all grown up."

"Don't," Jazz says, swinging around and pointing her finger at him, but Dmitri just laughs. It's the release of tension. Trundling across an endless frozen plateau in the middle of winter is enough to drive anyone mad. Nothing changes. A slight bump or a rise in the ice is cause for comment. Normally, it's hours of dead flat ice. They could be going in circles or about to drive off the edge of a cliff. Nick wouldn't know.

The banter dies when Bear starts talking about spikes in the electrical supply system and the heating pump on the engine block.

Hours pass like decades.

The GPS flickers in and out, giving results that broadly agree with the calculations Jazz has been maintaining. At times, it says they're hundreds of meters below the ice or somewhere high in the clouds, which doesn't lend much credence to their actual location in terms of latitude and longitude. Bear says, even with the storm, their location should be good to within a few kilometers.

"We're getting close," Jazz says, scratching yet another

equation into the margin on her map with the grease pencil.

For the past few hours, they've been counting down from a hundred kilometers. Now, Nick is genuinely excited. He cannot wait to crawl up onto a bunkbed and get some decent sleep. Closing his eyes at that moment is going to be bliss.

Bear grabs the radio handset. "*Vincennes*, this is US Expedition 104. Come in, over."

There's no reply.

Nick asks, "What if we drive right past them in the darkness?"

"We're not driving past them," Jazz insists, but how does she know?

"*Vincennes*. US Expedition 104," Bear says into the radio handset. "Are you reading me? Over."

Nothing.

Bear asks, "What's the plan, boss?"

"Okay, assuming the agreement between dead-reckoning and GPS has a margin of error of less than ten kilometers, then we're close. If we can't raise them, we'll stop and conduct a grid sweep. We'll circle at five hundred meters, winding back and forth over ten clicks until we find them."

"Comb the snow?" Bear says. "Okay. That'll work."

"How are we for fuel?" Dmitri asks.

Bear checks a gauge. "At the moment, we're good for roughly four hundred kilometers. At the moment, we could make the Russian base at *Vostok*."

"Good. Good."

"We could still end up missing *Vincennes* in the darkness," Nick says, leaning over the bench seat and pointing at the map. "I mean, we're assuming it's in this area, but we could be further east than we think. We could end up searching nothing but ice."

"We could," Jazz says, agreeing with him. "And if that

happens, we shift our search area over here."

"We can't search forever," Bear says, "We're going to burn through a helluva lot of fuel going nowhere while conducting our search, especially when we start pushing into that headwind. If we're wrong in our initial assumptions and there's nothing in the first search area, we'll have burned through two hundred clicks. That will put *Vostok* out of reach. After a second search grid, we'll be running on fumes. We won't have enough for a third."

Jazz says what they're all thinking.

"Fuck."

Bear continues with, "Then there's the difficulty of U-turns in our dead-reckoning. Without visual points of reference, we could end up with a lopsided pattern. What we think of as nice and uniform and square could be a kindergarten drawing with crayon going everywhere."

Bear leans on the steering wheel.

"We have no choice," Dmitri says. "Without radio contact, we have to do something. It only makes sense to search the area."

"Yeah, but he's right," Jazz says, surprising Nick by pointing at him. It seems she needed a moment to collect her thoughts as she goes on to say, "We could miss *Vincennes* in the dark. A helluva lot of people have died out here because they convinced themselves they were right about their location when they were wrong—dead wrong."

She slams her gloved hand on the dash. "Goddamn it!"

Bear says, "Yeah, the base only spans a few hundred yards. We can see less than fifteen yards in this storm. Even with a good search pattern, we could sail right past them and not even know it."

"There's another problem," Nick says.

"What?" Dmitri asks.

"Doesn't the lack of a response bother anyone? I mean, I get that we couldn't talk to them way back by the fuel dump, but now we're right on top of them, surely a radio signal can get through. If we're only a few miles away, they should be able to hear us, right?"

Bear looks at Jazz. Dmitri shakes his head.

Reluctantly, Jazz says, "Maybe the storm has slowed us more than I thought. We could be going into a search pattern too early."

Bear picks up the radio again.

"*Vincennes*, this is US 104 Lucille. We are in need of navigational assistance. We sure could do with an escort for the last few clicks. Come in, over."

Nothing.

"*Vincennes*, Lucille US 104. Sound off. Over."

"Let's try *Vostok*," Dmitri says. "They're nearby."

Nearby is a relative term in Antarctica. *Vostok* is hundreds of kilometers from *Vincennes*. Jazz nods. Dmitri reaches over the back of the bench seat and holds out his hand for the microphone. Bear hands it to him. Dmitri raises the mic to his lips and speaks clearly, saying, "Станция Восток. Станция Восток. Говорит американская экспедиция № 104. Проверка связи. Приём."

He releases the transmit key and listens. His finger is poised, ready to respond if there's a reply. Nothing.

"Станция Восток. Американец 104. Приём."

Through the crackle of static, a few words drift across the radio waves in Russian.

"...Американец... Восток... Слабый... Шторм."

"What are they saying?" Jazz asks.

"Ah, they're saying our signal is weak because of the storm."

"But they're receiving us," she says. "At a distance of roughly four hundred clicks."

"Yes."

Outside, nothing changes. Lucille continues on over the frozen plateau. Snow and ice whip past the headlights. The diesel engine hums. The cabin rocks. As always, the darkness is impenetrable.

Jazz draws a line from their position to *Vostok Station*, measuring the distance. She writes on the map, working through a series of calculations, taking into account wind speed, fuel consumption, time and distance. No one speaks. Finally, she breaks the impasse.

She sighs. "Bear, adjust your heading by twenty-two degrees north by northwest. Reduce speed to fifteen kilometers an hour. We're going to want to conserve what fuel we have in case we need to negotiate any ravines."

"Understood."

"Dmitri, tell *Vostok* we're lost. We cannot find *Vincennes* and are getting no reply over the radio. We are declaring an emergency and heading for *Vostok*. We have limited navigation and are going to need help finding them."

Dmitri is sullen. He nods reluctantly, lifting the microphone and speaking in Russian.

"Станция Восток, говорит американская экспедиция 104. Мы объявляем чрезвычайную ситуацию. Повторяю, черзвычайная ситуация. Мы не нашли Валькирию. Мы не можем связаться с Валькирией. Наши навигационные возможности ограничены. Восток, мы идём в вашем направлении. Просим помощи. Приём."

The radio crackles in reply with, "...Американ... ериканская экс... Восток..."

The three of them watch Dmitri with intense curiosity, observing the slightest twitch on his face. Whether it's the rise of his lips, the tightening of his jaw, or the way his eyebrows narrow, they're all desperate to understand what's being said.

"Восток, приём, как слышите? Мы объявляем чрезвычайную ситуацию. Идём в вашем направлении."

Again, the silence within the cabin is painful as they wait

for a reply only one of them understands.

"...Винсеннес... часов... ждите..."

"What is it?" Jazz asks.

"Ah, I'm not sure how much of what I'm saying is getting through to them. We might have to wait until we get closer."

"What did they say?" Bear asks.

"The storm. It's bad," Dmitri says. "I'm getting words without context. Words that don't make sense. I think they're saying stand by. Maybe they're in touch with *Vincennes*."

"Did they say that?" Jazz asks.

"I don't know," Dmitri says. "They spoke about *Vincennes*, but I can't make out all of their words."

"Jesus," Jazz says, burying her head in her hands. "I didn't want this. I did not fucking want this."

She looks up, taking a deep breath and steeling herself as she addresses Nick. "We can't fuck around out here. As much as I'd like to stop and search for *Vincennes*. We can't. If we miss them and run out of fuel before reaching *Vostok*, we're dead."

She's frustrated. She points out the side window, saying, "They could be there. They could be right fucking there!"

Bear looks ahead into the darkness, watching where they're going even though nothing has changed in days. Snow drifts have buried the ice. The drifts are visible as slight undulations. The treads of the snowcat crush them as they pass. Beyond that, what little they can see is utterly featureless.

"We could conduct a couple of passes," Bear says. "Lucille's good for it."

"I want to," Jazz says. "But what I want is fucking irrelevant. We might as well be at the bottom of the ocean. If we run out of juice and have to abandon the cat, we'll be dead within an hour."

Dmitri is still trying to reach the Russians at *Vostok Station*.

"Восток, говорит американская экспедиция 104. Мы идём на север, в вашем направлении. Наши навигационные возможности ограничены. Просим помощи. Приём."

Seconds later, the radio crackles back to life but no one is expecting a coherent answer.

"...Американ... ...вычайная ситуация... Жди..."

"Ah, it's more of the same," Dmitri says even though no one asks him to translate. "They can hear us, but they can't get full sentences from us. They're responding with terms like, stand by, emergency. Things like that."

"We are not standing by," Jazz says. "If we stay out here, we die."

For Nick, it's astonishing to see how Jazz has talked herself out of her initial idea of sweeping the plateau looking for *Vincennes*. He suspects her experience is overriding any wishful thinking, which gives him confidence in her decision. The journey to *Vostok* means a few more days stuck in this tin can, but he thinks she's right.

Bear asks, "What happened to *Vincennes*?"

"Oh," she says. "It could be something as simple as a guide wire came loose on the main antenna. Damn thing falls in the storm and—*boom*—they're off the net. I saw one crumple at McMurdo. It ain't pretty. Crushed the roof of the maintenance shed. It wouldn't be a problem if we had a decent GPS signal."

"*Vostok* it is then," Bear says, only he's no longer looking out the windshield. He's turned to face Jazz. Bear is trying to show his support for what is a frustrating decision. It's then Nick sees something ahead of them in the darkness.

Someone.

There's a man out there, looming in the headlights, just off to the passenger's side of the vehicle. He's standing knee-deep in the snow.

Dark eyes stare blindly into the storm.

Frozen arms reach for the lights.

Nick leans over the seatback, grabbing Bear by the shoulders as he yells, "Watch out!"

BEAR

Bear slams his boots on both the clutch and brake. Lucille comes to a sudden halt. He reduces the throttle to an idle and puts the snowcat in neutral.

"What the fuck," slips from his lips as they stare out of the windshield at the frozen figure caught in the headlights. Another fraction of a second and Lucille would have crushed him beneath her right-front tread.

For what seems like an eternity, no one moves. The rumble of the engine behind them is the only proof that time continues to unfold. Jazz is closest to the man, sitting over by the passenger's door. Dmitri is behind her, but he's barely breathing. Nick is seated behind Bear. He leans forward, whispering, "Is he dead? He's dead, right?"

Slowly, Jazz nods, but her eyes never leave the frozen corpse standing before them on the icy plateau.

Snow curls around the man's legs. Icicles hang from his outstretched arms. It's as though he's reaching for something from a shelf at head height, only there's nothing there. His eyes are open, staring into the distance. His skin is pale. It's almost as white as the snow rushing past the headlights. Ice clings to his cheeks. His hair is spiky. It's as though it froze while wet.

He's clothed, but he's not dressed for the weather. A lab coat flickers with the wind, but it's mostly frozen, moving only at the tips. The man's wearing jeans and a collared shirt with a flannel pattern.

His fingers seem to reach for them, longing for the light.

Bear mumbles. "How the hell does someone die like that?"

"Dee, you're with me," Jazz says. "Bear, you and Nick stay here."

Jazz reaches beneath the front seat of the snowcat and pulls out a pistol set in a holster. A thick black belt has been wrapped around the gun. Magazines sit in pouches on the belt. She hands it to Dmitri. His eyes never leave the dead man. With seasoned skill, he slips the gun from the holster and removes the magazine. First, he checks the chamber is empty. Then he quietly ejects five rounds from the magazine and slips them back into the magazine, ensuring they're free to move.

At the same time, Jazz retrieves an M4 Carbine from beneath the front seat. She checks the breach and the magazine, ensuring the first few rounds are loose and not frozen in place. She pushes the magazine up into the heart of the rifle. Both guns click softly as they're cocked.

Outside, the man hasn't moved.

"Ready?" she whispers with her hand resting on the door handle.

"Ready."

Without another word, they both exit the vehicle in a fraction of a second, moving like ghosts, barely making a sound. One moment they're there, seated within the cab of the snowcat, the next, they're outside standing on the metal treads with the doors closed behind them.

Jazz drops into the snow.

Dmitri leans against the front door, steadying his aim as the storm buffets him. He hasn't raised his jacket hood, so his hair is tossed around by the wind. There's no time to worry about the cold. He peers down the barrel of the Glock with his gloved finger

142

on the trigger. Nick's fired enough guns to know that's a bad position to be in. Even without the cold, firing a weapon while wearing gloves is crazy as there's no way to feel the tacit feedback as tension mounts on the trigger. Dmitri could pop off a shot without meaning to.

Jazz wades through the snow, making her way forward of the treads. She keeps the barrel of her M4 pointing at the corpse stuck in the ice. Even though she's barely ten feet away, she peers down the scope, examining his shoulders and chest.

Jazz edges closer and taps his frozen hands with the barrel, looking for a response. Nick is pretty sure he's dead, but, okay, he'd do the same. She uses the barrel of her M4 to shift the man's jacket, checking both sides of his chest, pulling it back far enough to see his shoulders. All the while, Dmitri never moves. If Nick didn't know better, he'd swear Dmitri was frozen too. The barrel of Dmitri's gun never wavers.

Slowly, Jazz comes up beside the frozen corpse. She circles around him, staying away from his outstretched arms. Her M4 is pulled hard into her shoulder, but she's no longer pointing it at him. She's directing her aim out into the shadows behind him, looking into the darkness. If there's anything else looming out there, she wants to know about it in advance. With one hand, she reaches back, feeling for and then searching his jacket pockets. She retrieves something, shoving it in her back pocket.

Nick's expecting her to retrace her steps, but she continues past the frozen corpse, stepping forward as though she were negotiating a minefield. To his horror, her outline disappears from the lights of the snowcat. With the wind and snow howling across the plateau, all Nick can see is a shadow turning from one side to another, scanning the distance. Dmitri still hasn't shifted his sight from the man.

Jazz returns, climbing into the cab of the snowcat. Dmitri seems reluctant to take his aim off the corpse, but he too withdraws to the relative warmth provided by Lucille.

"What the fuck was that?" Bear asks as Dmitri rubs his ears, trying to get some warmth back into them. He was only out there for a minute or two, but the skin is already bright red. He pulls a woolen beanie over his head, sitting it low over his brow as he shivers. He's still got the gun in his right hand. There's no way in hell he's putting that down.

"That," Jazz says, holding up a smartphone with a pouch stuck to the back of it containing several cards and IDs. "That's Lee Lao Chan, from China."

"He's a juror?" Nick asks in alarm.

"A scientist," Dmitri says, shocked to hear that name. "He specializes in quantum mechanics. What the hell is he doing out here?"

"I dunno," Jazz says, turning the IDs over in her hand.

"What happened to him?" Nick asks.

Jazz shakes her head.

"How the hell did he die standing up?" Bear asks.

Jazz shrugs.

"Wait a minute," Dmitri says. "This means we're close. Think about it. He's from *Vincennes*. He can't have gone far dressed like that."

Bear says, "This is good, right? I mean, not for him, but they've got to have search parties out looking for him. He's a scientist. They're going to go ape-shit with him missing."

"Yeah, I dunno," Jazz says with the M4 set between her legs. The barrel is pointing up at the roof of the snowcat. "I was using an infrared scope out there. I should have been able to see for at least a hundred yards in all directions—even with the storm."

"And?" Bear asks.

"Nothing. Either he's a long way from base, or no one's out looking for him."

"That makes no sense," Bear says. "They should be turning over every icy rock on the plateau trying to find this guy."

"He's been out here a long time," Dmitri says.

"I'm not sure about the scope sensitivity," Jazz says, "but there's no residual body heat coming off him."

"He's frozen?" Nick asks. "As in frozen solid?"

Jazz says, "There wasn't any difference between him and the background."

"How long does it take for a body to freeze like this?" Nick asks, only his choice of words is telling. *Body.* He's scared. What he means to ask is, *how long did it take him to freeze?* But the implication is that *him* could become *me,* and that's something he can't face.

"With this wind chill?" Jazz says. "I don't know. Hours? Maybe a day or two?"

Dmitri says, "Assuming he came from *Vincennes,* we have at least a general direction as it should be somewhere behind him."

"If he hasn't walked in circles," Bear says.

"He can't have walked that far," Jazz says.

"What are we going to do with him?" Bear asks.

"Nothing."

"We're just going to leave him there?"

"For now. Once we find *Vincennes,* we'll tell them where he is and they can dispatch a recovery team."

Jazz rummages around beneath the bench seat, pulling out a backpack. She digs into it, retrieving a helmet with night vision goggles raised high. She places another handgun on the seat between her and Bear, along with a tablet computer. The tablet is surrounded by thick, rugged plastic, making the screen appear ridiculously small.

Jazz points beyond the dead man, saying, "I saw a faint

glow on the horizon. It might be *Vincennes*."

"So we head over there," Bear says, readying himself. He's got his boot on the clutch and one hand on the gear shifter, ready to reverse Lucille and head around the body.

"No," Jazz says. "Dee and I will scout it out on foot. I want you to stay here with Nick." She looks at Dmitri, saying, "You up for this old man?"

A wicked grin breaks across Dmitri's face.

Jazz hands him the helmet along with a throat mic, saying, "This is an integrated warfare unit. It'll broadcast back here. You use the night-vision goggles. I'll stick with the infrared scope."

Dmitri doesn't bother taking off his beanie. He pulls the helmet over the thick wool. Once the throat mic is stuck below his jaw, he says, "Testing one, two."

"Coming through clear," Bear says, looking down at the tablet. He plugs it into a port on the dashboard. Nick leans forward, wanting to get a good look at the screen. Video streams in from both the helmet and the rifle scope. Two audio streams show up as squiggly lines at the bottom of the split image.

Jazz leans over, pointing at the controls on the tablet, saying, "You can switch between ambient noise and the throat mics, depending on what's easiest to hear."

"Got it."

Dmitri pulls the zip on his jacket, ensuring it's all the way up to his chin. He wraps the hood of his jacket over the helmet, closing it up. With the night vision goggles down in front of his eyes, an eerie metal cylinder protrudes from the fur lining his hood, making him look like an alien machine.

Jazz says, "We'll go in side by side. Ten meters apart. If there's any action, break wide and provide cover."

"Understood."

"Action? What action?" Bear asks.

Jazz shrugs.

"What about us?" Nick asks.

Jazz replies, "If we're not back in ninety minutes, head for *Vostok*. Under no circumstances should you try to follow us. Is that understood?"

"Oh, hell yeah," Bear says. "Understood."

She hands Bear the other gun, a nine-millimeter Glock Nick knows all too well.

Bear swallows a lump in his throat.

Jazz turns and kneels on the seat. "Can you pass me that black bag?"

Nick reaches over to one of the packs in the storage area. He wrangles a duffle bag from the bottom of the pile and hands it to her.

"Thanks," she says, pulling on the zip and dumping the contents on the seat. In between bits of survival gear are dozens of small flags wrapped in bundles held together with plastic ties. Bright day-glow orange pennants are attached to long thin metal wires. Jazz grabs a handful, tucking them under her arm, and zips up the bag, hoisting it over her shoulder.

"We'll leave breadcrumbs," she says, grabbing her M4 by the handguard wrapped around the barrel.

"And we're just going to stay here?" Bear asks, pointing at the corpse swaying in the gale-force winds. "With him?"

Jazz opens the door, saying, "He won't bite. I promise."

"You don't know that."

Jazz climbs out onto the treads of the snowcat as Bear repeats his point, yelling at her, "You don't know that!"

She smiles, slamming the door. Dmitri climbs out the rear of the vehicle. The two of them drop to the snow and move around in front of the snowcat, ignoring the human popsicle. They begin wading through the snowdrift into the darkness.

"Comms check," Jazz says.

"You're coming through clear," Bear replies, looking at the black and white infrared display in front of him. Nick rests his arms on the back of the seat, peering at the screen, fascinated by the image.

Jazz pushes a flag into the snow and ice, working it down to the point the madly flapping plastic is barely clear of the drift. Off to one side, a slight green smudge marks Dmitri moving in parallel with her.

"Goddamn, it is cold out here," Jazz says.

"I make it negative sixty-two," Bear says in reply. "Subtract another thirty with the wind chill."

"Continuing on."

Within twenty yards, they've disappeared into the storm. The video feed continues coming through, but it doesn't show anything beyond the haze of snow and ice tearing past them.

After several flags and at least a hundred yards, Bear says, "We're starting to lose you."

"Say again?" Jazz replies.

"Video is breaking up. Audio is patchy."

"Again?"

"We're losing you in the storm."

It seems Jazz doesn't care as she replies, "Copy that."

The fuzzy images begin to break up, coming in static strips and then pixelated chunks before finally they die.

"Jazz?" Bear says, talking into a microphone attached to the tablet. "Dmitri?"

Nick is quiet.

Up until now, the howling of the storm didn't bother him, but as the wind intensifies, he finds the cacophony of noise unsettling. The cabin rocks. Somewhere outside, a loose strap flaps, occasionally flicking against the sheet metal. As the wind shifts, the gusts catch the windshield wipers, causing the aluminum supports to vibrate.

Waves of snow and ice buffet the cabin, being driven at them by the ferocity of the storm. It's as though a giant has grabbed Lucille. He's got his hand over the cab and is shaking it. Within the cabin, odd things rattle. Nick hunts them out, shifting a ski pole away from the rear deck so it's no longer resting against metal.

Bear looks at his watch. He starts a timer.

"What are you doing?"

"You heard the boss," Bear replies. "Ninety minutes and we are getting the fuck out of Dodge."

"You're going to leave her?"

"You'd rather stay?" Bear asks, gesturing to the corpse standing a few feet from their ice-covered tractor treads. "You realize that's us, right? If we stick around here, we're as dead as that guy."

"But—"

"But nothing."

Bear buries his head in his hands, pushing his palms up against his eyes as though he's trying to clear a migraine.

"I am not cut out for this shit," he says, looking back at Nick.

"But you're a soldier."

"I'm an engineer. I'm the guy that sits back at base fixing things. I don't do," and he points at the dead man as he adds an emphatic, "*This!*"

"Who does?" Nick asks. For him, it's a serious question.

"Jazz. Dmitri. They're both special forces. They love this shit."

That's something Dmitri never mentioned to Nick, but it's no surprise given his physique. The idea of him pushing paper at the UN always seemed a little absurd. Nick has no doubt he really did work as an attaché for the Russians at the UN, but it was clearly a cover.

"You know why they assigned Jazz to this expedition, right?"

"No," Nick replies.

"She's the heroine of the Himalayas. Oh, she won't talk about it, but it's true. A couple of years ago, she was working as a US military advisor in India. Only she didn't train shit. It was a cover. Her team was there holding an advanced outpost, watching the conflict between India and China. Technically, she was supposed to be embedded with the Indians, but both sides knew the US had ground assets as informal peacekeepers. The idea was to try to stop two nuclear powers from going to war over a fucking glacier.

"Anyway, her team comes under artillery fire. Chinese troops are moving up the valley behind the barrage. They overrun the Indian forward position and a firefight erupts with the Americans. And fucking Jazz. What do you think she does?"

"I dunno," Nick says. "Pull back?"

"Like hell," Bear says, tapping at the windshield, pointing at her tracks in the snow. "She boxes the position. She works her way along a ridge line at night. Disappears almost ten miles behind enemy lines and negotiates directly with the colonel in charge of the Chinese battalion."

"Oh," Nick says, surprised. He's trying to be polite more than anything else. He has no idea what negotiate means in this context.

"Yeah," Bear says, "Only Jazz doesn't speak Chinese, but it seems the barrel of a gun is a universal language."

Bear laughs. "The Chinese account of that night is that their forward command was surrounded by hostiles. They said they took heavy fire from the hills and withdrew, realizing their flank was exposed. But that never happened. Before she melted back into the night, Jazz pushed her Glock into the guy's crotch, speaking softly to him, making promises he had no doubt she'd keep."

Nick laughs.

"So this is right up her alley," Bear says. "But it scares the crap out of me."

"Him?" Nick says, looking at the snow whipping past the frozen body. "He scares you? But he's dead."

"What if he's not?"

"That's ridiculous. Look at him. Besides, you've got a gun."

Bear picks up the Glock, examining it as he says, "Yeah, I could put a bullet in his skull. Just to be sure."

"No," Nick says, astonished that, for once, he's the voice of reason.

Bear fidgets. Nick would feel a lot better if he put the gun down. The barrel is facing forward so if there was a discharge, it would be stupidly loud in such a confined space, but all it would do is add some ventilation.

"How did you get your name?" Nick asks, wanting to distract him.

"Bear? Oh, yeah," he puts the gun on the bench seat, laying it on top of the tablet. "You really wanna know? You wanna see?"

"Sure," Nick replies, unsure where this is going.

Bear unzips his coat to his waist. He turns sideways, hoisting his shirt, pulling it up high so it's in front of his face, exposing his chest to Nick. "See that?"

Scars crisscross Bear's chest and belly. As it's cold, he drops his shirt before Nick has the chance to take a good look, but these aren't scratches. The pectoral muscle on his left side has been scraped away from his ribs. The claw marks are distinct, reaching down to his stomach.

Bear zips his jacket back up, saying, "It was a brown bear. I was hiking up in Alaska. Never even saw it. One moment, I'm stepping over a fallen log. The next, I'm lying on my back as a bear slashes at my chest, tearing open my jacket. All I remember is the smell. I was in shock. All I could process was the stench. Piss and shit. Rotten meat. Wet fur."

Nick is quiet.

"Its sheer strength was overwhelming. My girlfriend said it looked like I was trying to crawl away, but the truth is the damn thing threw me around like a rag doll. Somehow, I ended up on my front and it ripped open my backpack. All it wanted was lunch. We'd brought some freshly made ham rolls from a bakery just outside of Fairbanks. Once it got those, it trundled off with cling wrap hanging from its mouth.

"Jules is a Marine Corps nurse. She knew what to do. She whipped off my jeans and used what was left of my jacket to pack the goddamn hole in my ribcage to stem the bleeding. She tied the legs of my jeans around my chest, using them as a compression bandage. By this time, a couple of other hikers had stumbled across the carnage. There was no cell coverage so one of them ran back to the parking lot and called it in. Twenty minutes later, a stretcher is being lowered from a helicopter and I'm out of there. I would have died without Jules by my side.

"Anyway, that's it. That's why I'm called Bear. It started out as a lousy joke. Over time, the legend grew. I'd fought off a bear with my fists or something. The truth is, I ain't got no bravado no more. Oh, the military thrives on that egotistical alpha-male bullshit. You've got to be as tough as nails. Eat bullets for breakfast. Not me. I'm a mechanic. I fix stuff. I don't do the whole charge into battle thing."

He looks at his watch. Forty minutes have passed.

The tablet crackles back into life. Audio comes through first, followed by fleeting glimpses of video.

"Jazz?"

"Who else were you expecting?" is the reply, to which both

men smile. "Okay, we found it. *Vincennes* is eight hundred meters east by northeast of our position. We observed lights in the outer buildings but no movement within or between buildings."

Over time, the image comes through clearer. Jazz wades through the snow, running her hand over each flag as it comes into view. Dmitri is just behind her. Before long, Lucille's lights break through the driving snow and ice. The two men can see them approaching on screen and out the window.

Jazz and Dmitri climb up on the treads of the snowcat and clamber inside, brushing snow and ice from their jackets.

"Damn, it is cold out there," Dmitri says.

Bear asks, "What's the plan, boss?"

Jazz looks at him like it's a stupid question.

"We go in hot."

VINCENNES

Bear backs the snowcat away from the corpse and traverses a small mound, following the flags laid down by Jazz and Dmitri.

"I don't like this," he mumbles. "Nobody dies standing up. It ain't natural."

Everyone hears him. No one replies. Jazz looks down at the M-4 between her legs. Her hand rests on the guard. Her gloved fingers flex. It's not that she's ready for action. She's assuring herself it's there for protection.

Nick watches Lee Lao Chan out the side window. He's not expecting him to move. This isn't some dumbass horror movie, regardless of the hundred and thirty beats per minute rushing through his heart. As the man fades into the darkness, Nick wonders about all that's been lost. Unlike him, Lee Lao Chan wasn't a conscript. Being a scientist, he must have known the odds. Life in Antarctica is brutal, but the chance of gaining insights into life beyond Earth must have been exhilarating for him. What led him out here in the storm? Why wasn't he wearing survival gear? From what Nick understands, even crossing between buildings requires proper clothing. It's as though this guy just wandered out of a side door and into the night.

Lucille trundles on at a slow pace, inching forward as the team peer out into the darkness, unsure what to expect. Tiny orange flags are caught in the headlights as Bear follows the trail set down by Jazz. At first, there's a slight glow on the horizon. Buildings appear as blurs in the darkness, punctuated by the odd dim light.

"That's the operations center," Jazz says, pointing at a distant building set beside a spotlight mounted high on what looks like a telephone pole. "But I want to go to the general quarters first."

"Why?" Bear asks, reducing the throttle on the snowcat.

"It's closer."

That's not a real reason, but neither Bear nor Dmitri challenge her on that. It seems Jazz wants to know what's at her back rather than driving blindly into the middle of the base.

"Bring us to a halt twenty meters out."

Bear replies with an enthusiastic, "Copy that." It seems he's not keen on rushing in either.

With the buildings providing shelter from the wind, Lucille's spotlights reach further into the shadows. Stairs lead up to a door at the back of the living quarters.

"There," Jazz says, pointing.

Bear brings Lucille to a halt. Snow has piled up against one side of the building, burying its support beams.

Jazz tosses Bear a spare set of night vision goggles, saying, "If you need to go out there, use these."

"I'm not going out there," Bear replies, resting the goggles on the dash.

Jazz shrugs. She has her gloved hand on the door handle. "If anything comes out of that door other than us—shoot it."

Anything. Not anyone.

Nick needs to pee, damn it. His bladder feels as though it's bursting. He knows he doesn't actually need to relieve himself as he's barely had anything to drink in the past hour, but his nerves betray him.

Jazz sees him squirming a little. She ignores him, speaking to Bear. "I'm going on the wide mic so you can catch everything that happens in there, okay?"

"Okay," Bear replies.

"Anything goes wrong, and you hightail it to *Vostok*. Understood?"

"Understood."

Dmitri and Jazz exit Lucille. Snow whips around them. Jazz has her M4 pulled hard into her shoulder. Dmitri has his night-vision goggles down. He has both arms outstretched, with his elbows locked, pointing the pistol at the door to the living quarters. Beyond the spotlights, the darkness torments them.

From behind the bench seat, Nick fiddles with his trousers, slipping his penis into the neck of a pee bottle. Damn, the plastic is cold. He tinkles, relieving himself.

"Are you taking a piss?" Bear asks in disbelief.

"Say again?" Jazz asks, coming to a halt beside the door with the M4 pointing at the stairs.

"Nothing," Bear says, only now realizing he was transmitting.

Nick slaps him on the shoulder. Speaking under his breath, he says, "I couldn't help it."

"What's next?" Bear asks, having muted his microphone. "A nervous poo?"

"Don't joke about it," Nick says, embarrassed.

On the black and white split-screen, they watch as Dmitri reaches for the door. Ice has built up along the aluminum threshold, forcing him to jerk at the handle. Fine specks of snow rush down in front of them, being caught by an air curtain immediately inside the door. A sharp breeze blows down from a machine set above the doorway to keep the warm air from rushing out. As this is an emergency exit at the rear of the building, there's no staging area to insulate the interior from heat loss. The high-speed fan pushes a wall of air down to reduce thermal loss, but it stirs up the snow, making it impossible to see beyond the swirling white specks.

Jazz slides into the darkness, slipping through the invisible curtain of air. She raises her M4 in front of her. The two of them disappear into the building, closing the door behind them.

"Are you catching this?" Jazz whispers.

"Yeah," Bear replies, keying the microphone back to transmit. He's nervous. He's holding his gun all the time now, regardless of whether he's pushing buttons on the tablet or reducing the idle with the engine throttle. Nick's not sure whether Bear has chambered a round, but he suspects he has. The only positive is his fingers stay well clear of the trigger.

The lights are out. Immediately inside the living quarters, there are two doors, one on either side of the darkened corridor.

Jazz whispers, "Cover me."

Dmitri positions himself on an angle, with his back pressed against the external door so he's got a view down the empty corridor as well as at the internal door Jazz is preparing to open.

"On three," she whispers. "One. Two."

With barely any noise, she opens the door and steps inside, swinging her M4 up as she scans the room.

On the tablet, Nick and Bear watch as Dmitri maintains his view of the corridor. He's still got his arms out in front of him, with the barrel of his Glock threatening any approach from that direction. He edges sideways so he can peer into the room. He watches as Jazz moves around, but his attention remains on the corridor.

Jazz creeps through the room. Overalls and jackets hang from racks lining the walls. Boots have been shoved beneath a bench seat running around the room. Radios sit in chargers with small LED lights indicating battery levels.

"Clear."

Jazz steps back into the corridor. She creeps toward the room on the other side. The door is slightly ajar.

"Oh, man," Bear says, looking at the ghostly images being transmitted to them. "I've seen this movie. This shit does not end well."

"Shhh," Jazz replies. She looks briefly at Dmitri and nods. He acknowledges her, keeping his eyes on the corridor. Jazz pushes the door open. She rushes inside, raising her M4 as she turns, scanning the second room.

"Storage."

Shelving stretches from floor to ceiling. Boxes have been shoved in seemingly random spots, making it difficult to see through the aisles. Jazz takes her time, leading with her M4, checking for movement as she steps between the rows.

"This is not good," Nick says, feeling nervous.

Bear is still transmitting. He mumbles, "Beam me up, Sc—"

"Stay off-channel," Dmitri replies, cutting him off.

Reluctantly, Bear sighs.

Nick mumbles, "What about the lights?"

"Huh?" Bear says, looking up for a moment. He turns the Glock sideways so he can hit the mute button with his index finger and avoid transmitting to Jazz and Dmitri. "The lights are off."

"Not in there," Nick says. "Out here."

"What do you mean?"

"We don't know what's going on, right?"

"Right," Bear says, followed by a nervous and rushed, "Because nothing's going on. Everything's fine." Even he doesn't believe that. He's saying that because that's what he's supposed to say to put the dumbass civilian behind him at ease.

Nick says, "Well, is it a good idea to sit here with the engine running and our lights on? I mean, we're lighting up the night like a Christmas tree."

"W—What?" Bear says, stuttering. He's trying to process too much information at once. He's listening to Nick, looking nervously out the windshield at either side of the building and then back at the tablet, showing progress within the darkened quarters.

"I mean, moths are drawn to a flame, right?" Nick says. He's not trying to stir up controversy, but it seems to him as though leaving their lights on is a major flaw in the idea of sneaking into the base unnoticed.

"Fuck," Bear says. He keys the microphone, resting his Glock against the steering wheel as he speaks. "Ah, Jazz."

"Not now," she replies, whispering as she edges down the main corridor. "We've got lights ahead."

"Ah, Jazz," he continues. "Should we kill our lights?"

"What?" she says, coming to a halt. The way the camera view moves is telling. She's distracted. "Why?"

"Well," Bear says sheepishly. "Do we really want to attract attention before we know what we're dealing with?"

"All right," Jazz replies. "Shut them down."

She's barely spoken before Bear has killed the lights, but he doesn't cut the engine.

It takes a moment for Nick's eyes to adjust to the darkness. The rear door to the living quarters is barely visible through the driving snow. The aluminum rails lining the steps catch the ambient light from a distant spotlight over by the operations center.

Within the building, on the video screen, light seeps from beneath an internal door. Dmitri holds his gloved hand on a brass lever and pauses, looking up at Jazz for his cue. She's pulled her M4 back, pointing it down, allowing her to get close to the door. She nods. He twists and pushes the door open, standing back and allowing her to rush in with her M4 raised. Jazz turns both ways, scanning the room as she says, "Clear."

They're in a kitchen. The floor is sealed with scratched linoleum. Cheap chairs surround a rickety table. There's an empty fruit bowl.

"Where is everyone?" Dmitri asks in a whisper.

Jazz pulls one of her gloves off and cups her hand around the side of a kettle.

"Cold."

Dmitri crouches, looking carefully at a pot of coffee on the counter beside the fridge. Although Nick and Bear can't distinguish colors on their black and white screen, the light's on. It would be red for Jazz and Dmitri, but for them, it appears white. Within the glass carafe, there's little more than a stain, but the element is on, showing up as a brilliant white blob. Whatever coffee there was has long since evaporated.

Jazz doesn't say anything, but she clearly sees it as she reaches over, turning it off. Dmitri looks in the fridge. Like Bear, though, there's no way he's holstering his sidearm. He keeps his Glock in his hand as he pulls on the door. Nothing's going to jump out of the fridge. Nothing. Dmitri releases the handle and steps back, allowing the fridge door to swing open. Milk. Cheese. Mangos. Lots of foodstuffs in Tupperware. Labels on everything. Names and dates. No aliens.

Is that what this is all about? No one has said as much, but they must all be thinking it. Radio contact was lost. A stranger that froze to death on the ice. Next thing, an alien bursts out of a room or someone's chest. That's how these things go, right? Nick shakes that thought from his head. These are nothing but modern-day ghost stories designed to scare kids. They don't work on adults. Do they?

Jazz peers through a set of blinds at the yard between the living quarters and the operations building. Dmitri closes the fridge without comment. What the hell was he looking for? What was he expecting to find?

"What's the layout?" Dmitri asks, coming up next to Jazz. She turns the kitchen light off and points at the various buildings.

"Okay. We're in the living quarters. I don't think I've ever seen it empty. Everything's done in shifts so there are always people coming and going.

"That's the operations center. Staff of ten to twenty most days, but it backs onto the main research center.

"Over there's the quartermaster and mess hall. They're linked to operations by a walkway, so you don't have to go outside. Most of the labs are sub-surface, but there's a storage area at the back for ice cores and stuff like that.

"The low building beyond that snowdrift on the far side is the motor pool. There's only ever a couple of people in there. They maintain the tractors, run the generators, drive the snowplows, manage cabling, control the heating, stuff like that. Behind the motor pool, there's a radio tower and comms shack."

Dmitri nods, asking, "What are you thinking?"

"Where is everyone?"

"Could they be in the ops center?"

"Maybe. If something happened up top, they could have retreated beneath the ice. There's plenty of room down there, but I'm not seeing anything out of the ordinary other than the absence of staff. I mean, they've got power up here. There's no sign of storm damage, or structural failure, or a military attack. I've got two questions. Where did they go? And why?"

"So we go under the ice," Dmitri says.

"I want to sweep these buildings first," Jazz says. "It's important to understand what the hell happened up here before walking in down there."

"Agreed."

Jazz turns and heads back to the door, leaving the light off.

They make their way further down the corridor, checking closets and bedrooms as they go, looking under bunks and inside large cupboards. As they're both using infrared scopes, there's no need for flashlights. Neither of them make a sound as they creep through the dormitory.

Bathrooms are a dead end, which seems to trouble Dmitri. Although he's acting as backup for Jazz, bathrooms have him constantly looking around corners. Jazz edges open the empty stalls with her boot. No one's home.

At each point, they pause before opening doors, even if they lead back the way they came. Each movement is double-checked. There's near-constant chatter with Bear, although most of it is in a whisper.

Outside, the wind howls through the base, causing the windows to flex and creak. They return to the main corridor. Ahead of them, something falls. Whatever it is, it's heavy, making a dull thud.

Jazz comes to a halt with a raised fist. She listens for a moment before walking on. The soft squelch of her boots on the carpet comes through over the microphone.

Dmitri walks up next to Jazz. Without making a sound, he reaches inside a cabinet mounted on the wall and removes a fire ax. Jazz nods her approval. She inches down the corridor.

They're staring at a steel door leading to an external antechamber with a second door to trap heat. There are internal doors on either side. It's impossible to know where the noise came from.

"On the left is the auditorium," she whispers, more for Dmitri than Nick or Bear. "One entrance. The external fire exit is at the front, directly opposite the main door. Staggered seating. Four rows. Two aisles. Twenty seats per row.

"To the right is the ready room. It also doubles as storage."

"Copy that," Dmitri replies, keeping his bulky frame against the wall as they ease toward the end of the corridor.

Floorboards creak beneath their boots.

Jazz signals, pointing at one room and then the other, but Nick isn't sure which is which or what she intends. Dmitri, though, understands. One of the doors is slightly open. Dmitri crouches, pushing his back against the wall beside the open door. Jazz creeps to the far side of the door.

Dmitri rests his ax against the door jamb. He reaches around the corner and turns on a flashlight, sweeping it through the ready room, casting it in a wide swath, but he's not looking inside. Instead, he's facing the auditorium door, ensuring nothing and no one is coming out of there as Jazz stands in the open doorway to the ready room. She stares through the night vision scope on her M4. Clever. They don't need light to see. They're looking for any reaction to the light.

Jazz whispers. "Ready room clear."

They switch to the other side of the corridor. Dmitri pulls slowly on the handle. Jazz eases the door open with her boot. They repeat the process, with Dmitri down low, swinging the flashlight around while Jazz scans the room in infrared.

Immediately, there's a reaction. Something scurries behind a row of desks. Dmitri may not have seen it, but he heard it. He grabs the ax. Jazz rushes into the room, keeping her M4 trained in front of her. She keeps the front wall behind her while Dmitri moves along the other wall, approaching the desks.

They talk to each other in muffled whispers, saying things Nick can't make out.

Dmitri has his flashlight out again, but he's a distraction. Bait. He's allowing Jazz to move unnoticed behind the podium and flank whoever or whatever's in there. Nick's heart is about to burst through his chest it's beating so hard.

Plumes of heat coming from the ground interfere with their infrared vision. The internal heat must be on full. White air tumbles from vents on the ceiling. At the end of each row, a white mist rises from beneath the false floor.

Dmitri mumbles, "Lots of places to hide."

He flashes the light down the first row and then the second. As he's got his night-vision goggles partially raised, Nick and Bear only get a jerky vision of the roof from him. Without intending to, he's blinded them, leaving them only with the feed from Jazz and her M4. It's frustrating, but Bear remains silent.

Jazz covers Dmitri, scanning each of the rows with her infrared scope, looking for movement. A chair back rattles as someone or something scurries along the back row.

"Whoever this is," Jazz whispers. "I want them alive."

Dmitri doesn't reply. Even from where Jazz is, it's apparent he's shaking. He's got the light in his left hand and the ax in the other. Nick would have the gun out. He wants to scream at Dmitri. *The gun! Get your gun out. Use your gun.*

Dmitri holds the ax by its wooden neck. His gloved hand is up next to the heavy, steel head. He crouches, trying to make his big frame a smaller target. From what Nick can tell, Jazz is using him to flush out the game. She's scanning the far side of the room. She's expecting movement there, not near him.

"Hey," Dmitri says, quite loudly, looking down one of the rows. "It's okay. Don't be afraid. We're here to help."

He walks between the seats. His flashlight and his eyes are focused on someone crouching near the end of the third row. Their heat signature is apparent as they move, staying low between the folded seats.

"No one's going to hurt you."

Dmitri crouches, laying down his ax. He may not be going to hurt whoever this is, but Jazz has made no such promise. She keeps her M4 trained on them.

In a flash, someone leaps at Dmitri, knocking him backward as they scamper higher, rushing into the back row. Shots ring out. Over the feed, they come across as loud pops. A split second later, out in front of Lucille, those shots break like thunder from within the living quarters.

"Hold your fire," Dmitri yells.

"Fuck," Bear yells from within the cab of the snowcat. "Fuck. Fuck! FUCK!"

Nick says, "Well, if they didn't know we were here, they do now."

"What happened?" Jazz asks. From the way she speaks, Nick gets the impression her shots were accidental, probably the result of nerves and thick gloves getting the better of her. She rushes forward, but she's got her gun lowered, ruining their view of the auditorium. All Nick can see is the steps rushing past as she runs up the other side of the hall.

"She's over there," Dmitri yells.

"Where?"

A hazy blur lunges at Jazz. The M4 is knocked to the ground. It clatters on the stairs, coming to rest on its side. The view on the screen is disorienting, with the floor appearing like a wall. Boots rush into view, kicking the gun so it falls down another tier. Clomping boots now appear on the ceiling from the perspective of Nick and Bear outside in the snowcat.

As Jazz is hauled to her feet, she says, "That bitch scratched me."

Dmitri picks up the M4. Jazz snatches it from his hand.

"Where did she go?" he asks, but the camera mounted beneath the scope on the M4 is still facing the back wall.

"I'm bleeding," Jazz says.

"She's gone," Dmitri says. "Here, sit down. Let me take a look at you."

Jazz sits on one of the seats. She rests the M4 over the seat-back in front of her, leveling it at the door, giving Nick and Bear a clear view of the front of the room. If anyone comes in, all she has to do is squeeze the trigger.

"It's not deep," Dmitri says, examining her with the flashlight. "But as it's on your neck, there's a fair bit of bleeding."

"Fucking hell," Jazz replies. Her blood-soaked gloves are visible on the edge of the frame. In infrared, blood appears pitch black, staining her gloves. "What is wrong with these people?"

"Ah," Bear says from within the cabin of the snowcat. "Have we considered the possibility we might have walked into a biohazard?"

Jazz sounds annoyed. "I'm not turning into a *fucking* zombie, if that's what you're worried about."

"I'm just saying—"

"You watch too much shitty TV," Jazz says, cutting him off. She growls, "Stay off comms."

"I saw a med-kit in the kitchen," Dmitri says as they walk to the front of the room. "I suspect our friend is long gone by now. Let's get you down there and patched up."

They make their way back to the kitchen, checking each turn before moving forward. Nick can hear Dmitri rustling around, searching for bandages, but the view they have is either of the ceiling as seen from his goggles or the kitchen door as Jazz makes damn sure she's not going to be taken by surprise again.

Outside, the wind has taken on a distinctly eerie tone like that of moaning. With the lights off, Nick can barely see the outline of the hut in front of them. Lucille rumbles at a low idle. Bear dons the night vision goggles and looks around, peering out into the darkness. Snow swirls around the cat.

"Ah, I don't mean to be an alarmist," he says over the radio. "But you guys might want to come back to Lucille—like now!"

"What's going on?" Jazz asks.

"How many rounds does your M4 hold?"

"Thirty. Why?"

"You're gonna need them."

Neither Jazz nor Dmitri replies. They both scramble for the exit and out into the corridor, running for the emergency door at the rear of the dormitory.

"What's going on?" Nick asks, but he's not sure he actually wants an answer.

Bear doesn't say anything. He simply reaches up and flicks the toggle switch above the windshield, turning on the spotlights. It takes a moment for the sudden onset of brilliant white light reflecting off the snow and ice to subside. Shapes come into focus. Heads turn to face them. There are easily a dozen people standing in the snow. From what Nick can tell, they were originally facing the building. Now, they crowd around on all sides of the snowcat, bathing in its light. Like the corpse out on the plateau, they've got their arms outstretched, reaching for the spotlights, but they don't advance. There's movement in the shadows as more people join them, standing off at a distance.

Quietly, Nick says, "Oh, man. We are so fucked."

SANDRA

Jazz and Dmitri burst onto the landing outside the living quarters. They come to a halt at the top of the stairs, being caught in the glare of the spotlights. Easily ten to fifteen people stand between them and Lucille. There are more in the shadows.

"Talk to me," Jazz says, scanning the crowd with her infrared scope. Although the base staff are stationary, they light up as white shapes facing the cab of the snowcat. Warmth radiates within their upper torsos at least. Their legs are buried by the driving snow.

Jazz asks Bear, "What are they doing?"

"I don't know," Bear replies over the radio. "They're just standing there. Best I understand it, they came out after the gunshots."

"Why are they facing you?"

"I'm not sure," he replies. "They look like bugs drawn to an Alabama porch light."

Slowly, Jazz descends the stairs. Snow and ice crunch beneath her boots. She and Dmitri keep their weapons trained on the people standing in the snow. They switch from one person to another as they get close, trying to assess the threat, looking for any movement. The zombie-like base staff continue facing Nick and Bear in Lucille.

To get to the snowcat, Jazz and Dmitri have to pass within a few feet of these ghostly figures. They step slowly, carefully around them.

Bear has his gun out, but he remains within the cab of the snowcat. Nick's unsure whether he's going to fire through the windshield or if he'll open the door and shoot, but he's not climbing down from Lucille.

"Easy," Jazz whispers. "No sudden movements."

Dmitri follows close behind her, stepping in her boot prints. With each step, they sink into the deep snow. Jazz has the muzzle of her M4 barely an inch from the back of the head of one of the men standing directly in front of the lights. She circles around him, keeping her gun on him, but he doesn't so much as blink.

Jazz backs up, with the lights on the snowcat blazing behind her. She reaches out with a gloved hand for the treads, keeping her eyes on the closest person. She scoots inside the vehicle. Dmitri follows, closing his door quietly.

"Well, that was as creepy as hell," she says.

"Look at those fucking psychos," Bear says, leaning forward on the steering wheel to take a good look. He revs the engine, looking for a response. Lucille roars, but no one moves.

Nick mumbles, barely aware he's articulating his thoughts.

"We're afraid."

"Of course we fucking are," Bear snaps.

Fight or flight—that's all Nick has ever known. Any time he's been afraid, his response has been to lash out or run like hell. This, though, is different. For once, he has time to think. Fear makes people do dumb things. Nick is tired of doing dumb things. For once, he wants to do the right thing rather than being predictable. He wants to see beyond his own fears. He doesn't know what the hell is going on, but he knows their reaction isn't helping.

"W—Why are we afraid?" Nick stutters. "I think Jazz is

right."

Jazz twists in her seat to look at Nick. She doesn't say what she's thinking, so he elaborates. "Too much shitty TV, right? Look at them. I think we have this all wrong."

"I *am* looking at them!" Bear cries aloud, frustrated by Nick's comments. He gestures to the windshield with both hands. Snow sweeps across dozens of faces illuminated by the spotlights. Hair blows sideways in the wind.

"I am too," Nick says. "And I don't think they mean us any harm."

Dmitri has his gun up. He rests his hands on the back of the seat behind Jazz. The barrel of his Glock points at the metal roof. He says, "The woman in the lecture hall. She wasn't trying to attack us. She was trying to get away."

"She wasn't trying to attack *you*," Jazz says, feeling at the bandage on her neck.

Nick is lost. He's sleepwalking through the logic in front of him.

"They need our help."

"No, no, no," Bear says, taking his eyes off the figures standing in the snow and turning toward Nick. He throws his arm over the back seat. "Are you fucking mad?"

"They're going to die, right?" Nick asks Jazz.

"Out there in the cold?" she replies. "Yes."

Bear is adamant. "I say, we let them die. There's something wrong with them. Whatever it is, we don't want it."

"We don't have it," Dmitri says. "We're fine."

Bear glances across at Jazz and the large white bandage taped to the side of her neck. She's not impressed by the implication of his raised eyebrows. "I don't have it—whatever the fuck it is."

"What happened to them?" Dmitri asks.

"I don't know," Nick says. "But if we want to learn anything about what happened here, we have to help them."

"Fuck," Jazz says, leaning forward and hitting the dash with the heel of her palm. "Fuck this!"

"Why should we?" Bear asks.

"Because that could be us," Nick says.

Bear responds with, "This is some nasty shit!"

"This isn't supernatural," Dmitri says.

"Why not?" Bear asks, pointing at the bodies standing in the snow, illuminated by the spotlights. "Doesn't look natural to me."

"Because there's no such thing as the supernatural," Dmitri says. "There has to be some other explanation. Nick's right. The only way we're going to get any answers is by going back out there."

Bear says, "If we go back out there, that really could be us. Something caused this. How do you know that whatever caused this won't affect us as well?"

"It hasn't," Dmitri says.

"Shut the hell up," Bear snaps.

"Bear's right," Jazz says. "We could become caught up in this."

"We're already caught up in this," Nick says. "We're just not doing anything about it."

Dmitri agrees. "We're here, and we're fine. I'm with Nick on this. They're going to die out there. Just like Lee Lao Chan."

"We don't have much time," Nick says, swallowing the lump rising in his throat.

Nick's no hero, but he knows someone that is. Sandra is an ICU nurse. She's worked in ER and COVID wards. For a while, she even worked as a surgical nurse in a cardiac unit. As much as he wants to cut and run, she's his conscience. If she were here, she'd be appealing for reason over fear. This is exactly what she'd be saying. The funny thing is, if she were here, he'd be siding with Bear and arguing the reverse position. Without her, he feels compelled to take her point of view. Deep down, he knows he'll never see Sandra again. Is he compensating for losing her? Is this his guilt playing out? Hell yeah.

Bear says, "This is a freak show. I say we get the hell out of here."

Nick doesn't respond. Deep down, Nick's a coward. He's not brave. The real Nick wants to run and hide. But the real Nick is someone that makes this Nick sick to his stomach. The real Nick is a loser. Case in point, Sandra. The only way he is ever going to change is if, at some point, he stops and makes a change. Nick knows he needs to stop retreating from what's right. As hard as it is, perhaps this is how he begins.

With his gloved hand on the door handle, Nick says, "I don't think they're going to hurt us, but they are going to die."

He opens the door and is hit with a blast of cold air. To get down from the rear of the snowcat, Nick has to turn and slip his boots into the short metal ladder above the treads. That means turning his back on them. It's strange, but he doesn't feel any fear. He's defenseless, but he's at peace. Is this what Sandra feels when paramedics roll someone into the emergency room? When you've got a job to do, there's no time to be afraid.

"Jesus, Mary and Joseph," Bear calls out from within the cab. He's frustrated, but Nick doesn't care.

Nick steps onto the treads of the snowcat, shutting the door, and drops the last few feet to the ice. His boots crunch into the snow. Without any hesitation, he rushes to the closest person, a woman in her late 50s. She's wearing a thick jacket and jeans. Part of him is expecting the worst. If she lashes out with claws and a set of fangs, lunging at him like a vampire, he'd be shocked but not surprised. Sandra, though, seems to whisper in his ear, telling him that's absurd.

The wind swirls around him. Snow rushes past.

Nick ignores the woman's outstretched arms. He walks around beside her. After taking a deep breath, he drapes his arm over her shoulder and turns her, directing her toward the open door at the back of the living quarters.

"Come on. Let's get you inside."

Nick may not be a doctor or a nurse, but Sandra taught him kindness is as good as medicine. A couple of years ago, they were returning from a hot summer's day at Myrtle Beach. It was ten in the evening. They were driving down a quiet country road in her old convertible, taking a shortcut home when they came across an accident. Two cars had collided. One was turning, the other was going straight. The vehicles had spun to different sides of the intersection.

Steam rose from the crushed hood of a Cadillac pushed up against a street sign.

A Ford F-350 pickup truck lay on its side. Gasoline seeped onto the road. The windshield was shattered, hanging loose from its rubber seals.

'Get her,' Sandra yelled as they pulled up on the gravel at the side of the road. 'She's in shock.'

In that instant, she was a child not more than eight years old. From what Nick could tell, she'd been thrown from the truck. Blood ran down her legs as she stumbled on, walking toward oncoming traffic.

Sandra grabbed the overpriced first aid kit Nick always complained about from the trunk of her car. She ran to the overturned truck. The driver climbed out through the broken windshield. He was shaken but not visibly hurt. She directed him over to Nick and ran on to the Cadillac.

Nick took the two of them to one side and sat on the grassy bank of a drainage ditch. He dialed 911 as Sandra worked on the elderly couple in the Caddy.

Eventually, sirens sounded in the distance. EMTs were first on the scene, followed by a state trooper. Sandra praised Nick for looking after the father and daughter, but what had he done? Nothing. Sandra was the real hero. Was that the problem? Did he feel he had to be the hero? Did he resent her for being a nurse? Did she somehow make him feel small by comparison? Why the fuck did he ever compare himself to her? She never did that. It was all him. Standing there in Antarctica, he finally realizes his reaction was fucked up.

As much as he'd like to ignore that feeling of resentment, back then, he couldn't. Now, it seems childish. As it was, Sandra was covered in blood. There were stains on her knees, her sleeves, and her shoulder. Were it not for the disposable gloves she was wearing, the medics could have been forgiven for thinking she was one of the victims. Sandra talked with the paramedics as they rolled the injured couple away on gurneys. Now, in retrospect, Nick can see that young girl and her father weren't the only ones in shock. Being catapulted into that scene had thrown his mind into neutral. He idled along while Sandra hit the turbo boost.

Nick is ten thousand miles from South Carolina and yet he knows this is what Sandra would do. For once, he doesn't resent her for it. Instead, he admires her.

The wind bites at his cheeks. Snow races past.

Nick taps another man on the shoulder, getting his attention. The man looks at him in a daze, blinking rapidly. Nick shepherds the two of them toward the living quarters, gently pushing them on up the stairs.

Jazz has sprung into action. She has her M4 slung backward over her jacket with the barrel pointing at the ice. Like him, she's rounding up several people at once, working with Dmitri to get everyone inside the dormitory. Together, they herd a group of six people toward the stairs.

Even Bear has softened. He runs to the top of the stairs and directs people through the door and down the corridor.

For once in his life, Nick feels as though he's done something right. Somehow that gives him a warm feeling despite the cold. Sandra will never know how she helped save these lives, but she did.

Jazz yells to Bear.

"Keep them moving. There's a lecture hall at the end of the corridor. The heating is on in there."

"On it," Bear says, disappearing into the darkened hallway.

Lights flicker within the building.

Like sheep, the others follow without prompting. Dmitri takes Bear's place at the top of the stairs, brushing snow off jackets and trousers. Gently, he pushes people on down the corridor.

"I'll circle around Lucille looking for stragglers," Jazz says to Nick. "You kill the lights and the engine."

"On it," Nick says in mimicry of Bear. He climbs up on the treads of the snowcat and into the cab. Nick doesn't actually know what he's doing, but he looks around and finds the ignition switch. Nick turns off the engine, followed by the lights. Jazz waits for him by the front treads.

"You did good," Jazz says as he hops down. She pats her gloved hand on his thick jacket. "You're going to make an excellent juror."

"Thanks."

As they climb the stairs, Nick takes one last look back at the flurry of footprints in the snow and the now dormant snowcat, realizing just how different this could have ended. Yeah, Sandra would like this outcome, although she wouldn't stop to celebrate. She'd be busy tending to people inside. Perhaps that's what set him off the rails back then. She gave so much of herself to others. When she'd come home, all she wanted was some downtime, not a high maintenance man-baby. Nick could kick himself for being so shortsighted and selfish.

Nick and Jazz duck inside. With the lights on, the living quarters appear distinctly less evil than they did when shrouded in darkness and viewed through an infrared scope. If anything, the dorm looks a little too bland. Nick was expecting a no-expenses-spared Hollywood movie set. Instead, he got trailer-park chic. The carpet is so last century.

"Keep them moving," Jazz yells. As she's short, she tiptoes on her boots, looking across the sea of heads ambling along the hallway. Dmitri is standing by the kitchen, urging people on.

From the end of the corridor, Bear calls out, "Now what?"

Jazz thumps Nick on the chest. "Yeah, now what, genius?"

Nick wants to say, ask for a doctor or a nurse, but that's hardly practical. Hell, some of these people could be medical professionals and he'd never know it.

"Keep them warm," he yells back. "Grab some blankets. Strip off any cold clothing. Look for signs of frostbite."

Damn, for a moment there, Nick actually sounded competent. He turns to Jazz, asking, "What do you do for frostbite?"

"Depends on severity," she replies as they push past people to reach the kitchen. "But warming them up is a good start. We're gonna need painkillers. Lots of painkillers."

Dmitri hands her the first aid kit from the kitchen, asking, "So how do we break the spell?"

"Good question," Jazz says, leaving Nick with Dmitri as she pushes on toward Bear. "Figure it out."

"Okay," Nick replies, but he's clueless.

Dmitri moves between a bunch of base staff that have wandered into the kitchen. Their eyes are glazed. With stooped shoulders, they mull around, but they don't bump into each other. There's a semblance of cognition there, just not enough. Lips move, but no one speaks. It's as though they're mumbling to themselves.

"This one's a doctor," Dmitri says, looking at an ID in a purse he pulled from her jacket pocket. "But down here, she could be a doctor of anything."

The confused look on Nick's face prompts some clarification from Dmitri. "A doctor of astrophysics isn't exactly what we need right now."

"Ah, no," Nick replies, encouraging her to sit in a chair. The woman's face is pale, while her hands are red. Her fingers are starting to swell. Nick uses a little soapy water to remove her rings, placing them on the table beside her.

"How do we wake them?" Dmitri asks, looking into the eyes of one of the men. He moves his hands around in front of the man's face, trying to get a response.

"I don't know," Nick says, "but we have to try something." He searches through the cupboards and pulls out a large tin of instant coffee along with a five pound bag of sugar.

"Coffee? Really?" Dmitri asks, but Nick ignores him. He runs the water in the sink until it's warm. Then he mixes a heaped tablespoon of sugar along with a heaped tablespoon of coffee into a mug. The resulting concoction is more of a sludge than a liquid. Nick takes a sip. Damn, it's strong.

Dmitri laughs. "That's going to keep you awake all night."

"That's kind of what I'm counting on," Nick says. "Wake them up, right?"

Dmitri nods in agreement.

Nick cradles his left hand behind the woman's head as she sits at the table. He lifts the mug to her lips.

"Come on," he whispers.

Dmitri places his hand beneath her jaw, gently opening her mouth. Nick pours as Dmitri keeps her head back, trying to keep the fluid from running down her neck. The woman coughs, but swallows.

"That's it," Nick says. "A bit more. Come on."

"What are you thinking?" Dmitri asks.

"I dunno. I mean, I don't know what the hell I'm doing, but my girlfriend was a nurse. She was always going on about the strange things people do when they're in shock. She called shock the silent killer."

"You think this is shock?" Dmitri asks as they get the woman to swallow a little more.

"Maybe. Even if it's not, these guys haven't had anything to eat or drink for days. I'm hoping all they need is a pair of jumper cables to restart the engine, if you know what I mean. Some water. A bit of a sugar hit. The crunch of a caffeine buzz."

The woman's head turns toward him. She blinks, looking confused.

"Pass me a bottle of water," he says, putting the mug down. Dmitri breaks the cap on a bottle of water. Nick lifts it to her lips. "Here. Drink."

Slowly, the woman raises her hands, taking the bottle from him.

"Hey," Nick says, stepping back and making eye contact with her. He smiles. "Welcome back."

She chugs on the bottle.

"Easy," he says. "There's no rush. You're okay. Everything's going to be okay."

Water dribbles from her chin. At a guess, she's feeling numb. Her hands shake, which he takes as a good sign as previously they were still.

He asks Dmitri, "What's her name?"

"Dr. Adrianna Macmillan. United Kingdom."

"Adrianna," Nick says, resting his hand gently on her shoulder and looking deep into her heavily dilated eyes. "That's a beautiful name. How are you feeling, Adrianna? Do you know where you are?"

She speaks in a whisper.

"S—Sussex."

Nick grins. She's back and yet she isn't. As tenderly as he can, he says, "You're in Antarctica. You are at *Vincennes*. Do you know where that is?"

Adrianna nods. For a moment, he feels he's made some real progress, but it's quickly followed by her shaking her head in disagreement.

"It's okay. You're probably going to feel a little disoriented for a while. You're part of a multinational effort here in Antarctica."

At this point, Nick leaves out any mention of an alien spacecraft. The poor woman's got enough to deal with.

"What kind of doctor are you?" he asks.

"I—ah. I have a Ph.D. in astrobiology."

Nick nods, popping a couple of ibuprofen in her hand. He's still smiling, wanting to put her at ease. "You're not quite the kind of doctor we were looking for, but that's all right. Listen, I want you to take these, okay? You've been outside. You've got mild frostbite. As your hands warm up, they're going to sting."

Dmitri is over by the sink with a large metal pot. After emptying the tin of coffee and all of the sugar into the pot, he uses a spatula to mix in some warm water. "I'll get this concoction down to Jazz and Bear. Get them up to speed."

"Good," Nick says, starting to move onto the next person with his mug of sweetened, highly caffeinated sludge.

Adrianna grabs his arm.

"Hey," he says. "I'm not going anywhere, but I need to help these people. You understand?"

She nods, letting go.

"Everything's going to be okay," he says. Although he's sincere, his words are a lie. No one knows what the future holds, least of all him. If Adrianna stops and thinks about it, she'll realize that, but in the moment, lies are all any of them have.

DMITRI

Nick's tired.

Time is a blur.

There's so much to do and so little time to think. The team are busy dealing with what happened but not why.

It's been about six or seven hours since they gathered up the base staff in the living quarters and revived Adrianna. Since then, she's helped organize survivors. As far as he knows, there's no reason why some people woke easily while others are still catatonic even now, but it's been a long day. Nick has no idea what the time is. Outside, the storm is still raging in the perpetual darkness. Snow and ice whip past the buildings, shaking the double-glazed windows.

Knowing the layout of the base and its staff, Adrianna was able to identify nurses, doctors, and engineers. She sent them to work through the external buildings, looking for others, while Jazz and her team worked on those in the living quarters. The lecture hall has become a triage ward, with the seats being pushed down and used as impromptu beds. A couple of nurses have set up saline drips and health monitors they've dragged across from the medical suite. *Vincennes* was never designed to treat mass casualties. It's easier for the base surgeon to move between rows than it is to traipse between bunks in various rooms. The storage area opposite the lecture hall has been covered in plastic sheets and is used for surgery. So far, there have been three amputations.

"Colonel Buckley wants to see you," a uniformed soldier says to Jazz as she tends to one of the survivors.

"Okay," she replies, addressing Nick and Dmitri. "You guys stay here. Bear, you're with me."

Nick is exhausted. He slumps down against the far wall, sitting on the carpet tiles lining the floor.

Adrianna dumps a duffel bag on the ground and sits next to him, asking, "How are you holding up?"

"Me?" he replies. "I should be asking that of you."

She laughs. "I'm doing fine. I'm a little sore, but I'm okay."

"I'm beat."

"It's going to be a long day," she says.

"Wait? What time is it?"

"Last time I checked," she replies. "A little after eight."

"In the evening?"

She laughs. "The morning."

"Oh, damn," he replies, pushing his head back against the wall and looking up at the ceiling. Nick's got his arms resting on his knees. His fingers are shaking.

"Are you eating? Drinking?" she asks.

Nick turns and looks at her. "It's a little early for that, but what have you got?"

"I was thinking about water."

He smiles.

Adrianna says, "Keep your fluids up. Make sure you eat something. And be sure to get some rest. It's no crime to get some sleep."

"Yes, doc."

She hands him a bottle of water. Nick takes a sip and asks,

"Do you know what happened?"

"Mikhail thinks it was defensive rather than offensive."

"So they're not coming after us?"

"No. But we still don't have contact with the team under the ice. A lot of our equipment has been fried so we're still trying to piece things together. We need to get down there and find out what happened to the rest of the crew."

Nick nods.

"Oh," she says, hoisting the bag onto her lap and pulling on the zipper. "I've got something for you guys."

She rummages around, saying, "I had to guess on sizes, but there's several changes of clothing along with a bunch of toiletries like soap, toothpaste and shaving cream."

Adrianna hands the bag across to him. "I thought it might give you a lift."

"Thank you," Nick says, running his hand over the fuzz on his cheeks.

Nick's tempted to point out they've got their own stuff stowed away in the back of Lucille, but the prospect of going out into the cold again does not appeal to him at all. Already, he's feeling soft. In Antarctica, warm air is akin to the finest caviar.

As he gets to his feet, he says, "Thank you."

Nick grabs Dmitri, showing him the contents of the bag as though it were contraband. They head to the communal bathroom. After shaving and brushing their teeth, they shower in stalls barely two feet square. The flimsy plastic curtain between them is semitransparent, but Nick is beyond caring about privacy.

"Oh, damn," he says as hot water cascades over his head and shoulders. Steam rises around him. When he finally drags himself from the shower, the bathroom is like a sauna.

"Feels good, huh?" Dmitri says, drying himself.

"That," Nick replies, "is possibly the best shower in existence. I mean, like anywhere on the planet."

"Ha ha."

Nick rubs himself dry with a towel. "So you're Russian special forces."

"Was," Dmitri replies. "It's a young man's game. There's only so much punishment the body can take. They like to say, it's all in your mind, but that's a lie. Oh, it's a lie you believe when you're twenty, but a lie nonetheless. Pride only goes so far. Stubborn determination takes you further, but the body—it isn't fooled by bravado. Eventually, it catches up with you—catches up with me."

"Where did you serve?" Nick asks, getting dressed.

"Did I fire on Americans?" Dmitri asks, answering what he assumes is Nick's real question. "No. But I would have—such is the folly of loyalty. When you're young, you do as you're told. We weren't trained to think. We were trained to obey."

Nick nods but doesn't comment. For him, it's strangely comforting to put on clean, warm clothing. He's intrigued by Dmitri's blunt attitude. Back in Puerto Rico, Jazz warned him about being manipulated by the Russians, and he gets it. International cooperation is only ever in the context of national interests. Dmitri, though, seems genuine.

"You are in a unique position, Nick. In Russia, we have a saying: *У каждой дороги два направления—Every road has two directions.* You may have been dragged to Antarctica, but you get to choose where you go from here."

Nick sits on a wooden bench, getting dressed. He pulls on a pair of woolen socks.

"You don't trust me, do you?" Dmitri asks.

"Honestly, I don't know. I don't think I'm supposed to trust you. You're the enemy, right? Or has all that changed with this thing beneath the ice?"

Dmitri pulls a t-shirt over his head and shoulders, working his muscular arms through the sleeves as he says, "We need each other. We always have, but we've been too busy fighting each other to see that."

"Is that another Russian saying?" Nick asks, humoring him. "You know, in South Carolina, we have a saying."

"Oh, you do?" Dmitri asks, joining in and joking with him. "You have sayings?"

"We do. We say, the enemy of my enemy is probably still an asshole."

"Hah. I like that," Dmitri says. He grins, adding, "It's true."

They walk back out into the corridor to the sound of shouting from the lecture hall. Someone's yelling, "Where is he? Where the *fuck* is he?"

"Stay here," Dmitri says, pushing Nick to one side as he rushes down the hallway. To hell with that. Nick is hard on Dmitri's heels. They rush into the lecture hall to see a soldier dressed in fatigues. He has a thick winter jacket on with the hood pulled back. There's a Glock in his outstretched arm. He's pointing his gun at Adrianna, threatening to shoot her. Their eyes meet, and with the subtlest motion, Adrianna shakes her head. She wants Nick to flee, but he can't. It isn't a sense of bravery that keeps him there. He can't abandon her. Nick's still trying to process what the hell is happening and why.

Dmitri has his arms out, appealing for calm. Initially, he blocks Nick's view, hiding him from the shooter. Dmitri steps to one side, wanting to edge his way over to where his sidearm is resting on his jacket.

"Easy," he says, maintaining eye contact with the soldier. "What's going on here? We're all in this together. Let's work together. Talk to me."

Adrianna is shaking. She grabs her trembling arms, trying to settle them as she wraps them around herself.

"Is that him?" the soldier asks, gesturing at Nick with the barrel of his Glock. "Is he the new juror?"

"Let's slow things down," Dmitri says, still facing the soldier as he works his way around to his jacket. He's got his fingers splayed, appealing for calm.

"Fucking Russians!"

A single shot rings out.

Nick flinches at the violence being unleashed before him. In the confines of the room, the shot breaks like thunder, assaulting his ears and rattling his bones.

Dmitri clutches at his chest. He sinks to his knees, pausing for a second as he looks down at the blood staining his hands. The soldier has the gun trained on Dmitri's head, ready for a second shot. Nick rushes to Dmitri, grabbing him by his shoulders. He turns him, laying him gently on the floor. Blood soaks into the carpet.

Dmitri looks up into his eyes. "I—I."

Nick takes his hand and squeezes his fingers, trying to provide some comfort, but it's futile. Pathetic. Deep red blood sticks to his palm. Tears well up in his eyes. What the hell just happened? They were laughing just moments ago. How can death be so cruel?

"You," the soldier yells. "You're coming with me."

Before Nick can turn to face him, the soldier grabs Nick by his still-damp hair. Gloved fingers tear at his roots, threatening to rip clumps of hair from his head as Nick's dragged away. He has no choice. Nick can't pull himself free without losing part of his scalp. He grabs the soldier's wrist with both hands, but it's all he can do to crouch and follow along as he's dragged out into the corridor and through the entranceway with its double doors.

The soldier kicks the bar on the external door and it flies open, scraping across the snow on the landing. He grabs Nick's collar, dragging him behind him. Boots crunch on the ice. The wind whips around them. The sudden burst of an icy chill shocks Nick's body. The cold seeps into his bones. Already, his fingers are numb. Nick kicks with his feet, desperate to keep up with the soldier as he's dragged through the snow. He's expecting to be dumped out on the ice with a bullet in his head.

"Stop! Stop," he yells against the roar of the gale tearing across the frozen plateau. Spotlights break through the night, casting long shadows. Nick slips on the ice, scrambling, trying to break free. The soldier doesn't care, dragging him on by his torn shirt. He throws Nick in front of him, forcing him to keep up.

The soldier opens a door and swings Nick inside, sending him colliding with one of the bench seats lining the ready room. The air is knocked out of his lungs. Pain shoots through his ribs.

The soldier grabs Nick by his hair again, forcing his head back. For his part, Nick's doing all he can to avoid having his scalp ripped from his skull. He grabs the soldier's wrist. He can barely think through the pain wracking his head. He slides on the icy floor as he's shoved toward the internal door, only now realizing the soldier has let go.

The external door closes behind them. The soldier plants his boot in the center of Nick's back and shoves him forward, not allowing him to get back to his feet. Nick falls against the crash-bar on the internal door and stumbles through. He collapses on the linoleum floor of the operations center.

"Ah, there you are," a voice says. "I'm Colonel John Augustus Buckley, US Marines. It's nice to meet you, Nick. I see you're already acquainted with Sergeant Hillenbrand."

BUCKLEY

Nick is on his hands and knees, cradling his head, unsure whether the blood dripping on the floor is Dmitri's or his. He cries. Tears fall from his eyes as he rocks back and forth, trying to catch up with reality.

Colonel Buckley grabs him by the nape of his neck, jerking his head back and forcing him to look up.

"It's not polite to ignore basic pleasantries. What's your name, son? Your full name?"

The colonel's voice is deceptive. He's from one of the southern states. His accent is relaxed, making his words sound soft and warm. At a guess, Nick would think he's from Mississippi or Louisiana. Buckley smiles from behind a thin mustache, encouraging him to speak.

"Nick. Nicholas. Nicholas James Ferrin."

Nick stares at the overhead fluorescent lights, still trying to comprehend what's happening. Now that he's upright on his knees, the colonel lets go.

Buckley strides around in front of him, speaking with a voice as bitter as the storm outside.

"Do you know why you're here, Nicholas?"

"N—No."

"You're here to do your duty. You have a solemn duty to the

people of God's sacred Earth, Mr. Ferrin. Do you understand me?"

Nick nods. He looks around. Computer monitors line the walls, displaying dozens of graphs along with video images from throughout the base. Most of the shots are of the lights above an external door somewhere, revealing frozen stairs leading down to the ice. There are a few internal shots, but they're of empty corridors. On one screen, he sees Adrianna kneeling next to a body sprawled out on the floor. The images are monochrome. The blood seeping from Dmitri's chest is as black as coal.

"W—Why? Why did you kill him?"

The colonel ignores Nick.

"You have been called upon to serve your country, Nicholas. That is a noble endeavor."

Jazz is down on her knees not more than ten feet from Nick. Her hands have been bound behind her back with a plastic zip-tie. Blood drips from her chin, running in a steady stream from a cut on her forehead. Bruises have formed on her cheeks. Their eyes meet. She mouths the word, '*Don't.*'

Bear is beside her, kneeling on the linoleum floor with his hands bound behind his back. His face is black and blue. Large welts have formed on his cheeks.

"You're here to serve on the jury, Nick. Can I call you that, Nicholas? Nick is much more informal and relaxed. It's more appropriate, don't you think?"

Nick nods, still trying to focus through the haze of pain surging through his scalp.

There's a rhythm to Colonel Buckley's words. He speaks with deliberation. Every sentence is precise. Each word is pronounced with vigor.

"There's something I need you to do, Nick. As a member of the jury, I need you to authorize our response to the alien attack. Father has been disabled. We've got his core functions back online, but he needs your approval to proceed with our response. Do you understand me?"

Reluctantly, Nick nods.

Buckley walks over to Jazz. He places the barrel of his pistol under her chin, raising her gaze as he speaks. "You wouldn't lie to me now would you, Nick? Jasmine here, she lied. She told me you were dead. She said she lost you in the storm."

He rolls the barrel of the gun around her face, pushing it against her temple. Jazz doesn't flinch. Her head rocks as Buckley drills the barrel against her skull.

"Do you know what the punishment is for disobeying a lawful order, Nick? Dereliction of duty while in conflict? Do you know what the military does when a subordinate refuses a direct order in times of war?"

Jazz bows her head. Tears run down her cheeks, but she tightens her lips. She shakes her head, signaling Nick shouldn't respond.

"We're at war," Buckley says, pulling his gun away and turning on Nick. "We've been attacked. But we can stop them. You can stop them, Nick. You can be the hero."

He holsters his gun and offers Nick his hand. "Get up, son."

A thin trickle of blood runs down the side of Nick's head, curling around his ear and down his neck. Nick takes the colonel's hand and gets to his feet. He's unsteady, on the verge of falling.

"Easy," Buckley says, grabbing him by his shoulder. "Don't worry, boy. This will all be over soon."

"I—I don't know what you want from me."

"You will soon enough."

Buckley leads Nick around the side of an old-style computer console. A rickety keyboard and a green-screen monitor have been incorporated into a single, solid plastic case the size of a study desk. A trackball has been built into the surface, acting as a computer mouse. There's a woman seated in front of the console. She's hurt. Her left eye socket is swollen, closing over her eye. The skin on her forehead is purple with bruising. She looks dazed.

"Are you ready, Julia?"

She nods. Colonel Buckley pushes a large green button next to the trackball. Sergeant Hillenbrand stands at ease by the door. He has holstered his gun. He's got his hands clasped behind him. Rather than looking relaxed, it's as though he's waiting to die, accepting his fate.

A long metal stalk protrudes from the plastic casing. Buckley speaks into the microphone.

"Father, we have a quorum of the surviving jurors. I am requesting the execution of UN Emergency Contingency 57A."

Hundreds of lines of code scroll down the screen as a program starts. There's no graphical interface, just seemingly meaningless commands appearing automatically on each line. It's as though someone's typing in the background, entering text into a command prompt at an astonishing rate.

An electronic voice says, *"The detonation of the nuclear contingency requires the consent of the majority of jurors."*

"I have two of the three remaining jurors with me," Buckley says, nudging Julia.

Before she can speak, a feeble voice comes over the radio. "Don't do it, Julia."

Colonel Buckley ignores that comment. "Go ahead, Julia. Do—your—duty."

Julia puts her trembling hand on the computer monitor, steadying herself.

"Julia Duffie. United Kingdom. I vote yes."

No sooner has she spoken than the radio crackles with, "This is Anni Azizi, China. I vote no."

Colonel Buckley forces Nick's head down next to the

microphone. He's deceptively strong, forcing Nick to bend at the waist. Nick puts his hands out, smearing blood over the computer as he steadies himself.

"Say it, Nicholas. Vote. Say your goddamn name."

"No," Nick says. He surprises himself with a surge of strength that leaves him staggering away from the colonel. Nick might not be the most capable guy on the planet. He's not the sharpest or the smartest, the strongest or the bravest, but there's one thing Nick is good at—being as stubborn as a Sorrel pack mule.

"You will do this," Buckley says, lowering his head and glaring at him. "You will end this. Now."

"Fuck you!"

"Oh," Buckley says, grinning as he addresses Hillenbrand. "Looks like we've got ourselves a *bona fide* all-American hero. Goddamn, I am going to enjoy this."

Hillenbrand repositions himself, standing with his back to the door, blocking any chance of escape. Nick crouches, trying to assess his options. Jazz looks up at him with pity in her eyes. Yeah, he's totally fucked, but he's not going to die without a fight. Nick launches himself at Buckley. The colonel simply bats at Nick's head with the heel of his pistol, smacking him across the temple and sending him reeling.

Buckley uses the Glock like a pair of knuckledusters, with his fist wrapped around the pistol grip. He could shoot Nick if he wanted to, but he keeps his fingers clear of the trigger, using the butt of the magazine like a cold, hard hammer.

"What are you doing, Nicholas? Don't you know? You have a duty to perform, son. You're here to protect not only the US but humanity as a whole. Authorize that goddamn nuke!"

"Why are you doing this?" Nick asks, still reeling from being hit.

"Don't you get it? We have to stop them. We can't let these

things escape. We get one chance to stop this. One chance before tens of thousands of goddamn aliens come crawling out of that hole in the ice."

"You don't know that," Nick says.

Out of nowhere, he's struck again by the heel of the pistol, only this time, it rakes across his jaw, rattling his teeth. Blood swells within his mouth. He spits. Bloody mucus hangs from his lips, dripping to the floor.

"You think I'm the bad guy?" Buckley says, pointing the gun at the storm raging beyond the door. "What? You think I'm the devil?" He points his gun at the floor, saying, "I have seen the devil. The devil is down there beneath the ice. The devil hath no form but that like a man. The devil hath come here but for to deceive us. There is no other reason, Nicholas."

"You're not thinking straight," Nick says, staggering over near Jazz, trying to keep his distance from Buckley. "We need to understand what we're dealing with."

The colonel says, "Do you know what your problem is? Your problem is, you want to play by the rules. The devil also likes to play, but not by the rules. That's why he *always* wins. Is that what you want, Nicholas? Do you want the devil to win?"

Hillenbrand is enjoying this. He's smiling. Julia has slumped in her seat. It's not difficult for Nick to see that, given time, Buckley will beat him down. He'll end up like her, willing to surrender just to get it over with.

"This isn't right," Nick says, trying to appeal to reason. "You must see that. This isn't what was intended. You don't strong-arm a jury."

Buckley laughs. "You don't get it, do you?" he says, grinning. "You're white trash! The Russians didn't pick you because you represent the average American. They chose you because you're a chump. They chose you because they *knew* they could manipulate you. They think you're dumb. They think you're stupid, Nicholas. To them, you're a joke."

The blank look on Nick's face gets Buckley's attention.

"Oh, you really didn't know," he says, laughing. "Boy, you really are a fool."

The colonel turns his attention to Jazz. He points at her with his gun. "She knew, but she never told you, did she? Do you know why? Because she thought she could use you as well."

Jazz swallows a lump in her throat. Again, tears flow, but this time they're not shed out of pain. She's ashamed of herself. She struggles to make eye contact with Nick, mouthing the words, *I'm sorry.*

"How does it feel, Nick? How does it feel to be betrayed? Thirty pieces of silver. That's all it took to sway Judas. But these guys. These guys fucked you over for sport. For them, it was fun."

Nick falls to his knees, devastated by what he's hearing. Buckley reads him like a freeway billboard. The colonel crouches in front of him, sitting down on his haunches and looking him in the eye.

"You get it now, huh? They played you. They fooled you. They baited you like a bluegill in the bayou. They hooked you and reeled you in. Don't you see? You owe them nothing. Not a goddamn thing!"

"You're lying," Nick says, but he's deflecting, trying to shelter his own fragile ego. Tears roll down his cheeks.

"Am I?" Buckley says, holding his arms out wide, inviting a response. "I'm the only one that's being honest with you, Nicholas. You didn't seriously think the Russians picked you because they liked you, now did you? They despise you, son.

"Oh, the idea of a jury sounds good on paper. Don't let the elites hold power, right? Demand they convince the common folk. Pick people at random from each country in the UN Security Council. Only it's not at random. The Russians and the Chinese were never going to let that happen. For that matter, neither were we. What? Do you think we chose Chinese academics or communist party members? Hell, no. We picked the dumbest peasant fucks we could find.

"I've read your file, Nicholas. The Russians profiled the *shit* out of you. They monitored your house, your internet accounts, your work. Hell, they even bugged your goddamn bowling alley.

"When your girlfriend took out a domestic violence firearms notice, they calculated a 68% chance you would commit a felony within five days. When you started drinking and arguing with her, the probability jumped to 98%, and they closed in. They simply could not get to your house quick enough. They thought you were going to kill her.

"Don't you see? They needed you. They couldn't take a felon, but they could take anyone that walked right up to that line. And you. You dumbass! You let them. You gave them a goddamn puppet."

Jazz hangs her head. She's sobbing. Even Bear has tears in his eyes.

The colonel walks around Nick, saying, "What did she tell you? That you were doing your duty to your country? Shit, patriotism is a strike lure to a big old fat swamp bass like you. People like you see the Stars and Stripes and go all gooey inside. God, guts and guns, right? You've got it all wrong. You're being played for a fool. Patriotism isn't taking a swig of beer while the anthem is being sung at the Super Bowl. Patriotism is actually serving your country. You've got to get off your ass and do something for her.

"Don't you get it? They use that as bait because they think you're a sucker. They know patriotism will blind you to reality. Oh, good old Uncle Sam. Do it for Uncle Sam. And all the while, you're doing it for *them!*

"What do you think they say about you behind closed doors, Nicholas? They're treating you like a fool—like a fucking idiot!"

Colonel Buckley moves around beside him, resting his arm on Nick's shoulder, trying to be friendly.

"You can still be the hero, Nick. You can do this—for the right reasons—for all of us. You can do this for your country."

Buckley's right and yet he's not. Nick swallows the lump in his throat. He may be a fool, but he's determined not to be played. Not again. He's got to find some weakness in the colonel's argument. He looks at Buckley and asks, "Who's Anni?"

Oh, that strikes a nerve. The colonel doesn't like that question. He screws up his face in disgust. For the first time, Nick feels the balance of power shift. The colonel stiffens, stepping away from Nick, dropping all pretense.

"What gives you the right?" Buckley asks, pacing around him. "What makes you think you're better than me? Do you really think a washed-up mechanic from Shit Hole, South Carolina, is in a position to question the decisions of a decorated colonel in the United States Marine Corps?"

"Where is she?" Nick asks, ignoring him. "She's a juror, right? Why doesn't she agree with you? She's down there, isn't she? She's seen them. What does she know that we don't? Let me talk to her."

Nick might be a slow learner, but he does learn. Colonel Buckley has been peppering Nick with his distorted logic, denying Nick any breathing space. He hasn't given him the opportunity to consider anything in detail, pestering him to fold and give in. Nick is more than happy to return the favor.

"You want to kill us to save the planet," Nick says. "I get that. But you don't even know if it'll work."

Nick knows he's not the only one susceptible to reasoning. Like everyone at *Vincennes*, Colonel Buckley was caught in a trance. Like all of them, he's still in shock. He must feel blindsided, robbed of his dignity. Decades of experience compel him to fight back, but how can he justify his behavior? The military uses the threat of force far more readily than it uses force itself. He must know he's overstepped the mark. He's got to feel that through the fog of his mind.

Nick steps forward, saying, "I understand. Sacrifice is noble for a warrior, but we need to be sure. We don't even know if a nuke will dent the fender on this thing."

Buckley steps back. Nick sees an opening. It's subtle, but by moving toward the colonel instead of backing away, he gets the old man to hesitate.

Nick says, "If it thrives on energy, we could end up spreading radioactive contamination around the world. And for what? For nothing. If our nuke fails, we could provoke an all-out war."

"Don't," the colonel says, pointing his gun at Nick.

With his hands out in front of him, appealing for calm, Nick says, "We have to be sure. You want to be sure of a kill, right? The only thing worse than a wild tiger is one that's wounded. You don't want to wound this thing."

Colonel Buckley pulls back on the slide of the Glock, loading a round into the chamber. He stands beside Bear, pushing the barrel against his head.

"Do not fuck with me," Buckley growls. "I will kill him. Do you understand? You need to execute that command or I will pull this goddamn trigger."

"I don't want to die," Bear says. Tears stream down his cheeks. Snot drips from his nose.

Jazz is brutal. "Shut up."

Like Nick, she can see the weakness forming in the colonel's rationale. Nick holds his hands wide, inviting Buckley to shoot him instead.

"We're all dead anyway, right? A bullet in the head, or a nuclear explosion? Which is it going to be?"

Colonel Buckley backhands Nick with a closed fist, raking his knuckles across Nick's nose and cheeks. The sheer ferocity of his strike takes Nick by surprise, knocking him back. He staggers, falling into the computer console and onto the floor. A split second later, the barrel of the gun is pushed hard into his forehead.

"Give the command. Or I swear. I will pull this fucking trig—"

The door behind Sergeant Hillenbrand flies open, slamming into the wall. Although the operations center is shielded from the cold outside by a ready room, both doors are open. Snow billows within the command room. The temperature plunges below zero.

Dmitri stands there silhouetted by the spotlights lighting up the ice outside. Adrianna struggles to hold him. She crouches, with his left arm hoisted over her shoulder. She can barely keep him upright. Dmitri is holding a gun outstretched in his right hand. He's aiming at Buckley.

"Colonel," the burly Russian says. "You are relieved of command."

Buckley turns, caught mid-sentence. He begins to say, "Wh—" as a shot rings out. The sudden burst of noise within the room is deafening, causing Nick to grimace.

Eight grams of military-grade hardball ammunition accelerates to over a thousand feet per second. At that speed, it's traveling three times faster than the human nervous system. There's literally no time to react. The bullet catches Buckley on the back of his head, just behind his ear, splitting his skull open as it rips through the rear of his brain. The round clips the side of his skull like a baseball bat striking a watermelon. Fragments of shattered bone, blood, and grey matter spray across the computer monitors.

The colonel's lips move, but no sound comes out. For a second, he continues standing there with his eyes wide, unable to comprehend what has just happened. The shockwave rippling out from the bullet liquifies the remaining soft tissue in his brain, killing him before he can squeeze the trigger. His arms fall limp as he keels to one side. The gun clatters to the floor.

Adrianna loses her grip on Dmitri. The big Russian leans against the door jamb. He slides to the floor, saying, "Your services are—no longer required."

Sergeant Hillenbrand draws his sidearm.

Dmitri is in no position to defend himself. He slumps to his knees. The gun falls from his bloody fingers.

Jazz crash tackles Hillenbrand before he can fire. Although her arms are pinned behind her back, she has her head down. She charges, screaming as she collides with his waist. His gun goes flying from his hand, sliding across the floor.

"You bitch," Hillenbrand says, clambering back to his feet and pulling out a US Marine Corps fighting knife. Seven inches of hardened steel blade cut through the air in front of her.

Jazz faces him down, ready to fight, but without the use of her hands, the best she can hope for is a lucky kick. She dances, dodging the knife. Adrianna tries desperately to drag Dmitri back to his feet. Snow whips around inside the room.

Out of nowhere, three shots ring out in rapid succession.

The report from each shot is deafening. Bullets strike Hillenbrand in the upper thigh, waist, and lower ribs. They tear through his body like tissue paper. Hillenbrand grabs at the blood seeping from his clothing. He turns as another three shots thunder through the building, hitting him in the chest and shoulder. One last shot tears through his bicep, causing him to spin around. The knife falls from his grasp, and he collapses, slumping to the floor.

Hillenbrand lies crumpled on the linoleum, surrounded by a pool of blood.

"Easy," Adrianna says in the deafening silence. She kneels beside Nick. "It's okay. It's over. It's all over now. You can give me the gun."

It's only then Nick looks down at the Glock in his trembling hand. His finger is still on the trigger, poised to fire again. He can feel the grooves against his skin. Tension builds on the spring within the firing mechanism. His palms are sweaty.

"Just," Adrianna says, slowly peeling his fingers from the pistol grip. "Breathe. Nice deep breaths."

Suddenly, Nick can't get rid of that accursed thing fast enough. His fingers spasm, releasing the Glock, and he shuffles backward away from it.

Adrianna rests the gun on the floor. Nick looks down at his trembling hands. He's killed someone. His eyes focus on the fallen figure lying before him.

Blood soaks through the soldier's clothing. Hillenbrand was alive and now he's dead. He deserved it, Nick tells himself, but that doesn't seem to provide any solace. Taking a life is easy—too goddamn easy. He's always known that. Only now, he knows it's terrifying. A tiny metal slug reveals how utterly frail the human body is. Nothing that is done can be undone. Although it was Hillenbrand at the end of the barrel, what scares Nick is that it was once Sandra.

Blood sticks to his fingers. He wipes his hands against his trousers, trying to compose himself, but nothing he does can clean away the mess. No matter how hard he tries, it's always there. At best, he smears red blood over his palms. Nick is manic. He runs each of his fingers against his shirt, wanting to be clean but knowing he never will be. The best he can manage is to distract himself. He runs his hands up through his knotted hair. More blood sticks to them.

Adrianna cuts Jazz and Bear free with the knife.

Dmitri leans against the wall, sucking in air. He breathes in short bursts.

"Nick."

Nick pulls himself across the floor toward Dmitri. He could get to his feet, but his legs feel like jelly.

"Buckley said—"

"I know. I know," Dmitri says, gasping for breath. "One road. Two directions. Right?"

Nick nods. Although he's in shock, he's vaguely aware he needs to do something to help stop the bleeding. He reaches out, pushing his hand against Dmitri's jacket, trying to prevent blood from seeping out. Warm, deep red goo oozes between his fingers. This time, he shuts out the sensation, ignoring it.

"Get his jacket off," Jazz says, rushing over. She yells at Bear. "I need a major trauma kit. Now!"

"On it."

Whereas Nick is trying to be gentle with a dying man, Jazz is brutish. She shoves Nick aside. With a burst of raw energy, she rips the jacket off Dmitri's shoulders, peeling it from his arms. Dmitri slumps forward.

"Get his shirt off."

Nick starts unbuttoning Dmitri's shirt. Jazz throws the jacket behind her.

"Damn it," she says through gritted teeth. She crouches, grabbing Dmitri's shirt and wrenching it open. Buttons scatter over the bloodstained linoleum. "We've got to stop the bleeding."

For Nick, this might as well be a dream—a nightmare. He's in a daze. Jazz shoves a scrunched-up rag into his hands. She looks him in the eye and reiterates her last point. "Stop the bleeding."

Nick looks down at the torn material in his bloody hands.

"Get him on his side," she says, getting to her feet. "One hand on his chest, the other pushing the rag against the exit wound."

Jazz rocks Dmitri over, laying him on the floor. She makes sure Dmitri has one arm out in front of him and the other twisted behind his back.

"Exit?" Nick mumbles, kneeling behind Dmitri with the bunched-up rag.

He does as he's told, leaning over and sandwiching Dmitri's chest between his hands. Jazz was right. The small hole in Dmitri's chest lines up with a gaping wound on his back. Nick pushes the rag hard against Dmitri's shattered shoulder blade to reduce the bleeding.

"Where's that goddamn trauma pack?" Jazz yells, scrambling for one of the internal doors. She slips on the bloody floor, but doesn't fall. She looks back before disappearing into the next room. "Keep him talking."

Adrianna helps, kneeling beside Dmitri's head. She pushes the rag into the edge of the messy exit wound.

"Hang in there, buddy," Nick says.

"Don't look back," Dmitri says between labored breaths. "Look where you're going, Nick. Not where you came from."

"I will."

Dmitri grabs Nick's wrist, squeezing as he says, "I—I believe in you, Nicholas James Ferrin."

Dmitri's strength fades. His eyes close. His head slumps against the floor as his body goes limp. The surge of blood coming from his wounds drops to a trickle.

Nick cries.

His lower lip trembles as he speaks.

"Thank you, my friend."

Jazz comes running back into the room. She slides across the floor on her knees, pushing a heavy first aid kit in front of her. Adrianna is bawling. Jazz grabs a large gauze pad and tears it open. Nick hangs his head, and Jazz knows. She must know. Even so, she can't stop until all hope is gone. Jazz pushes the thick pad against Dmitri's chest wound, but the way the blood oozes rather than runs tells her he's dead.

JAZZ

Bodybags are carried out of the operations center and placed on bench seats in the ready room. A tractor pulls up outside, pushing a snowplow. Dozens of bodybags have already been stacked on a flatbed trailer hitched to the back of the Day-Glo orange chassis. Collecting the dead has become a job. Nick tries to count the bags, but they're not neatly stacked. The driving snow makes it difficult to see through the window. Heavy-duty, black plastic bodybags lie limp on a frozen aluminum tray. At a guess, the other bodies are base staff recovered outside, like that poor bastard Lee Lao Chan.

How many people have died?

How many more will die before this is over?

Nick is regretting not taking up the offer of solitary confinement in a US prison. Three meager meals a day, a jumpsuit, and a metal bench for a bed would be St. Regis Hotel in New York by comparison.

Nick feels a dull ache in his chest. It hurts to think of Dmitri being stacked alongside Buckley and Hillenbrand. For all that separated them in life, they're companions in death. Nick's scalp still aches, but the pain reminds him he's alive. Death humbles all. Life should hold more meaning, and yet there lies Dmitri—his body hidden by a black bag.

"Hey," Bear says, seeing Nick staring through the window

as the bodies are loaded onto the flatbed. "How are you holding up?"

As much as Nick appreciates Bear's concern, distracting him from the reality of death is poor comfort. Life itself is the great distraction. Nick's never thought about his own death before. Somehow, there's always been an underlying assumption that he'll continue on. He won't. Intellectually, he knows that, but it's easier to bury that aspect of reality than face it. Seeing the snow and ice resting on those black bodybags is confronting and leaves him feeling uneasy. As the bags are stacked, he loses track of which bodies are hidden within the rugged plastic. Once, they were distinct people. Not any more. Now they're just name tags. He turns away from the window. He has to.

Someone has wiped down the computer consoles and mopped the floor. Most of the blood is gone, but it's impossible to clean everything thoroughly. Thin red lines have seeped into the cracks, staining the plastic. Humanity is good at whitewashing shit. Nick wonders about the alien beneath the ice. Does it understand what it has unleashed? How does it reconcile life with death? Or does it too live in the delusion of the moment?

"We're going to be okay," Bear says.

One lie deserves another. Nick responds with a forced smile. He sits with his back to the window. It's all kinds of symbolism wrapped into a single act. Nick's got to move on. He doesn't want to, but there's nothing he can do to change the way the past has unfolded into now. He wonders if there's a body bag waiting for him in the near future.

"You okay?" Jazz asks, sitting next to him. She hands him a disposable cup of coffee. Bear leaves. Nick's not dumb. They're taking turns babysitting.

"Yeah, I'm fine."

"Liar."

That gets a genuine smile.

"He was a good man," Jazz says.

Nick sips at his coffee as a way of avoiding conversation.

"Listen," she says. "This is going to hit you hard, but that's okay. It's all right to feel anger, grief, regret. If anything, it's bad if you don't. At the moment, you're in shock. Everything's a blur, right?"

Nick nods.

Jazz is yet to drink from her cup. She warms her hands around it, saying, "It's important to understand everyone goes through what you're feeling right now. You're going to question what you did and didn't do. It's okay to feel numb one moment and pissed off the next. Feeling like shit is a way of mourning the loss."

Nick would rather not have this conversation. Jazz, though, is decompressing. She speaks from her heart.

"For thousands of years, we saw people die all the time. Children, parents, friends, grandparents. Whether it was through disease, old age, or by accident, everyone saw someone die. Most kids were born on the kitchen floor and died a few years later in their own beds. These days, life and death are hidden behind a hospital curtain.

"Death is never clean. People shun death because it's unpleasant. It makes us feel uneasy, but that's precisely why we shouldn't turn away. If we want to celebrate life, we have to accept death."

Nick watches the vapor rising from his coffee.

"Yep," he mumbles, feeling he needs to respond in some way.

Jazz isn't lecturing him. If anything, she's talking to herself. Speaking aloud is her way of dealing with Dmitri's death. Nick's a priest in a confessional booth. This is her shortcut to acceptance.

She stares at the floor. "We surround death with lies. We hide death in a nice, polished wooden casket. We send bouquets of pretty flowers. We talk about the dead looking down on us from heaven. Rarely do we face death for what it is—the quiet night that awaits us all."

Jazz isn't saying this merely for his benefit. This is her way of honoring Dmitri's life. If she were in a bar, she'd be raising a glass of whiskey.

Nick says, "He admired you, you know. I mean, I know he was Russian and always looking for an angle and all that stuff, but I think he genuinely admired you."

"Huh?" she says, sounding surprised.

"He said you were a hero."

"Well, I'm not."

"He told me you saved a lot of people in the Himalayas."

"Oh that," she says, laughing. "You know that's a joke, right?"

"A joke?"

"Yeah, my squad has played loose and hard with that over way too many beers. Yarns like that have a way of growing each time they're told."

Nick's confused. "Bear told me you snuck behind enemy lines?"

"I got lost."

She pauses, weighing her words. Nick can sense how deeply personal this is for her.

"It was dumb. I made a mistake. When you're up high in the mountains, it's easy for the cloud cover to descend, and all of a sudden, you're wading through fog."

"But," Nick says, "the Chinese captain or commander or whoever he was?"

Jazz grins. "He was taking a shit behind a boulder. I came sliding down the slope with my M4, and there he is, crouching over a turd with his pants down around his ankles."

Nick chuckles as Jazz continues.

"Oh, it was a steaming pile of shit, all right. He sees me and freezes. He's down on his haunches looking up at me with eyes as wide as saucers."

"What did you do?"

"I pointed my M4 at him and signaled with a gloved finger raised to my lips—*Be quiet or die.* And another squirt hit the rocks behind him." Jazz laughs. "I stood there stunned for a few seconds. And then I did the only thing I could."

"What?"

"I reached into my pocket and pulled out a packet of biodegradable disposable wipes."

"You handed him toilet paper?" Nick asks in disbelief.

Jazz has tears of laughter in her eyes as she continues. "What else was I going to do?"

"And what did he do?"

"He took them. He pulled out a wipe and cleaned his ass."

"All while you're training your gun on him?"

"Oh, by that time, I'd slipped a 37mm round into the M204 grenade launcher mounted beneath my M4."

Nick is laughing so hard he can barely speak. "I have no idea what that means, but I bet he shit himself. Again."

"He did," Jazz says, slapping him on the shoulder as she laughs.

"Then what happened?"

"I backed away, keeping my gun on him. Slowly, I disappeared into the mist. I retraced my steps and hightailed it the fuck out of there."

"Did they chase you?" Nick asks.

"I heard a lot of yelling in the fog, but it was in Chinese. I have no idea what was being said. I was expecting a firefight to erupt around me. I figured this was it. This was how I was going to die, but they pulled back."

"Oh," Nick says. "This is even better than the version Bear told me!"

"When I finally found my troop, they laughed their asses off. Apparently, the guy was a colonel. I saw he had gold shoulder boards, but I had no idea about his rank. Later that night, the Chinese lit up the hillside with mortar rounds and semi-automatic fire. They were zoned into a position neither we nor the Indians had ever held. I think they were saving face. They needed a tale of heroic battle to tell their command group. The unspoken agreement was we'd go our separate ways and never talk of this again."

Nick shakes his head, unable to wipe the grin from his face.

"And the best thing," Jazz says, "is that I was awarded the Silver Star for gallantry in action—for leading my troop safely out of an engagement that never actually took place. And for watching the enemy shit themselves!"

Nick slaps his legs, laughing as he says, "Oh, that is brilliant!"

"I know, right? All I did was get lost and then retreat from an enemy latrine!"

"Dmitri said we were lucky to have you on our side."

"He would," Jazz says, smiling.

Bear comes back over. Jazz gets to her feet. The two of them talk at length about logistics, losing themselves in details Nick doesn't understand. All he hears is a word-salad of military terms. He sips his coffee, reflecting on his conversation with Jazz. This is what death needs—the laughter and joy of life. Nick can imagine Dmitri joining in the banter. Perhaps that's the best way to remember him.

Jazz sits back down as Bear leaves. Her coffee is cold. She knocks it back regardless.

"What about you?" she asks. "How are you doing?"

"Me? I'm fine."

"You pulled that trigger. That ain't easy."

Nick rubs the back of his hand. "I haven't really thought about it."

"You should," she says. "In the military, we have after-action reports. It's important to get people talking about what just happened. Without that, you don't get closure."

"Ah-huh."

"It's crazy, isn't it?" Jazz says, looking down at her own bloodstained hands. "Squeeze your finger, and *Bam!* There's an explosion of violence. It's a contradiction, yah know. So little effort. So much damage."

Nick nods, staring at his boots.

Jazz says, "Nothing ever really prepares you for that moment. No amount of time on the range. You can pop paper targets all day long. Damn, it is different when there's a living, breathing human at the other end of the barrel."

"Yeah," is all Nick can say. Thinking about what he did is difficult. He'd rather bury that moment in the dark recesses of his mind. He doesn't think of it as shooting Hillenbrand, rather protecting everyone else.

"You did the right thing."

Reluctantly, he says, "I know."

Jazz says, "They like to tell us video games and movies have desensitized us. I guess they have. I dunno. I think they've lessened the act, but not what comes after. It's one thing to pull the trigger. It's another to see a life slip away. It's yet another to live on with that memory. It changes you."

He picks at his nails.

"I'm glad you didn't do that to her," Jazz says.

Nick turns in a start, looking at Jazz in alarm, unsure what she means. Deep down, he knows. He doesn't want to, but he does.

"Dmitri was worried you would," she says. "That's why we rushed from the airport with a police escort and sirens blazing. Your profile said, if pushed, you'd lash out. I'm glad you proved him wrong. I'm glad I was wrong. You're all right, Nick."

"What do you mean?"

Jazz looks sideways at him. "Your girlfriend. You pulled back from the brink. Not many people do."

"No, no," Nick says, shaking his head. He points at himself. "She fooled me. The chamber was empty."

"What are you talking about?" Jazz asks, squinting as she looks at him.

"Sandra emptied the magazine. She took the bullets out."

"We're talking about the Glock, right?" she asks. "The one you threw on the lawn?"

Nick nods.

Jazz says, "I watched the officers secure the scene. They bagged the magazine. There were at least seven or eight rounds in it. I mean, I didn't count them, but I could see it wasn't a full mag."

"What?" Nick says.

"The lead cop was wearing blue disposable gloves. He picked up the Glock and ejected a round from the chamber, being careful where he placed his hands. Dropped it into his palm. I guess he didn't want to smudge any fingerprints."

"I—ah." Nick tries to speak, but words refuse to pass his lips.

Jazz says, "It was a jacketed, hollow-point round. Nasty bitch."

Nick nods in agreement. His dad prefers bullets with a full metal jacket. In the misplaced bravado of his mind, Nick chose hollow point rounds for his Glock. More stopping power is a euphemism for more heartache and death, but that never mattered to him before now. Jazz talks through the details she observed as though she were recounting a football game. For Nick, her candor is confronting.

"He put the loose round in the same bag as the mag. The Glock went in a separate evidence bag. Zip-locked. You know, the kind you use for lunch."

Nick blinks rapidly, trying to recall what happened that afternoon. He ejected the magazine. He saw it was empty. Sandra had tricked him. He was so angry, but there was nothing he could do. At that moment, he was helpless. As much as he's ashamed to admit it, he wanted to kill her, but he couldn't. Was he lying to himself? Deep down, did some part of him want a way out? In that moment, did he cling to the only thing he could to save his ego?

"You really thought it was empty?" Jazz asks.

Nick's silent.

The magazine was empty. He's sure of it. But the weight. He remembers the weight of the magazine as a sensation. It was heavy at one end, almost falling from his palm. His Glock holds 17 rounds in a standard magazine. If it only had eight, the magazine would feel top-heavy.

"I—I guess I saw what I wanted to see."

Jazz is quiet.

"Lies, huh? The lies we tell ourselves."

The silence between them doesn't feel awkward.

"I was a big man, you know. Big ego. King of the castle and all that crap." He sighs. "She pissed me off. I wanted to hurt her. I wanted to but—"

"—but you couldn't."

"No," Nick says, looking away from Jazz. "Crazy, huh? I couldn't even be honest with myself."

"Hey," Jazz says, tapping his knee and getting his attention.

215

She pulls her lips tight, thinking carefully about what she's going to say. Nick beats her to it.

"A lot of people die because someone can't swallow their stupid, dumbass ego."

"They do," she replies in barely a whisper.

"Do you know what it all comes down to?" he asks. "Spite. I was acting like a spoiled child. I was so petty. In that moment, I wasn't thinking." He shrugs, adding, "I didn't care. The only thing that mattered was me."

Jazz starts to speak when Bear comes jogging back into the control room, interrupting them.

"We've found her."

"Who?" Jazz asks.

"Anni Aziz. She's barricaded herself in the L4 conference room beneath the ice. She said they're all down there."

"The jury?" Jazz asks. "They're alive?"

"Most of them," Bear says. "But they're catatonic, like the guys were up here."

Jazz gets to her feet but not without slapping Nick's leg. "Time to move on, soldier."

SCREWDRIVER

Jazz sits in the conference room just off the operations center. Adrianna, Bear, and Nick sit opposite her with Mikhail, the Head of Operations.

With straggly hair and a full beard, Mikhail could be a mad scientist. His demeanor, though, is nothing but professional. Nick has no doubt his stare could melt ice. He talks in hushed tones with Jazz before the meeting begins. A few notes scratched onto a page in a hurried scrawl reveal his temperament.

A couple of maintenance engineers work on a circulation baffle in a ceiling duct. Their name tags identify them as Phelps and Harris.

"Won't be long. Sorry for the interruption."

"No problem," Mikhail replies.

Harris climbs a stepladder and leans inside the duct. Nick overhears him talking to Phelps, saying, "Hey, that's crazy!"

"How do we stop this from happening again?" Mikhail asks the team, ignoring the maintenance crew.

Jazz points at a schematic diagram of the sub-surface base. "It's a good question. If we go down there and attempt a rescue, we could trigger whatever took everyone out up here."

Nick's distracted. It's the constant demand on his mind. He wants to zone out. He needs to. There's only so much his brain can handle. A mindless comedy on Netflix would be welcome right about now. He stares past Jazz, watching the maintenance crew. The ladder shakes as equipment is passed back and forth.

Mikhail says. "Okay. So, we have a core drill rig roughly half a mile south of here. It's little more than a hut on the ice. We use it to compare ice samples at depth, looking for any contamination—whether that's from us or them."

"And?" Jazz asks.

Mikhail smiles. "And the crew there weren't affected by the blackout. Whatever we got hit with, it was local."

"Nice."

"I've sent four snowcats out there with emergency supplies. We have in line-of-sight radio comms with them. I've got the team checking in every fifteen minutes. If we drop off, they'll send the cats back one by one to pick up the pieces."

"Okay," Jazz says. "So we have a contingency."

Harris backs down the aluminum stepladder, working his way out of the duct. He holds out his screwdriver, showing it to Phelps. Ah, for a bit of workshop banter. Being an electro-mechanic, Nick could lose himself in a powertrain refurb right about now. They're generally only done on older vehicles and take up to six hours. For him, there's something soothing about tracing wires and replacing parts. It's the focus. Nothing else exists anywhere in the world at that point in time. Nick is tempted to ask Harris if he needs any help. Watching the two men is therapeutic. They joke about the screwdriver.

"Can you tell me what happened?" Jazz asks.

"During the blackout?" Adrianna replies.

"Yes, what was it like. What were you aware of?"

There's a loose screw hanging from the screwdriver. That's what Harris was talking about in the vent. He shows it to his partner. Ordinarily, a loose screw would fall from the tip, but this one wobbles around like a drop of water clinging to a straw. It refuses to fall. Nick hears Harris ask, "Did you magnetize this?" To which Phelps replies, "No, not me."

"Uh, have you ever been hypnotized?" Adrianna asks Jazz.

"No."

"It's strange, but I was aware of everything that was happening. I just didn't care. The snow outside might as well have been sand at the beach."

"You didn't feel the cold?" Bear asks.

"No, it was like being at the fairground as a kid, walking around in a daze, looking up at all the lights. I mean, I knew it was wrong, but it didn't *feel* wrong. It was like watching a movie. I heard the gunshots and wandered outside expecting, I don't know? Fireworks?"

Nick is half-listening to the discussion, half-watching the maintenance crew. Phelps grabs a handful of screws from his toolbox. One by one, he hangs them from the screwdriver, much to Harris' delight. Two, three, four, and then five screws hang from the tip, forming a delicate chain. Screws dangle from the shaft of the screwdriver. They wobble, threatening to fall. The maintenance crew are like kids with a toy.

"Do you know what caused the blackout?" Jazz asks Adrianna.

"Magnets," Nick says, interrupting them.

Jazz looks at him in surprise. He points at the seemingly invisible maintenance crew behind her. Bear and Adrianna are confused.

Nick gets to his feet, saying, "We do this from time to time in my workshop back in South Carolina. If we need to get a loose screw out of a narrow gap, we'll magnetize a screwdriver."

Jazz and Adrianna are puzzled. Being a mechanic, Bear nods.

"May I?" Nick asks Harris, reaching for the screwdriver.

"Sure."

Nick carries the screwdriver back to the table with five screws dangling in a line from the tip. They're seemingly joined together by magic.

"What would it take to magnetize a screwdriver left lying in a toolbox?"

Mikhail says, "Ah, I'd have to check with one of the engineers, but the toolbox itself should have negated any such effect. The box should have acted as a faraday cage."

"Should have?" Jazz asks.

"Magnets are formed by a specific alignment of the electromagnetic field. For that to happen, it would need to pulse or surge in just the right way. Most iron isn't magnetic because the charges are chaotic. They cancel each other out."

"And this?" Nick asks, pointing at the screwdriver.

Mikhail asks the maintenance crew, "You didn't do this?"

"No."

"Have you seen anything else like this?"

"We've got burned-out motors all over the workshop. Does that count?"

Jazz says, "Could this be related to the blackout?"

"Maybe," Adrianna says. "Magnets don't normally affect people, but there have been experiments where they change the way the brain works."

"What kind of experiments?" Bear asks, intrigued.

"Magnets have been used to treat depression. Magnetic fields can induce nausea. They can leave people feeling confused and disoriented."

Jazz and Bear look at each other.

Adrianna says, "There have even been cases where they shut down one part of the brain but not another."

Nick asks, "What part of the brain?"

"If I remember correctly, there was one study where they

used a magnet to shut down speech. The person could sing lines from a song, but they couldn't say them until the magnet was switched off."

"What? Why?" Bear asks.

"We think of our brains as a single organ," Adrianna says, "but the brain is insanely complex. It's a conglomeration of different parts. Shut down one section, and another works perfectly fine."

"Well, I'll be damned," Jazz says.

"If we go down there," Bear says. "We have to be careful. Next time, we might not be so lucky. Next time, they might up the power. They could fry our brain cells."

Harris and Phelps go pale. Nick snaps them out of it, saying, "Thanks, guys. That was helpful, really helpful." He hands the screwdriver back to Harris. The two men pack up their equipment and leave.

Adrianna says, "I don't think we'll see the same response from them again."

"Why?" Mikhail asks, looking sideways at her.

"Maslow's hierarchy of needs."

"You're gonna have to explain that one," Bear says.

"We need to put ourselves in their shoes," Adrianna says. "We've got to think like them."

Jazz says, "They're not predictable."

"Everyone's predictable," Adrianna replies. "We've got to recognize we're dealing with an intelligent species down there, and it's going to have needs. It's going to have priorities."

"Go on," Mikhail says.

"Think about us. Our most basic needs are air, water, and food—in that order. Only after these are met do you get to things like having a home, or a job. And after that things like friends and family."

"Down here," Jazz says, "it's air, *warmth*, water, and only then food. I'd say shelter is more important than water."

"You see?" Adrianna says. "That's precisely my point. We have a hierarchy of needs. And it's variable. It depends on circumstance. What good is gold bullion if you're freezing to death?"

"And you think this explains their reaction?" Mikhail asks.

"It has to. Everyone is motivated by something. Understand their hierarchy of needs, and you'll understand their next move."

"I like that," Mikhail says. "And the blackout?"

"Self-defense," Adrianna says. "Notice there's been no follow up. No additional attacks. We are not under siege. This was a one-time event."

"They feel safe," Jazz says.

"For now."

"What do they want?" Mikhail asks.

"Put yourself in their shoes," Adrianna replies. "You're trapped under a mile of ice. What do you want?"

"To get out."

Adrianna nods.

Bear says, "Oh, that's bad."

"No shit," Jazz says.

Mikhail scrawls something on his notepad, not saying what he's thinking, but he seems to agree with the sentiment bouncing around the table. From where Nick is, he can see Mikhail's making a list of things to follow up on.

"How do they see us?" Jazz asks.

"Good question," Adrianna replies, raising her index finger as she pauses, thinking about her reply. "I suspect they're still trying to figure us out. Whoever or whatever is down there, they've been dormant for a helluva long time. Suddenly, we're knocking on the door. They wake to see a bunch of strange creatures tunneling through the ice toward them."

"So are we the good guys or the bad guys?" Jazz asks.

"That's what they want to know," Adrianna says. "Whatever happened down there, we got too close. We made them nervous as hell and they said, *Back off!*"

Jazz takes a deep breath. Her chest rises. She puffs up her cheeks and exhales slowly, saying, "This is not good."

"Okay," Bear says. "We shut everything down. We wait out the winter and hand this shit-storm over to the UN in summer."

"You think *they're* gonna wait that long?" Mikhail asks.

Jazz taps the table. "And in the meantime every one of our people down there dies."

Bear says, "We can't let these things escape."

"We may not have a choice," Adrianna says. "I mean, we're in control—for now. How long is that going to last?"

Jazz says, "I'm not leaving our people down there to die."

"You're going beneath the ice?" Mikhail asks.

"We go in quiet," Jazz says. "We leave that thing alone. We get our people. We get out."

Bear buries his head in his hands. He does not like this.

Adrianna says, "Then I'm coming too."

"No way, doc. This is now a military op."

"With an army of two?" Adrianna says. "You need an edge down there. Bombs and bullets ain't gonna cut it. You need someone with a scientific understanding of what's unfolding."

Jazz doesn't look impressed.

Nick says, "I'm coming too."

"Oh, hell no," Jazz replies. "You're on the jury. You're too valuable."

Nick laughs. He cocks his head sideways, raising an eyebrow as he says, "Me? Seriously? Come on. What am I going to do up here? Play Candy Crush?"

"We need a pack mule," Bear says.

Jazz is adamant. "It's too dangerous."

"A diverse team gives us the best odds for survival."

"Shut up, Bear."

"With a couple of Sherpas, we can travel light," he replies, ignoring her.

Jazz asks, "Have either of you ever gone abseiling or rappelled down a cliff?"

Adrianna raises her hand to shoulder height. Nick nods. Neither of them reply.

"For fuck's sake." Jazz is frustrated. The ire in her voice and the anger on her face suggests they have no idea what they're dealing with. She sighs, shaking her head in disbelief.

Nick says, "I'll carry your equipment—your ammo."

Jazz replies, saying, "You know you could die down there, right?"

"I could die up here."

Mikhail says. "Four is better than two."

"I cannot believe I'm agreeing to this," Jazz says. She brings up a computer interface.

"Father, what are the human losses?"

"*Twenty military staff. Thirty-two scientists. Five technicians. Two jurors.*"

"And survivors?"

"*Two military staff. Forty-one scientists. Twelve technicians. Nine jurors, seven of whom are trapped in the L4 conference room. At this point, there are only three functional jurors.*"

"Father, I need whatever imagery you can give me from the last 48 hours."

A series of thumbnail images are projected onto the screen at the far end of the room. There are several pages of photos containing fisheye-views of corridors, stairs, elevators, labs, and doors. They're sorted by timestamp.

Adrianna says, "Stop," as Jazz flicks between screens. "There!" She points. "The timestamp puts that about fifteen minutes before the blackout. That's someone from the sample retrieval team heading toward the airlock."

"Airlock?" Nick says, seeing nothing more than a boot disappearing behind a doorframe at the end of the corridor.

"Yes. There's a cavern surrounding the craft. It's partially submerged in a subterranean lake. We've taken samples from the water. All pretty standard stuff. Microbes with distinct genetic profiles. They've been trapped down here for millions of years, from long before the craft crashed. Their genes have diverged from those topside, but they're still clearly related."

"Is there anything else down there?" Jazz asks, rolling the computer mouse across the table to Adrianna, giving her control.

"Tube worms. Shrimp. Plankton. Squid. Several species of nudibranch."

"Nudes?" Bear asks, surprised.

"Not like that," Adrianna says, bringing up another set of images. "They're mollusks without a shell. Soft-bodied creatures like this."

On the screen, snake-like animals undulate through the water.

"Are those aliens?" Bear asks.

Adrianna laughs. "No."

"They look like aliens to me," Nick says, noting their squiggly curves and unusual antennae.

"We've sequenced their genes. They're terrestrial."

"Even that one?" Nick asks, pointing at a nudibranch that looks like an undersea porcupine made from Jell-O.

"Not alien," Adrianna says. "Those tips contain toxins, but they won't kill you. And he's tiny, barely the size of your pinky."

"What does it look like?" Jazz asks, changing the topic. By *it*, she means the alien spacecraft.

"You haven't seen it?" Adrianna asks, surprised.

Jazz shakes her head.

"You'd better show them," Mikhail says.

Adrianna brings up another folder and enlarges a photo. Temporary lights have been set up on tripods within an ice cave. Thick, heavily insulated cables lead back toward a generator. Spotlights reflect off the thin, silver edge of a spacecraft half-buried in blue ice, half-submerged in a subsurface lake. Dark water laps at a narrow, rocky ledge extending around the cavern.

Jazz, Bear, and Nick get to their feet and walk to the screen. Each of them says a single word, expressing their shared sentiment.

"Oh"

"My"

"God."

Adrianna brings up another set of images showing close-up pictures of the thin strip of the spacecraft reaching from the ice to the water. The interstellar vessel has settled on an angle of roughly thirty degrees.

"They told us it was crushed beyond recognition," Jazz says.

"It was."

"What do you mean—was?" Nick asks, turning to her in alarm.

"They're fixing it."

"They?" Bear says.

Adrianna nods.

"Since when?" he asks.

"Since we broke through into the chamber."

Bear states the obvious. "So we woke them?"

"Yep," Adrianna replies. "I figured you'd want to know what you're dealing with."

"Damn straight," Jazz says.

"Is anyone in there?" Nick asks, tapping the screen. "I mean, how could anyone be alive down there after all this time?"

"That's what we were trying to figure out," Adrianna says. "The working assumption is the crew are dead but there's some kind of artificial intelligence running the show."

"Assumption?" Bear asks. "I didn't think science worked on assumptions."

"It doesn't. This is new territory for us. We have to test our ideas."

Jazz says, "And testing your ideas caused the blackout?"

Adrianna screws up her face, pulling her lips tight. She nods but can't bring herself to say yes.

Bear says, "Well, they're working fast. That thing looks like it crashed yesterday, not hundreds of thousands of years ago."

Jazz says, "It doesn't look like it crashed at all."

"It looks like the ice formed around it," Nick says, astonished by what he's seeing.

Adrianna brings up another photo. "There are spare parts lying on the ground."

"Looks like junk," Nick says, pointing at the scraps. Curved panels and metal rods litter the ice near the craft.

"Best we understand it, they're using nanotech to repair their spacecraft in place."

"But?" Jazz asks.

"But it's stuck fast. There's too much ice on top of it."

She brings up an image of a woman standing beside the craft in an orange hazmat suit.

"That's me."

Nick takes a second look. Adrianna's standing beneath the rim of the spacecraft, next to a chunk of fallen ice. Her suit is inflated, making her arms and legs look rotund. Her nose and mouth are hidden behind a black gas mask, even though the suit includes a plastic visor covering her head.

"You've been down there?" Jazz says, turning toward her in astonishment.

"Oh, yeah. Several times."

"You are *definitely* coming with us."

Adrianna switches back to the original screen of thumbnails. "The airlock is at the end of that corridor. It's the boot that gives it away. We only wore those thick black boots when we were in hazmat suits. That's how I know they must have been going into the chamber."

"So the research team was in the cavern when all this went down?" Jazz says.

"Yes."

"Do we have any video?"

"Not from the blackout. These are the only images Father could recover."

"How did Father survive?" Nick asks. He's expecting Adrianna to answer when a voice sounds from the speakers in the ceiling.

"*I'm designed to survive a nuclear blast. My periphery devices were disabled, but not my core functions.*"

"Father," Jazz says. "What is the state of the containment lab?"

"*Containment has been breached. All levels are affected by water damage. The elevator is stuck on level three. Level four is entirely submerged.*"

"Can you start the pumps?"

"*Negative. Executive functions have not been restored*

within the lower bases."

"This is L4 from earlier today," Adrianna says, bringing up recent imagery. "This is where the airlock is located."

A body floats face down in a submerged corridor. Ice grows from the walls, choking the walkway. Lights glow from behind the glass in a door.

Adrianna raises her hand to her mouth. She wasn't ready for what she sees.

"This is not good," Jazz says.

"No shit," Bear says.

"And this is where the jurors are?" Jazz asks.

"And they're still alive?" Nick asks.

Mikhail says, "Ah, all the rooms are hermetically sealed. They weren't designed to be watertight, but they have independent vents. The idea was to contain any contaminants in case of a breach."

"Father," Jazz says. "Can we manually restart the pumps?"

An electronic voice replies. "*Unknown.*"

"Well, that's great," Bear says. "That's just fucking great."

Jazz says, "So we won't know if we can start those things until we get down there."

Bear says, "We're going to need tools, spare parts, hazmat suits, wetsuits, and oxygen cylinders, not to mention a fuck-ton of ammo."

"Well," Jazz says, looking at Nick. "It's a good job we've got ourselves a mule. All right, we're going to take a six-hour rest period. I recommend you bunk down here. There's no sense going back outside." She gets to her feet and dims the lights, saying, "Get some sleep. It's going to be a long day."

Day?

Nick rubs the grit from his eyes. He's insanely tired. It's already been a long day. In the back of his mind, he's vaguely aware Adrianna told him the time when she gave him the toiletries kit in the lecture hall, but that seems like a lifetime ago.

"What time is it?" he asks.

"Eleven in the morning."

"Damn."

Adrianna doesn't have to be told twice. She scrunches up her coat and uses it as a pillow, lying beneath the now darkened screen. Nick finds a spot near a floor vent and curls up. The carpet is thin but surprisingly comfortable. Within seconds, he's asleep.

ON BELAY

Spotlights illuminate the darkness. Snow and ice tear across the plateau, coming in sideways in the gale-force winds.

Even with his hood pulled almost to the point it's closed, it's hard for Nick to breathe in the intense cold. His cheeks feel as though they're frozen. His lungs are on fire. Six hours of sleep felt like six minutes. Staggering back out into a brutal antarctic winter is cruel. The tempest rattles his body, slamming into his jacket and threatening to topple him. Ice crunches beneath his boots. Everything beyond the fur lining of his hood is a blur.

Jazz leads the way to the maintenance building. She's doubled over, reducing her profile to the storm. The pack on her back sways with wind gusts.

Nick keeps his gloved hands on the guide wire, pushing his safety carabiner ahead of him. Snow races past low to the ground, hiding his boots from sight. Each step saps his strength. He's carrying four oxygen cylinders strapped to his pack. The weight is unbearable, and yet somehow, he staggers on. Occasionally, he stops, resting his arms on his knees to relieve a little of the weight for a moment. Within seconds, Bear is tapping his hip, yelling over the storm, wanting him to move on.

Fifty yards feels like fifty miles. The lights visible through the gloom never get any closer. Nick struggles, fighting against the tempest.

A gloved hand appears in front of the narrow opening in his hood. Nick looks up. Jazz is standing before him. Her eyes are hidden behind goggles. Wind buffets the fur surrounding her face. Her cheeks are rosy red. She's standing beside an open door. Light spills out from within the maintenance building.

Nick takes her hand. She says something, but he can't hear her over the roar of the storm.

He straightens, stepping out of the wind. Fluorescent lights flicker overhead. Nick staggers into the ready room and collapses on a wooden bench. The pack slips from his back. Metal oxygen cylinders clink together. He's past caring. Although the external door is open and the temperature is well below zero, he feels warm by comparison. Vapor rises like steam from his breath.

Bear stabs his feet at the steel grate in the entranceway, clearing ice from his boots. Snow swirls around him. For whatever reason, he wasn't wearing goggles. Ice has formed on his eyebrows. He grins.

"Feels good, huh?"

Nick shakes his head in disbelief. He chews on a thick peanut butter bar, trying to reclaim some of the energy he lost to the storm. Sesame seeds get stuck between his teeth.

Jazz helps Adrianna into the ready room, closing the door behind her.

"Everyone good?"

Nick offers a thumbs up. He can't muster actual words. His cheeks are too numb, and his mouth is full. Adrianna drops down next to him. She collapses on the bench seat, lying on her backpack.

"Do we really need all this stuff?"

Jazz says, "You're the one that wanted to come."

"I know, I know," Adrianna says, rolling over and almost falling on the icy floor as she gets back to her feet. "It gets easier from here, right?"

Jazz laughs, pushing through the inner door to the maintenance area. "You really have no idea, do you?"

Unlike the other buildings within the base, the maintenance area is four walls and a roof set on the bare ice. A raised walkway leads them between generators. Ducting hangs from the ceiling, disappearing into the ice.

"This is the site of the original drill hole," Jazz says. "The team widened it for utility access. Air is scrubbed and recirculated. Water is pumped down through insulated pipes. Sewage is pumped back. We're going to follow the conduits down through the ice. That will lead us to the maintenance bay on L2. From there, we'll restart the pumps."

It's only on reaching the duct that Nick realizes Bear and Jazz have been ferrying supplies between the huts for a while. Climbing ropes lie coiled on the ice, reaching back to anchor points on heavy machinery. Several sets of rope sit neatly on the casing of an idle backup generator. Climbing harnesses and crampons have been laid out on a metal walkway.

Jazz takes Nick's backpack, stacking it next to the other equipment. Bear helps Adrianna with her pack.

"Grab a helmet and leather gloves."

Nick folds back his jacket hood and dons a hardhat. He adjusts the straps, fixing the chin strap, and turns on the headlamp. His gloves are lined with wool, which makes them pleasant to wear.

"Now, slip on a pair of crampons," Jazz says, handing a pair of steel frames to each of them. She adds, "Kick hard enough into the ice, and these things will hold your weight on a vertical surface."

Nick turns the crampon over in his gloved hand, looking at the jagged metal spikes protruding from the frame. They're football cleats for a game played against zombies. He copies Jazz, fixing them over his boots and tightening the straps.

"Let's get you in your kit," she says.

Bear holds out a climbing harness. Nick steps into it. "Gotta get this fitted just right or you'll never have kids."

Nick lets out a nervous laugh as Bear tightens the waist belt. He cinches the straps around Nick's thighs, double-checking the clips.

Jazz leads them to a couple of climbing ropes dangling from an overhead walkway.

"This is our test rig. Once we get down in the hole, we're not going to be able to change much. It's important we get things right up here. Once we're hooked up, we'll transfer these carabiners to the climb-anchor, and we're away."

Jazz works with Adrianna while Bear follows her lead, helping Nick.

"We're going to descend on two lines, each of which uses double ropes. Nick, you'll be with Bear. Adrianna will descend with me."

Jazz fiddles with a thin length of cord, wrapping it around a leather loop in Adrianna's harness. Nick watches as Bear does the same for him, aware he may need to do this himself at some point.

"I'm making a French prusik with a little bit of paracord," Jazz says to Adrianna.

"Looks flimsy."

"Oh, it's a lifesaver," Jazz assures her.

At first, Nick assumes Jazz is providing them with instructions, but the quiver in her voice reveals she's speaking for her own benefit. Jazz is ensuring she's gone through all the proper safety checks. She winds the cord around the double ropes and leads it back to Adrianna's harness. Bear mirrors her motion on Nick's setup.

"I'm feeding this through the belay loop on your harness, but it's going to be set well below the belay device on the ropes.

The prusik is a backup. It'll slow your descent if you get in trouble. We're going to descend using military-grade belay plates and prusiks for safety. Keep one hand above the belay plate, the other above the prusik to keep it moving on the ropes. It won't do anything other than trail along. If you start to fall, the increase in load is going to cause your prusik to bunch up. It'll tighten and you'll come to a stop. Okay? You won't fall. You're going to be safe. Okay?"

Jazz is saying okay a lot, which elicits a nervous, "Okay," from Adrianna.

"Okay. There's a reason you've got a bunch of spare carabiners and slings attached to your harness. At no point do you ever release yourself from one without first hooking up to another rope or latching on to an anchor point. Understood?"

Adrianna nods.

Nick says, "Got it."

"If you need both hands free for whatever reason, raise your thigh and loop the main rope around your leg three times like this." Jazz demonstrates. "In essence, your leg then becomes a prusik. The friction will hold your weight. You'll find you can work away quite merrily with both hands without sliding down. Nothing fancy. Nice and simple. It works really well. When you're ready to move on, simply uncoil the rope. Okay?"

Jazz is doing all she can to reassure them they're going to be all right. Her reassurance, though, makes Nick as nervous as hell. He's standing on the ground, or at least he thinks he is. In reality, he's standing on a mile-high plateau of ice. In a few minutes, he's going to drop into a deep, dark hole within an ancient glacier. Yeah, that gets his heart beating a little faster.

Jazz says, "We're going to be making a multi-point descent. That means we've got one set of ropes we're going to use multiple times."

Yet again, Nick's heart beats faster.

"How many times?"

"Well, it's the best part of a mile down there, and we're on fifty-meter ropes, which equates to about a hundred and sixty feet, so..."

"So that's?"

"I dunno," Jazz says. "As many times as we need to reach the hatch."

Bear chimes in with, "Twenty points."

Back in the conference room, when Jazz asked if they'd rappelled before, Nick was naive. He imagined a single drop, not twenty consecutive drops.

"Umm, this might be a dumb question, but how do we use the same ropes over and over again?" Nick asks. "I mean, once you're at the bottom of the rope, how do you get the rope down to reuse it?"

"Good question," Jazz says, smiling with glee. "We come off the rope and hook up to a maintenance anchor point. We're using double ropes knotted on one side. That means we can feed the rope into the new anchor point, pulling it down on that side."

"And?"

"And at some point around halfway through, the rest of the rope will fall."

"Fall?"

Adrianna says, "Ouch."

"Yeah," Bear says, "You don't want your head sticking out when the rope comes down."

"It's perfectly safe," Jazz says.

"But it will hurt," Bear says. "It's like getting whipped by a cattle rustler."

"Wonderful," Nick says.

"Okay, sit back. Let your harness take your weight, and we'll check everything's in place."

Nick and Adrianna do as they're told, lifting their feet and dangling from the overhead walkway as Jazz and Bear fuss over their setup. To Nick's delight, his harness is comfortable. The weight is carried by his waist and thighs without crushing his groin.

"Good. Good," Jazz says.

Bear and Jazz hook onto the double ropes about twenty feet further down. They pull the coiled rope up, tie a prusik and hook in their own belay plates. They clip the packs onto carabiners attached to each climber's waist and unhook the test rig. Bear drags the ropes over to the anchor assembly beside the hole.

"Um, I don't mean to sound alarmist," Nick says, asking yet another question, "but shouldn't those ropes have knots in the end? You know, so we don't slide off?"

Jazz laughs. "Oh, you won't slide off. We're in front of you, remember."

"Yeah," Bear says, pointing a thumb at himself and saying, "We'll slide off."

"That doesn't seem safe," Adrianna says, picking up on Nick's concern.

"None of this is safe," Jazz says. "We're abseiling a mile deep through a glacier in complete darkness. Nothing about this is normal."

Adrianna says, "So we go fifty meters at a time and no more?"

"Fifty meters and no more, or it's nothing but air," Bear replies.

"Leaving the end without a knot sounds dangerous," Jazz says, "But it's not as dangerous as forgetting to remove a temporary knot when retrieving the rope for the next drop, so it's a risk we're going to have to take. If the rope gets jammed or stuck fifty meters above us, we're going to be in a world of pain, so this is the best approach."

Bear pats Nick on the shoulder, saying, "Don't go too far, and you'll be fine."

"This is going to be exhausting, huh?" Nick says.

"You'd better hope we don't have to climb out," Bear replies, grinning.

"Wait—" Nick says. "That's a possibility? I thought we were going to use the elevator?"

"If we can get it working. If not, Plan B is to climb out."

"How long will that take?" Nick asks.

"I dunno. A couple of days."

"Jesus."

"Oh, Jesus ain't gonna help you climb," Jazz says, laughing.

Bear tosses the ropes into the dark hole. He drags his pack across the ice, positioning it in front of the opening.

"ABC," Bear says, talking himself through his own safety checks as he looks at his harness setup. "Anchor, belay, climber—check. I'm good to go."

Jazz hooks onto a second line, saying, "We're going to use short ropes to enter the shaft so we don't drag you in behind us. Once we're down, you follow. Then we'll release from those and continue on the main lines. Remember, hold on tight to your belay plate. You're going to feel a tug once your pack goes over the edge. That's perfectly normal. Walk backward over the lip. When the line goes taut, release yourself from the short rope, and we'll get underway."

Jazz follows Bear, descending into the shaft. She steps beside the conduits and cables disappearing into the darkness. Nick and Adrianna look at each other, regretting their bravado in the boardroom. They clip onto the short rope, take up the slack and drag their packs over the edge. Immediately, the weight of the packs pulls the short rope taut. Nick staggers backward, edging into the shadows.

"That's it," Jazz says, looking up at them. "You're doing

great. This is the hardest part."

"Really?" Nick replies, leaning back and working with his crampons to enter the hole.

"Not really," Jazz says, "but you're doing it. You're on belay. You're going to be fine."

Under his breath, Nick whispers, "Liar."

DESCENT INTO DARKNESS

For almost ten minutes, they hang barely fifteen feet from the opening. Overhead lights illuminate the ice. Jazz is fastidious. She anchors her pack and uses her spare rope to clamber up and inspect them yet again. Once she's satisfied, they begin their descent.

"Bear and I will rappel to the fifty-meter mark and tie off down there. Once we're set, you'll follow. Understood?"

"Yep," Adrianna says on behalf of both of them.

Neither Jazz nor Bear is in a hurry. It's the darkness. It's intimidating. Humans have always been afraid of the unknown. The irony isn't lost on Nick. They're cautious at the least likely part of the climb to be problematic. If there is an alien down there waiting for them in the shadows, it's a mile beneath their boots.

Jazz continues talking to Nick and Adrianna as her lamplight recedes beneath them. The acoustics within the shaft are such that her voice carries. Although she's already a couple of stories below them, it sounds as though she's still up beside them.

"Friction is both your friend and your enemy. Friction slows your descent. It also heats the rope. Over time, it'll weaken it.

This is why we're descending in pairs with a gap between us. That gives the rope time to cool. Okay, we're at the first anchor point. You're good to follow."

Nick eases up on his belay plate. The double ropes slide effortlessly through the metal rings. Adrianna keeps pace with him on the other side of the conduits. The weight of their packs drags them down. The descent is easy—too damn easy.

Over the next few minutes, the ambient light around them fades. The ice goes from white to neon blue and then dark blue in the distance. Whereas his headlamp seemed robust near the surface, fifty meters down it barely illuminates the smooth curve of the ice.

Nick feels the weight beneath him lift as he approaches the end of the rope.

"And I've got your pack," Bear says, clipping it onto an anchor point beside the pipes. As Nick gets close, Bear grabs his legs, guiding him in against the conduits. Bear takes a carabiner from Nick's waist and tugs on the sling, clipping him into the wall. "And you're good to come off belay."

Once the anchor point has taken his weight, Nick releases his prusik along with his belay plate.

Bear is positioned slightly above Nick on a different anchor point. Nick's helmet collides with Bear's equipment belt. An ice ax rattles against the reinforced plastic on his hardhat, making it difficult to hear anything that's being said. Nick looks across. Adrianna swings below Jazz, colliding with her waist as well.

Nick's about to point out how impractical their position is when Jazz says, "Ready on the blue rope?"

"Feeding it through the next anchor," Bear replies.

"And go," Jazz says, followed quickly by, "Warning! Rope falling!"

Bear swings his leg out over Nick. He wraps his groin over Nick's helmet and turns to face the ice wall. Before Nick can react, he hears a sound that terrifies him. At first, it's a whoosh like that of the wind racing through an open window in a storm. Within a fraction of a second, there's an echoing, metallic sound—a hollow ring reverberating through the shaft. It's as though a steel spring has been struck with a hammer. Then comes the crack! Thunder breaks around them as the end of the rope whips past. Bear rocks in his harness as the loose rope thrashes around fifty meters below them. Ice cracks and breaks as the end of the rope collides with the walls. Broken ice fragments bounce off the conduits, ricocheting as they plunge to the bottom of the shaft a mile below them.

Ting! Ping! Bam! Boom! Zing!

For a moment, it's as though the shaft is collapsing, but the sound subsides as the ice falls away.

"Are we good?" Jazz asks.

"We're good," Bear replies. "Resetting the ropes."

"What the hell?" Nick says.

Bear swings away and descends slightly below him on the reset ropes. "Cool, huh?"

"So much for coming in quiet," Adrianna says. "If they didn't know we're here, they do now."

Jazz laughs.

"Remember," Bear says, tying a new prusik for Nick. "Set your prusik then your belay on the main rope. Only then do we transfer your pack from the anchor. But not you. You stay hooked into the maintenance anchor. Once we call out ready from below, release yourself from the anchor, and you're good to go. Got it?"

"Got it," Nick says, feeling a long way from the opening of the shaft already.

"Only thirty more to go."

"Wait. What?" Nick says. "You told us twenty."

"Twenty. Thirty. What's the difference?" Bear asks.

"How long are we going to be in here?" Adrianna asks.

Reluctantly, Jazz says, "Four or five hours."

"Fuck," Nick says. Bear releases his pack, and it once again swings below him, dragging him down. Even though he's anchored, it takes considerable effort to hold his belay plate in place.

After an hour, they've descended so far the maintenance room above them appears like a distant streetlight.

They continue their descent in pairs. First, Jazz and Bear. Then, Adrianna and Nick follow down the double ropes. Although it's efficient, Nick can't help feeling abandoned each time the two soldiers disappear into the darkness beneath them.

Jazz has them turn off their lights while they're waiting to descend to conserve electricity. Being trapped in the dark is terrifying. Nick watches as headlights recede below them.

It's the noises that are unsettling. Nothing sounds right. Bump against a metal conduit, and the resounding echo is utterly alien. Deep, throaty clinks reverberate along the steel. The sound races away from them, moving both up and down the shaft.

Each rappel takes ten to fifteen minutes to complete. The comfort found in repetition wears thin. Nick can't shake the feeling they're descending into a bottomless pit. With each crack of the rope rushing past, he feels as though the narrow shaft is going to collapse. Sweat breaks out on his brow in the cold. He's fighting a panic attack. Being crushed by millions of tons of ice is not how he thought he'd die.

"I can't do this," Adrianna whispers as Bear and Jazz disappear below them yet again, working deeper into the glacier. "I—I can't breathe."

"Hey," Nick replies softly. He reaches out a gloved hand, feeling for her in the dark. "I know. I feel the same. The air. It's—"

"There's no air," Adrianna says, gasping.

Their thick gloved fingers touch. Nick can't bring himself to say it's going to be okay. It's not. Dozens of people have died. What seemed simple up top is hideously more complex and dangerous now they're beneath the ice. Nick hasn't seen the sun in weeks. He wonders if he'll ever see it again.

"Ready?" is the call from below.

"Ready."

Nick and Adrianna reach up and switch on their headlamps. The sudden surge of light causes him to squint. Adrianna looks pale. Dark rings surround her eyes. Her cheeks are gaunt, while her lips are cracked. She looks at him and must see something similar as her eyes speak of resignation rather than resolve. They descend, but neither of them look down. They look at each other, keeping pace with each other.

"And I've got you," Bear says, once again taking Nick's pack at the bottom of the rope.

As a team, they go through the motions, clipping onto an anchor and then unclipping from the rope. The soldiers release the main ropes, shielding them from the lash as it whips past yet again. Jazz and Bear are unrelenting. They're methodical. Robotic. Once again, they disappear below them. Reluctantly, Nick reaches up and switches off his light. Adrianna follows, but not before locking eyes with him once more.

"We're trapped," she whispers. "If there's anything down there."

"There's nothing down there," Nick says, not wanting to have this conversation.

"But there is," she says. "We know there is. We've seen it."

For once, Nick would rather not have a scientist on hand. She's right. With the darkness looming over them, it's easy to panic. Nick balls his hand up into a fist, wanting to fight the fear. For now, they're still hooked onto the anchor point, awaiting word from below to proceed. Oh, how he longs to hear the call of ready. The only thing he can control is the rope feeding through his belay plate. It's poor comfort, but at least he gets to lose himself in the rappel.

"It wants to get out," Adrianna says, not content to let the conversation die. "You know that, right?"

"They'd use the elevator shaft," Nick says softly. "It's bigger."

"It is," Adrianna agrees.

"And we have to consider their needs, right?" Nick says, trying to use her own logic to calm her. "Maybe they need something. Like we need oxygen on the Moon. Maybe they can't just come up here after us. Maybe they need a spacesuit on Earth."

In the darkness, Nick hears Adrianna's tone of voice change as she composes herself.

"Maybe."

He asks, "How did they survive down there for so long? I mean, it's like hundreds of thousands of years, right? How is there anything down there?"

Adrianna seems resigned to defeat.

"We don't know. Machines wouldn't last that long, but life does. Life has thrived beneath the ice for millions of years. It may be that what we think of as a machine is somehow alive."

"Maybe they want something else from us," Nick says. "Maybe we've got this all wrong. We've read too many invasion stories and watched too many monster movies."

"I sure hope so."

A distant voice echoes up the shaft.

"Ready."

The two of them switch on their headlamps and continue their descent. This time, Adrianna smiles.

BACKPACK

Nick's backpack hangs several meters below him, swinging around on a rope attached to his harness, dragging him down into the darkness.

"And, I've got you," Bear says, pulling on Nick's pack. He drags it over to the conduits.

Nick uses his belay plate to come to a halt. The double ropes dangle below him, splitting apart as they flail around. He would feel a helluva lot better if there were knots in the end. Instead, the tips waver, teasing him. Let go. If he lets the rope run through his fingers, within seconds, there will be no rope at all. It's unnerving to think that death is so close at hand.

Bear takes Nick's backpack from him, attaching it to an anchor point on the wall. A metal spike driven into the ice takes the weight of his pack, relieving the pressure on his belay plate.

As the team descends, they use a variety of anchor points from trusses holding the conduits in place to anchors pounded into the ice during construction. Hearing metal creak and groan under weights never intended for it isn't reassuring, but more often than not, they're hooking into a cross member keeping the pipes against the ice wall.

Nick is tired. He wants to ask, how much further? But he's afraid of the answer.

Thin beams of light cut through the mist forming deep within the shaft. The original borehole is still visible, having been cut by a different drill head. When the shaft was widened, the construction crew must have used a slightly different process as the rest of the ice wall is smooth.

Lights turn with the motion of their helmets, illuminating random sections of pipe or the deep blue ice. Vapor drifts around the team. An eerie half-light surrounds them.

"Well, that's fifteen points down," Jazz says. "Congratulations! We're halfway."

Halfway? Rather than being an accomplishment, such a realization is exhausting.

Bear reaches out and grabs the double ropes, pulling Nick in toward an anchor point.

"A little lower," Bear says, reaching down and grabbing a carabiner on Nick's waist. Against his better instincts, Nick eases himself down. He watches as the end of the ropes dangle against his boots. Bear pulls on a sling, dragging one of Nick's carabiners over to the anchor point.

Nick's heart is pounding madly within his chest. On each previous drop, they stopped with at least a few meters of rope beneath them. This time, Bear's taken him right to the end. There's moisture in the air. His gloves slip, and he slides lower still. Nick's fingers tighten above the prusik. The end of the double ropes tap against his trousers, touching at his shins.

"A little closer," Bear says. "Can't—quite—reach."

Bear drags Nick's back against the conduits and pipes running down the length of the shaft. Nick's fingers are like an iron vice wrapped around the frozen double ropes. All the muscles in his body are tense.

Ice falls from an anchor point.

Ping! Bam! Zing! Bang! Boom!

Blue-white fragments of ice disappear beneath Nick's boots,

bouncing off the slick walls as they race into the pitch-black darkness.

Bear yells, "The pack!"

Before Nick realizes what's happening, Bear is swinging on Nick's harness. The increase in weight jerks at his belay plate.

"Goddamn it!" Bear yells.

Bear's released his anchor. He's got one arm around Nick's waist. The other is holding the length of rope attached to the loose backpack. The pack swings wildly below them, colliding with the ice wall. As it twists, it swings them around. The backpack ricochets off the ice, bouncing like a pinball.

An anchor in the ice has failed. A long metal screw has been wrenched from the wall. It dangles from the pack as it spins. Carabiners clash, crashing together. A cascade of ice plunges down the hole.

"Bear!" Jazz yells, but she's unable to complete a sentence. Everything's happening too fast.

Bear is untethered. He slips.

He grabs at Nick's harness, but his gloved fingers don't hold.

Bear slides down Nick's body, grabbing his legs and pinning them together as the double ropes slide up to Nick's thigh. It takes all of Nick's might to hold them there. No knots. Goddamn it! If there was a knot, he could let the rope run.

Bear has still got hold of the fallen backpack. His right arm is stretched out below him, gripping the rope, but the weight is dragging him down. He can only hold onto Nick with his left arm. His strength is failing. Bear slips from Nick's knees to his ankles. His armpit hooks over one of Nick's boots, providing some relief. The pack spins, bouncing off the conduits and colliding with the pipes, threatening to drag him into the darkness.

"Let it go," Jazz calls out.

"It's got our scuba gear," Bear replies.

Nick struggles with the way the double ropes reverberate above him. The tension on the ropes makes them difficult to grip. Bear wriggles beneath him.

Through gritted teeth, Nick says, "Can't—hold—on."

"Hang on," Jazz replies, seemingly ignoring him. She grabs the spare rope from another pack hanging on the ice wall.

The double ropes continue to slide through Nick's belay plate. No matter how hard he squeezes, the combined weight drags him down. The end of the double ropes slip past his waist. The prusik bunches, pulling tight, but with two men and a backpack, it can't hold.

"I've got it," Bear yells, swinging his legs wide and reaching for the wall. He tries to clip a carabiner onto a support truss but to do that he has to push to one side. Heat surges through the double ropes. Bear lifts the pack with one arm.

"Just—about—there."

Bear kicks against the wall, wanting to swing closer to the conduits. Nick twists with the motion. His helmet collides with the pipes, rattling his head.

To his horror, Nick feels the double ropes passing through the glove on his left hand. Once they're free of the prusik, the loose ends race toward the belay plate. Above that, his right hand squeezes tight. The muscles, ligaments, and tendons in his hand are failing. Cramps seize his arm. The heat of the friction reaches through his leather gloves. He can't hold it. He can't.

"Almost," Bear yells.

The aluminum carabiner strikes the truss. It rebounds, failing to close over the icy metal.

"Shit! Fuck!" Bear yells in that fraction of a second as the double ropes slip through the belay plate and from Nick's gloved fingers.

"No," Nick yells, scrambling with his hands, trying to grab the rope as it whips away from his harness.

Nick is weightless.

From his perspective, he doesn't fall. It's the ropes that race away from him, rushing up toward the surface. His body twists. His headlamp reflects off the glossy ice.

The backpack falls with him into the darkness.

Bear plunges down the shaft screaming. His hands reach for the conduits, grabbing for them, but that only causes him to rebound away from the pipes and wiring.

Bear reaches for Nick. His hands thrash about as he falls away. His eyes. Nick will never forget the look of disbelief in those eyes as the darkness swallows them. Bear slams into the ice wall. His arms flail about, desperately trying to grab hold of something—anything.

Nick falls along behind Bear.

The wind rushes past.

Chunks of ice fall beside him.

He's dead, and he knows it.

The rocks and ice at the bottom of the shaft are going to rush up at him, rising out of the darkness to pulverize his body. Nick's fingers reach for the slick ice rushing past.

Before he can react, his head whips forward toward his chest. Spasms ripple through his body.

Nick's helmet smashes into the ice. Cracks run through the thick plastic. The strap under his jaw goes taut, choking him.

Gloved leather fingers tear at the hair on the back of his neck.

"Got you," Jazz says, grunting. She's grabbed Nick by the back of his helmet, with her gloved fingers reaching up inside it, catching his hair. The helmet is wrenched half off his head. Nick chokes. Straps dig into his throat, cutting off his breathing. His legs dangle beneath him.

Bear plummets into the shadows. Occasionally, his

headlamp is visible, flickering as he tumbles into the darkness.

Within seconds, he's gone.

Nick reaches up with his hands, trying to grab hold of the conduits. He's desperate. Nothing. His gloved fingers slip, unable to grip the icy pipes. There's no air. He can't breathe. His crampons collide with the wall and he kicks. Metal spikes knock ice loose. Again and again, he strikes until one of his boots digs in. Nick pushes up. The crampon holds, relieving the pressure on his neck and allowing him to breathe.

"And again," Jazz says.

Nick raises his leg, kicking hard into the ice. His crampons bite, allowing him to push higher on unsteady legs. Jazz grabs the collar of his jacket and reaches under his right armpit.

"One more time."

Nick wrenches his boot free and digs in again, driving higher.

Jazz turns him, allowing him to push up off his crampons with ease. She's upside down, which confuses him. Like a circus performer on a high-wire trapeze, her legs are entwined in the rope above her, freeing her arms as she dangles within the shaft. She's attached her spare 25-meter static rope to an anchor and swung down in time to grab him.

"Can you reach that truss?"

"I—I think so," Nick says, grabbing a carabiner on a sling. He pulls it from his harness and reaches out, hooking it over the thin metal.

"Okay. I'm going to let go of you now. You're going to be okay. Okay?"

Nick has never wanted to be held more in his life, but he manages a shaky, "Okay."

Jazz releases him, and he swings in place beside the conduits.

The truss holds.

Nick's helmet knocks against the ice. He comes to rest hard up against the sewage pipe. Beneath him, there's nothing but darkness.

Whoosh! Wham! Boom! Bang! Kaboom!

It's heartbreaking to hear Bear falling to his death. Nick can only hope he's been knocked unconscious, sparing him from the terror. Jazz returns to join Adrianna on an anchor point fifteen meters further up the shaft. No one talks for the best part of a minute. All they can do is listen to the sounds ricocheting around them as their friend dies. The final thud is heartbreaking, echoing up the shaft.

Wah—boom!

In the silence that follows, Jazz cries. Tears roll down her cheeks. She wipes them away, smudging grit on her face.

Adrianna is the first one to speak.

"I—I'm sorry. I'm so sorry."

Jazz sniffs, ignoring the comment. She addresses Nick.

"I'm going to need your help with the ropes."

He nods, straightening his helmet.

Even though she said that, Jazz resets both sets of double ropes as he hangs below her. Over the next ten minutes, she barely speaks beyond a murmur. Anything she does say is directed toward the rappel, not them. She helps Adrianna and Nick tie their prusiks and attach their belay plates. Jazz reaches up and switches off their headlights. It's somewhat symbolic. She's prepared to do everything she can to get them out of here alive.

Yet again, Jazz leaves them hooked into their anchor points, only this time she descends alone. A solitary light glides below them, dropping into the darkness.

Nick is still in shock. Sitting there in his harness with his light off, surrounded by the darkness, two words tumble from his lips.

"He's gone."

This time, Adrianna reaches out, taking his hand. She doesn't speak. There's nothing she can say that will take away the pain.

Ten minutes later, a feeble voice calls out, "Ready." And with that, they're on the move again as though nothing happened.

Nick and Adrianna turn on their lights and descend slower than before.

At the stopping point, Nick helps with the retrieval of the ropes. He feeds the blue side through the next anchor and turns away as the black rope falls past. Although he's seen Bear do this a dozen times, he's not prepared for how the rope whips around when it comes to a halt. The weight of the ropes tugs against his gloved hands, but he keeps them secure.

"Good work," Jazz says, yet again helping him and Adrianna with their prusiks and belay plates. Nothing more is said. There will be time to mourn later. At this point, two words from Jazz is a pep talk. She's on autopilot. Like them, she wants to get the hell out of this goddamn shaft.

As Jazz descends further, Nick looks up. He can't see the light anymore. It's got to be there, but it's not even a solitary star in their bitter, dark night. The maintenance shed might as well have been swallowed by another dimension. *Vincennes* is a dream.

"How can she go on?" Adrianna asks as they wait in the darkness to descend to the next anchor point.

"She's got no choice."

"W—Why are we doing this? We don't know what's down there."

"Yes, we do," Nick says, feeling he owes Bear a debt to go on. "Survivors. We've got to help them. We're their only hope."

From the shadows, Adrianna nods. "We can do this," she

says as a voice calls out from below, urging them on.

"Ready."

Hours pass like days.

Each stage takes them deeper, but it feels as though none of them bring the team closer to the flooded research center. For Nick, they're descending into hell.

WATER

It's been five hours.

Nick's bladder is bursting.

Jazz dangles before a steel bulkhead set into the ice. Her headlamp flickers over the frozen door. Rather than entering a research station, it looks as though they're opening the blast door on an aircraft carrier.

Nick and Adrianna are on the main lines while Jazz has hooked up her spare rope to an anchor above the door. This allows the three of them to hang together in front of the entranceway.

Backpacks dangle below the team, disappearing into the darkness. Nick has no idea how much further the shaft extends, and he has no desire to find out. Somewhere down there lies the broken body of his friend.

"Once I'm inside, I'm going to need you to help me with my pack."

"Understood," Nick says, keeping a firm grip on his belay plate. The idea of slipping lower and having to climb back up is not appealing. Adrianna flips the double ropes around her thigh, locking herself in place. Nick does likewise, freeing up his hands.

The door opens inwards. Jazz turns a series of large metal handles strategically placed around the hatch, but it doesn't move. She pushes against the cold metal surface. It won't budge.

Nick grabs one of the handles on the doorframe and presses his shoulder hard against the steel.

"And push," Jazz says.

It's hard to apply any muscle as his body inherently wants to swing away from the hatch.

"Nothing's easy, is it?" Nick says.

Adrianna reaches over, saying, "Let me take your pack. That'll give you more freedom to move."

Their eyes meet. Nick goes to say something when she cuts him off. "I'll be fine."

Reluctantly, he agrees.

To counter the swing of the ropes, Nick removes his crampons, clipping them onto his harness, and plants his boots on the steel hatch. He grabs the handles around the outside of the door. He's standing sideways, hanging from the double ropes.

"Just like a leg press at the gym."

Jazz laughs. With mock disdain, she says, "You've never done a leg press at the gym."

"Hey," Nick says, pretending to be insulted. "I've walked past a gym. I've looked in the windows."

Jazz shakes her head, but he gets a smile.

Nick sets his legs and pushes. His boots leave prints on the frozen steel. Water seeps out from within the corridor.

Within seconds, the leak turns from a trickle into a torrent. Jazz shoves her pickax into the gap to wedge open the door. The water on the other side is waist-deep and runs for several minutes before the level lowers. As the pressure eases, Jazz wedges her helmet into the gap, allowing the water to run faster. Once she's inside, Nick hauls up her backpack. She drags it through the knee-deep water and onto the steps leading to L1. Nick passes the other two packs through to her.

"Damn, that's cold," Nick says, stepping into the water. A thin crust of ice has frozen around the edge of the walls. As the water recedes, the ice shelf collapses.

Adrianna looks at a half-eaten donut floating toward the door. "So much for containment protocols."

"Speaking of containment," Nick says. "I don't know about you, but I can't contain myself much longer."

"Just," Jazz says, unable to complete her sentence. She points at a nearby door with a stick figure on a brushed aluminum sign.

As Nick wades toward the bathroom, Adrianna says, "The plumbing is probably frozen."

He points at the door. "Which plumbing? Mine or?"

Adrianna shakes her head.

Nick says, "I'll leave something for future archeologists to find."

"Paleontologists," Adrianna says, correcting him. "And I'm sure they'll be thrilled."

"Anyone else need to?"

Jazz says, "I'll wait until we've found a working toilet."

"Okay," Nick says.

By the time he comes back, Jazz and Adrianna have dumped the packs on the stairs leading up to L1, getting them out of the water. In retrospect, he should have headed up there to the bathroom, but his bladder felt as though it was about to burst.

The two women have laid out the equipment on the steps. Ropes have been coiled. Crampons are stacked together. Carabiners and harnesses sit on top of each other.

"Hey, you know, what you did back there. Thanks," Nick says to Jazz, tipping his head toward the maintenance shaft. He's not sure what else he can say.

"You can thank me if we make it out of here alive," Jazz

says. "I only hope those goddamn pumps work. We lost the arctic scuba gear. If the pumps fail, the rescue is over."

The scuba gear isn't all they lost, but no one wants to mention Bear. For now, they have to press on.

"Is the water supposed to be so blue?" Nick asks, looking into the submerged staircase leading down to L3.

"Ultraviolet loading," Adrianna says, pointing up at the ceiling.

"Huh?"

"The lights," she says. "They saturate UV as a strategy to reduce microbial growth."

"Oh," Nick replies, as though that makes sense to him.

"Okay," Jazz says. "Enough sightseeing. Time to suit up."

They wade through the water and up the steps. Adrianna pulls a bunch of hazmat suits from her pack.

"Are these really necessary?" Nick asks.

"Yes. If we run into any kind of biohazard, these will keep us safe. Besides, they'll keep your feet warm and dry."

"Can't argue with that," Nick replies, sitting on the steps and pulling his boots off. He peels his wet socks from his feet. Adrianna hands him a fresh set of woolen socks. Although the hazmat suit is bright yellow, it has built-in black rubber boots.

Nick's glad to be rid of his boots. Jazz, though, keeps hers on, slipping them inside the suit. Her feet must be cold, but it seems she doesn't care.

Once Nick's climbed inside his hazmat suit, Adrianna fixes a respirator over his face and starts the flow of oxygen. She zips up his hood. In a matter of seconds, the suit inflates, leaving him feeling like the Michelin Man. The transparent plastic hood is oversized, leaning to one side on his shoulders, towering above his head.

"The suit uses positive pressure," Adrianna says as she

dresses. "So if you get any leaks, air will push out, preventing contaminants from getting in. We've got four hours on one tank."

"Four hours is all we need," Jazz says, zipping up her suit. "Okay, here's the game plan. Adrianna, you're going to sweep L1 looking for survivors. Nick, you'll work on the pumps. I'm going to go and get Father back online down here."

"We're splitting up?" Adrianna asks, unsure of herself.

Nick addresses Jazz. "You know when they do this in the movies, it's *always* a bad idea, right?"

"This ain't the movies," Jazz replies in a growl.

"Fair enough," Adrianna says, turning and walking up the stairs to the first level. Being in a bulky suit, she looks down at her feet as she mounts each step. She watches the fall of her rubber boots, wanting to avoid tripping.

"Wait," Nick says, grabbing her arm as she steps up beside him.

"What?" she says, turning toward him. The clear faceplate on her suit has ballooned, making her head look small in the oversized plastic hood.

Nick points at the top of the stairs. Fingers wrap around the edge of the wall. Jazz sees them as well. She pulls a handgun from her backpack.

"It's okay," Nick says, addressing whoever's up on the L1 landing. "You can come out. We're here to help."

Jazz steps away from the two of them, pushing herself hard up against the wall and aiming the gun at the top of the stairs. In her mind, help is a secondary priority.

Adrianna edges forward, repeating Nick's point. "We're from *Vincennes*. We came down here for you. We're going to get you out of here."

Straggly blonde hair appears followed by a bloodshot eye peering around the corner.

"It's okay," Adrianna says from behind the clear plastic

dome of her hazmat suit. She beckons the woman closer. The woman hesitates. Black gloved fingers are anything but reassuring. Adrianna steps up, slowly moving toward her. The woman removes her fingers, leaving bloody streaks on the wall.

"Please," Adrianna says.

"You. You," the woman says, stepping out in front of them. "You can't go down there. The crystal man."

"Easy," Adrianna says with both hands out in front of her. "You're safe now. No one's going to hurt you."

"You don't understand," the woman says. "You're in danger. The man. He's everywhere."

Jazz is barely breathing. She's got her gun trained on the center of the woman's chest. One sudden move, and she's protecting her team.

"What man?" Adrianna asks, stepping up toward her.

"The water man."

"There's no one down here," Adrianna says. She's close enough she can read the woman's name tag. "We're going to get you out of here, Elizabeth."

The two women lock eyes.

Adrianna has her hand within reach of Elizabeth's trembling fingers. "It's okay. Come with me."

Elizabeth takes her gloved hand. Slowly, Adrianna leads her down the stairs, but she won't go more than a few steps. She shakes her head, pulling against Adrianna. She's afraid of the water.

"Get me the med-kit and rations," Adrianna says to Nick.

Elizabeth sits on the steps, trembling, but not from the cold.

"Who is she?" Jazz asks.

"Dr. Elizabeth Montgomery. Physicist. She's from the UK."

Jazz puts her gun away. "Elizabeth, can you tell us what

happened here?"

She doesn't answer. Her eyes are fixed on the water lapping at the steps. Adrianna gives her something to drink, holding a bottle for her.

Nick asks, "What does she mean by the crystal man?"

No one answers.

Nick opens the first aid kit, giving Adrianna access to antiseptic lotion and bandages. Jazz is nervous. She keeps switching the way she's facing. One moment, she's watching them, the next, she's looking back at ripples on the water at the bottom of the stairs.

Adrianna bandages Elizabeth's hands.

"I need you to sweep that floor," Jazz says, sounding anxious. Adrianna doesn't reply. She bats her hand behind her as if to say, be patient.

"Listen," Adrianna says to Elizabeth. "You're safe here on the stairs, okay? I want you to wait here. I'm going to go and look for the others."

Elizabeth is reluctant to let go of Adrianna's hand, but she does. A soft squelch betrays Adrianna's steps as she approaches the top of the landing. Nick doesn't like this. They should stick together, but with limited oxygen, there's not enough time. As much as he understands Adrianna's concern, who's to say they haven't already been exposed to toxins or whatever. Their hazmat suits might be entirely redundant.

Jazz wades through the water, moving along the corridor on L2. Tiny fish dart away from her. Tiny transparent bodies scatter before reforming as a school and turning behind her. They're barely visible beneath the lights. Flickers of silver appear and then disappear as they move in a shoal.

Nick steps down into the icy cold water. The pressure of the water closes over his hazmat suit, but there are no leaks. It might be cold, but his feet are dry.

Jazz points at the cupboard beside the stairs leading to L3. "You'll find the sump pumps in there."

"On it."

As much as he doesn't want to turn his back on Elizabeth, Nick knows he has to. Now is not the time for nerves. Jumping at shadows makes no sense. Although he may feel as though someone's watching him, intellectually, he knows that's silly. Of course, someone is watching him—that someone's Elizabeth. Nick's got a job to do. He needs to focus.

Nick opens the maintenance room. It's barely a cupboard. Thick pipes run between floors. Unlike the bathroom, where exposed pipes beneath the sink have cracked as water froze within them, these pipes are insulated.

A steel grate sits over a gap between floors, allowing him to peer into the submerged L3 utility room below. Water drips onto his suit from L1. Nick runs his gloved hand over the various labels, wanting to understand the setup—electrical, sewage, air, water, drainage. Oval windows allow for inspection beside the access ports. He rubs one, looking for movement beyond the glass. There's a pressure gauge on the drainage line, but he's not sure about the reading. What's kPa in real measurements?

He opens a locker. A bunch of electrical sump pumps sit on a shelf. A variety of fire hose attachments hang from custom fittings.

Someone's standing behind him, but his hazmat suit makes it difficult to see beyond about 180 degrees without turning around. Nick's not sure who it is, but they're quiet, watching over his shoulder. So long as they don't annoy him, he doesn't care.

"Man, this place is kitted out," he says, picking up a bulky Y-shaped brass fitting. "Look at this. It's a heavy-duty three-way fire-point connector with brass ball-valves. This is hardcore. I haven't seen something like this since my days with the NYFD."

Nick screws the Y-connector onto the main pipe and links a few sections of hose together. He's methodical. Jazz is rubbing off on him. He reaches beneath the water and shifts the grate, leaning it to one side. Nick lowers a pump, submerging it in the shaft leading to L3. As soon as the hose goes slack, he knows he's on the lower floor. He grabs another pump and repeats the process.

"Here goes," he says, plugging the pumps into electrical sockets on the ceiling.

The fire hoses inflate with water. He opens the valves, allowing water to pump into the drainage line.

"All right," he says, clapping his gloved hands together. "Not bad for an amateur."

Nick doesn't think anything of the person standing behind him. Adrianna's probably come back from L1. Jazz might have finished her sweep of L2. Perhaps Elizabeth got bored and is looking to help. It doesn't matter. He's preoccupied, watching bubbles flicker beneath the glass viewpoint in the pipe.

"Our kPas are up," he jokes. "Whatever that means."

Nick's expecting some long-winded explanation about international standards from Adrianna, but if it's her behind him, she's quiet.

There's some chalk in the toolkit. He reaches down and scratches a mark on the wall, wanting to see how quickly the water recedes. His mind is preoccupied. There's a helluva lot of water to shift. Now, it's a question of the differential. Somehow, water is seeping in. So long as he's pumping water out faster than it's coming in, the water level will recede. Given it's taken time for the base to fill up, he hopes the pumps will win out over the leak. Ideally, he needs to find that leak and plug the hole.

Nick steps back, admiring his handiwork.

"What do you think?" he asks, turning around.

Elizabeth is still sitting on the stairs. She's huddled under a blanket, but her eyes aren't on him. She's looking at the ghostly apparition beside him.

Nick stands perfectly still. His eyes move, surveying the shape next to him.

A tiny fish darts through the water suspended beside him. It swims innocently through the shoulder of what appears to be a transparent man. The fish has no regard for where it is within the column of water forming the outline of a human. Nick shuffles backward, wanting to get inside the utility cupboard. Water ripples around his legs.

What the hell?

Is this what Buckley saw? What was it he said? *The devil has no form but like that of a man.* Is this what he meant? Is this what scared him into wanting to detonate that nuke?

Nick's heart pounds in his chest, threatening to break through his ribs.

The watery semblance of a man steps forward. Legs and arms move even though there's no substance to them, nothing beyond the cold, clear water. Light reflects off smooth curves. Shoulders, arms, biceps. It's as though the statue of David has been brought to life in crystal.

Nick bumps against the concrete wall inside the narrow utility room.

"W—What are you?" he asks. He reaches his hand out, wanting to grab the door, but the creature is too close. He'll shut him inside with him. A transparent hand mimics his motion, reaching for the handle.

Nick stops. He splays his fingers wide, holding up his open hand in a sign of friendship, at least as he understands it.

"Hello?"

The alien figure copies him. Water drips from a transparent elbow as the ghostly hand aligns with Nick's glove.

Nick reaches forward, touching gently against the watery hand before him. Contact is made. The creature feels firm. Nick was expecting his hand to pass through the water, but it doesn't.

Their eyes meet. How can this thing see or move or touch? There's no substance beyond the thin, almost crystalline exterior. Tiny bits of fine silt circulate, being suspended within the watery man.

"What are you doing?" Adrianna asks, coming down the stairs behind Elizabeth.

The alien water creature collapses, splashing against Nick's suit. Ice-cold water swirls around his legs. He looks down. Tiny fish dart away from his boots.

"Tell me you saw that?"

"Saw what?" Adrianna asks. "Have you found something? There's nothing up there on L1."

"Ah," Nick replies, looking at the water dripping from his gloves.

"Hey, you got it working!"

"Yes," he says, turning and pointing at the chalk mark. Already, the water level has dropped a couple of inches. Ripples of water lap over his ankles.

Jazz comes back, but unlike him, she has no regard for the water, allowing it to splash rather than wading through it. She's oblivious.

"Everything good?"

"Yeah, fine," he replies.

Nick is intimidated by the two women. Adrianna's smarter. Jazz is braver. He wants to say something about what he saw, but he's afraid of coming across stupid. He's never felt this way before. Normally, Nick's self-assured. In hindsight, he realizes his confidence was misplaced and arrogant. Now, he feels naked. He knows he should say something, but he doesn't. They'll think he's seeing things, letting his imagination run wild.

"Did you find anything?" Jazz asks Adrianna.

"What?" Nick says, feeling defensive. "Me? No."

"Not you," Jazz snaps, pointing. "Her."

"Bodies," Adrianna says.

Jazz doesn't say as much, but as she's returned alone, that was all she found as well. "Father is back online."

"Okay," Nick says. He's nervous. Jumpy. He wants to tell them about the watery man, but how? They'll think he's gone mad. Elizabeth is quiet. She knows. They exchange looks. Her raised eyebrows scream, '*Not so crazy now, huh?*'

Jazz asks, "Is there any way we can speed up those pumps?"

"No," he says, "but once we get down a level, I can double them up and extend them."

"Good."

Adrianna sits on the stairs beside Elizabeth, comforting her.

Jazz goes through the backpacks, organizing more of her equipment. She dumps the spare climbing gear on the stairs and sorts through a dizzying array of weapons and ammunition.

Nick watches as the water recedes. As soon as it has dropped below floor level, he shifts over to the stairs leading down to L3. Nick sits with his feet in the water, moving a few steps at a time, keeping his boots wet. It's a token gesture. He's not sure what happened by the maintenance cupboard, but whatever that creature was, it meant him no harm. In his own way, he's trying to invite it back. He'd love nothing more than for it to appear so he could say, See? I'm not crazy.

The water is clear, but it's not pure. Tiny bits of silt swirl around his boots. Schools of twenty to thirty transparent fish swim past. Occasionally, they examine the black rubberized soles of his boots. He can see a thin spine, intestines, and the flick of a tail.

"They're blind," Adrianna says, sitting beside him.

Ripples of water roll away from her boots.

"They can't see?" he says, surprised. The way they move

suggests they can.

"They feel their way through the water. They can sense movement, changes in pressure, electrical impulses, things like that."

"Huh."

"Are you okay?" she asks.

Nick asks her, "Have you ever seen something you couldn't explain?"

"Oh, sure. All the time. That's the thing about science. It's not about having answers. It's about asking questions."

"But what if you saw something impossible?"

"Everything starts out impossible," Adrianna says. "For thousands of years, flight was impossible. The Greeks had Icarus flapping a pair of wings, but flying was for the birds.

"As much as we admire the Wright brothers, they flew for a mere twelve seconds. They got twenty feet off the ground, that's all. They didn't even clear the sand dunes on the beach. But suddenly, something that had been impossible became possible. The rest is history.

"Can you imagine if they saw an A380 or an F-16? Or a helicopter flying on Mars? I think they'd laugh. To them, such machines would be ridiculous, but it all came from challenging the impossible."

As well meaning as she is, Adrianna isn't helping.

Nick moves down a step, dipping his boots once more in the receding water.

Adrianna joins him.

"What do you think's in there?" he asks.

"In the water?" she replies, clarifying his question. "Oh, lots of organics. Nutrients. Microbes. Plankton. It looks clear, but it's teeming with life."

"It sure is," Nick says, laughing.

With the water at waist level on L3, Jazz pushes past them, wading down the stairs. The air in her suit rushes up as she steps out into the corridor. She's so buoyant her boots barely touch the floor. Jazz is in danger of keeling over, but she continues on, using her hands to push the water around her.

"Let's get some more pumps going."

"On it," Nick says. He heads down to the L3 maintenance room and sets up another two pumps. Nick shifts the grating and drops them down to L4.

Bodies float past. Yeah, Nick would much rather see a transparent body than a real one. Conflicting thoughts gnaw at his conscience. Whatever that thing in the water is, it was down here when this happened. It caused this. Why the fuck are you waving hello, Nick? If he felt dumb before, now he feels like an imbecile.

Adrianna steers the bodies into an empty room but not before one bumps into the maintenance door. Blank eyes stare up at Nick. A crab emerges from the mouth of a dead scientist. Adrianna grabs him by his shoes, pulling him into the next room. Out of sight/out of mind has always been the best way for humanity to deal with death. Being confronted by a dead body makes Nick uncomfortable, but it's important. Bear is lying alone in the shadows at the bottom of that damn shaft. He deserves better. So does this guy. But he's pushed into a room, and the door is closed. It seems the living need to ignore the dead. Stop and think about it too long, and he knows he'll crumble.

Nick tells himself that if the team can rescue those trapped in the conference room, it'll mean something for those they've lost. It's a hollow victory for the dead, but it is a victory nonetheless. Passing the light of life on to another is the best anyone can hope for.

Nick has to focus. He takes a mental inventory of the equipment in the utility room. A screwdriver could make for a poor man's ice ax. A tape measure is useless. Coils of electrical wiring could be used as rope.

Vertical blades of ice have formed on the walls of L3 as the water began to freeze. To Nick, this level looks like the inside of a hive.

"It's just ice," he says quietly to himself as he heads back up the stairs to get a few extra lengths of fire hose. Nick wants to extend the pumps from L2, so they reach down to L4. The electrical cords are long enough. Someone somewhere ensured that long before the base was built. He just needs some extra hose. Nick drapes several thick hoses over his shoulder. Brass fittings clink together. Elizabeth hasn't moved. She's still sitting on the upper stairs next to the backpacks.

With a firm hand sliding along the rail, Nick heads back down to L3. Adrianna and Jazz are nowhere to be seen. A transparent figure stands beside the utility room, waiting for him. As Nick is coming down the stairs, he expects the watery man to look up at him, but the position of the transparent head remains the same. As soon as Nick's boots touch the floor, the alien walks toward him. Nick backs up, slipping into the utility room. The only ripples are from his boots. Seemingly crystalline legs move through the water, but there are no corresponding waves.

"W—What do you want?" Nick asks with a trembling voice. He's standing knee-deep in water. "What do you need?"

Nick's trying to recall the hierarchy Adrianna described in the conference room, but his mind is blank. The watery man holds up his hand just as Nick did on L2. Nick copies him, noting the roles are reversed.

"You want us to understand," he says. "But we need you to understand us. You may thrive here in the water. We can't. We have to rescue our people."

Nick points at the next set of submerged stairs.

"We have to go down there. Our people are trapped down there."

He lowers his hand, taking a good look at the transparent figure. The alien is bald, but he has eyes, a nose, ears, and a mouth, or at least the faint outline of them. Grit floats in the water, moving as though stirred by an unseen current.

The aquatic man points, but on a different angle. He's pointing in another direction down on the lower level. It seems he understands at least part of what Nick is saying.

"What the hell are you?" Nick asks from behind the safety of his mask and his hazmat suit.

"Have you got those pumps going?" Jazz calls out, sticking her head out of a room further along the corridor.

Nick turns, saying, "Almost."

Although the inflated hood on his hazmat suit is clear, the sides aren't. He loses sight of the creature. When he turns back, the watery man is gone. Ripples undulate across the surface of the water. If there's one thing alien movies have taught him, it's to be afraid of the unknown. Nick feels on edge. Why him? Why isn't this thing appearing to Adrianna or Jazz? Why doesn't it appear when they're all present? What is it trying to accomplish? It's not trying to stop him, even though he's restricting its movement by draining the base.

Nick turns off the pumps, extends them with the extra hoses, and drops them down to the next level. He hooks up the electrical system and starts pumping. Now, he's running four pumps. Two go into the drainage pipe, the other two into sewage.

"And we're good," he says as the others join him by the next set of stairs. The water recedes at a steady rate. "Did you figure out what jammed the elevator?"

Adrianna says, "A body."

Not a scientist or an engineer.

Not a man or a woman.

A body.

RESCUE

With the water receding, Nick hauls the medical pack down to the lowest level within the base—L4. Ice clogs the corridor. It's grown in wings, forming baffles that reach out from the walls, choking the walkway.

"I found the leak," Adrianna says, wading toward him. "Over by the airlock. It's iced-over so we won't be fighting more incoming water."

"That's good to hear," Nick says.

"Which one's the conference room?" Jazz asks.

Adrianna replies, "Oh, on this level, they're all conference rooms."

"What?"

Jazz starts chipping away at the ice, trying to reach the nearest door. The outer layers of ice have formed thin sheets and come away easily. In closer to the walls, the ice is like concrete. She hacks at the slab, barely making any progress. Her climbing ax scratches rather than breaks the hardened ice.

"Wait," Nick says. He points along the corridor at one of the rooms down to their left. Mentally, he's tracing the line shown to him by the creature in the water. "They're in that room over there."

"What?" Adrianna says.

"How do you know that?" Jazz asks. "That's skipping three or four other rooms."

"I—I can hear them," Nick says, lying. "They're banging on the walls."

The two women stand still. Water drips from the ceiling. Ice groans as the water level drops. Pumps hum in the background. They look at each other.

"Damn, you've got good hearing," Jazz says, wading forward. Water sloshes around her. She positions herself several doors down and points, asking, "This one?"

"Yes. I think so."

She begins chipping away at the ice. "This is going to take a while."

"We're getting low on oxygen," Adrianna says. "Forty-five minutes left. We need to get in there. Quick."

"I'll see if I can find something we can use for leverage," Nick says. He leaves the women in the corridor and tugs on the door to the utility maintenance area. Sheets of ice fall free, splashing in the water. Behind the cabinet, he finds a length of three-quarter-inch steel pipe. As it's painted red, it must be leftover from the installation of the fire suppression system. It's five feet in length. It'll work nicely as a crowbar.

Nick and Jazz work together, hacking at the ice.

A dim light shines through the ice, coming from a window in the door. Someone's banging metal on metal on the other side.

"Goddamn," Jazz says, turning and looking at Nick. "They're in there, all right."

Nick wedges the pipe into a crack and pulls, breaking a section of ice free.

"Anni?" Jazz calls out. "Anni Azizi? Stay where you are. We're coming."

The water is still waist-deep, but there's so much ice the volume of water in the corridor is dropping fast.

Jazz targets the window, clearing the ice away from the glass. Anni smiles from the other side. She's an elderly Asian lady wearing a traditional headscarf. Her weathered face speaks of a harsh life working on a farm. Like Nick, she shouldn't be here in Antarctica.

"We're going to get you out of there," Jazz yells. "Hold tight. We'll have you topside within the hour."

Anni jumps for joy, pointing at the others. Nick cranes his neck. Bodies lie on the boardroom table. Some of them sit slumped in chairs.

"Are they dead?" Adrianna asks.

"Father says they're alive," Jazz replies.

Nick hacks at the ice, but he's exhausted. His muscles ache. Sweat drips within his hazmat suit. It's frustrating not being able to reach up and wipe it away.

Jazz is also tiring. Her blows glance off the ice. Adrianna takes over with the ax, giving Jazz a break, but she barely scratches the thick slabs that have grown around the edge of the door.

Nick widens his stance, throwing his strength behind each blow. The ice is like granite. With each strike, the pipe shudders, jarring his hands. Pain shoots up his arms and into his shoulder. The *wahaika* hanging around his neck swings wildly. It's heavy, resisting the impulse to move, reacting to each strike.

Why the hell didn't he leave that goddamn trinket topside? It's annoying. Its motion, though, causes his mind to cast back to the *Te Kaha*. Hah! This is what Eddie meant by *mana*. Nick can still hear the growl with which Eddie pronounced the word as *mun-nah*.

In Nick's mind, he's alone—and yet he's not. Eddie knew. Everyone stands alone, and yet they don't. Nick isn't here in Antarctica representing some nebulous concept of *The World*. It's about people. He's here for Commander Simonds, Ensign

Temuera, Eddie, and everyone else he met on the *Te Kaha*. Damn it, he's here for Dmitri and Bear.

Mana.

Mun-nah!

As much as he wouldn't admit it while he was on the *Te Kaha*, for Nick, *mana* was hokey Maori bullshit. Oh, he respected it as important to their culture, but it was meaningless to him. Like any other indigenous group, Nick thought of the Maori as outdated and archaic. To his mind, *mana* was a relic of past glory. *Mana* was overwhelmed by European conquest. *Mana* might as well be a Greek tragedy or a statue of the Virgin Mary from the fifth century. It's history. Nothing more. Now, though, he feels it in his bones. *Mana* is the strength of everyone that brought him to this moment. It's humanity stripped bare. For Nick, *mana* is—us, not me. With that, he grits his teeth and strikes at the ice with renewed strength. Pain is nothing. Fatigue is an imposter. All that matters is the precision of his strike.

The *wahaika* hanging around his neck fights the ice. It swings in response to each blow, refusing to relent. Nick finds his rhythm. The motion of the *wahaika* drives him on, counteracting the stubborn ice, giving him resolve. He settles into a steady pace. Jazz and Adrianna step to one side, sensing the vigor in his stride. They're silent. They don't want to break his concentration. For once, Nick's not dreaming of heroics. He's a warrior.

Nick uses the pipe like a spear to chip at the ice. When cracks appear, he uses the length of pipe as a crowbar to break off large chunks. What seemed impossible is now inevitable. Sweat is a reward. Aches are a matter of pride. Nothing can stop him. Nothing will.

By the time he's cleared around the door, the water is lapping at his ankles.

"Damn," Jazz says as Nick finally steps back, kicking fallen ice away from the door. "Nice work."

Nick leans on the steel pipe, pushing it hard against the floor as he bends over, catching his breath.

Jazz tugs on the frozen handle, pulling at the door. Anni pushes from the other side. Adrianna prepares a couple of bottles with an electrolyte drink to help revive those inside. The door opens in starts, moving a few inches at a time until it's wide enough to squeeze through. Jazz is in danger of popping her hazmat suit as she shimmies inside the room. Nick uses the pipe to pry the door open further.

Water pours in through the door, flooding the floor to a depth of a couple of inches. The pumps, though, are doing their job.

Rousing the jurors from their slumber is an arduous process. Some of them respond like they're drunk, slurring their words.

"We don't have time for this," Jazz says. "Get them mobile and get them into that goddamn elevator. The medics can deal with them up top."

"Understood," Nick says, walking them in twos toward the elevator. His muscles ache, but pain has never felt so good. Elizabeth helps him, holding the elevator door open.

"You? Did you see him?" Anni asks as Nick escorts her to the elevator. Given she's barely five foot four, and he's in an oversized hazmat suit, it's difficult to hear her. It's the rubberized plastic. It squeaks and squishes with each step.

He leans forward. "The crystal man?"

"Yes. He saved us."

"I don't understand," Nick says, coming to a halt in front of the elevator.

"He herded us into the room."

"Okay, we're ready to go," Adrianna says, brushing past Nick in her hazmat suit. She helps the last person into the steel cage. Several jurors slump to the floor. They sit on the grating in a daze. They're still waking from their slumber.

"I'll take the next one," Jazz says.

"We're out of oxygen," Adrianna says. "We should all go together."

Jazz has tears in her eyes. She's emphatic. "I said, I'll take the next one."

She's standing in front of a flatscreen panel beside the elevator. Father's displaying stats on the underground research center.

A week ago, Nick wouldn't have cared. Bravado makes for a nice cliché etched into a tombstone. Back then, he would have waved goodbye, pushed the button, and ridden to the surface without any regret. If asked, he would have said she's got her own free will. Jazz is an adult. She knows what she's doing. She's a soldier. Now, though, something breaks inside him. He can feel it—her grief. He may not understand why, but *mana*. Clichés be damned—they're all in this together.

Nick steps out of the elevator knowing he only has a few minutes worth of clean oxygen in his tank. Nick, you're a fool.

"Take care of them," he says to a bewildered Adrianna standing beside Anni. Nick leans in and slaps the button for *Vincennes*. The doors close as he steps back onto L4.

"What? No way," Adrianna says, jumping out into the corridor. The doors close, and the elevator rises.

"You should have gone with them," Jazz says.

"What's wrong?" Adrianna says, seeing the tears streaming down Jazz's cheeks.

Jazz points at the wall screen.

Adrianna says, "I don't understand."

Nick scans the list of names. Father's highlighted those that went into the chamber during the outage. Beside each name is the term deceased. One name catches his attention—Jon Danes.

He taps the screen. "Jon was her fiancé."

"Oh, I'm so sorry," Adrianna says.

"He wasn't supposed to be here," Jazz says, fighting back more tears. "Jon was supposed to be on rotation. He was supposed to be on R&R visiting his folks in England. He knew I was wintering here. He must have shuffled the schedule so we could be together."

"Jazz," Adrianna says. "There's nothing you can do."

"Oh," she replies, laughing through her tears. "You really don't know me, do you? There is something I can do, all right. I can end this."

"What?" Nick says. "No!"

Jazz ignores him. She grabs at the zip running diagonally across her hazmat suit, pulling it from her left shoulder to her right hip. The suit deflates. Jazz rips the mask from her face. She swings the oxygen cylinder from her back, dumping it in the ice and slush on the floor. Unlike Nick, she's wearing her boots beneath her suit, allowing her to walk away through the water.

As she steps out of her suit, Adrianna steps in front of her, stopping her, saying, "Please. Don't do anything stupid."

Jazz is cold in reply. "A word of advice, Adrianna. Don't get in my way."

A red light blinks on the valve on the side of Nick's mask. He's out of air.

"Damn it!"

Nick unzips his hazmat suit.

"No, no, no," Adrianna says. "There could be contaminants."

Nick doesn't care. He can't. He has no choice. He drops the oxygen cylinder from his shoulder. Nick ties the arms of the suit around his waist, wearing it as a pair of baggy trousers.

Jazz disappears up the stairs at the far end of the floor.

"You don't understand," Adrianna says with her hands out, trying to stop Nick. "It's not the big aliens we need to worry about. It's the little ones. The microbes."

Nick points back at the elevator, saying, "They're not dead."

"Not yet," Adrianna says. "But everyone else down here is. You don't get it. There could be pathogens in here we know nothing about."

"But you haven't found anything, right?" Nick says, turning back to her briefly as he walks after Jazz. "After months of trying, you haven't found any alien microbes."

Reluctantly, Adrianna agrees.

He points at her, saying, "What are you going to do when your air runs out?"

"Goddamn it," she says, unzipping her suit in a fit of fury. She drops her mask and oxygen cylinder and copies him, wrapping her upper suit tightly around her waist. She ties off the arms in a knot. "If something bursts out of my chest, you're the first one it's going for. You know that, right?"

Nick laughs, jogging down the corridor. Water splashes from his boots.

Jazz is up on L2. She has one M4 slung over her back and another leaning on the stairs. She checks the movement of the magazine and the latch on the grenade launcher, making sure neither has frozen in place. An ammo belt hangs over her shoulder, only the pouches are oversized. They've been stuffed with flashbangs and fragmentation grenades.

"You cannot wage war," Nick says, appealing for calm.

Jazz pulls her hair back into a ponytail.

"I'm going to get him back," she says. "No one and nothing is going to stop me."

"These are creatures from some other world," Adrianna says. "Hell, we don't know what they are. For all we know, they're machines. You can't kill something that's not alive."

Jazz transfers M4 magazines full of ammo into a lightweight backpack. She shoves a couple of scrunched-up body bags into her pack, working with her fist against the thick rubberized plastic.

"We're not leaving anyone down here," she says, fighting back tears. "Not Jon. Not Bear. Not those poor saps we found floating in the water. No one. Do you hear me?"

"Okay, so we go back up in the elevator and bring a recovery crew down here," Adrianna says.

Jazz replies, "You and I both know that's not going to happen. Mikhail isn't going to let anyone else back down here before spring. By then, this whole place will have frozen over. No. We're here now. We do it. We collect the bodies and stack them by the elevator."

"And if we run into trouble?" Nick asks.

"Leave that to me."

Adrianna says, "You know this is like a villager going up against a nuclear-powered aircraft carrier in a rickety wooden canoe, right?"

Jazz doesn't care.

"They're thousands of years more advanced than us," Adrianna says. "I doubt our weapons would even scratch that craft."

Nick says, "And what if there are, I dunno... Things? Monsters? Aliens?"

"Do you see this?" Jazz asks in reply. She holds up a thick, curved metal plate. "This is an M18A1 Claymore. *Alien* would have been a helluva lot shorter movie if they'd carried a few of these bad boys on the *Nostromo*."

"This is madness," Adrianna says.

"I didn't start this," Jazz says. "But I sure as hell will end it." She points at the wall of ice leading to the airlock at the bottom of the stairs. "I'm only going in there for the bodies. If they let us retrieve our dead, it's all good. If they want a fight, I'll give them one."

"Jazz, please," Nick says. "This is an intelligent species."

"That killed at least two dozen scientists, soldiers, and engineers. And indirectly killed at least forty more topside when it fried their brain cells!"

"We don't know what happened in there," Adrianna says, pointing at the airlock leading to the subterranean lake.

Jazz hoists a pack over one shoulder and picks up the spare M4.

"Well, let's go and find out."

CONTACT

Machinery whirs around them. Clunks resound through the walls of the airlock. The overhead light fades to dim red as the air pressure increases.

Adrianna says, "Try to yawn. You need to equalize the pressure in your ears."

Jazz winds the handle on the outer hatch. She pushes on the steel plate. Hinges creak. With her M4 out in front of her, she steps forward, pointing the barrel into the darkness.

"No light?"

"Must have lost power," Adrianna replies in a whisper.

"Can you restore it?"

"I don't know. I can try."

"What's the layout?" Jazz asks, turning on a flashlight mounted on the side of her M4.

"Ah," Adrianna says. "You're on the edge of a lake that varies in depth from 100 to just over 350 meters. It's roughly two kilometers wide and thirty kilometers long. It links to dozens of other similar subsurface lakes. The cavern we're in is on the southeast shore. We're in an open area that spans roughly a football field, but most of that is covered by the lake. There's a thin strip of bedrock running to your left. Follow that."

Nick steps over the edge of the airlock. A thin sheet of ice breaks under his boots, giving way to the rocks beneath. Adrianna reaches out for him, holding onto his shoulder as she steps down into the darkness.

She follows close behind him, saying, "Watch your step."

The darkness doesn't scare Nick. He's always been able to separate the fear of the unknown from the empty darkness. Why be afraid if there's nothing out there? Only this time, there is something out there. This time, it's something from another world. This time, it's already killed a helluva lot of people. He swallows the lump rising in his throat.

Jazz is already thirty feet ahead of them, leaving the two of them to feel their way in the darkness. Her flashlight illuminates dead spotlights mounted on aluminum stands. She follows the wires running along the ground to an industrial battery pack the size of a desk.

"Plenty of juice," she says. "They must have blown the lights."

As his eyes adjust to the dark, Nick notices something blue in the water. There's a shimmer on the edge of his vision like that of a faint neon sign.

"What's that?"

"Bioluminescence," Adrianna says. She crouches, running her hand through the water. A blue shimmer trails behind her fingers.

"That's normal?"

"Perfectly," she replies. "In a world without light, you have to create your own."

"And that's from—from Earth, right?"

"Yes. We see this everywhere from Tasmania to Hawaii. Most of the time, it's overlooked because we're too busy shining streetlights and headlights everywhere, but this has been around for hundreds of millions of years."

Rocks crunch softly beneath his boots. "What causes it?"

"Bacteria. It gets incorporated into plankton, jellyfish, even squid. They use bacteria to create a cold light. There's even a species of shrimp down here that vomits light."

"It vomits light?"

"Oh, yeah."

"Why on Earth would anything do that?" Nick asks, watching as water drips from Adrianna's fingers. The point at which each drop hits the lake glows in a soft, neon blue. It's as though the water has been electrified.

"Oh, light can attract mates or confuse predators. There are lots of reasons to glow. Camouflage. Enticing prey."

"But you said those tiny fish back there were blind," he says as they walk on around the edge of the lake.

"They are. That's all the more reason for these things to give off light. It's like passing notes in class knowing the teacher can't see you."

The more his eyes adjust to the ambient light, the better he can see. A blue glow laps at the rocks around the edge of the lake. Above them, the ice isn't quite as dark as he first imagined. It catches some of the glow, casting it back at them.

Long, dark legs pass through the water, casting shadows. Thin spikes cling to the rocks barely a foot beneath the surface.

"What the hell is that?" Nick asks, stepping back and pointing.

Adrianna scoops up a handful of water and sprinkles it across the surface of the lake, causing a soft glow. A spider-like crab, easily four feet in length, holds still, watching for movement. After a few seconds, it creeps along the rock face below the water's edge, disappearing back into the depths.

"Jesus," Nick whispers. "And that doesn't scare you?"

"No. It's not after me. I'm not a fish."

"This shit is freaking me out."

"This shit, as you so aptly put it, is nature."

Further along, part of the ceiling has collapsed, scattering frozen blue/white ice on the dark bedrock. The two of them pick their way over the rubble. Ahead, Jazz sets up a couple of claymore mines on a boulder of ice the size of an SUV.

"What are you doing?" Adrianna asks.

"Think of it as an insurance policy."

"You can't fire explosives in here. The pressure surge could cause the cave to collapse. We'd be buried under a mile of ice!"

"We should be so lucky," Jazz replies, linking the claymores together.

"I'm serious."

"So am I. Don't worry, doc. This is just a contingency."

The gap between the boulder and the shoreline is barely a foot wide. Nick pushes his back against the ice as he shimmies past. Something moves in the water. Something big. Twenty feet below the surface, something glows. It swims along beside them before retreating into the shadows.

"Did you see that?" Nick asks.

"Don't start," Adrianna says, not impressed with either of them.

"Does any of this seem strange to you?" Jazz asks, flashing her light across the rocky ground as it curves around the lake.

Nick replies, "All of this seems strange to me. What I want to know is, what seems normal to you?"

"Nothing. That's the problem."

"What were you expecting?" Adrianna asks, coming up beside Jazz.

"Bodies."

Jazz waves her M4 around. The flashlight illuminates dark bloodstains on the ice.

Under his breath, Nick mumbles, "Fuck."

Jazz follows the trail. Smeared frozen red blood leads down to the dark water.

"Are you thinking what I'm thinking?" Jazz asks Adrianna.

"God, I hope not," Adrianna replies as the water is disturbed roughly forty feet from shore. They step back, staying away from the edge of the lake.

Quietly, Jazz asks, "Where's the spaceship?"

"Uh, it's another hundred yards that way."

"We're not going to make it," Jazz says.

"What? Why?" Nick asks, hating the darkness around him. Spotlights. Right now, he'd love nothing more than to flick the switch on a set of massive floodlights. For once, the darkness terrifies him.

Jazz replies under her breath.

"We're being hunted."

Jazz pulls a grenade from her ammo belt and slips it into the launcher mounted beneath her M4. She moves slowly, trying not to make any sudden moves or too much noise.

"By what?" Nick asks.

"I don't know, but don't get too close to the water."

Nick looks around. There's barely ten feet of rocky ground between the ice wall and the lake. What the hell constitutes too close? As soon as Jazz said that, Nick was ready to put a couple of miles between himself and this goddamn cesspool. He reaches for the ice, running his hand along the frozen surface. He has to crouch to stay close to the wall.

"What's down there?" Jazz asks Adrianna. "Could it be alien?"

"I—I don't know. I don't think so. We did hundreds of samples. We never once came back with anything other than terrestrial DNA. There were a few previously undocumented species of bacteria. We were able to identify trace amounts of fecal matter from animals like shrimp and squid, but they're all related to known species topside. Nothing extraterrestrial."

A splash of water echoes through the cavern. Waves ripple against the rocks, glowing as they reach the shore.

"Something's in the water," Jazz says, peeling the flashlight from the side of her M4. Nick can hear the sound of duct tape being pulled loose and it terrifies him.

Jazz hands Adrianna the flashlight. "You and Nick continue on. I'll lag behind. That'll allow me to flank whatever that thing is."

"What?" Nick says in alarm. "We're the bait?"

"Since you put it like that," Jazz says, smiling in the half-light. "Go. I've got you covered."

"I am not liking this," he replies, staying well away from the water. The glacial ice meets the bedrock at about waist height. In close to the wall, the ceiling of the cavern is barely five feet high, forcing him to bend over as he inches on. His hand remains in contact with the ice, trailing along the smooth surface as rocks crunch softly beneath his boots.

Adrianna flashes the light around, running it over the waves, but that hurts rather than helps their night vision. Immediately afterward, nothing is visible beyond the gloom.

"Keep the flashlight off the water and on the rocks," Jazz says. "Pretend you haven't noticed."

"We really are bait," Adrianna mumbles in the darkness.

"We're gonna die," Nick says.

"Great," Adrianna says. Sarcasm hangs from her lips. "Thank you for that astute observation."

Nick gets more nervous with each step. He's sweating in the cold. His fingers tremble. His rubber boots feel like lead weights. He's got to say something, if only to keep his mind turning over.

"Where does all this water go?"

Adrianna says, "This lake is part of a maze of interconnected ravines and lakes hidden beneath the ice sheet. It's a network bigger than the Grand Canyon. We know so little about what lives down here."

"What did you expect down here?" he asks.

"Microbes," she replies. "Nothing like those fish or that crab."

"What else could have made it down here?"

"I don't know, but it would have been trapped here for a helluva long time. Four hundred thousand years is plenty of time for natural selection to come up with a few oddballs."

In the quiet of the cave, even a whisper travels hundreds of yards.

"We've got this all wrong," Adrianna says softly. "There are three of us down here."

Nick's confused. "Of course there are. You, me, and Jazz."

"No," Adrianna says, peering out at the glow on the water. "Us, that alien spacecraft, and them."

"Them?" Nick says as water swirls near the shore.

"An entire ecosystem full of predators and prey."

Blue lights flicker on the waves.

Adrianna sounds nervous. "Umm, I'm not so sure the blackout was intended for us."

"What do you mean?" Nick asks, no longer interested in seeing an alien spacecraft. Right now, he'd like to see the inside of that elevator again.

"That was a threat response, only we never threatened it. We were observers."

Before he can say anything, there's a splash of water out in the deep. Bioluminescence lights up the spray. Waves rush in toward the shore.

"What was that?" Adrianna asks.

"It was big," Nick replies. "That's what it was."

From the darkness somewhere behind them, Jazz speaks. The way her voice carries, Nick could swear she was next to them, but she's not.

"If shit goes down, hit the deck and douse your light."

"Got it," Adrianna says.

The ledge narrows, forcing them near the water's edge.

"Sweet Jesus," Nick says, backing up against the ice. "Did you see that?"

"See what?"

"An eyeball," Nick replies. Panic seizes him. "In the water. An eye the size of a basketball racing along beneath the surface. Watching us."

"Exactly what did you see?"

"A big, black, long thing with big-ass eyes."

"If you could be more specific," Adrianna says, reaching out and resting her hand on his forearm.

"You think I'm mad, don't you?" Nick says a little too loud. "You think I'm making this up. I didn't imagine that."

"No, it's just—"

The water beside them explodes, showering the bedrock and ice with spray—blue phosphorescence rains down on them. Out of the darkness, tentacles lash through the air. Adrianna drops the flashlight. It rolls into the water. Immediately, it's grabbed by a long, thin, flexible arm and dragged into the depths.

Nick and Adrianna lie flat on the rocks, soaking wet.

Tentacles strike around them, searching the foreshore. Rocks are dragged back into the water. An eerie blue glow fills the cavern.

"I see you," Jazz yells, lighting a red flare. Pungent smoke cascades from the burning tip. A blood-red glow reflects off the water. Jazz is roughly eighty yards away, back by the collapsed ceiling. "You wanna dance? I'm over here, big boy."

"Run," Adrianna yells at her.

Jazz drops the flare at her feet. She's not going anywhere. She backs up against the ice boulder at the narrowest point on the path.

Waves roll into the shore, kicking up hints of bioluminescence, but the creature is gone. A blue trail follows its wake as it swims beneath the water, racing toward Jazz.

"You can't kill that thing," Adrianna says, getting to her feet. "It's too big."

"The hell I can't."

Jazz is illuminated by the eerie red light coming off the flare. Clouds of smoke surround her, hiding her boots from view. She holds a wide stance, scanning the water as she peers through the night-vision scope on her M4.

"She'll be okay," Nick says, hoping rather than knowing that.

"No, she won't," Adrianna replies. "The water—her shots won't go more than a few feet. They'll splinter and deflect when they hit the water. Within five feet, they'll be nothing more than pebbles sinking to the bottom. She's not going to hit a goddamn thing."

If Jazz knows this, she doesn't care. She fires a burst of three rounds into the lake, barely fifteen feet from where she's standing. Water is kicked up by each thundering impact. The spray glows with neon-blue bioluminescence. The report from each shot is deafening. Chunks of ice fall from the ceiling.

"No, no, no," Adrianna mumbles, sheltering beside Nick. "She's going to bring the cave down on us."

Silence descends on the cavern. In the quiet, Nick dares to believe it's over. Whatever that creature was, it must sense the raw power standing on shore. Perhaps the shockwave from the bullets scared it away. As the seconds pass, he breathes a little easier.

Jazz pushes her back against the ice, crouching as she surveys the smooth, dark surface of the lake. Before she can react, a tentacle erupts from the water, lashing out at her M4. The rifle is ripped from her hands.

"It's a squid," Adrianna whispers.

"A what?" Nick replies.

"Giant squid!"

Jazz has her Glock out. She fires several shots, but her bullets are no match for an animal the size of a school bus. As if it senses how vulnerable she is, the creature rises from the deep. Thick arms reach through the air, surrounding her. Suckers squirm, threatening to attack. Jazz ignores them, keeping her gun trained on the body of the animal as it floats just below the surface. A large, bulbous eye examines her. Tentacles wave around her. They're longer and thinner than the arms, with thick pads at each end. In the flickering light of the flare, they look utterly alien—only they're not. Water drips from the arms as they sway.

Jazz growls, "Come on, you asshole!"

Behind her, the creature's arms grab at the boulder, rocking it off the ground, cutting off any means of escape. To Nick's horror, Jazz steps forward. Her boots splash in the water.

She holsters her sidearm, yelling, "What the hell are you waiting for?"

Bubbles rise to the surface. The creature positions itself in front of her. It might have missed Adrianna and Nick. It's not going to miss Jazz.

The lake explodes as the animal launches itself out of the depths. Water erupts from around the squid, soaking the shoreline. The aquatic creature rises from the lake. It opens its circular mouth, rushing in toward the boulder. A massive, sharp beak snaps at the air.

Jazz drops into the water below the creature. She has a clacker in her hand. It's a small device that looks like an oversized switch. With her hand above her head, she plunges beneath the waves.

Both Adrianna and Nick have their hands over their ears.

From beneath the water, Jazz squeezes the clacker, firing the claymores. Three synchronized explosions rip outward through the cavern. Fire erupts from the ice. Each antipersonnel mine releases seven hundred steel ball bearings at over a thousand feet per second. Blisteringly hot metal screams through the cavern, perforating the arms and tentacles of the squid. Chunks of flesh are torn from the creature.

Slabs of ice fall from the ceiling, crashing into the water, sending waves racing across the lake. Within seconds, it's over. The acrid smell of explosives chokes the air. Smoke hangs low over the lake. The flare dies. An eerie blue gloom descends. Severed tentacles float on the surface of the lake. Black ink seeps across the water.

Adrianna runs toward the shattered boulder. Jazz grabs at the rocks along the shoreline. Nick reaches in, helping her out of the icy cold water. His ears are still ringing, making it difficult to hear.

"Are you okay?"

"Fine."

Jazz shivers as she crouches by the edge of the lake. She clings her arms around her, trying to warm herself.

Adrianna is in a daze. She lifts a shredded length of squid up, holding it out before them. Suckers pulse on the arm, reluctant to die.

"Calamari, anyone?"

"Not funny," Nick says.

"Really not funny," Jazz says, dripping wet. "What the hell

was that?"

"*Mesonychoteuthis*," Adrianna says. "The Antarctic Colossal Squid. We picked up DNA samples in the water, but I didn't think it would be that big. Or that aggressive. A big old boy like that only thinks about two things—sex and food."

Jazz laughs. "I guess I should be grateful it was hungry and not horny."

"This air pocket probably served as a hunting ground for it."

"Is it dead?" Nick asks, looking out at the still water on the lake.

"Probably not."

"Damn," Jazz says.

"It'll be back," Adrianna says, dropping the severed limb on the ground. "We've got to get you out of here."

"Wait," Nick says, seeing movement on the lake.

From out of the haze, a watery figure approaches. At first, only his head is visible above the surface of the lake, then his shoulders, arms, and torso. The alien figure rises out of the water as he approaches the shore. Blue bioluminescence sparkles around him, lighting up his arms and legs. Tiny fish swim within his torso.

"What the hell?" Adrianna says as the man comes to a halt a few feet from the rocks.

"It's okay," Nick says. "This is the crystal man."

CRYSTAL MAN

"So A—Anni? And Elizabeth?" Jazz says, kneeling on the rocks, trembling in the cold.

"Yes," Nick replies. "They saw him in the research center."

"And you?" Adrianna asks. Her words are followed by a fine vapor in the frigid air.

Nick is relieved rather than scared. "Me? I thought I was going mad."

Adrianna steps over the rocks, peering carefully at the watery shape. She examines his legs, his arms and hands, pointing in astonishment. A blue tinge in the water causes the apparition to glow.

"Not possible."

"B—B," Jazz says, shivering uncontrollably. "Beau—Bee. B—Beautiful."

"It's not beautiful," Adrianna says. "It's not even alive. This isn't real. At best, it's a projection—a distraction." She turns her attention to Jazz. "We cannot stay here. That water is a shade under three degrees. We have got to get you out of here."

Adrianna crouches in front of Jazz, turning her back on the crystal man. She straightens her up, pulling at her jacket, wanting to get it off her. "We need to get you back inside the base and get you into dry clothing."

"B—But." Jazz points at the shimmering blue figure.

"No buts." Adrianna peals the soaking wet jacket from Jazz, tugging it free of her arms. "He's not going anywhere, right? He can wait. You can't. You'll die from hypothermia if we don't do something."

Nick's unsure if it's the soft light, but Jazz looks pale. Her skin is turning blue.

"Wait," he says. "Look."

The ghostly figure crouches within a foot of the shore, pointing at Jazz. The alien is matching her gesture, holding his finger a few inches from hers.

"Whoa," Adrianna says, shifting on the rough gravel.

Jazz leans forward, still holding her gloved finger out.

Adrianna says, "I'm not sure you want to do that."

Nick is shaking, but not because of the cold. Jazz touches the luminescent watery finger. A blue tinge runs down her arm. Within seconds, it envelops her entire body. Then it retreats as quickly as it came.

"What the?" Adrianna says.

"I'm dry," Jazz says in surprise. She withdraws her finger as the watery man stands upright again. "How is that possible? I— I'm still damn cold, but my skin, my clothing—they're dry."

"I don't under—" Adrianna turns to Nick. "What exactly did you see inside the research center?"

"Ah, it followed me. It was interested in what I was doing with the pumps. It didn't look like this, though. It wasn't blue. It was just water. Back there, it looked like a see-through store-front mannequin brought to life."

"And?"

"And it pointed at the room with the jurors. When we were on L3, it pointed at the room down on L4."

Adrianna steps in front of the glowing figure, matching its

posture and asking, "Do you understand me? My words?"

"I don't get it," Jazz says, getting to her feet when there's no reply. "If that thing is from outer space, why does it look like us?"

"It doesn't," Adrianna says. "This is mimicry. It's adopting a shape we'll recognize—something to lower our stress levels. You know, like a zookeeper dressing up as a panda or a wildlife camera operator wearing a penguin suit."

"So it thinks we're dumb?" Jazz asks.

"Less intelligent," Adrianna says. "Easily fooled. It thinks it's dealing with animals. From its perspective, it is. It's treating us the way we'd treat a chimp. It knows there's at least some intelligence. It's trying to assess how much. I think it's worried about freaking us out."

She holds out her arm, moving her hand in a vast circular motion involving her forearm, elbow, and shoulder. It's as though she's cleaning a window. Although the watery man has none of these joints, being nothing more than a shell, he copies her motion with precision.

Nick asks, "What the hell are we dealing with, doc?"

"A communication gap. It's copying us, trying to figure us out. See the way it moves its mouth as though it's trying to speak? It probably doesn't realize we rely on sound waves. It thinks we read lips."

"So it's trying to say something?" Nick asks.

"It knew I was cold," Jazz says.

"It must have sensed your body temperature dropping outside the range it normally observes."

"This is amazing," Nick says, leaning over the water and taking a good look from the side. A tiny jellyfish darts up within the column of water forming a human shape. Neon blue tentacles pulse, driving it on. Thin strands glow, dangling below the gelatinous blob. The jellyfish is oblivious to where it is.

"This isn't them," Adrianna says. "This isn't what they look like. This is a projection—an attempt to appeal to our reason."

"Why?" Jazz asks. "What do they want?"

"To get the hell out of here."

As if in response to what Adrianna said, the cavern lights up. In the distance, the thin edge of the spaceship glows in a rainbow of colors.

"See that?" Adrianna says, pointing. "They don't know how much light we can see, so they're circling through the spectrum."

"So are we?" Nick asks.

"Are we what?" Jazz asks.

"Are we going to let them out of here?"

"Whoa," Jazz says, holding her hands out and signaling they should slow things down. "Is that really what's happening here?"

"Yes," Adrianna says. "Look!"

The watery humanoid holds up an index finger on one hand and both his index and middle finger on the other. Slowly, he brings them together. All three fingers point at the icy ceiling.

"What the hell does that mean?" Nick asks.

"One plus two equals three?" Jazz says. "Is he teaching us to count?"

"It's not counting," Adrianna says. "Communicating, remember? It wants us to understand something about the number three."

"Is this like preschool for aliens?" Jazz asks. "Start with a little basic arithmetic?"

"I don't know."

Adrianna holds up her right hand, raising three fingers in a Girl Scout salute. The transparent man pulls his hands apart, holding them out wide. Slowly, he brings his hands together again. One finger raised on one hand. Two fingers on the other.

"Okay, it's not the number three," Adrianna says. "It's one

thing made up of two parts."

"One and two," Jazz says. "But not three."

Nick rubs his head. "Oh, man. I am so confused."

Jazz says, "They must think they're dealing with a bunch of idiots."

"They are."

Adrianna says, "Whatever this is, it's something they need from us. It's something they're confident we can figure out."

"They've seen us at work, right?" Jazz says. "They've seen our subsurface base. They know at least a little bit about what we're capable of accomplishing. I mean, digging through a mile of ice and all."

"Yes," Adrianna says. "They know we have machines and that we can harness electricity to drive our technology. They've got to be communicating within the bounds of what they think we'll understand. I doubt he's signaling something about dark matter or string theory. Whatever he means, it's something we can understand with our current level of tech."

"So one plus two is something other than three," Nick says.

"One and two," Adrianna replies. "Forget about three."

"What the hell is one and two if not three?"

"I dunno."

As if he can sense their confusion, the blue facsimile of a man gestures with one hand. He keeps his two fingers still, while moving the other away until it reaches arm's length. He repeats the motion a few times.

"Three minus one is two," Nick says, shaking his head. "That's all I'm getting out of this."

"Wait," Jazz says, watching him repeat his movement. "Perhaps his motion is intentional. One can move, but two can't. Two stay still."

"One moves, two remain," Nick says. "Is he talking about us? Does he want one of us to leave?"

"No, that's not it," Adrianna says. "Why is one in motion while the other two aren't?"

"They're different," Jazz says. "Whatever one is, it's not the same as two."

"Yes," Adrianna says. "One is affected by an external force. The other two aren't."

"So they're neutral?" Nick asks.

Adrianna copies the glowing man, but she moves one finger in several directions. She keeps two of her fingers still, while raising the other, lowering it, and even passing it in front of the others.

The watery figure repeats his motion, ignoring the different directions. He only ever moves his finger one way.

"It only ever goes left," Nick says.

"Right, from his perspective," Adrianna says.

"Oh," Jazz says, getting frustrated. "I know what this is. These are giraffes. Each finger is a long-neck giraffe."

"Penguins," Nick says. "We're in Antarctica. They've got to be penguins."

Jazz counters with, "Caterpillars. Worms."

Adrianna does not look impressed.

"Come on," Jazz says in her defense, throwing her arms wide. "Three fingers could represent anything. Bananas. Birds. You name it."

"But they don't," Adrianna insists. "They represent something simple. Three simple things with a simple, clear distinction between them. Notice how he only ever moves his finger in one direction. That's deliberate. There's got to be a simple explanation, we're just missing it."

"We're talking to an alien," Nick says, feeling exasperated.

"There's nothing simple about this. I mean, look at him. He's playing a game of charades without any categories. His fingers could describe anything. Those could be three churros, but only one gets dipped in chocolate."

"And yet it's not," Adrianna insists. "He's using a simple form of communication because he knows this is simple. Think about it. We're complicating this. Not him. We have to simplify our thinking. What's the simplest thing you can make something out of?"

Off the top of his head, Nick says, "LEGO."

"Why?"

"Because it's a kid's toy. They're just a bunch of blocks but you can make anything out of them."

"Oh," Adrianna says. "Now we're getting somewhere. And what's the simplest thing in the universe? What's our equivalent of LEGOs?"

Jazz shrugs. She says a tentative, "Atoms?"

Adrianna has a glazed look in her eyes. She stares past them, lost in thought.

"That's it!" Adrianna copies the motion of the crystal man, holding three fingers up and moving one away from the others. "It's an atom. It's made up of one proton and two neutrons. The proton can be influenced by an electromagnetic field, but not the neutrons. In his example, they stay where they are."

"What?" Jazz says.

"Wait," Adrianna says. "What's the atomic number for oxygen?"

"Oxygen?" Nick asks, surprised by the notion.

"You're asking us?" Jazz says, pointing at the two of them.

"Is it eight or ten?" Adrianna asks.

"Seriously," Jazz says. "You think either of us know that?"

"Eight," Nick says. He smiles at Jazz, adding, "High school

chemistry. It was the one class I didn't sleep through."

Adrianna reaches down and cups some water in her hands. Slowly, she lets it drip in front of the shimmering figure.

"Okay, let's see if this works."

Adrianna holds up a single finger on each hand, keeping her hands separate. Then she lowers her hands and brings them together, holding four fingers up on each hand. Now, though, instead of having her hands next to each other, she puts her wrists on top of each other, interlacing her fingers.

"I need this thing to understand the number eight."

"Eight protons," Nick says. "Oxygen."

"Yeah. Forget about neutrons for a moment," she whispers, repeating her motion. "Let's talk about water. Two hydrogen atoms and one oxygen atom. Come on. H_2O. You're made out of water. You must understand it as a molecule."

The transparent watery figure copies her. It crouches, scoops up some water, and lets it drip from its fingers. Then it holds up one finger on each hand.

"That's it," Adrianna whispers. "Two hydrogen atoms. Now oxygen. Show me oxygen."

Rather than tucking in its transparent thumbs, they disappear. The four fingers on each hand become eight, which is jarring to behold. The watery man holds his hands together, displaying sixteen fingers in all.

"Oh, that's cheating," she says. "But yes. Eight protons, eight neutrons. Okay, smarty pants. I couldn't do that, but yep, that's a water molecule."

"So we're speaking the same language?" Jazz asks, getting excited.

"Yes."

The watery hands return to normal, and the creature repeats its earlier motion, holding up a single finger and bringing two fingers on the other hand up next to it. Again, one finger is pulled away from the others.

"Okay, so we've got one proton and two neutrons," Adrianna says.

"That's hydrogen, right?" Nick asks.

"Tritium," Adrianna says. "It's an isotope of hydrogen. He's telling us they use tritium to power their spacecraft. They must run that thing on fusion. That's what they need. He's asking us for tritium."

"And they can't just get that down here?" Jazz asks.

"No," Adrianna says. "Tritium is rare. And it doesn't last long. Its half-life is something ridiculously short, like ten or twelve years. I'm pretty sure it's only made high in the atmosphere or in outer space. They must be starved of it down here."

Jazz changes the tone of the discussion.

"We need to get out of here—now!"

"But we've only just started talking," Adrianna says.

"You don't understand. We have tritium."

"What? Here in Antarctica?"

"Yes."

"I don't get it?" Adrianna says. "Why would we have tritium at *Vincennes*?"

Jazz looks her in the eye, saying, "It's in the bomb."

JURY DUTY

The storm is getting worse.

The wind howls across the frozen plateau.

Snow races past the windows, being caught in the spotlights for a moment before disappearing into the darkness.

After descending through the ice, wading through a flooded research center, and then creeping along a darkened cavern next to a subterranean lake, it's strange to be back up top. For Nick, it's as though he's teleported between worlds. Reality is a blur. He longs to return to the Earth he never left. Antarctica is a helluva long way from South Carolina. He might as well be on Mars. Or Hoth.

Outside, someone crosses from the maintenance building. They're tethered to a guide wire, but they're struggling to make any headway against the wind. Whoever it is, they've got their hood down. Ski goggles hide their eyes. Gloved hands pull on the wire. With each step, their legs disappear into the haze of snow and ice whipping past low to the ground. Nick doesn't want to go back out there any time soon. It's depressing to think spring is still months away. Even with heavy over-trousers and thick gloves, the hurricane-like winds pick up loose shards of ice, hurling them at arms and legs. Even a glancing blow stings.

Air circulates from floor grates within the building. Initially, it's warm, but that doesn't last. Most of the jury have their down-filled vests on.

"Look, I get it," Nick says, walking to the front of the room. "No one wants to be here."

There's plenty of latitude as to what he means by *here*.

Here in Antarctica. Here at *Vincennes*. Here in the auditorium as part of the jury. Here as in having escaped death beneath the ice and wondering if it's all about to happen again.

Nick flicks through his orientation binder. Hundreds of pages pass beneath his fingertips. He's looking for the biographical outline of the jurors. From memory, it's an appendix. His hand rests on a page full of photographs. He looks around, trying to match faces with names.

Someone says, "I just want to sleep."

Jazz says, "There'll be time for sleep later. Right now, we have a problem—and I'm not talking about an alien spacecraft stuck beneath the ice. Your responsibility has changed."

"How so?"

"Father, explain the purpose of *Vincennes*."

From the speakers in the ceiling, a disembodied electronic voice speaks.

"*Vincennes was established on the principle of maritime law to avoid jurisdictional conflicts arising between member states of the United Nations Security Council. The extraterrestrial vessel was declared a derelict. Recovery was governed by the agreed laws of oceanic salvage.*"

Jazz asks, "Why is that no longer the case, Father?"

"*The presence of an intelligent life-form indicates ownership. In such a case, salvage rights extend over cargo but not the vessel itself. This also changes the status of the operation from recovery to rescue.*"

"No *fucking* way," the Frenchman Jacques Lamar says.

"I say we nuke it," Bradley Hoggard says, but he's British.

He can't pull off an American accent. He's being a smartass. Everyone's seen the movie *Aliens*. Oh, yeah, that's funny, Brad. Dust off and nuke it from orbit. It's the only way to be sure, right? Julia might nod in agreement, but no one else is impressed.

Nick scans the profile page. Each of the five permanent members of the United Nations Security Council has two representatives on the jury. Nick matches faces to names as he reviews each background.

China

• Bao Xi, an English Teacher at Hubei Central High School.

• Anni Azizi, a villager from the Uyghur region in north west China.

Russia

• Petrovich Andrey Vavilov, a railway engineer from Moscow.

• Kalai Noyan, a goat farmer from Lake Baikai (Siberia/Mongolia).

France

• Jacques Lamar, a dentist from Riems.

• Samira Ayoub, a shop assistant from Toulouse (Moroccan descent).

United Kingdom

• Bradley Hoggard, an accountant from Milton Keynes.

• Julia Duffie, a barmaid from Armagh in Northern Ireland.

United States of America

• ~~Chad Smith, a television producer from Atlanta, Georgia.~~ Deceased.

• ~~Ebony Chambers, a fitness instructor from Pine Bluff, Arkansas~~. Deceased.

Chad Smith died from a pulmonary embolism a day before the blackout. Ebony died in the subsurface base. She was one of the bodies shoved into an empty room. That leaves only one juror representing the US—Nick. America only gets one vote.

Jazz says, "That storm out there isn't likely to subside for months. With the main antenna down, we're cut off from the outside world. We can get messages out through the Russians over at *Vostok*, but it's basic stuff. There's no way to transmit scientific data."

Julia asks, "What about the spacecraft?"

"With confirmation of an active extraterrestrial intelligence, Father has instructed Mikhail to lock down the main shaft. Any decision to continue has to be endorsed by the jury."

"You want to go back down there?" Bao Xi says, pointing at the snow and ice whipping past the window. "Are you mad?"

"We need to help them," Adrianna says. "We have no right to plunder their spacecraft."

"You have no right to be in here," Bao replies, indignant. "You're a scientist, not a juror. You must leave."

"She's not going anywhere," Nick says, holding out his hands and appealing for calm.

"Who put you in charge?" Bao asks, pointing at him.

"No one."

"Then why should we listen to you?"

"You shouldn't," Nick says. "You should listen to her." He points at the frail, elderly woman sitting beside Bao.

Anni Azizi shrinks in her seat. She really doesn't want to be here, regardless of how here is defined.

Nick is blunt.

"If it wasn't for Anni, we wouldn't be having this discussion. We'd all be dead."

Nick stares directly at Brad. There's no time for subtlety. "If it wasn't for Anni, you'd have got your precious thermonuclear explosion, and the world would have one helluva mess on its hands."

Jazz says, "We don't even know if a nuke would damage this thing. Hell, it can fly between stars. It's survived under a mile of ice for hundreds of thousands of years. Would one of our nukes even scratch the paintwork?"

Bao turns to Anni and speaks rapidly in Chinese.

"No," Jazz says, marching up the aisle toward them. She has one hand on her sidearm and the other outstretched toward Bao, signaling for him to stop. "There will be no private discussions. This is a jury setting. If you have something to say, say it to everyone."

Anni looks at Jazz with tears in her eyes.

"Whatever he said, it's not true. Do you understand?" Jazz beckons for Anni to join her. "You're safe. We're going to make it out of here alive, okay? You did the right thing down there. Keep doing what you think is right."

Anni takes her hand. Jazz leads the frail old woman to a seat at the front of the room. Bao is fuming, but he remains silent. His eyes speak of murderous rage.

Nick looks down at the profile page. Anni is eighty-four. She comes from a family of twelve and has nine children, forty-seven grandchildren, twenty-nine great-grandchildren, and two great-great-grandchildren. What the hell is she doing in Antarctica?

Anni is wearing a traditional, ornate, Muslim headscarf,

hiding her hair from sight. Her skin is dark and wrinkled.

She smiles at Nick, appreciating his support. Anni adjusts her headscarf, making sure any stray strands of hair are tucked away. That seems to antagonize Bao.

"You want us to listen to her?" Bao asks. "Look at her. She's a peasant. She's a religious old fool. She knows nothing of spaceships and aliens."

"She's the only one that kept her mind intact down there," Adrianna says. "You might think she's weak, but she was the strongest among us."

Bao folds his hands across his chest, smarting at that remark. He tucks his chin down. He's a volcano caught between eruptions.

Nick laughs.

Staring at the list, he finally understands. The whole damn thing is a joke.

"What's so funny?" Bao asks through gritted teeth.

"The jury."

Jazz looks worried. She stares at Nick with a furrowed brow. If she could, she'd say something, but it seems she doesn't want to be too vocal in front of everyone else.

"What do you find funny?" Jacques asks.

"Don't you get it?" Nick says. "It's been staring you in the face all this time—the jury itself!"

Brad says, "We're here to represent our countries."

"Are we?" Nick asks, raising an eyebrow. "I thought we were here to represent all of humanity. Or is all this just a show?"

No one speaks.

"It's the list that gives it away." He taps the thick pages in his binder. "Do you know what I think?"

Bao is acidic in his reply. He snarls. "No one wants to know what you think."

"Exactly," Nick says, pointing at him. "And yet, here I am—on the jury along with you."

Bao is quiet, but it's apparent Nick's comment stung. Bao gets it. Whether he likes it or not, they're in this for the same damn reason.

Nick sets down the binder. "I think the jury started out as a good idea. When news of this discovery first broke, someone somewhere was sent scrambling trying to figure out how the hell this could be managed on a global stage. They knew nations would bicker. Damn, are we good at that. They knew the small guy would be ignored. Again, we are so *fucking* good at stepping on the little guy. That insight was a no-brainer.

"They debated who they could trust. Governments? Hah! They're driven by too many conflicting ideologies. What about the military? Hell, no. They're lapdogs. They'll do whatever they're told. How about religious leaders? Nope. There are too many of them and they never agree. What about scientists? Meh. Too sterile. No heart. No emotion."

Adrianna glares at him with a raised eyebrow. Hey, this isn't his logic. He's trying to walk through someone else's reasoning.

"Every combination they came up with revolved around an elite group. Class systems have done us no favors over the centuries, so they settled on the idea of an impartial jury of peers. With the best of intentions, they wanted to give the everyday man and woman a say in these decisions.

"It sounds good in theory, right? But there are lots of problems with this concept. How big should the jury be? How are jurors selected? At random? From a pool? Who has the right to challenge selection?

"The biggest problem was, how could the jury be structured so decisions could actually be reached. The last thing anyone wanted was to drown this discovery in a quagmire of indecision.

"Although the idea of a jury was embraced, I bet the initial recommendation was ignored. How do I know that? Simple. There's no way two people could ever represent an entire country. But then could ten? Twenty? A hundred? Ten thousand? It seems the jury was a great idea destined to fail.

"And then there's the countries involved. It makes sense to limit this to the permanent members of the UN Security Council as that follows historical precedence. It also keeps the jury manageable. At least, that's what they told themselves. The reality is, it makes the whole notion of a jury a farce. What about India or Indonesia? Or, I dunno, Somalia? Do they not count? Are their voices not to be heard?"

No one speaks.

"But what sealed it for me was seeing the mix of jurors."

Nick tears a page from his binder. He holds it aloft, crumpled in his fist.

"From the start, the decision-making process confused me. If the nations involved down here agreed on something, decisions were made without the jury. If there's no argument, there's no need for deliberation, right? It was only when there was contention that issues were brought to the jury. If everyone agreed, they just did whatever the hell they wanted. The jury was only ever here to settle arguments.

"Doesn't that strike you as a flaw? It's one helluva loophole. Let's say France is the only dissenter. Okay, so America and China bribe the French to keep an issue away from the jury. In this way, substantial issues can be railroaded through. I suspect the really thorny problems were always going to be resolved by horse-trading behind the scenes.

"The jury provides the UN with plausible deniability. It allows the Security Council to appear open and transparent while the real decisions are being made behind closed doors.

"Looking at the history of judgments reached by the jury, America and the UK almost always side together. Russia and China formed another voting block. Split decisions came down to

France."

Samira Ayoub lowers her head. She knows.

Nick says, "Often, it came down to a shop assistant from Toulouse, born in Morocco. No offense, but doesn't that strike you as bizarre?"

Samira nods.

Jazz leans against the wall with her arms folded across her chest. She's relaxed. Nick can see she's fascinated by the dynamic forming within the room.

"Oh, there were a few jury decisions where the Russians broke ranks, or the Americans shifted their priorities, but it's only ever the women that dissented. It's only ever Ebony, Samira, Anni, or Kalai that swayed the vote. Why?"

Nick unfolds the crumpled paper, stretching it out on the desk in front of Anni. He taps the page, asking, "What do you notice about your fellow jurors? In particular, the women."

"This is bullshit," Bao says. "Why are we listening to him? He knows nothing. He's only just arrived. He's never sat in deliberation."

Anni, though, remains focused. She examines the sheet of paper.

"We have simple jobs. No education."

"Yes," Nick says, raising the page so everyone can see it. No one can read it from more than a few feet away, but they all know what's on it.

"Anni is a villager. Ebony taught yoga. Kalia is a goat farmer. Samira worked in a grocery store. Julia's a barmaid."

"Stripper," Julia says, correcting him.

"But this is representative," Brad says, holding his hands out in exasperation. "I'm an accountant. Bao is a teacher. Petrovich is an engineer. Jacques is a dentist. We come from a broad cross-section of society."

"Is that what they told you?" Nick asks. He opens his arms wide, mimicking Brad. He wants to make sure the dried bloodstains on his shirt are apparent. "Because I was told something else."

Petrovich says, "Duty — *Я выполняю свой долг.*"

"I do my duty," Kalia says, translating for him. "He understands English, but it is difficult for him to speak."

This is the first time the stocky Russian has spoken at all. He's balding but has a full beard reaching halfway down his chest. Petrovich looks as though he could benchpress a Lada.

"What is your duty if not to do what's right?" Nick asks. "Think about it. Why did they pick Anni and Kalia, or Samira and Julia?"

Kalia knows. She turns sideways in her seat, looking at her Russian companion as she says, "So they could push us around."

She's not intimidated by Petrovich, regardless of his scowl.

"Yes," Samira says. "They pressure us. They tell us what we should say."

Nick says, "You were chosen because they knew you could be steamrolled into decisions."

Anni nods. She keeps her head facing forward, but she makes sure the others notice her agreement, loudly saying, "Mm-hmm."

"But they were wrong," Nick says.

Anni sits up straight and proud. She has her feet flat on the floor and her hands on her thighs. Her body language screams, *Finally!*

"I don't buy your argument," Brad says. "We made our own decisions. No one forced us to do anything."

"And yet, here you are," Nick says. "No one came here willingly, did they? Like me, you were all threatened with solitary confinement."

Bao says, "Petrovich is right. We are here to do our duty."

"Our duty?" Nick asks. "Or are we pawns in a game of chess being played between countries?"

"This is absurd," Bao says. "We are the jury. We make the best decisions."

Nick says, "You get *pushed* into decisions."

Looking at the women before him, it's clear they agree. They're sick of losing arguments to these guys. From what Nick can tell, the women have been talked down too many times. Oh, he knows precisely how it would have happened. He did this to his girlfriend all the time. Nitpick a point. Get angry at some other insignificant detail. A raised voice is not an appeal to reason, but it gets the same result. Before long, Sandra started caving. And Nick knew it. He knew precisely what he was doing. He reveled in it. Gaslighting her was a sport. He could read the exasperation on her face. Arguing became too hard. Arguing with him was like talking to a brick wall. It's strange, but being on the other side of this, Nick can see it all too clearly.

Bao is angry. Of course he is. That's par for this particular golf course. He says, "If you're so smart, then why are you here?"

"Oh, but I'm not smart," Nick says, tapping his chest. "Do you want to know why I'm here? Like all of you, I was picked by a committee in *another* country. The Russians picked me because they knew I'd be a pain in the ass for the Americans. They wanted to disrupt the US agenda. And they were right about me. I'm an ornery, cantankerous fool."

Nick looks over at Jazz. Her eyes fall away from his. She stares at the floor, biting at her lip.

"I'm here because I'm an asshole."

Brad says, "No arguments there."

"Father," Bao says. "What level of agreement is required for this proposal?"

The answer echoes from the speakers in the ceiling.

315

"A change in the fundamental operational priority from recovery to rescue requires a unanimous decision."

"And what, exactly, would rescue look like?" Bao asks Jazz. "What are you proposing?"

"They need tritium."

"Do we even have that?" Brad asks.

Jazz speaks with dry deliberation. "It's a component of the bomb."

Brad explodes. He's on his feet in an instant. He points at Jazz, shouting, "You want to give them the bomb? As a goddamn present? What are you? Insane?"

The two men at the back of the amphitheater are fuming with anger.

"Father, this is Bao Xi. I vote no."

"Bradley Haggard. I vote no."

The women are quiet.

Father says, *"I need a vote from each member of the jury to complete documentation for this decision."*

Anni shakes her head. Kalia buries her head in her hands. Samira is on the verge of crying. Even Julia is sad.

Jacques is silent. His defiance angers the other men. They glare at him. Although only one vote of dissent is required to break the proposal, the tension between the men is obvious. Jacques tightens his lips. His nostrils flare. Even if he doesn't agree, he could go on the record by voting yes. His silence reveals his shifting allegiance. This isn't about the vote. He feels betrayed.

"He knows," Nick says, pointing at Jacques. "He's not fooled by this charade."

Jacques gets to his feet. He turns to face the others. "Nick's right, isn't he? The women were brought here to be patsies. But us? Us men? We are the assholes. We're here because of our loyalty. Only loyalty means being egotistical. Prideful. Predictable."

"Horse-trading," Nick says.

"Yes. Even within the jury selection itself. We are compromised. We shouldn't even be here."

Bao gets to his feet, yelling from the back of the room. "We are the jury! We have a duty—a responsibility!"

"To who?" Jacques asks. "To our country? Our people? Or to be honest with ourselves?"

Bao snaps off his words. "Do not question my integrity."

"Are you making your decision out of reason? Or anger?" Jacques asks. "Is it humanity you serve or your own ego?"

"Damn you," Bao says. "You're a traitor!"

The women on the jury cringe. They've all known their own Bao over the years. They know when reason is gone.

Jazz says, "Let's just cool it for a moment."

For all Bao's bluster, her ability to remain calm speaks of authority. In the midst of the heated argument, she's relaxed. It seems all Bao understands is brute force. Although Jazz doesn't threaten him, it's clear she could, which is something the other women couldn't do. He sits, slamming his hand on the table in disgust.

"We need to debate," Anni says. That she's the first jury member to speak following Bao's outburst is significant. The Chinese delegation is divided, but that was always the intent. Nick doesn't know if Bao and Anni were selected by the Americans, the English, or the French, but they were picked to ensure chaos for the Chinese. From what he can tell, it seems only one juror in any pairing is loyal to their country. No one selection committee trusted another country enough to pick a balanced pair of jurors. If humans are good at anything, it's trolling each other. This time, though, it might actually be for the best.

"Debate is good," Anni says, repeating her point, speaking over Bao as he mumbles and swears under his breath.

"I agree," Samira says.

"Me too," Kalai says.

"Let's do this properly," Julia says.

Nick nods and remains silent. Now is the time to shut the fuck up. He missed this point far too often with Sandra, but the tells are the same—an appeal to reason, a desire to be heard, a yearning for justice and equality.

Nick leans against the wall and slumps to the floor. He rests his arms on his knees, ready to listen.

Brad says, "I don't see the need for this."

Jacques says, "I do."

Bao folds his arms over his chest yet again. He may try to shut them out, but he can't. Everyone gets a vote. His is only one voice. Technically, he's already blocked the resolution, but the women will have their say regardless.

Petrovich may shake his head, but like Jacques, he has not cast a vote either way.

THE DEBATE

Jacques addresses Brad and Bao, saying, "Stick to your vote if you must, but we need to discuss this before finalizing our decision. There must be proper deliberation."

Kalia says, "I would like to hear from the scientist." She turns in her seat, looking toward Bao and asking, "If there's no objection?"

Bao flicks his hand in the air. His head sinks. If he had a smartphone, he'd be staring at the screen in defiance. As much as he may want to ignore the discussion, he can't. He too is curious, he just won't admit it.

Adrianna says, "From a scientific perspective, that spacecraft is buried treasure. It's something that will spur on research for decades, if not centuries to come."

"But?" Samira asks, sensing Adrianna's reluctance to unduly sway the jury.

"Science is full of uncertainty. Questions drive us on."

"And?" Anni asks, following Samira's lead.

"We may not be able to learn that much at all."

"I don't understand," Julia says.

Adrianna clarifies her point. "Imagine if an F-22 fighter was sent back to Roman times. How much could they learn from it? They'd be impressed by what they saw, but they'd have no idea how to replicate even the most basic parts, like the glass canopy or the rubber wheels. Oh, they could copy the shape, but they'd never master the construction techniques. A computer circuit board might as well be a piece of jewelry to them. No one in that age would be able to refine fuel for an F-22 or fly it. It's doubtful it would change their technological progress at all. If anything, they'd worship it. Within a hundred years, it would be a relic. Just a bunch of rusting spare parts bouncing between monasteries like the bones of the saints."

Jacques asks, "And you think that's what will happen here?"

"It's not inconceivable," Adrianna says. "Oh, we can learn from their metallurgy and basic design, but the gap between us and them is probably measured in tens of thousands of years. They can fly between stars. We can barely make it to the Moon. It could take hundreds of years to unlock the fundamentals behind their technology."

Brad says, "But we can reverse-engineer this stuff, right? I mean, once we've got our hands on it, we can figure out how it works."

"It's not that simple," Adrianna insists. "We have to reverse-engineer entire industries, not just individual components. Imagine a Bedouin tribesman in the Arabian desert. He could be as smart as Einstein, but he's not going to be able to reverse-engineer an iPhone because an iPhone is a conglomeration of technology backed by numerous different industries. We need to understand *how* these parts were made. Most of the components on that thing represent breakthrough-physics for us, so it's not going to be easy."

"But we can do it," Brad insists with the kind of confidence and ignorance Nick once reveled in.

"Can you reverse engineer a wooden ax handle?" Adrianna asks.

When no one replies, she says, "It's not just a stick. It's a very specific piece of wood. The length, the thickness, the run of the grain, the strength of that particular type of wood, the absence of knots, the lathe process, the curve of the handle, the width of the head. These are all important. Why don't splinters form on the handle when it's under stress? I have no idea.

"You see, none of these points are accidental. They're all by design. Get just one of them wrong and the ax will break.

"Even simple things are a lot more complicated than we think. Can you describe the mechanics of how a toilet flushes? There's a lot more engineering involved than you realize.

"When it comes to the alien spacecraft, there are millions of parts to consider. The problem is, each one of them has so many factors, we don't know which points are important and which aren't. Get that wrong and we'll run into a dead end."

"But?" Samira says, wanting to draw more reasoning from Adrianna.

"But a working version—with some kind of crew—that's different."

"So," Julia says, "from your perspective, this improves our position."

"Slightly."

"And yet?" Samira says, coaxing Adrianna on. Nick likes her style. Samira may not say much, but when she does it carries weight. Like him, she senses the complexity lying beneath the surface of this discussion. She genuinely wants to understand the scientific position.

Adrianna swallows the lump in her throat. "We have the ability to take what we want, but do we have the right?"

"Oh, please," Bao says from the back of the room. "Spare me your liberal morality. We need to make a rational decision here."

Brad agrees. "Next, you'll want to sit and hold hands and sing *Kumbaya* around the campfire."

Adrianna shakes her head.

Jazz says, "Hang on. Disagreements between a couple of drunks leads to a bar-fight. Between nations, it leads to war. Between interplanetary species, it leads to what? Extinction?"

"It's a real concern," Adrianna says. "You have to remember, to them, we're an alien species."

"But this is our world," Bao says. "Our planet. They came here."

"But it's not our world," Adrianna says. "This is not about us. Think about our history. For far too long, we assumed the cosmos revolved around us. We could see the stars turning above us, the sun and moon passing over our heads. We thought we were the center of the universe, but we were wrong.

"This is not our world by any measurable definition. As a species, we've only been around for a couple of hundred thousand years. Cyanobacteria have been here for at least 2.4 billion years! That's over ten thousand times as long as us!

"We're one animal species among roughly nine million others—*trillions* of others if you count archaea and bacteria. Every one of them has a stake in calling Earth its home.

"Our civilization is a few thousand years old, and yet we only just harnessed electricity in the last hundred and fifty years. We're the snotty-nosed punk kid that won't be told what to do. We know it all. Only we don't. We're not even close."

"They have no right," Bao says.

Adrianna replies, "They have every right to their own autonomy. They came here long before we emerged as an intelligent species. They may have struggled to survive beneath the ice, but they predate us on this planet. Remember, we're not dealing with aliens down there. Regardless of whether there are biological or mechanical entities resurrecting that craft, we're dealing with remote descendants. They've adapted to suit that environment just as we did on the African savannah."

"This is bullshit," Bao says.

Jacques says, "Personally, I'd rather not start a war over technology we may not even be able to harness."

"We're at a crossroad," Nick says. "Right now, this decision is confined to these four walls. We've got to think about what happens beyond here. Whatever we decide, it changes everything out there—for better or for worse. Once Pandora's Box is open, we may never get a chance to close it again."

Julia addresses Nick. "There is an argument to be made that this decision isn't ours to make. You said it yourself. We don't represent humanity's best interests. We're the result of infighting between nations. Perhaps we should leave this to the UN?"

"So we abdicate our responsibility?" Jacques asks.

"Is it really our responsibility?" Julia asks. "I mean, no one foresaw this damn thing awakening. Are we really capable of making a decision of this magnitude?"

"And what rights do these creatures have?" Adrianna asks. "If you defer this decision, who's going to represent them before the UN? What legal standing will they have?"

"I say *fuck those assholes*," Jacques replies, pointing at the far wall. "They played us. They used us like pawns. We have no reason to trust them. This is our time—our moment. This is our opportunity to prove them wrong. It's our chance to make the right decision."

Nick says, "If we leave this to the UN, they may propel us down a path to war. I think Jacques is right. We need to decide this here and now, while we still can."

"They attacked us," Brad says.

"They haven't continued their attack," Jazz replies. "Best we understand it, they were defending themselves."

"We spoke to them," Nick says. "We conversed through sign language. And then we left. They made no attempt to stop us."

"So they're not going to invade our world?" Julia asks.

"No. We invaded theirs," Nick replies.

Bao asks, "What about the treasures? Adrianna said it's a treasure chest down there. Should we really give that up?"

Brad asks, "What if it includes the cure for cancer?"

Nick replies, "What if it doesn't? What if we're too pushy and things escalate into war."

"Forget about war with them," Jacques says. "What if that war is between us? What would another world war look like? If we end up squabbling over the spoils of an alien spacecraft, billions will die."

Brad says, "So we solve cancer and kill each other in World War Three. Great. That's just bloody great."

"There's too much uncertainty," Anni says. "How can we know what we should do? We cannot."

"Principle," Jacques says. "We cannot be guided by a crystal ball we don't have, but we can be guided by principle."

"Which principle?" Nick asks.

Bao says, "We must seek what is best."

Adrianna replies, "Define best."

Brad says, "The best decision is the one that does the greatest good for the greatest number of people."

"People?" Anni asks in reply, challenging his notion. "What about them? What about their best interests?"

Bao says, "We cannot lose this opportunity. We have a duty to future generations to learn all we can from this spacecraft."

Jacques turns in his seat. "What about you, Petrovich? You're quiet. Too quiet. What do you think?"

Petrovich nods and speaks in Russian.

"Правда многих злит"

Kalia translates. "He says, the truth makes many angry."

"Не имей сто рублей, а имей сто друзей."

"His words are—it's better to have a hundred friends than a hundred rubles."

"My English," Petrovich says. "It is slow."

Kalia confers with him in Russian. "Petrovich understands what we're saying, but finding the right English words doesn't come easy."

"It's okay," Nick says. "I get it. The spacecraft. That's the rubles. We have an opportunity to make friends instead of riches, right?"

"Yes. Yes," Petrovich says, grinning from behind missing teeth.

He speaks to Kalia in Russian. *"Никто не жалеет о новых друзьях"*

"Petrovich says, no one regrets having friends."

Jacques says, "That's what we've forgotten in all of this. We've looked at this as a transaction. Either we take the spacecraft or we let it go, but there's a third option before us. We could establish a relationship with another space-faring species."

"Hang on," Adrianna says, holding out her hands. "This isn't a trade. We can't assume they'll see it that way. We have no guarantee about how they'll respond. For all we know, this is like a tribe in the Amazon returning a downed pilot to a US aircraft carrier. The US would be grateful, but they wouldn't give the tribe an F-16."

Anni says, "So we are faced with a dilemma. We are being asked to do the right thing with no offer of reward."

Adrianna nods.

Bao listens intently. He's got his elbows on the table in front of him. His chin rests on his hands.

"So much uncertainty in all outcomes but one," he says. His point isn't vehement agreement, but it is a concession. He asks, "What would a rescue entail?"

Adrianna says, "From what we understand, they lack nuclear materials. Their spaceship uses a fusion drive. We can disarm the bomb and give them tritium along with a bunch of enriched heavy metals like uranium 235. That should allow them to kick-start their engine. Whether that's enough to break out of the ice, I don't know. They should have enough to fire up their drive."

"In practice, what does that mean?" Brad asks.

"Imagine the sun erupting beneath the ice."

"Oh."

In his thick Chinese accent, Bao says, "It feels wrong to give up control."

Kalia says, "We never had control. What we are losing is the illusion of control."

Jacques says, "We could be on the verge of losing what little control we have right now and not even know it. We need to make a clear decision while we can still make a decision."

"We cannot wait for the UN," Kalia says.

Anni says, "The best decision for us is the best decision for them. We must let them go."

"They won't forget us," Samira says. "We may not know what they'll do, but we know what they will take with them—the knowledge that humanity honors freedom."

Brad says, "Okay, so we vote."

Nick is fascinated by the shifting dynamic. Without conferring, Brad and Bao have softened their position. It seems Brad is keen to get out in front of the pack.

"Father," he says. "Bradley Hoggard. On the decision to move from recovery to rescue, I vote yes."

One by one, the jurors vote for the rescue, with Bao recanting his earlier no vote.

All eyes settle on Nick.

"What?" he says before the realization hits. "Oh, yeah. Father, this is Nicholas James Ferrin. I vote yes."

FREEDOM

The twenty-minute descent back into the ice is terrifying.

On the way up, Nick barely noticed the elevator ride. It was the adrenaline high. He was buzzing after First Contact. If he ever gets to see the stars again, he knows he'll never look at them the same way. Far from being distant points of light, they're life-givers. Somewhere around some other star, hundreds of thousands of years ago, an intelligent space-faring civilization set its sights on Earth. Had one of their probes not crashed, humanity would have continued on oblivious, thinking it was alone in the cosmos. Going back down through the ice in the elevator, though, is different.

Descending beneath the glacier is unnerving. Nick's never been one for claustrophobia, but this is different. The elevator is a cage. Even the floor is little more than steel mesh with the odd reinforced bar. The lighter the weight, the more it could transport, or at least that was the thinking during construction.

Ice glides past the open sides of the elevator. A single LED light on the crossbar above them illuminates the darkness. Steel rails mounted against the glacier guide the elevator on. Blue ice fades into the darkness beneath Nick's feet, giving him flashbacks of Bear plunging down the utility shaft. With no harness or rope, he feels as though the steel mesh beneath him is about to collapse. To keep himself sane, he keeps a gloved hand on a rail.

The ice is alive with noise.

Zing! Ping! Zoom! Bang! Boom!

Adrianna told him the sounds were nothing to worry about, but she remained topside. She said ice is a type of rock. Like all rocks, it can stand immense weights bearing down on it. Creaks and groans are to be expected. And yet they're not as far as Nick is concerned. They come out of nowhere, overwhelming the sound of the winch. Although noises like this have existed on Earth for eons, they sound alien to him. Apparently, tiny fragments of ice can sound like a glacier collapsing, but it's an acoustic illusion. Echoes within the shaft amplify the slightest noise. Nick should have asked for earplugs.

Even Jazz is silent on the descent. It's the awe—the sheer majesty and power inherent in an ice sheet that dwarfs mere humans. Some people feel small before the immensity of the heavens, but that seems like nothing when descending through a mile of ice. At 25 million gigatons, the Antarctic ice sheet is intimidating. Standing beside a ten-megaton thermonuclear warhead resting on the floor of the elevator is nothing compared to the deep blue ice.

A light appears at the bottom of the shaft.

The elevator comes to a halt out of alignment with the floor. The doors open. Nick and Jazz carry the bomb on a stretcher between them. The electronic fuse has been removed. The nuclear material is encased in a dome rising above an aluminum block. They step up and off the elevator.

"And they'll know what this is?" Nick asks.

"Oh, yeah. Uranium doesn't get enriched to this level in nature. This stuff has only one practical use. They'll know, all right. They'll be very aware we were prepared to bomb them if needed."

The two of them pass through the airlock and out onto the rocky ground surrounding the lake. The crystal man is waiting for them, standing just offshore.

The cavern is alive with activity. Bioluminescence glows around them. Streams of water rise in the air like geysers, only there's no spray. Columns of water press against the underside of the ice shelf like pillars within an ancient Greek temple. Like the crystal man, they defy human reason, being part of an artificial alien construct. The spacecraft turns in place. Its disc-shape allows it to move, melting the ice immediately around it as it rotates. Lights flicker from its thin rim.

"Someone's been busy," Jazz says.

They put down the stretcher and step back. The crystal man walks onto the rocks. This is the first time Nick's seen him separate from water. He walks around the nuke, looking down at it with eyes that don't exist.

"Time to go," Jazz says, backing up.

"That's it?" Nick asks. "That's all?"

"We need to get the hell out of here."

The crystal man holds up one hand. Nick copies him, only this time Nick does a Vulcan greeting, splitting his fingers into groups of two, forming a V between them.

"This isn't from here," he says, stepping back toward the airlock. "Well, it is. But if you take anything from us, let it be that. Peace out."

"What the hell do you think you're doing?" Jazz asks, closing the hatch and cycling the airlock. "We ain't got time for games. We've got to get back up top before they decide to fire up their engines."

The inner hatch opens and they run for the elevator. Wearing a hazmat suit over Antarctic survival gear makes running difficult. Thick rubberized boots thunder down the hallway, splashing in the ankle-deep water.

Once they're in the elevator and heading up, Jazz radios ahead.

"*Vincennes*, package delivered. We're returning to the

surface."

"Copy that," is the reply. "Evacuation is underway. *Vostok* confirms two snowcats inbound with supplies. The Russians are sending inflatable shelters and fuel for our portable generators. Connor's hooked up the medical center to a couple of tractors. He's dragging it out to the drill site."

The elevator shakes.

Ice falls from above. Shards of ice shatter on contact with the steel cage, showering them with fine fragments. Nick grabs the steel mesh, holding on as a tremor passes through the glacier.

"Not good," Jazz says, locking eyes with him. "Ice resists downward pressure, but it's lousy under shear movement. Any sideways stress and the shaft will collapse."

"And you decided to tell me this now?" Nick says as the cage rocks.

Chunks of ice plummet from above. On hitting the steel mesh, they disintegrate. Bursts of blue-white ice explode like fireworks immediately above his head.

"It wasn't a problem before now," Jazz yells over the noise. Already, the roof of the cage is sagging against the support struts, being bent inward by each thundering impact.

"Come on," Nick whispers amidst the confusion.

Slabs of ice come away from the walls around them, plunging down the shaft. Below them, part of the shaft collapses inward. Boulders of ice clog the dark hole. Metal bends and snaps, being brittle in the cold. One of the rails twists, breaking away from the carriage. The elevator shakes but continues on. It swings, colliding with the ice.

Slowly, the light at the top of the shaft grows bigger.

Jazz climbs out of her hazmat suit. She yells at Nick, but he can't hear her over the sound of ice breaking. He sheds his suit, leaving it crumpled on the grate. Ice slides past. As they approach the surface, the size of the individual ice crystals become smaller—finer. Down deep, they're as big as his fingernail. Up close to the surface, they're like wood grain. They're close to the base. Damn close.

"Ready?"

Jazz dives out before the elevator has cleared the ice. Nick follows as the surface reaches waist height. He rolls across the ground, feeling tremors reaching through the ice.

"Gotta go," Jazz says, offering him her hand.

Cracks form in the ice floor inside the maintenance building. A diesel generator slides toward the shaft. The metal frame above the elevator buckles. Cables break. The cage falls, plunging into the darkness.

Jazz runs for the door. Nick is hard on her heels. The ice shifts beneath his boots. He has no idea where he's going beyond anywhere other than here. Jazz is running so fast she collides with the bench seats in the ready room, scrambling for the external door. She throws it open and rushes out into the storm.

By the time Nick reaches the external door, she's disappeared into the gloom.

What the hell? Where is she?

The storm howls across the frozen plateau. Spotlights illuminate little more than the snow racing across the plain. Buildings are a blur in the night.

The wind hits Nick like a freight train coming out of the darkness. It's not possible to see the ground, just a haze of snow and ice being kicked up by the hurricane-force winds. Nick tumbles. His legs and arms flail as he struggles to figure out which way is up. The wind pushes him along the ice like a hockey puck. His hood has blown back, exposing his face to the vicious cold. No goggles. He had a pair hanging around his neck, but they're gone, having been ripped off by the storm.

Nick rolls over, turning his back to the wind. He pulls his hood over his head, wanting to protect himself from the driving snow and ice. A cascade of fine snow pours down the back of his neck, freezing him to his core. Splinters of ice pelt his back, tearing at his jacket. Beneath him, the plateau shakes.

The spotlights mounted on the buildings scattered throughout *Vincennes* struggle to break through the darkness. Nothing looks right. Nick can't even tell where the maintenance building is and he left it seconds ago. He's rolled forty to fifty feet in the storm. Where the hell is Jazz?

Nick struggles to his feet, crouching. Hurricane-walking. He keeps his waist bent and his head down, but that means he can't see where the hell he's going—as if there was anything to see.

Cracks run through the ice beneath his boots, forcing him to widen his stance. The wind drives hard against him, determined to topple him yet again. He staggers on, blind to where he's going. The cold lashes his face, freezing his cheeks. Looking up, all he sees is the blur of snow and ice screaming past.

Is this it?

Is this how he dies?

When Jazz and Dmitri told him about the scientist that died within a few feet of one of the buildings down here, he didn't really believe them. Why the hell didn't that guy just go back inside? He could see the lights. Why didn't he head toward the lights? At the time, it seemed dumb, but now he understands. Even with a dozen spotlights around the base fighting against the night, the storm makes it impossible to judge distances. Nick can barely focus on his own gloved hands, let alone anything else. He could stumble up to a spotlight on a pole instead of above a doorway. What then? Besides, what safety is there inside? The whole base is about to collapse into the ice.

Life is small in Antarctica. Back in South Carolina, life was large. Hot wings and beers. Buddies over for a barbecue. Bowling on Sundays. Baseball in summer. Football in winter. But it was all an illusion. Out on the ice, there's no doubt life stops at the end of his fingertips.

He's dying.

His mind gravitates to Sandra, but not because he loves her—because he should have loved her. All bravado is gone. Ego is meaningless. The things people do for their political parties or country pale compared to what is done for just one other person. Standing there in the full force of the storm, regret is all he has left. His life is what he made of it, and he made nothing of it. And she was right there. She was so close and yet always a world away.

Nick falls to his knees. He curls up on the ice, trying to stay warm. It's not that he's accepting his fate. He has no choice. The cold saps his strength. Nick conserves his fading energy. He's got one last surge, but where should he direct that? Which light is closest? And where the hell is Jazz?

Jazz.

She had to be going for a snowcat.

Nick pushes his hands against his knees. He staggers on trembling legs, staying low as he turns, looking out into the darkness. He's looking for two lights, not one. Two lights close together, just above ground height.

There.

Nick rocks forward, wanting to be sure of each step. Without a guide wire, it's too easy to lose his footing and go tumbling across the plateau. Every couple of feet, he looks up, trying to judge the distance. At a guess, the snowcat is more than fifty yards away. If he can just get there.

Nick fights the storm. Snow whips around him, blinding him as it's caught in the lights. He takes another step, and the metal tracks of the snowcat come into reach of his gloves. Nick can't believe what he's seeing. Ice-covered metal treads never looked more beautiful. He can see Jazz inside the cab, flicking switches as she powers up the diesel engine. Nick was never more than about fifteen feet from the snowcat. The angle it's parked on had its lights pointing away from him. The lights he thought he saw were little more than the headlights reflecting off the snow as it rushed past. Had he wandered off in another direction, he would have been lost—and in an Antarctic storm, with an alien spacecraft breaking through the ice, lost translates to dead.

Nick clambers up over the treads and pulls on the door handle. He collapses on the bench seat.

"You made it."

Nick can't talk. His face is too cold. It's all he can do to shut the door behind him. Adrianna is in the backseat. She wraps a woolen blanket over his shoulders, but the cold has seeped into this bones.

Jazz says, "We were just about to come and get you."

If Jazz had turned the tractor around, she would have crushed him before she found him.

"Mm—My," he says, struggling against the cold.

"What is it?" Adrianna asks, pushing his hood back and brushing snow from his hair as he huddles under the blanket.

"Myrtle. I—I want to go to Myrtle Beach. Please."

Jazz laughs. "Well, I ain't your Uber Driver, but okay. Myrtle Beach it is." She engages the treads, causing the snowcat to lurch forward. Windshield wipers flick back and forth in a futile effort to improve visibility.

The ice sheet tilts beneath them, leaning to one side. Jazz guns the engine. Metal treads bite at the ice. The snowcat climbs the slope before rocking as it falls back to the plateau.

They drive into the storm. Jazz's already on the radio, talking to someone at the remote drill site, but Nick's still trying to get warm. He looks back. Huts disappear, falling into the gaping hole opening up in the ice. Light pours out of the chasm, illuminating the clouds. The snowcat accelerates, racing across the plateau, leaving *Vincennes* behind. Thirty miles an hour might seem slow, but it's a mile every two minutes, allowing them to clear the area above the lake.

"Just in time for the fireworks," Jazz says. "I hope you guys are right about these things. Because whatever's down there, it's now free to explore a world full of humans."

"You saw how they repaired their ship," Adrianna says. "Once we woke them, once they realized there was an intelligent species up here, they were always going to break out and look for tritium."

"You really think so?" Jazz asks.

"I do," Adrianna replies. "The only question was, would we stand for or against them."

STARRY NIGHT

The drill site is in the lee of the plateau to the south of *Vincennes*. Although the Antarctic ice sheet looks flat, it undulates, varying in height by a few meters over the span of kilometers. It's enough to protect the site from the harsh katabatic winds. Spotlights crisscross the ice. Snow flies past, but without the same vicious bite it had back at *Vincennes*.

Snowcats sit idling as people move between them and the team building a temporary shelter. Several of the cats have dragged diesel tanks across the ice to ensure the survivors have enough fuel to make it through the winter. Tractors approach, pulling two elongated huts. It's going to be a cramped couple of months on the ice, but at least it'll be warm.

"Are you okay?" Jazz asks. "You haven't said anything since we left."

"Just decompressing, you know?" Nick replies. "The last few weeks have been a long decade."

"Oh, they sure have," Jazz says. She steers her snowcat into a gap between the others. The cats are parked in a semi-circle, providing light for the engineers working on the impromptu camp beside the drill site.

The wind drops. At first, it's the flapping flags and loose tarpaulins that benefit, but as the driving snow subsides, people hop down out of their snowcats. They walk around, looking up at the night sky.

"Look," Jazz says, pointing. She kills the lights within the cab. "Stars!"

They climb out of the snowcat.

Standing on the treads, Nick is able to look out over the crew fixing guide wires on a radio mast. Above them, the Aurora Australis lights up the night. Curtains of light flicker in the cool air. It's far brighter than the display they saw by the fuel dump. Streamers of green, yellow, orange and purple reach up hundreds of thousands of feet above them, dwarfing them.

One by one, lights around the camp are switched off. It seems everyone wants to enjoy the majesty unfolding above them. The stars are radiant. Nick doesn't recognize any of the constellations. Jazz stands in front of the snowcat, having dropped down onto the ice.

She says, "I've never seen anything like this."

"Me neither," Nick replies. He suddenly becomes aware she's talking about something other than the aurora. Jazz points at the horizon. Rather than dissipating, the storm swirls around them, forming a wall of cloud. It's as though they're caught in the eye of a hurricane.

One of the stars is in motion. Nick feels sick. He knows what's happening before the pinprick of light grows in size. Within a minute, the temporary base is illuminated with enough light to play a game of football. Shadows shrink as the alien spacecraft descends to within a few hundred meters of the plateau.

Adrianna says, "It's beautiful."

The vessel rotates above them. A kaleidoscope of colors circle the rim of the alien spaceship.

"What do they want?" Nick asks, hopping down off the treads of the snowcat and joining her.

"I don't know," she replies. "Contact, I guess. They want to see who rescued them. I mean, this is more their style, right? They're the dominant star-faring species. They get to initiate these things, not us."

Jazz asks, "Should we be worried?"

Adrianna laughs. Nick gets it. For her, the question is ridiculous. They're standing beneath a massive vessel capable of flying across the endless darkness between star systems. This is no derelict, abandoned hundreds of thousands of years ago. The paintwork is fresh, for lack of a better term. The UFO hangs in the air, defying gravity.

Snow swirls in front of Nick. At first, he's confused as there's no wind. Legs appear, followed by arms and a torso, shoulders, and a head.

"Oh, hello," Adrianna says, standing beside Nick.

Rather than being made from snow, a humanoid appears as thousands of snowflakes caught within a snow globe, only the globe is in the shape of a mannequin. Flakes swirl around, caught within the invisible bounds of a technology beyond human comprehension. The ghostly figure raises its hand, holding its palm up beside its chest.

Nick starts to raise his hand, but Adrianna stops him, reaching out and gripping his forearm. "Wait. We don't know what this means."

Nick asks, "What's wrong?"

"Whatever meaning this gesture meant down there, it's different now. You need to understand that. The power dynamic has shifted. Remember, there's nothing in front of you. Nothing but snow. You're communicating with someone—something up there. It's asking you a question. Are you sure you want to answer?"

"They wouldn't hurt me," Nick says.

"They may not even understand the concept of hurt," Adrianna replies. "Pain might be an entirely terrestrial phenomenon. They came to Earth looking for something—looking for life. For them, this might be like catching bugs in a glass jar."

"It came back for me."

"It did," Adrianna says. "Not for Anni or Jazz. Or me. You. Think carefully about this. It might not be something you can undo."

She releases his forearm. Nick stares into non-existent eyes. Slowly, he raises his hand, matching the pose before him. On Earth, such a gesture is a sign of friendship. It's a greeting. At the very least, the alien must understand that.

What choice does Nick have? He can't ignore the apparition. He's not going to go running off into the storm. Curiosity gets the better of him.

Nick blinks. In that instant, his body soars hundreds of feet in the air. The acceleration causes his knees to buckle. Beneath his feet, snowcats and tents sit on the ice. People appear as dark blots loosely grouped together on the plateau. Before he can react, he's standing inside the heart of the spaceship.

"Ah, okay," he says, watching as vapor forms on his breath. "Not what I was expecting."

Conduits wind past him, packed in bundles on the walls. Junctions split cables, allowing them to run in different directions. His boots rest on six-inch pipes instead of a walkway. He's been brought in through a hatch in the outer skin of the craft. Behind him, a circular hole provides his last glimpse of Earth. The hatch closes by shrinking rather than sliding shut.

"Where are you?" he asks. In the back of his mind, he can imagine Adrianna's reply. Nowhere. There's no crystal man because there never was a crystal man, only a crude representation of a human form.

Lights pulsate in a crawlspace, urging him on. Nick crouches, working his way forward. There's no floor as such, just a network of pipes.

"This way, huh?" he says, feeling nervous. "You know, I was expecting a welcoming committee or something. Anything."

As he shuffles along, the lights behind him fade, leaving only one option—to continue on.

He says, "It would be nice to talk about this."

The tunnel isn't straight. It curves, rising and falling. At points, Nick has to haul himself up to another level. Lights guide him. They fade as he passes various points, discouraging him but not preventing him from going the wrong way.

"You know, a simple *thank you* would have been enough."

He emerges in a chamber full of specimens preserved in some kind of gooey liquid.

"What is this place?" he asks, resting his hand on a glass enclosure. Inside there's an ostrich, only it's huge, reaching up twelve to fifteen feet in height. Nick could tickle its underbelly but not much more. Vast clawed feet give way to dark brown feathers covering a body the size of a small car. Bubbles rise slowly within the thick fluid surrounding the flightless bird.

"I mean, those drumsticks rival anything on *The Flintstones*."

As a joke, his humor falls flat, but it's comforting to speak aloud.

The neck of the flightless bird is covered in white feathers. Its head has a fine blue plumage. Its beak is intimidating, but it's the top of its skull that takes him by surprise—it's been removed. Clean cut. Thousands of tendrils reach into the fluid, peeling away from the ceiling. They converge on the animal's head. The bird's skull has been cracked open like a hard-boiled egg, exposing the brain. Red tendrils reach into the soft tissue.

"Okay, that's creepy."

He walks past a sea lion. Like the ostrich, the top of its head has been removed. Blood has seeped into the fluid immediately in front of its eyes but no further. Rather than mixing, it's suspended. Tendrils probe the mammal's brain. Its flippers look as though they're frozen mid-stride. It's as though the animal was captured as it swam along.

"This is quite the zoo you've got here," Nick says, walking on.

He pauses beside a mammoth. To call it an elephant is wrong. It's clearly not, and it's not just the fur that reveals that. The tusks are astonishingly long. They curve like the branches of a low-hanging tree. Besides, its body shape is all wrong for an elephant. Instead of a raised saddle-back like that of a horse, the mammoth's hindquarters slope like the back of a giraffe. Again, tendrils wind their way through the liquid and into an open skull.

"This is starting to freak me out," Nick says, squeezing between specimen cylinders, looking for animals he recognizes. Most of them are alien to him. There's a monkey-like creature with arms as long as its body, a bear that's clearly not a bear but rather some kind of giant anteater with a long snout and claws like meat cleavers. He sees birds and bats, plants and insects. Most of them are oversized.

Nick comes to a halt before a cylinder with a hairy man standing erect. He's seen exhibits like this at the Smithsonian. Were it not for the occasional bubble rising slowly through the clear liquid, Nick wouldn't realize the caveman was submerged. Whatever this fluid is, it's not water.

The caveman is holding a wooden spear. Rather than having a beard, it's as though there's no distinction between the hair on his head and that growing from his cheeks, his chin, neck and chest. If anything, his hair looks like the mane of a lion. It merges, forming almost a hood as it sits on his shoulders. Black skin. Black hair. Clearly defined stomach muscles. Broken nails. He's an astonishing specimen.

Scars line the man's chest. Skin is peeling from his shoulder, exposing the texture of the muscle beneath. Unlike his other injuries, this appears to be the result of the way he's been preserved.

"I don't understand," Nick says, resting his hand on the glass.

Like the others, the caveman has had the top of his skull removed. Tendrils wind their way over his brain. His eyes. The whites of his eyes. They seem almost hollow, but they're not. Dark pupils seem to move, following Nick as he steps forward.

"You're collectors," he says, feeling the hair on his arms rise with that realization.

A thick gooey liquid surges from the floor, surrounding his boots.

"No, no, no."

Nick tries to run, but a glass cylinder slides up from the floor, cutting him off.

"Wait," he yells, pounding on the smooth surface. "You're making a mistake. Stop! Don't do this. Please."

Already, the warm fluid has reached his waist, impeding his motion. He looks around, trying to gauge the height of the cylinder. Nick jumps, wanting to reach the upper edge, but the goo holds him back.

"You can't do this to me," he yells as fluid swells around his chest, reaching up over his shoulders. Like quicksand, the more he fights, the tighter it grips.

"I'm begging you. Don't."

Tendrils reach from the ceiling, wrapping around his throat and under his jaw, holding his head in place.

A tear rolls down his cheek.

Nick knows what's coming. Deep down, he's always known—ever since he pulled that goddamn gun on Sandra. Regardless of what happened after that, nothing was *ever* going to be the same again. Granted, he didn't expect to be dragged to Antarctica, but there are some tickets for which there is no return journey.

When the handcuffs were released, he knew something was wrong. Horribly wrong. He should have been bundled into the back of a police car and carried off to jail, not to the airport. He should have been sent before a judge, not placed on a jury. What? Did he really think being dragged onto a military transport was going to improve his situation? Hah. What a joke. Nick may not have known these events would lead him here to the cargo hold of an alien spacecraft, but he always knew he'd die. He could feel it—even while he was on the C-5 Galaxy. It was the disassociation with reality. He'd been torn from one world into another. He was never going back.

Nick was given a choice. Jazz told him he could spend his time in solitary confinement or with them in Antarctica, but choice is a curse in itself. Choice is an illusion. Choices are always limited by the options available. Choices are as fleeting as the vapor rising from a cup of coffee. No, his fate was sealed when the Russian intelligence service settled on him as their patsy and drove out with Jazz to collect him. Nick was too dumb to see it, but death was waiting for him. It was just a question of how and when. What other outcome could there ever be? As soon as he stepped away from his home, he knew he'd never go back. He felt it in his bones.

A dome descends, closing over his head. Sharp edges dig into the skin above his eyebrows, extending around his head and above his ears. He wants to scream, but the thick goo is lapping at his chin, threatening to go into his mouth. It's all he can do to purse his lips and suck in what little air is left within the cylinder. The pressure of the fluid closing over his chest makes breathing a chore.

A surge of pain pulsates through his skull. In an instant, the bone is severed. His skullcap is removed. Blood squirts from a vein somewhere near his right eye, splashing on the inside of the cylinder. He can see the thin stream pulsating in time with his madly beating heart. Tendrils reach into his brain, following the curves and crevasses of his grey matter. They wind around the lobes, reaching down to his brain stem. The last thing he sees is the eyes of the naked male hominid opposite him. He's watching. Although he never blinks, his eyes are locked on Nick. He knows. Somehow, he's conscious. There's pity in those eyes.

Darkness descends.

From behind him, a familiar voice says, "You be careful down there, bro."

"What?"

Nick's confused. He's standing in the galley of the *Te Kaha*, holding the *wahaika*. The Maori war ax hangs around his neck. Light reflects off the polished greenstone. Nick's back on board the New Zealand naval frigate operating in the South Atlantic, only he's not. Nick's not fooled. He knows precisely where he is. He's deep within an alien spaceship, but all he sees is the gunmetal grey walls of the warship.

Eddie's a big man. Physically, he's six foot four in height. He's got the biceps and shoulders of a grizzly bear. Ornate tattoos curl around his forearms. Black lines swirl over his muscles like vines. Tendrils.

"Remember us down there, my brother. Don't forget us. Don't forget your *mana*."

Eddie places his huge hand around the back of Nick's neck and pulls him close. They touch foreheads, looking down at each other's boots. Eddie holds him there for a second. It's as though he's imparting something to him. Strength. Nick can feel the warmth radiating through his skin. There's a shared sense of might and determination. *Mana*. In that moment, Nick's determined to do Eddie proud. For once, duty calls to him.

He closes his eyes and breathes deeply, only he can't. There is no air within the cylinder, only a thick sludge oozing down his throat. He chokes, convulsing.

A woman's voice says, "She doesn't have a name."

Nick blinks.

Instead of being inches from Eddie, Nick's staring into a desiccated human skull. Darkened eye sockets pierce his soul. The smooth curve of the bone above the brow reaches back to where the girl's skull knitted together shortly after birth. A gaping hole marks where once there was a nose. Yellowing teeth reach up into the lower skull and down into the jawbone. To him, they appear unusually long.

"She had one," the lab technician standing beside him says. "But I don't know what it was."

The young woman works in the biology department within his high school. She prepares lessons for teachers, preps dead rats and frogs, along with the odd cow's eye. Dissection is fun for some, nauseating for others. For Nick, it's a horror movie minus the screams and jump-scares.

"Sad, huh?" she says, looking at the skeleton.

"We call her Lucy," he replies. Nick can't stand to think of the collection of pale bones before him as anything other than human, but she looks like a prop from a movie or a Halloween decoration. She's suffered. She lost her life. She shouldn't lose all of her identity. She deserves something, at least.

"Lucy's a good name," the technician says, nodding in agreement.

The single burst of a siren announces class is over. Children begin flooding the corridor. Nick can hear them beyond the solid wooden door. He should go. He's done his job. He's transported her back from the administration block. He's got to get to his history class, but he can't leave. Not yet. He needs to know more about her.

"How do you know?" Nick asks. "I mean, I believe you, but how do you know she's a girl? How can you tell?"

He gestures to the thin, aging bones hanging before him. A

chain leads up from a screw in the center of the girl's skull. It attaches to a metal frame that reaches behind and then below the skeleton. Even though he knows the screw was inserted long after she died, it looks painful. Nick can't help feel as though that screw was twisted into his own skull. His palms go sweaty at the thought he too might end up as a specimen in some laboratory somewhere. Such a thought is terrifying.

"Look at her hips," the woman says. "See how they open outward. It's the shape that gives it away. Also, look how small her ribs are."

Boney arms hang limp from hollow shoulder sockets. Thin wires hold her lower ribs in place. Seeing through her ribcage to her spine is unnerving. Legs hang from smooth hips. Her feet are limp. They're a seemingly random collection of bones ending in stubby, boney toes.

For Nick, it's disturbing to see what amounts to his own body mirrored before him. It's as though he himself has been stripped bare in an acid bath. Is this what will happen to him? As much as he doesn't want to admit it, one day, all he'll be is a bunch of bones like Lucy. Although he doesn't say anything to the lab tech, he longs for something more.

"How did she die?" he asks.

"She drowned. A flood struck her village, sweeping away her home in the middle of the night. They found her a few days later, hundreds of miles downstream."

It's difficult for Nick to see the collection of bones before him as once being a living, breathing human being, but she was. He wants to. Although it means nothing to her, it is important to him. For years, she was just like him. She laughed. She played. She went to class and wrote notes in textbooks. At lunchtime, she kicked a ball around or sat in the shade of a tree. She hung out with her friends after school. She ate dinner and probably loved candy. Who doesn't love candy? And now she's dead. Now, she's the star of his anatomy class. Now, she is an example of the intricate network of bones everyone has hidden from sight.

"Bye, Lucy."

Memories, that's all these are.

Nick is dying on an alien spacecraft, but his mind is clinging to anything it can in a vain hope of surviving. For whatever reason, his brain is racing through past thoughts and feelings, desperately trying to find answers. There's no escape. He's become Lucy—a specimen on display for others to peruse at their leisure. Instead of a high school, he's been caught up in an interstellar zoological expedition.

Nick's angry.

It's not fair.

Why should his life end like this?

Tendrils squeeze around his brain stem, flexing as they enter his spinal cord. They wind their way around the medulla at the base of his brain. His heartbeat stutters, becoming irregular. Nick feels as though he's choking, but he's already submerged in the thick, goo-like fluid and has been for several minutes. It's a reflex reaction to the way the thin alien probe is interacting with his cerebellum. He can feel them inside his head. They're stealing his memories.

"*We are at the twenty-two-yard line, and we have a flag on the field. Second down!*"

"Read it, Nick. Read it carefully."

Rage overwhelms him and yet it doesn't. For once, Nick can see himself as he actually is, reacting rather than thinking. Although a host of memories flood his mind, he feels detached from them. There's something, someone else beside him, someone lurking in the back of his mind, probing his thoughts. His reactions are being examined. These alien creatures are curating the neurons firing within his brain, scrutinizing his memories.

"You fucking bitch!"

Rage demands retribution, not reason. Anger consumes him, or it did. Now, though, he's an observer. He sees through his eyes and yet he doesn't. It's as though he's sitting beside himself. Like the alien inside his head, he's a witness to these memories.

Sandra stands beside the door. She's trembling. All he knows is vengeance. That bitch has ruined his life. Or has she? He's been slighted, and yet he's done this to himself.

Nick has lashed out without any regard for balance or understanding. Nothing matters beyond the adrenaline surging through his veins. To his mind, anger is righteous. It's not, but no opinion matters other than his own.

He throws a glass bottle, but now he's horrified by his actions.

[*No, no, no.*]

Nick's drunk. His thoughts are a blur of white-hot fury. His thinking is dull, or it was when this happened. Now, he sees nothing but arrogance and stupidity.

The glass bottle shatters against the door frame. Splinters scratch the paint, digging into the wood. He doesn't care, but he should.

[*What are you doing?*]

"Get out! Get the fuck out of my house, you goddamn whore!"

[*Stop!*]

Sandra runs for the car. She pops the trunk and tosses her suitcase in, slamming the metal lid shut. The young teen looks up in alarm.

[*James, I'm sorry. I—I. I didn't mean this.*]

Any thoughts of sorrow he has now are worthless. Nothing can make up for the terror of those few seconds. In that moment, he wanted to kill Sandra. He would have happily left James as an orphan.

Inside the house, Nick kicks over the coffee table in anger, sending magazines flying. Empty beer bottles roll across the carpet.

[*Stop this madness, you idiot!*]

"You want my goddamn guns?" Nick mumbles under his breath. "Well, you can have the fucking bullets!"

[*Walk away!*]

Nick rifles through the drawers in the kitchen. Adrenaline surges through his body. The artery in his neck pulses with a surge of anger. The car door slams outside. His fingers wrap around the pistol grip of his favorite handgun, squeezing tight.

[*Jesus, this is fucked up!*]

With grim resolve, Nick pulls back on the slide, loading a round from the magazine as he marches to the front door. He sees the bullet. He feels it slide into place. He knows the gun is loaded.

Within the depths of an alien spacecraft, Nick wonders about himself. Who would do this? Him. He would. Any other conclusion is a lie. There's no escaping who he chose to be.

[*This is stupid. You're not tough. You're not "Being a man."*]

His feet pound on the wooden floor, echoing through the empty house like thunder.

[*You're a goddamn coward hiding behind a gun.*]

The car engine roars to life after a few false starts. Sandra throws the gear shift in reverse, but before she looks over her shoulder and races down the driveway, she sees Nick standing in the doorway with the gun.

[*Fuck you, Nick!*]

He raises the Glock, peering along the barrel, lining up the sights.

"No, no, no," Sandra says, pushing her son's head down below the dash of her old convertible. She reverses along the

352

drive.

Nick hasn't shot anyone before, but he's thought about it. A lot. He's trained for this moment with paper targets at the gun range. They say killing someone is hard, but that's a lie. It's as easy as squeezing a trigger.

[*You think you're the shit.*]

[*You think you're such a big man.*]

[*You're small, Nick. You're tiny.*]

His finger tightens on the thin, curved, precision-machined metal, but he doesn't pull the trigger.

[*Don't do it!*]

In his memory, Nick waits, but not out of pity. No, he's leading the shot, anticipating the motion of the car, making sure he's not going to miss.

Although Nick's reliving a memory on an alien spacecraft rising high above the Antarctic plateau, he fears he'll go through with it. The past cannot be changed, but it feels fluid. It feels as though he's reaching back in time.

Nick stares down the barrel of the gun. His fingers should tremble, but they don't. He knows precisely what he's about to do.

The car tires squeal on the concrete.

Nick hesitates. He hates himself for it, but life should be measured by something other than a mere eight grams of lead being accelerated to over a thousand feet per second.

[*You're an asshole!*]

Sirens sound in the distance.

In that instant, his thinking is the same then as it is now. Within the confines of the spacecraft, words echo within his mind.

[*Fuck this shit!*]

[*Pulling a trigger is simple.*]

[Killing someone shouldn't be so goddamn easy.]

The convertible is halfway down the drive. Nick and Sandra lock eyes. She knows something he doesn't. She's tricked him. She emptied the gun. Only she didn't. He saw the bullet slide into the chamber. He lied to himself. In that moment, he couldn't accept any other way out. Pride demanded something other than cowardice. He couldn't be honest with himself, but then, when was he honest with his own thoughts and feelings? Ego is a mask. Pride is vanity. Arrogance is avoidance.

Onboard the alien spacecraft, regret rocks his mind, and yet he can die in peace knowing Sandra will live on. She didn't deserve his crap. All she wanted was to love and be loved. As the darkness descends and his thoughts fade, he dies content in the knowledge she has survived. He only hopes she can make something of the life he once sought to steal from her.

The alien monster, or machine, or whatever the hell it is, struggles with his thoughts. It's perplexed. Nick doesn't know how, but he can feel that response to his memories. It seems it expected intelligence. All animals have some degree of smarts, but it's confused by his raw emotions. That's something it didn't anticipate. He's haunted with regret and it can sense that.

It's the contradiction of his life that leaves this star-faring entity puzzled. Hell, it ain't alone. Looking back at his life, Nick is bewildered. He wasted the opportunities before him. He squandered them like a pile of chips at a casino.

If he were to live just one more day, he'd want to spend it relishing the little things. The quiet of the morning. The call of birds in the trees. The way dew lies on the grass. The smell of coffee wafting through the air. The feeling of warmth on his cheeks as he walks out into the sunshine. The wind rustling through the leaves. The bright sun causing him to squint. Far from being annoying, it would be a joy to behold. These are the sensations he was robbed of by his own arrogance. What he thought of as focus and determination were petty. They blinded him to the magnificence of a world teeming with life.

For Nick, there is nothing more.

His heart stops.

Oxygen no longer flows through his brain.

Sandra will live on. That's all that matters now.

In the end, it's not hope he clings to but the thought that life on Earth is bigger than his own ego.

The End

EPILOGUE

"Do you have any batteries?" a nurse asks, rummaging through a desk drawer. "My mouse died."

"Here," Sandra says, finding a couple in the cluttered junk box beneath her workstation.

Twelve beds surround the central nursing desk—three on each wall, with an internal hallway running off-center through the middle of ER. After a busy afternoon, it's been a quiet night. The curtains are drawn back on most of the beds. As each unit is separated only by a thin plastic curtain, the team likes to rotate bed allocations. As much as possible, they separate patients to provide at least a semblance of privacy. At the moment, beds one, five and seven are in use.

There's a television on, but the sound is turned down. It's mounted behind the central desk on a wall covered in pigeon holes, smack in the middle of ER. No one's sure who put it there or what purpose it serves as the only way the nurses can watch it is if they turn away from their patients. As the curtains are drawn, there's no way patients can see it. Even if they could, the screen is only visible to roughly half of the beds. For Sandra, it's background noise. It helps pass the time but little else. Anything's preferable over silence while trying to whittle away a ten-hour weekend shift.

"What do you make of it?" Dr. Jeannie Sopori asks, leaning

357

on the high front counter. She's standing in the walkway with her back to the empty waiting room.

"Huh?" Sandra says, looking up from her paperwork. A quiet Sunday night is ideal for catching up on the chaos of a crazy Saturday. Sandra's been typing up notes. She wants to get ahead of the admin team on Monday. From their perspective, failing to complete records is lazy. It's not. If anything, it's a sign of how goddamn busy they were yesterday. Sandra never signed on for clerical duty, but it comes with the territory.

"The UFO?" Dr. Sopori says.

Sandra raises an eyebrow as if to say, *Are you serious?*

Dr. Sopori looks to the screen behind her. "Haven't you seen it?"

"No," Sandra replies. "Too busy. Last night, we had a bus rollover on the highway. Thankfully, there were no fatalities, but we had to split patients between here and Georgetown. Keeping track of who went where and what claims are due is a nightmare."

Sandra swivels in her seat. The padding has worn flat, but it's better than standing.

"*...having crossed Mexico, the craft is currently over the Gulf and expected to make landfall near Lafayette in Louisiana.*"

"And this is for real?" Sandra asks, surprised.

"I guess."

"What does an alien spacecraft want with Cajuns?"

"I don't know," Dr. Sopori says. "Hot sauce?"

Dr. Sopori is from Chennai in India. She's known as a bit of a prankster in the quieter moments, prompting Sandra to glare at her.

"It's not me," Dr. Sopori says, raising her hands in defense. "I swear. How am I going to fake that?"

"If you're playing some dumb movie in the background to wind me up, I swear."

Dr. Sopori laughs. "Honest. It's been on TV all day. They've been tracking this thing up the west coast of South America since about two this afternoon."

"Hmm," Sandra says, not convinced. She wants to turn back to her paperwork. It's not going to complete itself, but she allows herself to indulge in a moment's distraction.

Fighter planes take off from some unnamed airbase in one of the southern states. They roar into the sky with missiles hanging from their underbellies. Afterburners glow in the twilight.

"How many planes have they launched?" Sandra asks.

"Um. I don't know," Dr. Sopori says. She shrugs. "All of them, I think."

Sandra laughs, shaking her head.

"No, I mean it," Dr. Sopori says. "They've been doing this for hours now."

Sandra cocks her head sideways, making her disbelief apparent.

"I'm serious," Dr. Sopori says. "My cousin works as a triage nurse up at Shaw. She said they've recalled everyone back to base. They're pushing everything they have into the skies."

Sandra rolls her eyes. Her tone of voice is dry.

"We are *not* under attack from an alien warship."

"I didn't say that."

Sandra turns her back to the television. UFOs won't be considered a legitimate excuse by admin. She continues typing up her notes.

"Do you want a Pepsi?" Dr. Sopori asks.

"No, I'm fine. Thanks," Sandra replies. The doctor wanders off into the waiting room. A coin drops within a vending machine, followed by the clunk of a can of soda.

"...*flights grounded across the Continental US. We are*

being told the President is monitoring the situation from the bunker beneath the White House... At this point, we are told there is no cause for alarm."

Sandra's still not convinced. This could be some alternate opening for the movie *Independence Day.* When does Will Smith arrive on screen?

As she finishes entering an online form, she glances back at the television. Sandra's half-expecting Dr. Sopori and the others to come waltzing in laughing at her. Mentally, she's ready to respond. *Ha ha. Very funny. It's not April 1st. I know you're bored. Go play Candy Crush or something. I've got work to do.*

Suddenly, a sharp, high-pitched whine comes from bed seven. Sandra is out of her seat and on her feet in a fraction of a second. Her hand slams the large red intercom button on the counter.

"Code Blue on Seven. Code Blue on Seven."

She rushes out of the nursing station, catching her hip on the edge of the bench. A jolt of pain surges through her, but her own pain will have to wait. Someone's dying. Nothing matters beyond the Code Blue.

Sandra throws back the curtain. Her nice quiet teenaged boy was waiting on x-ray results. He fell from the roof while setting up a spotlight over his driveway. He's been in here for a few hours now. Mild pain relief. Nothing serious. Dr. Tao was treating him before the evening shift change. If anything, he fractured rather than broke the bones in his left arm. Why the hell has he gone blue?

Bubbles form on his lips.

"I need a crash cart," she yells, rushing up to his bedside. In a single motion, she kicks the emergency release pedal, disconnecting the hydraulics that make the gurney comfortable. The bed drops. Buttons go flying as she tears open his shirt, exposing his chest. With her hands positioned one over the other and her fingers interlaced, she starts CPR. At five foot four in height, Sandra is on her tiptoes, driving hard against his chest with all her weight. His body convulses.

"Airway check," she yells to the other nurse rushing in. Sandra is already hitting two beats per second, crunching down on his sternum with the rhythm of a jackhammer breaking concrete. "I am not losing this kid!"

"What the hell?" Dr. Sopori says, running in beside her.

"Allergy," Sandra says. She's guessing, but with fifteen year's experience, her assessment has got to be damn close.

The other nurse says, "LMA tube ready."

That's Sandra's cue. She comes to an abrupt halt. The second nurse inserts a plastic tube to open the teen's airway. She follows up with an oxygen mask.

"And go," the nurse barks.

Sandra returns to pummeling the teenager's chest. "Where the hell is that goddamn defibrillator?"

Young bones bend and flex beneath her outstretched palms. This guy is going to have some serious bruising on his chest tomorrow.

"Ampenthadazanol," Dr. Sopori says, checking the patient's chart.

The second nurse applies plastic paddles on either side of his chest as Dr. Sopori yells, "Who the hell gave him Ampenthadazanol?"

Dr. Sopori runs out of the unit and into the nurse station, calling out, "Hold on that defib. He needs a shot of adrenaline first."

Sandra keeps driving hard. Sweat beads on her forehead. With her elbows locked, she uses her weight to thrust down time and again. Each compression sends his abdomen rising, causing his legs to flex on the gurney, but there's no sign of consciousness.

Dr. Sopori runs back into the medical bay. She unzips the

361

man's jeans. The second nurse helps her work his pants down.

Sandra ignores them, refusing to slacken her pace. She's tiring from the initial burst of adrenaline, but she forces herself on. The explosion of energy required to keep two hearts pumping saps her strength, but she's determined not to break her stride.

Dr. Sopori talks through what she's doing so there's no confusion. This way, she and both nurses have absolute clarity about what is being done to save the teen's life.

"Point seven five milligrams of adrenaline administered to the left thigh, aiming for the femoral artery." With that, Dr. Sopori slams the injector into his leg muscle and squeezes the tube. "And ready on that defibrillator."

"Ready," the other nurse says.

"Clear," Sandra says, stepping back away from the gurney with her hands raised high.

Kah-thunk.

The teen arches his back for a moment before falling onto the mattress again. To Sandra's relief, a tiny blip appears on the medi-monitor. At first, his heartbeat is irregular, but within seconds it finds its rhythm. She takes a deep breath.

Dr. Sopori pats her on the shoulder, saying, "Well done."

"Oh, you too," Sandra says.

With the patient regaining consciousness, the second nurse removes the breathing tube. She leaves the oxygen mask over his mouth and leans in, talking softly to him, telling him he's going to be okay. He's oblivious—dazed, but alive.

Sandra steps back, letting Dr. Sopori continue to examine the man. The doctor pushes her fingers against his neck, looks at his hands and fingers for swelling, and shines a light in his eyes, checking for a response. He coughs and moans, which is a good sign. If his ribs weren't cracked when he came in, they damn sure are now. Once he's stable, Sandra will have to get him back down to the x-ray dept.

"Dr. Tao has some questions to answer," Dr. Sopori says, turning the patient's chart around so Sandra can see the notes. "Ampenthadazanol. What the hell is he doing giving that to someone with a history of allergies?"

"Oh, yeah," Sandra says, relieved they've saved the man's life. She'll leave the arm wrestling with Dr. Tao to Dr. Sopori.

It's several hours before Sandra's shift ends. She types up an emergency intervention report, wanting to capture all the details while they're fresh in her mind. The teen is transferred to the ICU as a precaution, but he's sitting up and chatting as he leaves.

It's just after ten in the evening when Sandra walks out of ER. Her shoulders are stooped. Her keys hang from her hand. She wants nothing more than to collapse on her bed. Dinner can wait for breakfast. Her son had better be home. She does not need any of his shit tonight.

There's a chill in the air, but the stars are out, competing with the flickering, failing lights in the staff car park. Sandra drops her keys. She's drained. They feel like lead weights as she picks them up.

Sandra starts her old convertible. For once, the engine immediately roars to life. It's as though it fears her wrath.

It's a beautiful night in South Carolina. The flick of a switch on the dash causes the soft-top to fold backward into a compartment hidden above the trunk. The mechanism squeaks, but she ignores that. Although her convertible is second-hand and eight years old, the soft-top is more than a gimmick to her. After an intense shift, she needs to relax. She pulls her hair back into a low ponytail so it doesn't catch in the wind and zips up her jacket. Sure, it'll be cool on the highway, but the feeling of freedom is worth it. Her little car, with dents in the fender and rust coming through the bottom of the passenger's door, is a work of art. To her, it's a Lamborghini.

Sandra turns on the radio.

"...clogged with traffic as people flee metropolitan areas."

"Oh, you have got to be fucking kidding me," she says, realizing this is a report on the UFO. For her, that dumb thing ceased to exist as soon as bed seven went blue. After what Sandra's been through tonight, she has neither the time nor the patience for unhinged paranoia. Too many people have been watching too many dumbass alien invasion movies. Sandra's lived through disasters before. COVID. Atlantic storms. Forest fires. The solution is always the same. *Don't panic. If you haven't been told to evacuate, stay off the roads. Hunker down. Stay home. Get some sleep. You'll need your strength on the other side.* She'd love to have the microphone in that radio station. She'd tell everyone to chill out.

The reporter is happy to inflame things further.

"Hysteria has gripped the nation. We have reports of sightings along the East Coast. At the moment, they're unsubstantiated, but they're coming in fast."

"Oh, please," she says to no one but the radio. "If they're unsubstantiated, what the hell are you reporting?"

Sandra turns on the sat-nav in her car. Red lines sprawl across the map around her. "Great. That's just great. It's Sunday night, people. Where exactly do you think you're going?"

Sandra sighs. She turns toward an old country road that bypasses the highway.

"What is wrong with you people?" she mumbles, turning off the radio.

The wind whips over the windshield as she races along. Loose strands of hair dance around her face, but they don't bother her. There are no streetlights. On either side of the road, trees hide the stars from view, darkening the night. High above, though, a thin speckle of stars shine down upon her. They're beautiful.

After a few minutes, Sandra reaches open farmland. The

road is raised above the surrounding fields. The stars are brilliant. They're so close she could reach out and touch them. Her convertible has never felt so small. She doesn't care. The magnificence of the entire universe is out there, just beyond the reach of her headlights.

A fighter jet races overhead.

Although it's probably over a hundred feet in the air, it feels as though it scrapes the distant treetops. The roar of the engine is deafening. The aircraft came from behind her, out to her right. It banks as it cuts across the road and rises into the night. Wings tilt as the craft turns. Tiny navigation lights blink. Twin engines glow in the darkness.

"What the hell?" she mutters, gripping the steering wheel. Her eyes follow the dark silhouette as it gains altitude.

Thunder breaks around her again. One, two, three, four fighter jets scream across the farmland in front of her, trailing each other. They're separated by less than a second. As Sandra's further down the road, they're so close the jet-wash buffets her car. Turbulent, swirling air rocks the open cab of her convertible. The wind lifts junk food wrappers from behind the front seats.

"Sweet Jesus," she says, hunching over the steering wheel. To her, it feels as though the planes could have clipped her car. They were probably still well above the road, but damn that felt close.

She yells in anger. "I hope you guys are having fun!"

The aircraft bank as they race into the distance, peeling to one side and climbing high into the night. The roar of jet engines lingers long after the fighters are a mere smudge against the stars.

"Not cool," Sandra says, shaking her head. "Seriously, that's not funny. Go scare someone else."

Bugs splatter on her windshield, being attracted by her oncoming headlights. The highway would have been a cleaner ride.

Sandra's still annoyed at being buzzed by a bunch of flyboy adrenaline-junkies. She eases off the gas and adjusts her rearview mirror, leaving it angled to one side. If there are any more aircraft, she wants some warning.

Floodlights illuminate her car from directly overhead. Unlike those of an intersection or a rural town, they move with her rather than simply passing beside her. The intensity grows, blinding her with a blue/white light. The night turns to day.

Sandra slows her car to a crawl. She flicks the switch on the dash to raise the soft-top. Nothing happens. Her car engine splutters. Gravel crunches beneath her tires as she trundles along at ten miles an hour, hugging the shoulder of the road. Sandra doesn't dare stop. The light is so bright she can barely see beyond the hood of her car. Is this like a police helicopter or something? She's waiting for someone to call out to her over a bullhorn. What is this? Prank-a-nurse day? Maybe they're looking for an escaped criminal. But why the jets? She's confused, but she knows she needs to drive out the other side of the light.

There are vehicles ahead. They've stopped. If she squints, she can make them out—a pickup truck and a luxury car. Sandra doesn't know the makes and models, but they've been in an accident. Probably after being distracted by the low flying fighters. Perhaps this is what the helicopter's looking for. The chopper must be a paramedic flight responding to a 911 call. Being on the scene already, she can help.

The luxury car has a distinct, deep burgundy paint job. The hood is crumpled. It has popped open, obscuring the occupants in the front seats. Steam rises from the radiator. Fluid leaks onto the road.

The pickup is lying on its side. Gasoline drips onto the brightly lit concrete. The front windshield has shattered. The glass is a spider web of cracks and splinters. It's hanging from the rubber seals surrounding the metal frame of the cab. A child wanders into the middle of the road. She looks dazed. Her arms hang limp by her side.

"Get her," Sandra yells at Nick, pulling over on the side of the road. "She's in shock."

What?

Nick?

Gravel skids beneath her tires as she hits the brakes too hard, bringing the car to an abrupt halt. She throws the shifter into park and pulls on the handbrake. She wants to ask Nick, *'How did you get here?'* But people are hurting. Sandra turns on the hazard lights.

Blood drips from Nick's fingers. Sandra notices, but she's distracted. Too much is happening at once. Her mind is already responding to the emergency in front of her.

She has her seatbelt off and the door open. One foot is already out on the gravel by the time her mind has registered that Nick is there with her. She's moving on instinct.

Sandra pops the trunk and grabs her first aid kit. This isn't a ten-dollar special from CVS. Sandra carries a full emergency response kit. It's only a couple of steps removed from what would be in the back of an EMT vehicle. Add some oxygen cylinders and her little red convertible is an ambulance. Nick hates this thing. It's a waste of money. She loves it. For her, it's the chance to help someone in need. She slings the heavy bag over one shoulder and jogs toward the luxury car.

Sandra is as fit as the next suburban mom. She can run to the local street corner but not much further. Yoga on a Saturday morning is more fun than running around the block. An exercise bike in front of the TV makes her feel better, but it's a light workout at best. The bag bounces awkwardly on her shoulder as she runs. Within twenty feet, Sandra's feeling the exertion. For her, this is a sprint with twenty-five pounds weighing her down.

An overweight man crawls from the cab of the pickup. He

looks dazed, but he's conscious and coherent. For now, that's enough. Her mind is already running to triage. He could be harboring serious injuries like internal bleeding, but he's breathing and mobile. No matter how badly hurt he is, right now, he's low on the list. He should be okay until the paramedics land.

"Get them off the road," she calls out to Nick.

Nick?

He's still sitting in her car.

Sandra runs toward the luxury sedan, breathing hard. Her shoes pound on the concrete. She comes to a halt, standing in front of her bright red convertible.

"What?" she says, bathed by the headlights, looking at the open back of her own car. She reaches out, touching the smooth paint on the hood. "I—I don't understand?"

Sandra turns, looking for the luxury car and the pickup. Nothing. The road is clear. Where the hell did the pickup truck go? Where's the child? What about the guy crawling out of the cab?

Is this a dream?

It's a memory.

Sandra's confused. Her mind is playing tricks on her. She's reliving a moment from last spring, only now it's gone, having evaporated like a mist.

"Sandy."

Sandra blinks in the blinding lights raining down upon her from above.

"Nick???"

Fingers reach from the passenger's seat, touching the door trim. Deep red blood smears across the leather upholstery.

"Nick!"

Sandra runs around the side of the car. The door is open. Nick has one foot out on the side of the road. It's as though he's trying to stand but can't. It's then she sees his head.

"Oh, dear God," she says. "Don't move. Do you understand me? Stay exactly where you are."

Sandra slings the first aid kit from her shoulder and onto the ground. She unzips it, but her eyes never leave his head.

"Major trauma. Head injury," she mumbles, talking herself through what she sees. "Exposed brain tissue. Patient is conscious and coherent."

She rummages around with her hands, feeling for the things she needs, knowing precisely the shapes and weights of the heavy trauma pads, bandages and saline solution packs.

Nick's breathing is shallow and rapid. His skull has been sliced open, exposing his brain. Blood seeps from the bone, matting what's left of his hair. Cranial fluid oozes around the folds of grey matter making up his cerebral cortex, soaking into the gap between hemispheres. Thin red veins cover the folds of his brain, creeping up from below.

"I—I—I."

"It's okay," she says, taking his hand for a moment. "Easy. I need you to sit still, okay? Don't nod. Don't speak. Just breathe. Focus on your breathing. Slow, deep breaths. In and then out. Just keep doing that. You're going to be fine."

"L—Liar."

Her hands tremble. She is not capable of dealing with an injury this severe. He's going to die. All she can do is comfort him—be with him. It feels strange helping someone that once tried to murder her, but she can't turn away. It's just not in her nature. If nothing else, she has to be true to herself.

Sandra smiles, trying to reassure him with something other than words. Nick smiles back. He knows. He seems at peace with what's happening to him. He's dying, but that doesn't bother him. Her Nick would be panicking. He'd be freaking-the-fuck-out. What is going on?

Sandra breaks open a tube of sterile saline solution and cleans around the exposed bone.

"What happened? Who did this to you?" But she quickly corrects herself with, "No. Don't say anything. Just stay still."

Forget about keeping him calm—Sandra needs to keep herself from hyperventilating. She wipes a tear from her cheek with the back of her wrist.

Focus.

Sandra rips open the plastic on a large gauze pad and positions it behind his head, resting what's left of his skull on the pad and then on the seat.

"Relax," she says. "Nice deep breaths. I know this is hard, but I need you to relax. Keep your head straight but let the muscles in your arms and legs go limp. I need you to slow things down for me."

"I—I'm sorry," he says with tears streaming down his cheeks.

"I know," she says, towering over him.

Sandra leans around, getting a good look at his wound. She stands in the footwell of her car, wanting to understand the way his skull has been severed. If anything, she's surprised how little bleeding there is.

She sees the upturned skull cap in his other hand, resting in his lap. The inside is pink. Torn membranes lie crumpled within. Sandra goes to take it from him but thinks better of it. Which way is forward? If she puts it on the wrong way she could damage his brain tissue. Besides, it looks as though there's fine grit in it. That could be ground bone or some other contaminant. She could inadvertently bring on a clot or introduce a microbial infection. She's not qualified for this. Nick needs a surgeon. For once in her nursing career, Sandra feels helpless.

Nick's arms, legs and chest are covered in thick goo. It's been wiped from his face. Smeared would be a better description than cleaned. He's wearing a heavy arctic jacket. It's the kind Sandra's only ever seen in places like Canada or the Dakotas. Nick doesn't own a jacket like this. For South Carolina, it's serious overkill. She pushes the hood of the jacket down away from his neck, making sure the thick lining is well clear of his exposed brain.

Sandra uses tweezers to pick bits of loose fur from around the bone. Nick grimaces at the slightest touch. His eyes dart around, looking for something, but he keeps his head still. Sandra pulls back a flap of skin on the far side of his head. It hangs loose, no longer resting on his grey matter.

"You're going to be okay," she says as darkness creeps in around her and the temperature drops. She's never seen an injury like this and has no idea how to treat him. That he's still alive is astonishing. All she can do is reduce blood loss and keep his wound clean. The hospital is only fifteen minutes away. There's no point in calling an ambulance. She'll be back there before they could arrive.

Nick's in shock. He needs an infusion of intravenous fluid to stabilize him, but that's beyond the scope of her medical kit.

"T—Thank you."

"Easy," she says, looking deep into his eyes.

Given the severity of his injuries, talking is good. Head injuries are notoriously difficult to assess. Exposed brain matter is normally fatal. Rather than being the result of blunt force trauma, his skull cap has been surgically removed without damaging his brain. Although that makes no sense, it gives her hope.

Sandra's seen a lot of awful injuries as a nurse. She's watched as patients have slipped away, holding their hands and talking softly with them until the end. She knows the names of everyone she's lost. Most of them were drugged up by the time they passed, so at the very least it was peaceful. Death never comes easy, but it can be free from pain and panic. This, though, is different. To her, Nick's injury is horrific. It should be fatal, and yet it's not. There's no sign of saw teeth cutting through the bone. The edges are smooth. His skull cap has been removed, but by what?

How is he still alive?

Sandra uses another sterile bandage to pack the hollow that's formed between the rear of his skull and his brain. She tries to stop blood from pooling there.

Nick reaches out with feeble fingers, touching lightly at her leg, pushing against her pants just below her knee. She understands. He's trying to find some reassurance. Touch is life.

"It's okay. I'm not going anywhere. I'm going to get you to the hospital."

Sandra isn't looking forward to the drive back. She's going to have to manage changes in acceleration carefully. Turns will be difficult. Gently, she lowers his seat, resting it as far back as possible, hoping he continues to retain control of his neck muscles. At best, it's set at an angle of thirty degrees.

The wind swirls around her, something that's been strangely absent for the past few minutes.

Red and blue emergency lights paint the trees and fields in splashes of color. EMT vehicles rush in from both directions, confusing her. There are dozens of them, but their sirens are off. Normally, that's an indication they're carrying a patient and trying not to distress them. In this case, though, it's clear they're coming for Nick. How did they know he was here?

Helicopters circle overhead, bathing the sports car with their spotlights, but they remain up high. These aren't low-flying police helicopters trying to catch a criminal on the run. They seem to be aware they need to keep their distance and not kick up any debris. It's like they know he's down here.

The light is different. It's not as intense.

Sandra looks up, craning her neck and peering into the

darkness. The stars have long since vanished from sight, all except one. It moves toward the horizon, streaking away into the night.

Paramedics throw open the back of their vehicles, grabbing gurneys and rushing in toward them. Only one's needed, but it seems they don't realize that yet.

Sandra steps back as they run to Nick's side. To her surprise, the medics are wearing full hazmat suits. Thick yellow rubberized plastic squelches as they jog over. Oxygen cylinders bounce on their backs.

"Don't worry," one of them says, hidden behind a bulky black mask. "We're here to help."

"What is going on?" she asks, but no one answers. They're too busy talking among themselves and focusing on Nick. Radios crackle with instructions.

One of the medics climbs into her car, standing half in the footwell and half on the driver's seat as he applies a neck brace. Medics crowd around, reaching in and raising Nick out of the vehicle and onto a gurney, handling him with care.

Like her car seat, the gurney is set on an angle, allowing him to lie back but without laying him flat.

Nick keeps his eyes facing up. Whatever he's been through, he has the presence of mind to keep his head straight. His fingers slip out from beneath a white sheet as they wheel him away. Sandra takes his hand and walks along with the medics.

Behind her, a convoy of military trucks pulls up. Soldiers climb out in chemical warfare suits. Some of them are carrying guns. Others unload portable barricades. They begin setting them up around her convertible at a distance of twenty feet. Someone's got what looks like a fancy handheld video camera. They scan her car with a UV light.

The speed with which everything is happening leaves Sandra bewildered. Shock catches up with her.

Nick squeezes her fingers. This time it's his turn to say, "It's going to be okay."

ΛFTERWORD

Thank you for taking a chance on *Jury Duty*.

Regardless of whether it's *Contact, Alien, ET,* or *The Thing,* alien stories are about us. *The Day the Earth Stood Still* makes this abundantly clear in its title. We are the subject. Oh, we think these stories are about some creature that blends into the jungle or has acid for blood, but it's our responses, our reactions, our limitations and emotions that are being explored. The unknown is a dark mirror. The reflection we see is that of ourselves stripped bare of the usual pretense and theater.

Having written over a dozen stories on the subject of First Contact, I love exploring the motivation aliens might pursue and their potential nature, but these kind of stories always circle back to us and our behavior when confronted with the unknown. *Jury Duty* examines the dark side of humanity—how we abuse each other and troll ourselves. It's also a redemption arc. The only way anyone learns to care about anything is by looking beyond themselves.

One potential criticism of this story is that the protagonist perpetuates domestic violence. As someone who grew up dodging machetes and axes, this isn't something I take lightly and don't intend to glorify. We can't fix problems we ignore. I hope this story goes some way to highlighting how domestic violence is normalized far too often instead of being dealt with honestly.

Domestic violence doesn't always end in murder—that's simply the extreme that makes it into the news. It's my ribs being bruised after being thrown across the kitchen and into the dining table. It's being punched while on the phone to a friend. It's someone screaming at you, telling you over and over that you're a loser, a bastard, and a string of expletives I cannot bear to type. It's knowing which floorboards creak in the hallway. It's climbing out the bedroom window when you hear him starting to yell. It's hiding under the bed in the spare room while he stalks you in a drunken stupor, calling out time and again, *"I'm going to fuck'n kill you!"* It's waiting until silence descends before skulking out of your own home. It's walking for hours in the dead of night to reach the safety of a friend's house. It's not something I take lightly. It's also not something I can ignore.

Too often, our heroes rely on violence to solve problems. It's not difficult to see how domestic violence arises when violence is glorified for entertainment. Here in Australia, our equivalent of the Super Bowl is called State of Origin. When these games are played, domestic violence spikes by 40%. The same is true in England when the World Cup is being played, regardless of where the host country might be.

These are games!

They're entertainment, that's all.

And yet, they become the catalyst for violence against women and children. For me, stats like this highlight how difficult it is for some men to separate fiction from reality. Adrenaline starts pumping and the lines become blurred.

Violence is the failure of reason. Even when it comes to something like law enforcement where violence is often unavoidable, it should be the position of last resort, not the default reaction. When it comes to entertainment, it should stay on the screen or in the text of a page in a book.

When it comes to domestic violence, the reality is that it's too goddamn easy for assholes to get away with everything right up until the point of murder—and then it's too damn late. Domestic violence stems from self-centered arrogance. It's selfish. It's the abuse of trust and the exercise of raw power over others. Is it unforgivable? Is it irredeemable? Can someone recognize and shed that toxic persona? That's the question I wanted to ask in *Jury Duty*.

Is Nick a hero? Or is he a flawed human stumbling through life with excess baggage he desperately needs to unload? Should Sandra forgive him? Having lived through something similar, I don't think she owes him anything.

I think our idealized stereotype of the all-conquering seemingly-divine hero is a mistake. Too often, stories get caught up in a messiah-complex. Some authors are too willing to overlook flaws in their desire for an epic story. No one is perfect. Perfection is a trope we need to retire.

My last few novels have been criticized for being slow, which I find comical. Movies have desensitized us to character arcs. These days, we're expected to care about a character right from the explosive opening. Action! Action! Action! That's all that matters. You'll figure out the characters as we go—is the mantra. Personally, I think that approach is flawed. I struggled to care about anyone in *Rogue One* until I watched it a second time. Don't get me started on *Tenet*.

When I first came up with the idea for *Jury Duty*, I realized I couldn't teleport Nick to Antarctica. It was going to take time to get him from South Carolina to *Vincennes*. Rather than seeing this as a problem, I realized it was an opportunity to develop some depth of character.

Given the problematic opening, where Nick loses all respect in our eyes, his protracted journey to Antarctica was ideal. As his life slips further out of his own control, he begins to realize he was never in control anyway. When the action does come, it hits hard and fast. If you cared about Dmitri and Bear, then the opening chapters succeeded. If you worried whether Jazz or Nick might die, then the novel wasn't slow—the pacing was just right and drew you into the story.

Besides, I wanted to establish a sense of utter isolation in Antartica. Giving the reader an appreciation for how difficult it is to reach an inland base during winter helps give the novel a sense of claustrophobia on the ice.

As with all my novels, I try to ground my concepts in realism. Fiction is, by definition, fictitious, but can be (loosely) plausible if based on actual science. It's impossible to list every point in this book, but here are some of the more interesting facts woven into the narrative.

The crashed UFO is based on an asteroid that exploded above the ice of Antarctica 430,000 years ago, showering the continent with tiny metallic debris. As this was an airburst event rather than an impact, there was no crater, but it left me wondering, what if that was more than a metallic meteor? The remnants were scattered across a large section of the continent. They were barely a hundred microns in size, no bigger than the width of a human hair, and buried beneath the ice for hundreds of thousands of years until we discovered them.

In this story, the alien spacecraft is part of an automated sample return mission akin to the kind of device we would use to retrieve rocks from Mars or Enceladus. Operating at extreme distances, it needs to be autonomous and able to conduct repairs/maintenance. It has AI decision-making capabilities when selecting samples, and this leads it to release Nick at the end of the novel when it realizes its dragnet has swept up a sentient being.

Life on the ice is extreme. Explorers venturing into the Arctic wilderness of Baffin Island in Canada need between three thousand and five thousand calories a day. To reach this, they'll eat sticks of butter. Danish explorer Mille Porsild said, '*You actually get so hungry that eating a stick of butter or eating a piece of jerky with a chunk of butter in between is quite delicious.'* She even described sticks of butter as her *'snack of choice.'* I can't speak for you, but I think I'd be sick if I ate that much butter in one sitting.

Living in Antarctica is like being on another planet. Summer is four months of unrelenting sunlight, while winter is four months of darkness. In between, the days grow shorter or longer at an astonishing rate. The last day of sunlight each year is only about 40 minutes long. Imagine sunrise occurring at noon and sunset happening just before one in the afternoon. Such rapid, extreme variations play hell with the circadian rhythms of the scientists and engineers stationed there.

Nick's story about the high school skeleton is one from my own life. As far as anecdotes go, it was macabre but human. Back in the 1980s, little thought was given to the ethics of using the actual skeleton of a teenaged girl killed in the flooding of Bangladesh to teach biology. I doubt the poor girl's family consented to whatever process stripped her to the bone and saw her shipped to a high school on the other side of the world. We were told she was thirteen when she died. I couldn't help but feel she'd been cheated twice. She'd died prematurely and then been sold to another country. With the heartache she endured, I'd like to think she would have enjoyed our impromptu tour of the school and the laughter that ensued. It sure beats being stuffed away in a closet. I wonder where she is now. I hope her remains have been repatriated to Bangladesh and buried with respect. If she's still in a biology lab somewhere in New Zealand, I hope some other high school students take pity on her and show her some kindness. I'm sure she'd appreciate another school tour.

Long before the arrival of Europeans in New Zealand, the Māori were fierce warriors, specializing in brutal ambushes that would wipe out entire tribes. Taking prisoners was rare. The *haka* developed as a form of deterrent—a way of warning against the devastating consequences of war. These days, the New Zealand All Blacks perform the *haka* before international rugby matches. Although these exhibitions honor Māori culture, there's no doubt they also fire up the players for the game. Māori culture is built around the concept of mana, which can best be described as honor blended with humility. Māori society places emphasis on *iwi* and *whānau*, meaning the unity of the tribe and caring for family. I tried to show these attributes in the character Eddie, who's loosely based on a couple of people I knew in New Zealand. I grew up hunting deer and boar in the *Ureweras* so I find the historical quote about the Māori songbird from that region fascinating.

In this novel, a series of electromagnetic pulses are used to disorient the base staff, effectively putting them in a catatonic state. Although such an effect is fictitious, the idea is based on the use of (TES) Transcranial Electromagnetic Stimulation to alter brain activity in medical treatments. During the Cold War, the Soviet Union developed an electromagnetic weapon capable of inducing a variety of effects on the brain, including causing it to go into a dormant state. Side-effects included nausea, disorientation and confusion—which tied in well with this story.

Ice is a type of rock. The design of the subsurface ice station was based on the US Army's excavation in Thule, Greenland and the subsequent scientific research into the viability of tunneling through ice.

The description of the sounds that were made during the descent through the ice were taken from a video made by Dr. Peter Neff who dropped a piece of ice 90 meters down a borehole on the Taylor Glacier in Antarctica. The visual descriptions were based on the WATSON project, searching for microbes embedded deep within the ice in Antarctica.

When it came to abseiling, I drew heavily on a number of online resources as well as some of my own experience climbing in the Rockies. As a writer, I had to decide whether to be glib and say they just hooked up and magically made it to the bottom of the shaft, or whether to go into detail. I decided on the latter as it is improbable such an undertaking would be taken lightly with civilians along for the ride. Also, I felt it helped the reader better understand the stakes and appreciate the danger involved.

Life is resilient. Researchers in Antarctica were astonished to find a complex ecosystem well over a mile beneath the ice. Surveys conducted through bore-holes have revealed *"small mobile animals such as shrimp and crustaceans called sea fleas... tube worms, stalked barnacles, [and] hydroids, which are related to jellyfish... In order to survive, these organisms would have to feed on floating material from other animals or plants... it is impossible for plants to photosynthesize in the sunless seawater... the direction of the currents beneath the ice shelf suggests the nearest plant life is up to 1,000 miles away."*

Bioluminescence is astonishing. Yes, there really is a species of deep sea shrimp that vomits light. Remarkably, 90% of our oceans are yet to be explored. What we have seen is awe-inspiring. We humans are clumsy. We throw up lights everywhere, drowning out the way nature teases out the darkness. You can find bioluminescent waves in California and the Chesapeake Bay on the Atlantic. Allow your eyes to adjust to the darkness and you'll find the water looks like something from Avatar.

Mesonychoteuthis hamiltoni is known as the Antarctic Colossal Squid. Although giant squid are real, the prospect of one attacking a human are slim to none. Large squid can be aggressive, though. The USS Stein was attacked by an unknown species of squid estimated to be upwards of 150 feet long. The squid disabled the ship's sonar, forcing it back to port. Humboldt squid are known to attack scuba divers off the coast of California.

Giant squid evolved to survive in almost complete darkness at immense depths. These are depths and pressures comparable to those found in the lakes beneath the ice in Antarctica, but as far as we know, those lakes have only ever held microbes and small creatures. There is, however, a network of canyons and lakes beneath Antarctica that dwarfs the Grand Canyon, so there's plenty of room for biodiversity to occur on par with what we see in the depths of the ocean. *Mesonychoteuthis hamiltoni* has the largest eyeball of any animal, reaching beyond the size of a dinner plate to that of a beach ball.

I'd like to thank those beta-readers who have helped refine this novel: John Larisch, LuAnn Miller, Bruce Simmons, David Jaffe, Petr Melechin and Didi Kanjahn.

Pavel Ananyev helped with the Russian translations, including the radio transmissions to ensure they were plausible.

Thank you again for taking a chance on *Jury Duty*. Novels like this are not possible without your support. Please take the time to leave a review online and tell a friend about this unique science fiction story. If you're interested in future releases, subscribe to my email newsletter.

Peter Cawdron

Brisbane, Australia

Printed in Great Britain
by Amazon